THE MAMMOTH BOOK OF

HEROES

THE MAMMOTH BOOK OF
HEROES

*True Tales of Courage from
Ancient Times to September 11, 2001*

Edited by Jon E. Lewis

CARROLL & GRAF PUBLISHERS
New York

Carroll & Graf Publishers
An imprint of Avalon Publishing Group, Inc.
161 William Street
16th Floor
NY 10038–2607
www.carrollandgraf.com

First published in the UK by Robinson,
an imprint of Constable & Robinson Ltd, 2002

First Carroll & Graf edition 2002

Collection and editorial material
copyright © J. Lewis-Stempel 2002

ISBN 0–7867–1067–5

Printed and bound in the EU

These are deeds which should not pass away,
And names that must not wither
Byron, *Childe Harold*, Canto III, Stanza lxvii

You ready? Let's roll
Todd Beamer, United Airlines Flight 93

We can be heroes/Just for one day
David Bowie, "Heroes", *Low*

For my hero, Tristram
For my heroines, Freda and Penny

CONTENTS

INTRODUCTION

At some point in the late 20th century, heroism died in the Western world. There were individual heroic acts, certainly, but the age was not sympathetic to the heroic ideal. "Whatever happened to all of the heroes?" sang the English punk band The Stranglers. "No more heroes anymore", was the anthemic reply. This observation was not confined to the nihilist edge of British pop culture in the oil-crisis ridden 1970s. "They're hard to find", lamented a major American weekly magazine about heroes in August 2001.

Rarely, of course, has a statement been proven so wrong. A bare three weeks later, on September 11, Islamic terrorists flew passenger planes into the World Trade Center and the Pentagon with the loss of thousands of lives. As the terrorists presumably intended, the Western world changed on September 11 – but not in the way they wished. The decadent West did not roll over on its back; instead it rediscovered some old-fashioned virtues. Duty, compassion, faith, altruism, and greater even than these, heroism. What will always be remembered about that day is the valour of firefighters, police and rescue services in the avalanche of death, and the bravery of the passengers of flight UA93 as they sought to overcome their hijackers. The commentators ceased to remark on heroism's demise, only on its importance to modern life.

The strange death and resurrection of heroism requires some explanation. Once upon a time, even as late as the 1950s, every little boy and girl was brought up on a diet of heroes and heroic deeds: Columbus sailing the ocean blue, Florence Nightingale, the Alamo, Rorke's Drift, Harriet Tubman . . . An appreciation of the heroic was part of the training for life, and had been since humankind could first tell stories or pass down remembrances (think of the world's body of heroic literature and legend, from *Beowulf* to *The Odyssey*). The heroic started going out of fashion in the West in the 1950s, with the advent of the "teenager". Until that decade, youth had always been a minaturized carbon-copy of its parent, but the new phenomenon of "teenage" set youth against parent. In effect, this turned teenagers against the heroic – for parents are always the first heroes of children – and their parents' essentially conservative value systems . . . and eventually all value systems. The point was neatly made in the 1953 film *The Wild One*, the quintessential teen movie. Marlon Brando's motorcycle boy is asked "What ya rebelling against?" "Whaddya got?" he replies.

It was all downhill for heroism after the 1950s, although the 1960s offered the contradiction of simultaneous revolutionary iconoclasm and heroic labour for noble ideals (the black civil rights movement, for example). But, when the optimism of the 1960s was murdered by Hell's Angels at the Rolling Stones' Altamont concert, the slip-slide of heroism became a fullscale runaway. The nadir was reached in the cynical, consumerist, cocaine-fuelled 1980s. In *The Talmud* the question is asked, "Who is a hero?" And the answer is, "He who has conquered his evil inclinations." Evil inclinations were more applauded than conquered in the 1980s, when money and fame were the only gods. Thus, there were scarcely any heroes in that age, only *anti*-heroes and celebrities. The emblem of the anti-heroes, or amoralists, was Gordon Gecko, the company trader in Oliver Stone's 1987 *Wall Street*; the emblematic celebrity was every wannabee prepared to humiliate themselves on *Blind Date* or *Oprah* for their statutory Warholian 15 minutes of fame. No one got famous for good works anymore, only good looks, shopping, self-abasement, scandal and, preferably, victimhood. Of course, if you could do all five – like Madonna or the Princess of Wales – you could reach that stellar state of renown once reserved for the likes of Jesus Christ, George Washington, Joan of Arc, or Winston Churchill.

And so did heroism bump along abysmally for twenty years, until September 11 2001, when suddenly there were heroes galore. They had of course been there all along; it was just that the West had been blinded to them by the reflected tawdry dazzle of money and *Hello!* celebrity. *They* being the people who faced adversity – death even – to help others. And they did it not for the dollars or the pounds – hell, they were often poorly paid – or for the exposure on the TV but because of a sense of public duty, decency even. *They* were people like firefighters and rescue workers at Ground Zero. And when the West learned to see heroism again – for that is what happened on September 11 – it could see it everywhere, in the men and women who push the boundaries of science and human endeavour, in those who stand firm for their rights against tyranny, in those who serve to protect us. Of course, it was lost on no one that in valuing heroes the Western world was valuing what was best in itself.

There were some less obvious lessons in September 11. How, for instance, to explain the heroic acts undertaken by "ordinary" people, the combative passengers of Flight UA93 in particular? And, why were some people heroic but not others? The answer lies, in all probability, in Nurture as much as it does in Nature. Certainly, some people seem to be born risk-takers (and nobody was ever a hero without taking a risk), but heroism also rests on the psychological foundations of self-confidence, self-esteem and empathy; a hero-in-waiting, after all, must not only feel that she or he can affect the outcome of a given situation but must wish to do so. Self-confidence, self-esteem and empathy are qualities learned in childhood. This leads full-circle to why previous generations were fed of an evening on the deeds of heroes. Heroism can be learned. Those "non-professionals" who acted heroically on September 11 almost certainly did so because they were taught cardinal virtues at their parents' knee.

The learned nature of heroism means more than the enabling of the individual to act heroically. (Though it might be argued that many individuals would profit more from reading Ernest Shackleton's *South* or M.R.D. Foot's account of the Second World War resistance fighter Witold Pilecki – extracts from both of which appear on the following pages – than any amount of counselling or analysis.) A society educated in heroism will become heroic itself. The citizens of Britain endured alone the tyranny of Hitler for a whole year between the fall of France and the outbreak of fighting in Russia. They did so because as children they were taught about the defeat of the Armada, about Henry V at Agincourt, about the frostbitten Titus Oates sacrificing his life so that his fellow explorers at the South Pole might have a better chance to live. ("I am just going outside and may be some time", said Oates.) Heroic "primers", recounting such deeds used to be commonplace. The greatest of these was Thomas Carlyle's "On Heroes, Hero-Worship and the Heroic in History" which was a philosophical examination of heroism, but also a book of *moral* instruction by historical example, a book by which Carlyle intended to shape a nation's (Britain's) character, indeed.

It would be egotistical and rash to compare this book with Carlyle's, but its purpose, above the provision of the time-honoured "good read", is an avowedly moral one: to show, by illustration from the past, what heroism is, what it looks like, and why we should and could emulate it. If you want, it's a DIY book of heroism, with handy best-case examples from Ancient Greece to September 11, 2001, ranging through war to science to exploration to sport. Some of the examples are sure to irk, even to provoke, for heroism crosses political boundaries; the heroic don't always fight for the same causes (Ron Kovic was heroic in his struggle against the Vietnam war, just as Lt.-Col. Joe M. Jackson was in fighting it), but the *way* they fight is the same: selfless, dutiful, virtuous (never for the dollars), constant and always against the odds, be these odds superior numbers in battle, the opinion of the crowd, the forces of Nature.

There is one outstanding component of heroism, which is even greater than these. This is courage. For that reason, this anthology also presents many stories of courage, so that this quality may be seen clearly and often. Courage and heroism are, of course, quite distinct: the heroic is always courageous, but the courageous is not always heroic. Courage can be bought for money, it can be generated by self-interest. The pugilist Tom Hickman showed immense courage in his bare-knuckle fight with Bill Neate in 1821, but it was prompted solely by the size of the purse and desire for reputation. He makes these pages because his endurance and his "self-possession" (as Hazlitt has it) in battering, bloody round upon round was something to behold. And still is.

Hickman's courage, then, was physical courage. There is another sort, which is moral courage, the arguing of one's beliefs. Everyone vaunts physical courage (the Nazis did, Stalin did), but moral courage – such as that shown by Emile Zola in defending the Jewish Dreyfus in the anti-semitic France of 1898 – is more problematic. In general, the society which values moral courage is itself moral. The societies of Hitler and Stalin never did and never were. Even so, it is always the threat of physical pain up to and including death which tests human bravery most absolutely, most perfectly. Since this threat is most often found in war, I have included a number of battlefield stories.

A last comment. This volume is not intended to be read page to page. It is, instead, a book to browse, to dip into; the contents list will direct anyone in search of particular examples. There is no great over-arching order, only that which seems to me to provide variety and thought-provocation. That said, I have consciously put the epic of the Spartans at Thermopylae at the beginning, since this is surely the benchmark of heroism, the event by which all heroic deeds are to be judged.

And a final hope. I hope that the reader will be left enlightened in the heroic landmarks of our past and depart inspired by them. Ralph Waldo Emerson once wrote, "whoever is heroic will always find crises to try their edge." He might equally have written, "Crises will always find us, but we will only get the edge on them by being heroic." The hero resides in us all.

THE SPARTANS AT THERMOPYLAE

Charlotte Yonge

It was in 480 BC that Xerxes of Persia led his army into Greece, to be met by the Spartans in the narrow gorge of Thermopylae. Although the Spartans were defeated, their stand at Thermopylae inspired the Greeks to later victory and entered the annals of history as the byword for steadfast courage against insuperable odds.

"Stranger, bear this message to the Spartans, that we lie here obedient to their laws."[1]

There was trembling in Greece. "The Great King," as the Greeks called the chief potentate of the East, whose domains stretched from the Indian Caucasus to the Ægæus, from the Caspian to the Red Sea, was marshalling his forces against the little free states that nestled amid the rocks and gulfs of the Eastern Mediterranean. Already had his might devoured the cherished colonies of the Greeks on the eastern shore of the Archipelago, and every traitor to home institutions found a ready asylum at that despotic court, and tried to revenge his own wrongs by whispering incitements to invasion. "All people, nations, and languages," was the commencement of the decrees of that monarch's court; and it was scarcely a vain boast, for his satraps ruled over subject kingdoms, and among his tributary nations he counted the Chaldean, with his learning

1 *Simonides: Epitaph on the tomb of the Spartans who fell at Thermopylae.*

and old civilization, the wise and steadfast Jew, the skilful Phœnician, the learned Egyptian, the wild freebooting Arab of the desert, the dark-skinned Ethiopian, and over all these ruled the keen-witted, active native Persian race, the conquerors of all the rest, and led by a chosen band proudly called the Immortal. His many capitals – Babylon the great, Susa, Persepolis, and the like – were names of dreamy splendour to the Greeks, described now and then by Ionians from Asia Minor who had carried their tribute to the king's own feet, or by courtier slaves who had escaped with difficulty from being all too serviceable at the tyrannic court. And the lord of this enormous empire was about to launch his countless host against the little cluster of states the whole of which together would hardly equal one province of the huge Asiatic realm! Moreover, it was a war not only on the men, but on their gods. The Persians were zealous adorers of the sun and of fire; they abhorred the idol-worship of the Greeks, and defiled and plundered every temple that fell in their way. Death and desolation were almost the best that could be looked for at such hands; slavery and torture from cruelly barbarous masters would only too surely be the lot of numbers should their land fall a prey to the conquerors.

True it was that ten years back the former Great King had sent his best troops to be signally defeated upon the coast of Attica; but the losses at Marathon had but stimulated the Persian lust of conquest, and the new King Xerxes was gathering together such myriads of men as should crush down the Greeks and overrun their country by mere force of numbers.

The muster-place was at Sardis, and there Greek spies had seen the multitudes assembling and the state and magnificence of the king's attendants. Envoys had come from him to demand earth and water from each state in Greece, as emblems that land and sea were his; but each state was resolved to be free, and only Thessaly, that which lay first in his path, consented to yield the token of subjugation. A council was held at the Isthmus of Corinth, and attended by deputies from all the states of Greece, to consider of the best means of defence. The ships of the enemy would coast round the shores of the Ægean Sea, the land army would cross the Hellespont on a bridge of boats lashed together, and march southwards into Greece. The only hope of averting the danger lay in defending such passages as, from the nature of the ground, were so narrow that only a few persons could fight hand to hand at once, so that courage would be of more avail than numbers.

The first of these passes was called Tempe, and a body of troops was sent to guard it; but they found that this was useless and impossible, and came back again. The next was at Thermopylæ. Look in your map of the Archipelago, or Ægean Sea, as it was then called, for the great island of Negropont, or by its old name, Eubœa. It looks like a piece broken off from the coast, and to the north is shaped like the head of a bird, with the beak running into a gulf, that would fit over it, upon the mainland, and between the island and the coast is an exceedingly narrow strait. The Persian army would have to march round the edge of the gulf. They could not cut straight across the country, because the ridge of mountains called Œta rose up and barred their way. Indeed, the woods, rocks, and precipices came down so near the seashore that in two places there was only room for one single wheel track between the steeps and the impassable morass that formed the border of the gulf on its south side. These two very narrow places were called the gates of the pass, and were about a mile apart. There was a little more width left in the intervening space; but in this there were a number of springs of warm mineral water, salt and sulphurous, which were used for the sick to bathe in, and thus the place was called Thermopylæ, or the Hot Gates. A wall had once been built across the westernmost of these narrow places, when the Thessalians and Phocians, who lived on either side of it, had been at war with one another; but it had been allowed to go to decay, since the Phocians had found out that there was a very steep, narrow mountain path along the bed of a torrent by which it was possible to cross from one territory to the other without going round this marshy coast road.

This was therefore an excellent place to defend. The Greek ships were all drawn up on the farther side of Eubœa to prevent the Persian vessels from getting into the strait and landing men beyond the pass, and a division of the army was sent off to guard the Hot Gates. The council at the Isthmus did not know of the mountain pathway, and thought that all would be safe as long as the Persians were kept out of the coast path.

The troops sent for this purpose were from different cities, and amounted to about 4,000, who were to keep the pass against two millions. The leader of them was Leonidas, who had newly become one of the two kings of Sparta, the city that above all in Greece trained its sons to be hardy soldiers, dreading death infinitely less than shame. Leonidas had already made up his mind that the expedition would probably be his death, perhaps because a prophecy had been given at the Temple at Delphi that Sparta should be saved by the death of one of her kings of the race of Hercules. He was allowed by law to take with him 300 men, and these he chose most carefully, not merely for their strength and courage, but selecting those who had sons, so that no family might be altogether destroyed. These Spartans, with their helots or slaves, made up his own share of the numbers, but all the army was under his generalship. It is even said that the 300 celebrated their own funeral rites before they set out, lest they should be deprived of them by the enemy, since, as we have already seen, it was the Greek belief that the spirits of the dead found no rest till their obsequies had been performed. Such preparations did not daunt the spirits of Leonidas and his men; and his wife, Gorgo, was not a woman to be faint-hearted or hold him back. Long before, when she was a very little girl, a word of hers had saved her father from listening to a traitorous message from the King of Persia; and every Spartan lady was bred up to be able to say to those she best loved that they must come home from battle "with the shield or on it" – either carrying it victoriously or borne upon it as a corpse.

When Leonidas came to Thermopylæ, the Phocians told him of the mountain path through the chestnut woods of Mount Œta, and begged to have the privilege of guarding it on a spot high up on the mountain side, assuring him that it was very hard to find at the other end, and that there was every probability that the enemy would never discover it. He consented, and encamping around the warm springs, caused the broken wall to be repaired and made ready to meet the foe.

The Persian army were seen covering the whole country like locusts, and the hearts of some of the southern Greeks in the pass began to sink. Their homes in the Peloponnesus were comparatively secure: had they not better fall back and reserve themselves to defend the Isthmus of Corinth? But Leonidas, though Sparta was safe below the Isthmus, had no intention of abandoning his northern allies, and kept the other Peloponnesians to their posts, only sending messengers for further help.

Presently a Persian on horseback rode up to reconnoitre the pass. He could not see over the wall, but in front of it and on the ramparts he saw the Spartans, some of them engaged in active sports, and others in combing their long hair. He rode back to the king, and told him what he had seen. Now, Xerxes had in his camp an exiled Spartan prince, named Demartus, who had become a traitor to his country, and was serving as counsellor to the enemy. Xerxes sent for him, and asked whether his countrymen were mad to be thus employed instead of fleeing away; but Demartus made answer that a hard fight was no doubt in preparation, and that it was the custom of the Spartans to array their hair with especial care when they were about to enter upon any great peril. Xerxes would, however, not believe that so petty a force could intend to resist him, and waited four days, probably expecting his fleet to assist him; but as it did not appear, the attack was made.

The Greeks, stronger men and more heavily armed, were far better able to fight to advantage than the Persians with their short spears and wicker shields, and beat them off with great ease. It is said that Xerxes three times leapt off his throne in despair at the sight of his troops being driven backwards; and thus for two days it seemed as easy to force a way through the Spartans as through the rocks themselves. Nay, how could slavish troops, dragged from home to spread the victories of an ambitious king, fight like freemen who felt that their strokes were to defend their homes and children?

But on that evening a wretched man, named Ephialtes, crept into the Persian camp, and offered, for a great sum of money, to show the mountain path that would enable the enemy to take the brave defenders in the rear. A Persian general, named Hydarnes, was sent off at nightfall with a detachment to secure this passage, and was guided through the thick forests that clothed the hillside. In the stillness of the air, at daybreak, the Phocian guards of the path were startled by the crackling of the chestnut leaves under the tread of many feet. They started up, but a shower of arrows was discharged on them, and forgetting all save the present alarm, they fled to a higher part of the mountain, and the enemy, without waiting to pursue them, began to descend.

As day dawned, morning light showed the watchers of the Grecian camp below a glittering and shimmering in the torrent bed where the shaggy forests opened; but it was not the sparkle of water, but the shine of gilded helmets and the gleaming of silvered spears! Moreover, a Cimmerian crept over to the wall from the Persian camp with tidings that the path had been betrayed; that the enemy were climbing it, and would come down beyond the eastern Gate. Still, the way was rugged and circuitous, the Persians would hardly descend before midday, and there was ample time for the Greeks to escape before they could thus be shut in by the enemy.

There was a short council held over the morning sacrifice. Megistias, the seer, on inspecting the entrails of the slain victim, declared, as well he might, that their appearance boded disaster. Him Leonidas ordered to retire, but he refused, though he sent home his only son. There was no disgrace to an ordinary tone of mind in leaving a post that could not be held, and Leonidas recommended all the allied troops under his command to march away while yet the way was open. As to himself and his Spartans, they had made up their minds to die at their post, and there could be no doubt that the example of such a resolution would do more to save Greece than their best efforts could ever do if they were careful to reserve themselves for another occasion.

All the allies consented to retreat, except the eighty men who came from Mycæne and the 700 Thespians, who declared that they would not desert Leonidas. There were also 400 Thebans who remained; and thus the whole number that stayed with Leonidas to confront two million of enemies were fourteen hundred warriors, besides the helots or attendants on the 300 Spartans, whose number is not known, but there was probably at least one to each. Leonidas had two kinsmen in the camp, like himself claiming the blood of Hercules, and he tried to save them by giving them letters and messages to Sparta; but one answered that "he had come to fight, not to carry letters," and the other that "his deeds would tell all that Sparta wished to know." Another Spartan, named Dienices, when told that the enemy's archers were so numerous that their arrows darkened the sun, replied, "So much the better: we shall fight in the shade." Two of the 300 had been sent to a neighbouring village, suffering severely from a complaint in the eyes. One of them, called Eurytus, put on his armour, and commanded his helot to lead him to his place in the ranks; the other, called Aristodemus, was so overpowered with illness that he allowed himself to be carried away with the retreating allies. It was still early in the day when all were gone, and Leonidas gave the word to his men to take their last meal. "To-night," he said, "we shall sup with Pluto."

Hitherto he had stood on the defensive, and had husbanded the lives of his men; but he now desired to make as great a slaughter as possible, so as to inspire the enemy with dread of the Grecian name. He therefore marched out beyond the wall, without waiting to be attacked, and the battle began. The Persian captains went behind their wretched troops and scourged them on to the fight with whips! Poor wretches! they were driven on to be slaughtered, pierced with the Greek spears, hurled into the sea, or trampled into the mud of the morass; but their inexhaustible numbers told at length. The spears of the Greeks broke under hard service, and their swords alone remained; they began to fall, and Leonidas himself was among the first of the slain. Hotter than ever was the fight over his corpse, and two Persian princes, brothers of Xerxes, were there killed; but at length word was brought that Hydarnes was over the pass, and that the few remaining men were thus enclosed on all sides. The Spartans and Thespians made their way to a little hillock within the wall, resolved to let this be the place of their last stand; but the hearts of the Thebans failed them, and they came towards the Persians holding out their hands in entreaty for mercy. Quarter was given to them, but they were all branded with the king's mark as untrustworthy deserters. The helots probably at this time escaped into the mountains; while the small desperate band stood side by side on the hill still fighting to the last, some with swords, others with daggers, others even with their hands and teeth, till not one living man remained amongst them when the sun went down. There was only a mound of slain, bristled over with arrows.

Twenty thousand Persians had died before that handful of men! Xerxes asked Demaratus if there were many more at

Sparta like these, and was told there were 8,000. It must have been with a somewhat failing heart that he invited his courtiers from the fleet to see what he had done to the men who dared to oppose him, and showed them the head and arm of Leonidas set up upon a cross but he took care that all his own slain, except 1,000, should first be put out of sight. The body of the brave king was buried where he fell, as were those of the other dead. Much envied were they by the unhappy Aristodemus, who found himself called by no name but the "Coward," and was shunned by all his fellow-citizens. No one would give him fire or water, and after a year of misery he redeemed his honour by perishing in the forefront of the battle of Platæa, which was the last blow that drove the Persians ingloriously from Greece.

"LET'S ROLL"

Toby Harnden, Daily Telegraph, 18 September 2001

On the humdrum morning of September 11 2001 fanatics from the Al-Qaeda terror group hijacked four American airliners. Of these, two were flown into the Twin Towers of the World Trade Center in New York, while another crashed into the Pentagon — all symbolic targets, all full of human life. The terrorists' plan to use the fourth plane, flight UA93, as a flying bomb went awry when its passengers and crew staged a fight back. As a result of this resistance, led in part by passenger Todd Beamer, flight UA93 crashed not into the capitol, its probable intended target, but a lonely disused quarry in Pennsylvania, thereby saving hundreds, even thousands of American lives. There were no survivors aboard flight UA93 itself.

America discovered another posthumous hero yesterday when a computer executive emerged as a leader of the passengers who tackled hijackers at the controls of Flight 93. The last recorded words of Todd Beamer were: "Are you guys ready? Let's roll." Minutes later the Boeing 757, which officials think was heading for the Capitol in Washington, crashed near Shanksville, Pennsylvania, with the loss of all 44 on board.

Mr Beamer, 32, who worked for Oracle Corporation in New Jersey, had telephoned a GTE Airfone operator and told her one passenger had been stabbed to death and the two pilots injured. One hijacker appeared to have a bomb strapped to his waist.

The operator, Lisa Jefferson, took the call at 9.45am. By this time Mr Beamer and others on board knew from other mobile phone calls that two planes had crashed into the World Trade Centre.

Some passengers were being guarded in the first class section, but most, including Mr Beamer, had been herded into the rear. He told Miss Jefferson that a group of men planned to "jump" the hijackers.

"We're going to do something," he said. "I know I'm not going to get out of this." Together, he and Miss Jefferson recited the Lord's Prayer and the 23rd Psalm: "The Lord is my shepherd . . . Though I walk in the vale of death's shadow, I fear not, with You at my side."

After Mr Beamer said "Let's roll", Miss Jefferson heard screams and an intense scuffle before the line went dead. It was just before 10am and moments later Flight 93 plunged into a corn field.

Unlike other passengers, Mr Beamer did not call a loved one to say goodbye. Instead, he made Miss Jefferson promise to telephone his pregnant wife, Lisa and their sons David, three, and Andrew, one. "Tell her I love her and the boys."

Mrs Beamer said: "When the plane started to fly erratically, he said he knew he wouldn't make it out of there." Her husband's heroism had "made my life worth living again".

Vice-President Dick Cheney said he believed the terrorists were intending to crash Flight 93 into the Capitol, while the primary target of Flight 77, which devastated part of the Pentagon, was the White House.

James Smith, a Capitol Hill staffer who studied with Mr Beamer at Wheaton College, Illinois, said it was "incredible" that his former classmate's actions might have saved his life and those of hundreds around Congress.

"He was a real athlete, a basketball player who hung around the jocks at college. But he was a quiet, smart guy with a nice smile. You always got the sense that he had done his homework."

The hijackers appear to have found themselves against at least five powerful men determined to strike back.

Jeremy Glick, 31, was a college rugby player and judo champion. He telephoned his wife, Lyzabeth, to say there was talk of "rushing" the hijackers. After telling her he loved her, he said: "We decided we're going to do it."

Mark Bingham, also 31 and a former college rugby player, Thomas Burnett, 38, a California businessman, and Louis Nacke, 42, a weightlifter with a Superman logo tattooed on his arm, are also believed to have taken part.

"He [Mr Nacke] was a warm, smiling individual who jumped right into every situation, a guy who couldn't do enough for you," said Robert Weisberg, his father-in-law.

After tackling the hijacker guarding them, all five would have had to charge up the aisle to storm the cockpit.

The body of a male crew member, bound hand and foot, was found yesterday. Earlier, the body of a flight attendant was found with her hands bound.

THE HABIT AND VIRTUE OF COURAGE

Aristotle

Written by the Greek philosopher in 350 BC.

. . . by doing the acts that we do in our transactions with other men we become just or unjust, and by doing the acts that we do in the presence of danger, and being habituated to feel fear or confidence, we become brave or cowardly . . . for by being habituated to despise things that are terrible and to stand our ground against them we become brave, and it is when we have become so that we shall be most able to stand our ground against them.

THE FACE OF COURAGE

M.R.D. Foot

*The Nazi holocaust produced the 20th century's darkest moments;
it also produced its most shining examples of moral and physical
courage. Witold Pilecki was a Polish army officer who determined
to break into the Nazi death camp at Auschwitz to set up a
resistance movement there.*

Pilecki, though still only a junior officer in his middle forties,
was someone of enormous force of character, even in a
society that teemed with people of strong character and intense
individuality. He belonged to a body called the *Tajna Armia
Polska*, the Secret Polish Army; a body that was merged
eventually in the AK, the Home Army. It would be misleading
to say he played a prominent part in the TAP, because as every
Pole knew it was indispensable not to be prominent, for anyone
working clandestinely against an occupier; but he was extremely
active. Several much more senior people knew and trusted him,
and he was aware of a great deal that was going on.

Reports of the camp under construction at Oswięcim – as the
Poles called Auschwitz – reached and impressed him, and he
conceived a daring plan to do something about it. The plan was
so daring that for several weeks his colonel hesitated to approve.
It was simply – most daring plans are simple – to let himself get
arrested, and sent to Auschwitz as a prisoner. Having got there,
he was to send out reports of what was really happening inside
the camp, to see whether he could organize resistance, and then,
if he could, to escape.

On top of the military difficulties of these tasks, the personal ones were severe. He had married a dozen years earlier, and had a daughter; but Poland's crisis was such that merely personal troubles just had to be brushed aside. Mobilization overrode the marriage tie; his heart could and did stay with his wife and child, but his body had to go elsewhere.

A little time had to be spent on arranging the essential details about communication; a very few addresses, reckoned perfectly safe, which he had to memorize, and a safe, simple password system by which a messenger could establish good faith, were all that were needed. The TAP was a brisk and efficient body, though its leaders were already on the run from the Gestapo. It could clear up promptly business of this sort, over which café-conversationalist resisters in Bucarest or Paris could dally for months, even years.

And by a stroke of luck, Pilecki secured a false identity which, he reckoned, ought to earn him a sentence to Auschwitz, his first objective: the identity of Tomasz Serafiński, a reserve officer who had gone underground instead of reporting to the Germans as ordered. Pilecki did not know – he did not need to know – where Serafiński had gone. He found out instead enough about Serafiński's past to survive cross-questioning in his new character; and he knew that the German secret police, as methodical as they were cruel, had secured a list of all the peacetime officers in the Polish army, active and reserve. To be on this list, and (like the other 19,600) not to have surrendered oneself, would – he reckoned – be crime enough to merit consignment to Auschwitz.

His reckoning proved correct.

It was not difficult to get arrested. He just failed to run away down the nearest side street, one early morning in September 1940 when the Germans made a routine rush-hour check on people walking into central Warsaw to work. He shortly found himself, with a thousand companions, lying face down on the damp sawdust floor of a nearby riding school. Their hands were stretched out flat in front of them, palms down. Machine guns covered them from the galleries. SS-men walked among them, whipping those who fidgeted. Pilecki did not fidget.

Two days later, he was received (as Serafiński) in Auschwitz, and became prisoner number 4,859. In his own words, as he and his companions were marched from the railway station into the camp:

> On the way one of us was ordered to run to a post a little off the road and immediately after him went a round from a machine-gun. He was killed. Ten of his casual comrades were pulled out of the ranks and shot on the march with pistols on the ground of "collective responsibility" for the "escape", arranged by the SS-men themselves. The eleven were dragged along by straps tied to one leg. The dogs were teased with the bloody corpses and set onto them. All this to the accompaniment of laughter and jokes.

They reached the camp as glum, they thought, as could be; marched in under the slogan *Arbeit macht frei* (work sets you free); and were then made glummer still by being made to strip, and to have *all* their hair, body hair as well as head hair, shaved off, and to put on the prison uniform of striped canvas.

Pilecki was lucky enough to get an indoor job, as one of the cleaning staff for his hut; but lost it before long, as the German criminal in charge of the but would only employ on his staff those who, like himself, habitually clubbed their fellow-prisoners before speaking to them. Not only did he lose his soft job, as well as many other illusions, promptly, he soon almost lost his health, which in such a camp was equivalent to losing one's life.

On 28 October 1940, a man ran away from an outside working-party, and was found to be missing at the noon roll-call. All the prisoners were kept standing at attention on the parade-ground from noon till nine in the evening; in an icy north-east wind that bore heavy rain and sleet, turn and turn about. Anyone who moved was liable to be shot – 200 died of exposure. Pilecki was among several hundred more who collapsed, but was nursed back to a semblance of health in the camp hospital, and rapidly returned to work.

The work consisted of building more huts to hold the increased numbers of prisoners who were expected, to store the belongings they brought with them, and in the end to dispose of them and their bodies.

All Nazi concentration camps were run by the SS. Most existed for two reasons: as prisons to sequester those the SS wanted out of the way, and as factories to provide the SS with profits. For this peculiar organization, originally Hitler's small personal bodyguard, grew to be a state-within-a-state of an unusually intricate kind; financing itself in part from the products of its slave labour; and with its own private army, the *Waffen-SS*. Through this army's ranks a million men passed; it provided the hard core of Nazi Germany's armed forces, nearly forty divisions strong, and included many crack units. Some of its weapons and equipment were, for economy's sake, turned out by the camps that were under SS control.

At and near Auschwitz there were a few arms factories; but the Auschwitz-Birkenau group of camps existed for a third reason also, more secret and more sinister. Here among other places, here above all, the SS proposed to get on with the *Endlösung*, the final solution of the Jewish problem: the killing of all the Jews they could catch. As Himmler put it to Rudolf Hess, the founder-commandant of Auschwitz, in the late summer of 1941, "The Jews are the sworn enemies of the German people and must be eradicated. Every Jew that we can lay our hands on is to be destroyed now during the war, without exception."

The method chosen was by cyanide gas poisoning. At Auschwitz and Birkenau, as at other extermination camps such as Treblinka, Maidanek, Sobibór, windowless concrete huts were built, with nozzles in their ceilings, into which Jews – or any other prisoners of whom the SS wanted to dispose – were herded, naked, in large crowds; believing they were to have a shower. They were showered with cyanide gas, their bodies were then hauled and shovelled across to the building next door, also prisoner-built, where they were cremated. On the way from gas chamber to crematorium, the bodies were checked for gold teeth or for rings, which were removed (it was simplest to remove ringed fingers with a garden chopper), to keep the SS profits up.

It took time, again, for a scheme of this size and this elaboration to get moving. Auschwitz was founded in 1940, the big killings did not start there till 1942; in January 1945 it was overrun by the Red Army. Twelve hundred prisoners were left in it at that moment, all too ill to move; in Birkenau there were about 5,800 more invalids, two-thirds of them women.

Something approaching four million people had been killed in the complex meanwhile, during the 1,688 days of Auschwitz's existence.

During Pilecki's first three months in the camp, nearly 3,000 more prisoners joined it; they were only the beginners. By the summer of 1944 the Auschwitz-Birkenau group of camps had about 130,000 current inmates, sometimes 140,000; but the rate of turnover was very high. For instance, during that summer 437,000 Hungarian Jews were admitted to the camps, almost all of whom were killed when, or soon after, they arrived. In such cases people would be sent straight from the train to the gas chambers, pausing only on the way to undress – several large huts were filled, quite full, with their clothing. They were spared the body-shave Pilecki had gone through; their head hair was shorn after death, on their way to the crematoria, and made into mattresses, to keep the SS profits up.

Nearly a thousand prisoners were employed in the *Sonder-kommandos*, the special squads that ran the actual process of extermination. All were Jews; they were housed, in the end, in the crematorium attics. Each squad worked a twelve-hour shift, turn and turn about with its alternate; about once a quarter, each squad was itself led into the gas chambers by its successor. "The members of the *Sonderkommando*, speaking many languages and dialects, could quieten down those being driven to their death, and this they did in the knowledge that they would gain nothing by behaving differently and that by kindly treatment they could at least mitigate the anguish of the victims' last moments." The death squads themselves knew only too well what awaited them.

All this apparatus of terror was under the guard of about 3,250 SS men. They never moved unarmed, seldom moved singly, and had all the usual adjuncts of a terror camp: tracker dogs, lighted electrified fences, torture chambers, above all, atmosphere. As Pilecki's example showed us, from the moment they came under SS guard, prisoners were aware that their captors were entirely ruthless. The inmates were encouraged to believe that, as the crematorium squads mostly came to do, they should accept their fate as stoically as they could. They were there to die; they might as well die in a calm and orderly way.

Yet, diabolical as their captors were, they were not diaboli-

cally efficient. And in the early months of the camp, they even
now and again let people out; it was still just possible to
persuade even a member of the Gestapo that he might have
made a mistake.

As early as November 1940, two months after his arrest,
Pilecki was able to send his first report out of Auschwitz to
Warsaw. It was memorized by one of his earliest recruits, a
perfectly innocent and inoffensive citizen who had friends in
Warsaw powerful enough to persuade the Germans that he had
in fact been arrested in error. He was made to swear the
customary oaths that he would reveal nothing about what went
on inside the camp, but was a good enough Pole and a good
enough Catholic to know that oaths sworn under duress have no
value. When he made touch with Pilecki's superiors, he talked.

There was not yet much to say. At this date the gas chambers,
and the whole Birkenau camp, were no more than gleams in
Himmler's and Eichmann's eyes. But at least Home Army
headquarters now knew that Auschwitz was a concentration
camp, and a cruel one (there were no mild ones); and that
Witold Pilecki was at work inside it, seeing what he could do
about resistance.

What could he do? First of all, continue to report: for which
he seized every opportunity, however glancing, that appeared
safe. Some of the SS garrison's laundry, for example, was done
for them in Auschwitz town. The SS did not want to demean
themselves by carrying laundry baskets; they contented themselves with searching the baskets very thoroughly (such baskets
forming a well known means of escape), and providing a vigilant
armed guard for the prisoners who toted them. Over the
months, their vigilance relaxed a trifle. The camp laundry
squad had meanwhile had a chance to assess the characters
of the few town laundry workers whom they saw, and, given
luck and daring, could slip written notes to them. Any Pole
could be relied on to be anti-German, so the notes got passed on
to any address they bore.

Any such system bore risks of interception, at any and every
stage; people who will not run risks cannot hope to win battles.
In 1942–4 a considerable body of intelligence about what was
going on inside the camps got passed out of Auschwitz and
Birkenau, reached Warsaw safely, and was passed on thence to

Stockholm, whence it reached London from March 1941. The London Poles passed the news on to MI6, which passed it to the foreign office; thence it went to Washington, Moscow, and any service departments that needed it. Some of it the Poles used straight away in their propaganda.

The trouble was that the news was, on the whole, too bad to be credible; and most people who heard it, did not take it in as true. Moscow was disinclined to believe anything that emanated from the London Poles, on principle. In Washington and London, everyone in authority, however bellicose towards Nazism, had been brought up to believe mass murder to be utterly beyond the pale of civilized behaviour, and imagined Germany still to be a civilized state. The sheer incredulity of distant senior men lay, unknown to Pilecki, as one obstacle across his path.

Much closer obstacles were only too obvious. The main starting task was to do anything he could to encourage his fellow prisoners not to kowtow, any more than they had to, to the terrorist regime under which they had to live. As most of his fellow prisoners were Poles, this task was not insuperably difficult. In carrying it through, he was able to gauge something of his companions' characters, and to estimate which could be most useful for more advanced work.

He had had to abandon most of his preconceived ideas about what he would do, as soon as he discovered how hard conditions in the camp really were: a process of adapting idea to reality, painful enough in one's teens, that can be excruciating in manhood, especially on the morrow of a great national disaster. He wanted to set up a secret grouping among the prisoners that would be ready to try to wrest power from the SS, the moment there was a nearby allied armed force to help. He did take in that there was no probability, no outside likelihood even, that the prisoners could seize power all by themselves: the SS had too many machine guns, and were too quick to use them. He hoped for a Russian or an Anglo-American parachute landing in force; or failing that, for a coup by Polish partisans.

There were in fact some Home Army partisan groups in the neighbourhood, now and again, though they were neither strong in numbers nor heavily armed. The Home Army's weakness in arms, compared to similar groups in France or

Greece or Yugoslavia, arose from two causes: Poland lay at the extreme limit of air range from Anglo-American territory, and the Russians forbade aircraft on supply sorties for the Home Army to land on soviet airfields. The few aircraft that could manage the round trip – even from Brindisi, when Brindisi became available late in 1943, it was a ten-hour flight – therefore had to take up most of their load with petrol, to get them there and back. France and Yugoslavia both got about 10,000 tons of warlike stores by air, through links with SOE and its American opposite number, OSS (the Office of Strategic Services); Poland only got 600 tons.

The People's Army does not seem to have operated in the parts of Poland annexed to the Reich. The official soviet attitude to the camps was in any case, to a western eye, slightly odd. Theoretically – in Marxist-Stalinist theory, that is – no prisoners were ever taken from the Red Army; a Red Army man's duty was to fight, never to surrender. The Germans and their satellites took over six million uniformed prisoners all the same (four-fifths of whom, by the by, succumbed in German hands: another huge item for the butchers' bill). Every single survivor who was returned – usually forcibly, by the other allies – to the USSR after the war, automatically did a punishment spell in a Siberian labour camp. All camps, of whatever kind, were looked at askance by the Russians: except for their own. And the existence of their own was inadmissible.

But we must get back from these strategic and political generalities to the hard particular facts of Pilecki's Auschwitz career. By Christmas 1940 he had already chosen his first five clandestine leaders; he added two more groups of five in the following spring. An attack of pneumonia, brought on by standing naked on parade for some hours in February while his hut and clothes were disinfested of lice, put him for a month into the camp hospital, where he organized a highly efficient cell. It was (as Peulevé later found in Buchenwald) a part of the camp well adapted for resistance and deception, and the Auschwitz hospital secured, by devious means, a wireless receiver: this freed prisoners in the know from dependence on Goebbels' propaganda bulletins, which were all that the camp loudspeakers ever provided in the way of news. There were no newspapers within the camp.

All the attempts to organize resistance were not, of course, confined to Pilecki and his groups. Several senior Polish officers set about organizing intelligence networks, with varying degrees of success. Unhappily, some among them – some even of the senior officers who became involved in Pilecki's own groupings – occasionally found they had to stand on their dignity, and insisted on receiving orders only from people senior to themselves. Such petty resentments, pathetically out of place in an SS camp, were ineradicable in the old Polish officer caste.

There were differences between Polish prisoners on more important matters than rank: they did not all see eye to eye in politics. Differences in political viewpoint grew more widespread, as the racial composition of the camp's inmates changed. At first the prisoners were nearly all Poles, with a sprinkling of senior Germans, but over thirty nationalities were represented eventually; particularly Russians and Ukrainians, as well as hordes of Jews from several different states. Pilecki preferred dealing with Poles, as communication was so much more easy through a common language and common customs, but by no means imposed any sort of racial bar. In any case, while he was in the camp it remained very largely Polish in its prisoner population.

The communists among the prisoners at first lay low; after 22 June 1941 they hurled themselves into the resistance struggle, not with any outstanding effect. The German communists in Buchenwald and other camps often held dominant positions; the Polish communists, starting later in the struggle, were not as a rule as successful. One subsequently well-known politician, Jozef Cyrankiewicz, already – though ten years younger than Pilecki – an eminent socialist, took a leading part in the politico-military fusion that Pilecki's tact and ability and common sense had created by the time Cyrankiewicz reached the camp in the autumn of 1942. He later drew apart from the right-wing elements whom Pilecki had persuaded to co-operate with the socialists; threw in his own lot with the left-wingers, and became prime minister of the new communist-dominated Poland after the war.

Such actual military organization as Pilecki was able to set up was necessarily slender and tentative; and conditions, as well as people, in the camp changed so fast that he found he had to set up different groups to cope with different contingencies. By night, with the prisoners locked in their huge huts, a different set of fighting men would be needed from the grouping that would apply during the day when prisoners were scattered at work, some inside the camp and some outside it.

A good deal of intricate, deadly secret planning was done on these necessarily conjectural lines, everyone in the early stages taking the utmost care to bring nobody else into the plot who was not wholly to be trusted. The one vital necessity was armament: which was at first glance unavailable.

Reflection showed some possibilities. A daring quartet of prisoners managed to fake up a key to the SS clothing store; and on 20 June 1942 dressed as two officers and two warrant officers, used another faked-up key to visit the arms store, stole a visiting senior officer's car, and drove away in it, being smartly saluted by the sentry, who did not bother to look at their forged passes. One of them, called Jaster, bore a report of Pilecki's which he delivered in Warsaw. Rumour swelled their numbers; the incident greatly cheered the prisoners who remained behind. They had a few rough weapons ready enough to hand: pick helves, spades, hammers, mauls, hand axes, a few two-handed felling axes: no use against an alert sub-machine-gunner, but not perfectly useless in a scrimmage, or at night. One or two attempts at mass break-outs were made with these hand weapons, all with ill result; though nine men out of one party of fifty did get clean away, and over 600 prisoners escaped altogether, one way and another. Over half of these 600 were soon recaptured, humiliated and killed.

Himmler himself visited the complex on 17–18 June 1942; watched a party of Jews reach Birkenau; saw most of them gassed; inspected the artificial-rubber works run in Auschwitz town by camp labour; asked to watch a woman being flogged; promoted Hess a rank; and went away.

Pilecki by now had four battalions of followers organized, about 500 of whom knew him by sight and name as a secret camp resistance leader: the secret was becoming much too open for comfort. He had a fairly settled job, so far as anything in Auschwitz was settled, in the tailor's shop; and all his 500 friends were vigilantly on the watch for Gestapo informers, of whom there were many. He began to feel uneasy; before he left, he had one more macabre scheme to carry through.

The SS had a weakness for black pullovers, which they had knitted for them by women prisoners. There were quite a lot of women in Auschwitz, and hundreds of thousands died in Birkenau which was primarily a women's camp: endless opportunities for intrigue, corruption and romance resulted. Hess himself had a prisoner mistress, though he had his own wife and small children living with him just outside the main gate; his conduct was widely enough known for him to have no hold over the misdemeanours of his own men.

Pilecki's organization exploited the double SS weakness, for pretty girls, and for warm clothes, and with the help of their hospital friends, occasionally supplied the SS with pullovers or greatcoats bearing typhus-infected lice. A very few SS died as a result.

More direct action could be taken by men who were tired of life. At Sobibor camp, near Lublin, the *Sonderkommando* of about 300 in the innermost camp decided one day to break out. SS men visited the tailor's shop one by one, to collect uniforms they had left there for pressing before they went on leave. A prisoner stood behind the shop door with a spade, and hit each SS man as hard as he could on the back of the head. When the tailors had collected fifteen corpses, and a pistol from each, the whole squad rushed the gate of the inner compound; got to the main gate; rushed that too, and were out in the open. Half of them were brought back by the surrounding peasantry, because they were Jews. A few got away. Himmler was so put out that he had the whole camp closed down.

This escape was not till 14 October 1943; by which time Pilecki was well away from Auschwitz.

His escape was straightforward. He decided to leave in the spring of 1943; for another body of four escapers from Auschwitz, who had got out on the previous 29 December, included a dentist called Kuczbara who knew too much about him, and had fallen back into Gestapo hands on 20 March. So it was dangerous for him to stay, and he was anxious also to impress in person on his superiors in Warsaw the readiness of the camp to rise, and the need for some positive partisan demonstration to give it the signal to do so.

He handed over military command to Major Bończa, and all
the innumerable liaison details he carried in his head to Henryk
Bartosiewicz – both were his friends – and was ready to leave.
He secured – this was child's play to someone by now so
experienced underground – a forged pass to join the bakery
squad: the bakery was outside the wire. By now he had left the
tailor's shop for the parcel office, and he faked illness on Easter
Saturday, 24 April, to get out of that. Hospital friends discharged him in time to join his bakery squad on the next
Monday/Tuesday night – like Peulevé, he was supposed to
have typhus, but in this case he was not really ill at all. The
prisoner boss of the bakery group was bribed with a piece of
chicken; and a friend in the locksmith's squad produced a key to
the bakery door. Two companion bakers were to leave with him;
all had plain clothes beneath their camp uniforms.

After several sweltering hours – Pilecki had never been in a
bakery before – one of them cut the telephone wires, another
unlocked the door, and at a moment when none of the SS was in
sight they all went through it: and ran.

It was a fine night for escape, dark and pouring with rain, and
they got to the bank of the Vistula – several miles away –
unchallenged. They had everything they needed except food.
"This had crossed their minds in the bakery, but at the last
moment, in the heat of the dash for freedom, they had forgotten
to grab a few loaves." Pilecki moreover was racked by sciatica.
Luck stayed with them: they found a dinghy on the river bank,
padlocked, and by a miracle the bakery key opened the padlock.

They hid in a wood all day on Tuesday, and in another wood
farther east all Wednesday. Next night, with a priest's help,
they crossed into the General Government, kept south of
Cracow, and came on 2 May to a safe address at Bochnia, a
town some twenty miles east of it. There Pilecki inquired for the
nearest Home Army unit, and found it, by a singular freak, to be
commanded by Tomasz Serafiński whose name he had been
using in captivity.

Cracow District of the Home Army could not be got to take
any interest in Auschwitz. Pilecki persevered, and went to main
headquarters in Warsaw. There they had "a heap of files", with
all his reports in them and others; but could not be persuaded
that the risks of an action against it were worth the running. If

ever there were a countrywide rising, he was assured, Auschwitz would not be forgotten; and that was all.

He turned to other duties; fought through the Warsaw rising of August–September 1944; survived even that catastrophe; and spent the rest of the war, under a different false identity, in a prisoner-of-war camp in Germany. Auschwitz had been an experience so shattering that he was looking for no more adventures; having lived through that and the Warsaw rising was, he felt, enough.

Or was it? When the Third Reich crumbled quite away, he moved southward in the crowds of what were pathetically named "displaced persons", and reported to the Polish army in Italy. It was put to him that someone of his almost uncanny tenacity in adversity would be just the man to go back into Russian-occupied Poland on a mission for the Polish government-in-exile, in London.

He went; was arrested almost immediately he got there; and was executed in 1948 – no one outside the Polish and Russian secret police forces is quite sure when, or where. His wife and daughter, who still live in Poland, do not even know where he is buried.

THE HEROINE OF THE PLAYGROUND

Maurice Weaver, Daily Telegraph

On July 8 1996 a modern scourge visited St Luke's School in Wolverhampton, England, when a madman ran amok. A teenage nursery assistant, Lisa Potts, was all that stood between a group of infants and their sure slaughter.

A nursery assistant who was badly injured trying to save children from a machete attacker relived the horror in court yesterday, swinging the blood-stained weapon over her head to show how he slashed his way into the kindergarten.

Lisa Potts, 20, who was still a teenager when Horrett Campbell struck at St Luke's infants' school in Blakenhall, Wolverhampton, on July 8, described the panic as he attacked during a teddy bears' picnic in the playground. "He didn't say anything at all," she said.

"His teeth were gritted with anger, as if in a laugh. It was crazy. The children were hanging on to my skirt and some of them went underneath the skirt, they were so frightened. He just struck right down, going for my head and I put my arm up to protect."

Campbell, 33, an unemployed welder, from Villiers Court, a block of flats overlooking the school, faces seven charges of attempted murder – four of adults and three of children. The prosecution at Stafford Crown Court alleges that he planned a massacre on the lines of those carried out at Dunblane by Thomas Hamilton and in Tasmania by Martin Bryant.

Police found two newspaper cuttings in his flat about Tasmania, the court heard. Richard Wakerley, prosecuting, said: "He told police that those murderers had been driven to indiscriminately kill others, just as he had been compelled to do what he did." He felt an affinity for them, claiming that he, like them, was "misunderstood by society". He also thought that the children at St Luke's had once jeered at him.

While Hamilton and Bryant used guns, he did not have access to one. Two dismantled toy guns and drawings of gun parts were also found at his home.

Campbell, sitting in the dock between two warders, has expressed a readiness to admit six charges of inflicting grievous bodily harm with intent and one of attempted grievous bodily harm with intent. But the prosecution has rejected the offer, quoting evidence of lengthy premeditation of the crime, the "fearsome" nature of the weapon and his aiming at the victims' heads as proof that his intention throughout was to kill.

Miss Potts, who has received awards for her heroism, received the most severe injuries of all as she tried to push the children, aged 3.5 to 4.5, to safety under a rain of blows from the machete's 16in blade. She is still unfit to return to work.

Mr Wakerley said: "You may well be astonished by the courage of that young girl . . . but for her action this tragedy could have been so much worse."

Miss Potts was asked if she felt able to demonstrate how Campbell made his attack. She put on plastic gloves, took the machete from a court usher and swung it high over her head in a downward chop. "It was like that," she said. "They had great force."

The judge, Mr Justice Sedley, asked: "They were overarm blows?" Miss Potts agreed: "They had great force." The machete still carried various words inscribed by Campbell, including the phrase "you filthy devils", and a swastika. Another inscription was "666 marks the Devil".

During the attack Horrett carried a sports bag containing a Fairy Liquid bottle full of petrol. He wore a tweed deerstalker with two screws sticking out like horns and a black cross on the side.

Mr Wakerley told jury members that, even if they considered that Campbell had been mentally unbalanced at the time of the attack, he could still be found guilty of attempted murder.

Miss Potts described how Campbell had first hit two mothers who were waiting in the playground as the children prepared to go home. Then he turned on the children, slashing Francesca Quintaine, four, so violently that he sliced off her ear, tore open her face from ear to mouth and broke her jaw.

Miss Potts said: "I was clearing up and putting things into a basket and saw a man running from the corner of the fence. He went to attack one of the mums who was walking to collect her kid from the infants. He was carrying a machete. He came to the mum [Wendy Willington] and basically belted her over the head.

"She was lying on the floor and then I heard Miss Halles [Dorothy Halles, the nursery head teacher] say: "Quick, grab some of the children." I started running with them. The man leapt over the fence and attacked one of the other mums, Surinder Chopra.

"He came again with it and went down on to her head. It was crazy from then on. Children were holding on to my skirt and some of them went underneath. They were hiding with fright.

"I started running with the children to try and get into the nursery door, but before I knew it the man came at me with the machete. As I started to run in, he lashed out at Francesca – straight across the face. Her face just opened.

"I was just running for the door and had two children under my arm. I got inside the nursery and dropped the children and as I went to shut the door his foot was in it and he was inside. I pushed one of the children into the dressing-up area behind the door and put my arms around the others as he attacked me again. He came again with the machete and started attacking my back. I think he hit me twice. I realised as I turned round that he was going for the little boy. The other children had run off to the outside door.

"He went for Ahmed [Malik] across the head. I went to pick him up and he cut my arm again. There was another blow to Ahmed on the arm as he fell to the floor. I couldn't pick him up. I ran around the side of the water tray in the nursery and I then felt the blow on the head. That's the one I felt the most."

Despite being hit, she continued running. "I didn't look back," she said. It was only when the children were safe that she realised she was covered in blood. Miss Potts was sliced six times in all, including the blow to her head which chipped the skull.

THE FRONT OF THE BUS

Kai Friese

December 1 1955. The American South was a segregationist land where black people were required to sit at the back of the bus. However, Rosa Parks refused the seat allocated her by prejudice. It was a moment of pure history; the beginning of the end of legal segregation in America.

It was Thursday, December 1, 1955. The workday was over, and crowds of people boarded the green-and-white buses that trundled through the streets of Montgomery. Rosa Parks was tired after a full day of stitching and ironing shirts at the Montgomery Fair department store. She thought she was lucky to have gotten one of the last seats in the rear section of the Cleveland Avenue bus that would take her home.

Soon the back of the bus was full, and several people were standing in the rear. The bus rolled on through Court Square, where African-Americans had been auctioned off during the days of the Confederacy, and came to a stop in front of the Empire Theater. The next passenger aboard stood in the front of an aisle. He was a white man.

When he noticed that a white person had to stand, the bus driver, James F. Blake, called out to the four black people who were sitting just behind the white section. He said they would have to give up their seats for the new passenger. No one stood up. "You'd better make it light on yourself and let me have those seats," the driver said threateningly. Three men got up and went to stand at the back of the bus. But Rosa Parks wasn't about to move. She had been in this situation before, and she had always given up her seat. She had always felt insulted by the experience. "It meant that I didn't have a right to do anything but get on the bus, give them my fare and then be pushed around wherever they wanted me," she said.

By a quirk of fate, the driver of the bus on this December evening was the same James F. Blake who had once before removed the troublesome Rosa Parks from his bus for refusing to enter by the back door. That was a long time ago, in 1943. Rosa Parks didn't feel like being pushed around again. She told the driver that she wasn't in the white section and she wasn't going to move.

Blake knew the rules, though. He knew that the white section was wherever the driver said it was. If more white passengers got on the bus, he could stretch the white section to the back of the bus and make all the blacks stand. He shouted to Rosa Parks to move to the back of the bus. She wasn't impressed. She told him again that she wasn't moving. Everyone in the bus was silent, wondering what would happen next. Finally Blake told Rosa Parks that he would have her arrested for violating the racial segregation codes. In a firm but quiet voice, she told him that he could do what he wanted to do because she wasn't moving.

Blake got off the bus and came back with an officer of the Montgomery Police Department. As the officer placed Rosa Parks under arrest, she asked him plainly, "Why do you people push us around?"

With the eyes of all the passengers on him, the officer could only answer in confusion. "I don't know. I'm just obeying the law," he said.

Rosa Parks was taken to the police station, where she was booked and fingerprinted. While the policemen were filling out forms, she asked if she could have a drink of water. She was told that the drinking fountain in the station was for whites only. Then a policewoman marched her into a long corridor facing a wall of iron bars. A barred door slid open. She went inside. The door clanged shut, and she was locked in. She was in jail.

Parks decided to challenge her arrest in court. As a show of support, black people in Montgomery organized a boycott of the city's bus service.

Rosa Parks woke up on the morning of Monday, December 5, thinking about her trial. As she and her husband got out of bed, they heard the familiar sound of a City Lines bus pulling up to a stop across the road. There was usually a crowd of people waiting for the bus at this time. The Parkses rushed to the window and looked out. Except for the driver, the bus was empty and there was no one getting on either. The bus stood at the stop for more than a minute, puffing exhaust smoke into the cold December air as the puzzled driver waited for passengers. But no one appeared, and the empty bus chugged away.

Rosa Parks was filled with happiness. Her neighbors were actually boycotting the buses. She couldn't wait to drive to the courthouse so that she could see how the boycott was going in the rest of Montgomery. When Fred Gray arrived to drive her to the trial, she wasn't disappointed. Rosa Parks had expected some people to stay off the buses. She thought that with luck, maybe even half the usual passengers would stay off. But these buses were just plain empty.

All over the city, empty buses bounced around for everyone to see. There was never more than the usual small group of white passengers in front and sometimes a lonely black passenger in back, wondering what was going on. The streets were filled with black people walking to work.

As Rosa Parks and her lawyer drove up to the courthouse, there was another surprise waiting for them. A crowd of about five hundred blacks had gathered to show their support for her. Mrs Parks and the lawyer made their way slowly through the cheering crowd into the courtroom. Once they were inside, the trial didn't take long. Rosa Parks was quickly convicted of breaking the bus segregation laws and fined ten dollars, as well as four dollars for the cost of her trial. This was the stage at which Claudette Colvin's trial had ended seven months earlier. Colvin had had little choice but to accept the guilty verdict and pay the fine.

This time, however, Fred Gray rose to file an appeal on Rosa Parks's case. This meant that her case would be taken to a higher court at a later date. Meanwhile, Mrs Parks was free to go.

Outside the courthouse, the crowd was getting restless. Some of them were carrying sawed-off shotguns, and the policemen were beginning to look worried. E. D. Nixon went out to calm them, but nobody could hear him in the din. Voices from the crowd shouted out that they would storm the courthouse if Rosa Parks didn't come out safely within a few minutes. When she did appear, a great cheer went up again.

After seeing the empty buses that morning, and this large and fearless crowd around her now, Rosa Parks knew that she had made the right decision. Black people were uniting to show the city administration that they were tired of the insults of segregation. Together, they could change Montgomery. They could do some good.

HERO WORSHIP

Thomas Carlyle

The Scottish historian Thomas Carlyle (1795–1881) was the most eloquent writer on heroes and heroism since the Ancient Greeks. Here he promotes his belief in hero worship as the foundation of good society.

And now if worship even of a star had some meaning in it, how much more might that of a Hero! Worship of a Hero is transcendent admiration of a Great Man. I say great men are still admirable; I say there is, at bottom, nothing else admirable! No nobler feeling than this of admiration for one higher than himself dwells in the breast of man. It is to this hour, and at all hours, the vivifying influence in man's life. Religion I find stand upon it; not Paganism only, but far higher and truer religions, – all religion hitherto known. Hero-worship, heartfelt prostrate admiration, submission, burning, boundless, for a noblest godlike Form of Man – is not that the germ of Christianity itself? The greatest of all Heroes is One – whom we do not name here! Let sacred silence meditate that sacred matter; you will find it the ultimate perfection of a principle extant throughout man's whole history on earth.

Or coming into lower, less *un*speakable provinces, is not all Loyalty akin to religious Faith also? Faith is loyalty to some inspired Teacher, some spiritual Hero. And what therefore is loyalty proper, the life-breath of all society, but an effluence of Hero-worship, submissive admiration for the truly great? Society is founded on Hero-worship. All dignities of rank, on which human association rests, are what we may call a *Her-oarchy* (Government of Heroes), – or a Hierarchy, for it is "sacred" enough withal! The Duke means *Dux*, Leader; King is *Kön-ning, Kan-ning,* Man that *knows* or *cans*. Society everywhere is some representation, not *in*supportably inaccurate, of a graduated Worship of Heroes; – reverence and obedience done to men really great and wise. Not *in*supportably inaccurate, I say! They are all as bank-notes, these social dignitaries, all representing gold; – and several of them, alas, always are *forged* notes. We can do with some forged false notes; with a good many even; but not with all, or the most of them forged! No: there have to come revolutions then; cries of Democracy, Liberty and Equality, and I know not what: – the notes being all false, and no gold to be had for *them*, people take to crying in their despair that there is no gold, that there never was any! – "Gold," Hero-worship, *is* nevertheless, as it was always and everywhere, and cannot cease till man himself ceases.

I am well aware that in these days Hero-worship, the thing I call Hero-worship, professes to have gone out, and finally ceased. This, for reasons which it will be worth while some time to inquire into, is an age that as it were denies the existence of great men; denies the desirableness of great men. Show our critics a great man, a Luther for example, they begin to what they call "account" for him; not to worship him, but take the dimensions of him, – and bring him out to be a little kind of man! He was the "creature of the Time," they say; the Time called him forth, the Time did everything, he nothing – but what we the little critic could have done too! This seems to me but melancholy work. The Time call forth? Alas, we have known Times *call* loudly enough for their great man; but not find him when they called! He was not there; Providence had not sent him; the Time, *calling* its loudest, had to go down to confusion and wreck because he would not come when called.

For if we will think of it, no Time need have gone to ruin, could it have *found* a man great enough, a man wise and good enough: wisdom to discern truly what the Time wanted, valour to lead it on the right road thither; these are the salvation of any Time. But I liken common languid Times, with their unbelief, distress, perplexity, with their languid doubting characters and embarrassed circumstances, impotently crumbling-down into ever worse distress towards final ruin; – all this I liken to dry dead fuel, waiting for the lightning out of Heaven that shall kindle it. The great man, with his free force direct out of God's own hand, is the lightning. His word is the wise healing word which all can believe in. All blazes round him now, when he has once struck on it, into fire like his own. The dry mouldering sticks are thought to have called him forth. They did want him greatly; but as to calling him forth –! – Those are critics of small vision, I think, who cry: "See, is it not the sticks that made the fire?" No sadder proof can be given by a man of his own littleness than disbelief in great men. There is no sadder symptom of a generation than such general blindness to the spiritual lightning, with faith only in the heap of barren dead fuel. It is the last consummation of unbelief. In all epochs of the world's history, we shall find the Great Man to have been the indispensable saviour of his epoch; – the lightning, without which the fuel never would have burnt. The History of the World, I said already, was the Biography of Great Men.

Such small critics do what they can to promote unbelief and universal spiritual paralysis: but happily they cannot always completely succeed. In all times it is possible for a man to arise great enough to feel that they and their doctrines are chimeras and cobwebs. And what is notable, in no time whatever can they entirely eradicate out of living men's hearts a certain altogether peculiar reverence for Great Men; genuine admiration, loyalty, adoration, however dim and perverted it may be. Hero-worship endures forever while man endures. Boswell venerates his Johnson, right truly even in the Eighteenth century. The unbelieving French believe in their Voltaire; and burst-out round him into very curious Hero-worship, in that last act of his life when they "stifle him under roses." It has always seemed to me extremely curious this of Voltaire. Truly, if Christianity be the highest instance of Hero-worship, then we may find here in Voltaireism one of the lowest! He whose life was that of a kind of Antichrist, does again on this side exhibit a curious contrast. No people ever were so little prone to admire at all as those French of Voltaire. *Persiflage* was the character of their whole mind; adoration had nowhere a place in it. Yet see! The old man of Ferney comes up to Paris; an old, tottering, infirm man of eighty-four years. They feel that he too is a kind of Hero; that he has spent his life in opposing error and injustice, delivering Calases, unmasking hypocrites in high places; – in short that *he* too, though in a strange way, has fought like a valiant man. They feel withal that, if *persiflage* be the great thing, there never was such a *persifleur*. He is the realised ideal of every one of them; the thing they are all wanting to be; of all Frenchmen the most French. *He* is properly their god, – such god as they are fit for. Accordingly all persons, from the Queen Antoinette to the Douanier at the Porte St. Denis, do they not worship him? People of quality disguise themselves as tavern-waiters. The Maître de Poste, with a broad oath, orders his Postillion, "*Vabon train*; thou art driving M. de Voltaire." At Paris his carriage is "the nucleus of a comet, whose train fills whole streets." The ladies pluck a hair or two from his fur, to keep it as a sacred relic. There was nothing highest, beautifulest, noblest in all France, that did not feel this man to be higher beautifuler, nobler.

Yes, from Norse Odin to English Samuel Johnson, from the divine Founder of Christianity to the withered Pontiff of Encyclopedism, in all times and places, the Hero has been worshipped. It will ever be so. We all love great men; love, venerate and bow down submissive before great men: nay can we honestly bow down to anything else? Ah, does not every true man feel that he is himself made higher by doing reverence to what is really above him? No nobler or more blessed feeling dwells in man's heart. And to me it is very cheering to consider that no sceptical logic, or general triviality, insincerity and aridity of any Time and its influences can destroy this noble inborn loyalty and worship that is in man. In times of unbelief, which soon have to become times of revolution, much downrushing, sorrowful decay and ruin is visible to everybody. For myself in these days, I seem to see in this indestructibility of Hero-worship the everlasting adamant lower than which the confused wreck of revolutionary things cannot fall. The confused wreck of things crumbling and even crashing and tumbling all round us in these revolutionary ages, will get down so far; *no* farther. It is an eternal corner-stone, from which they can begin to build themselves up again. That man, in some sense or other, worships Heroes; that we all of us reverence and must ever reverence Great Men: this is, to me, the living rock amid all rushings-down whatsoever; — the one fixed point in modern revolutionary history, otherwise as if bottomless and shoreless.

THE DARLINGS OF THE LIFE-BOATS

E. Cobham Brewer

Grace Darling, daughter of William Darling, lighthouse-keeper on Longstone, one of the Farne Islands. On the morning of 7 September 1838, Grace and her father saved nine of the crew of the Forfarshire steamer, wrecked among the Farne Isles, opposite Bamborough Castle (1815–1842). Wordsworth has a poem on the subject.

The Grace Darling of America. *Ida Lewis (afterwards Mrs. W. H. Wilson, of Black Rock, Connecticut). Her father kept the Limerock lighthouse in Newport harbour. At the age of eighteen she saved four young men whose boat had upset in the harbour. A little later she saved the life of a drunken sailor whose boat had sunk. In 1867 she rescued three men; and in 1868 a small boy who had clung to the mast of a sailboat from midnight till morning. In 1869 she and her brother Hosea rescued two sailors whose boat had capsized in a squall. Soon after this she married, and her career at the lighthouse ended. (Born 1841.)*

Grace Darling
William Wordsworth

'Twas on a lonesome lighthouse,
There dwelt an English maid,
Pure as the air around her,
Of dangers ne'er afraid.

One morning just at daybreak,
A storm-tossed wreck she spied,

Said Grace "Come help me father,
And launch the boat" she cried.
Her father cried "Tis madness
To face that raging sea,"
Then up spoke brave Grace Darling,
"Alone I'll brave the sea."

To the rock men were clinging,
The crew of nine all told,
Between them and the lighthouse,
The seas like mountains rolled.

One moment prayer, Heaven guide her,
She reached the rock at length,
She saved the storm tossed sailors,
In heaven alone her strength.

Go tell the wide world over
What the English pluck can do,
And sing of brave Grace Darling,
Who nobly saved the crew.

Chorus
She pulled away o'er the raging main,
Over the waters blue,
"Help! Help!" she could hear the cries
Of the shipwrecked crew
Bold Grace had an English heart,
And the raging seas she braved,
She pulled away with the dashing spray,
And the crew she saved.

LIEUTENANT PHILIP CURTIS WINS THE VICTORIA CROSS

Anthony Farrar-Hockley

Philip Curtis served with the Gloucestershire Regiment during the Korean War of 1950–3. The exploit for which he was awarded a posthumous Victoria Cross occurred during the regiment's famous stand at Imjin River on 22 April 1951.

The dawn breaks. A pale, April sun is rising in the sky. Take any group of trenches here upon these two main hill positions looking north across the river. See, here, the weapon pits in which the defenders stand: unshaven, wind-burned faces streaked with black powder, filthy with sweat and dust from their exertions, look towards their enemy with eyes red from fatigue and sleeplessness; grim faces, yet not too grim that they refuse to smile when someone cracks a joke about the sunrise. Here, round the weapons smeared with burnt cordite, lie the few pathetic remnants of the wounded, since removed: cap comforters; a boot; some cigarettes half-soaked with blood; a photograph of two small girls; two keys; a broken pencil stub. The men lounge quietly in their positions, waiting for the brief respite to end.

"They're coming back, Ted."

A shot is fired, a scattered burst follows it. The sergeant calls an order to the mortar group. Already they can hear the shouting and see, here and there, the figures moving out from behind cover as their machine-guns pour fire from the newly occupied Castle Site. Bullets fly back and forth; overhead, almost lazily, grenades are being exchanged on either side; man meets man; hand meets hand. This tiny corner of the battle that is raging along the whole front, blazes up and up into extreme heat, reaches a climax and dies away to nothingness – another little lull, another breathing space.

Phil is called to the telephone at this moment; Pat's voice sounds in his ear.

"Phil, at the present rate of casualties we can't hold on unless we get the Castle Site back. Their machine-guns up there completely dominate your platoon and most of Terry's. We shall never stop their advance until we hold that ground again."

Phil looks over the edge of the trench at the Castle Site, two hundred yards away, as Pat continues talking, giving him the instructions for the counter attack. They talk for a minute or so; there is not much more to be said when an instruction is given to assault with a handful of tired men across open ground. Everyone knows it is vital: everyone knows it is appallingly dangerous. The only details to be fixed are the arrangements for supporting fire; and, though A Company's Gunners are dead, Ronnie will support them from D Company's hill. Behind, the machine-gunners will ensure that they are not engaged from the open, eastern flank. Phil gathers his tiny assault party together.

It is time; they rise from the ground and move forward up to the barbed wire that once protected the rear of John's platoon. Already two men are hit and Papworth, the Medical Corporal, is attending to them. They are through the wire safely–safely! – when the machine-gun in the bunker begins to fire. Phil is badly wounded: he drops to the ground. They drag him back through the wire somehow and seek what little cover there is as it creeps across their front. The machine-gun stops, content now it has driven them back; waiting for a better target when they move into the open again.

"It's all right, sir," says someone to Phil. "The Medical Corporal's been sent for. He'll be here any minute."

Phil raises himself from the ground, rests on a friendly shoulder, then climbs by a great effort on to one knee.

"We must take the Castle Site," he says; and gets up to take it.

The others beg him to wait until his wounds are tended. One man places a hand on his side.

"Just wait until Papworth has seen you, sir –"

But Phil has gone: gone to the wire, gone through the wire, gone towards the bunker. The others come out behind him, their eyes all on him. And suddenly it seems as if, for a few breathless moments, the whole of the remainder of that field of battle is still and silent, watching amazed, the lone figure that runs so painfully forward to the bunker holding the approach to the Castle Site: one tiny figure, throwing grenades, firing a pistol, set to take Castle Hill.

Perhaps he will make it – in spite of his wounds, in spite of the odds – perhaps this act of supreme gallantry may, by its sheer audacity, succeed. But the machine-gun in the bunker fires directly into him: he staggers, falls, is dead instantly; the grenade he threw a second before his death explodes after it in the mouth of the bunker. The machine-gun does not fire on three of Phil's platoon who run forward to pick him up; it does not fire again through the battle: it is destroyed; the muzzle blown away, the crew dead.

DANIEL IN THE LIONS' DEN

The Bible

This incident is from the twilight of Daniel's life. Although a Jew, Daniel had been given high office by Darius of Persia, who valued his wisdom and his organizational ability. From "The Book of Daniel", Chapter 6.

It pleased Darius to set over the kingdom an hundred and twenty princes, which should be over the whole kingdom;

2 And over these three presidents: of whom Daniel *was* first: that the princes might give accounts unto them, and the king should have no damage.

3 Then this Daniel was preferred above the presidents and princes, because an excellent spirit *was* in him; and the king thought to set him over the whole realm.

4 q Then the presidents and princes sought to find occasion against Daniel concerning the kingdom; but they could find none occasion nor fault; forasmuch as he *was* faithful, neither was there any error or fault found in him.

5 Then said these men. We shall not find any occasion against this Daniel, except we find *it* against him concerning the law of his God.

6 Then these presidents and princes assembled together to the king, and said thus unto him, King Darius, live for ever.

7 All the presidents of the kingdom, the governors, and the princes, the counsellors, and the captains, have consulted together to establish a royal statute, and to make a firm decree,

that whosoever shall ask a petition of any God or man for thirty days, save of thee, O king, he shall be cast into the den of lions.

8 Now, O king, establish the decree, and sign the writing, that it be not changed, according to the law of the Medes and Persians, which altereth not.

9 Wherefore king Darius signed the writing and the decree.

10 ¶ Now when Daniel knew that the writing was signed, he went into his house; and his windows being open in his chamber toward Jerusalem, he kneeled upon his knees three times a day, and prayed, and gave thanks before his God, as he did aforetime.

11 Then these men assembled, and found Daniel praying and making supplication before his God.

12 Then they came near, and spake before the king concerning the king's decree; Hast thou not signed a decree, that every man that shall ask a *petition* of any God or man within thirty days, save of thee, O king, shall be cast into the den of lions? The king answered and said, The thing *is* true, according to the law of the Medes and Persians, which altereth not.

13 Then answered they and said before the king, That Daniel, which *is* of the children of the captivity of Judah, regardeth not thee, O king, nor the decree that thou hast signed, but maketh his petition three times a day.

14 Then the king, when he heard *these* words, was sore displeased with himself, and set *his* heart on Daniel to deliver him: and he laboured till the going down of the sun to deliver him.

15 Then these men assembled unto the king, and said unto the king, Know, O king, that the law of the Medes and Persians *is*, That no decree nor statute which the king establisheth may be changed.

16 Then the king commanded, and they brought Daniel, and cast *him* into the den of lions. *Now* the king spake and said unto Daniel, Thy God whom thou servest continually, he will deliver thee.

17 And a stone was brought, and laid upon the mouth of the den; and the king sealed it with his own signet, and with the signet of his lords; that the purpose might not be changed concerning Daniel.

18 ¶ Then the king went to his palace, and passed the night

fasting: neither were instruments of musick brought before him: and his sleep went from him.

19 Then the king arose very early in the morning, and went in haste unto the den of lions.

20 And when he came to the den, he cried with a lamentable voice unto Daniel: *and* the king spake and said to Daniel, O Daniel, servant of the living God, is thy God, whom thou servest continually, able to deliver thee from the lions?

21 Then said Daniel unto the king, O king, live for ever.

22 My God hath sent his angel, and hath shut the lions' mouths, that they have not hurt me: forasmuch as before him innocency was found in me; and also before thee. O king, have I done no hurt.

23 Then was the king exceeding glad for him, and commanded that they should take Daniel up out of the den. So Daniel was taken up out of the den, and no manner of hurt was found upon him, because he believed in his God.

24 q And the king commanded, and they brought those men which had accused Daniel, and they cast *them* into the den of lions, them, their children, and their wives; and the lions had the mastery of them, and brake all their bones in pieces or ever they came at the bottom of the den.

25 q Then king Darius wrote unto all people, nations, and languages, that dwell in all the earth; Peace be multiplied unto you.

26 I make a decree, That in every dominion of my kingdom men tremble and fear before the God of Daniel: for he *is* the living God, and stedfast for ever, and his kingdom *that* which shall not be destroyed, and his dominion *shall be even* unto the end.

27 He delivereth and rescueth, and he worketh signs and wonders in heaven and in earth, who hath delivered Daniel from the power of the lions.

28 So this Daniel prospered in the reign of Darius, and in the reign of Cyrus the Persian.

THE CHARGE OF THE LIGHT BRIGADE

F.E. Whitton

Why the British Light Brigade was sent on its melancholic death ride against the Russian army at Balaklava will now never be known with certainty. Yet nothing can detract from the valour of the Light Brigade as they spurred their horses into the very muzzles of the Russian guns, an endeavour which produced gasps of disbelief from enemy and friend alike on that Crimean battlefield – and has much the same effect on a reader a century and half later.

From the edge of the plateau the plain below was spread out like a stage, and to the group of French and British officers who had galloped to this "gallery" – as we may call it – it was clear that a long day's fighting was at hand. The Russian field army had climbed over the horizon to the east, and was advancing menacingly up the two valleys into which the plain was divided, in the direction of the little port of Balaklava.

It was a raw, cold morning on that 25th October 1854, and, peering through the mist, Lord Raglan and his staff – and with them some of the French higher command – could see that the Russians had already achieved a disconcerting success. The plain that lay some six to seven hundred feet below the "gallery," formed by the edge of the plateau, was bisected by a kind of hog's back, surmounted by a post road, running almost at right angles to the foot of the plateau, up which it wormed its way to cross the high ground before sinking into Sevastopol, down to the left rear of Lord Raglan and his companions. Below, to their right, was the narrow cove of Balaklava, enclosed and almost hidden by low hills, and this was the British base. The value of the hog's back lay not so much in the fact that it provided a natural rampart to the little port of Balaklava, some two miles from it, as that it covered the best route, a regular roadway from the harbour, across the low ground to the post road, and thence by the zigzag to the summit, where the bulk of the British army was in position facing Sevastopol. With the hog's back road – or the Causeway Heights, to give it its proper name – once lost, all supplies from Balaklava would have to be diverted to a much inferior route, to crawl as best they could over steep and broken ground up to the summit of the plateau by the Col of Balaklava.

To strengthen the natural rampart of Balaklava the Causeway Heights were crowned by six earthworks, garrisoned by Turks, and within them were some naval 12-pounders which had been lent by H.M.S. *Diamond*. Unfortunately, the Causeway Heights did not turn towards the coast-line and so afford protection to the right flank of Balaklava; on the contrary the line of forts could be seen "in enfilade," so to speak, from the edge of the plateau, stretching some three miles towards a jumble of mountains behind which the Russian field army was known to be. It follows that the farthest work – No. 1 Redoubt – was completely in the air, and was very likely to be rushed by the enemy suddenly appearing over the horizon; and if No. 1 Redoubt fell, the others might be mopped up in succession. Assistance from Balaklava would be impossible; for the garrison there was very small and it had its own inner position to defend. The main French and British forces were up on the plateau investing the southern portion of Sevastopol, and considerable time would be required to transfer any appreciable strength to the plain below. The Russian field army would, therefore, have things its own way, for a time at least, and the only opposition it would at first encounter would be that provided by the British Cavalry Division – comprising a heavy and a light brigade – whose camp could be seen at the foot of the plateau, just underneath where Lord Raglan and his staff were gazing anxiously down at the plain below. Small wonder that they were anxious.

No. 1 Redoubt put up a fine resistance, but it was soon over, and then, to the horror of Lord Raglan and his companions, the

Turkish soldiers could be seen streaming out of the next three works, a disordered rabble running madly towards Balaklava. The Russians promptly occupied the abandoned redoubts, withdrawing, however, from No. 4 as being too far forward, but not until they had rendered it unserviceable. Such was the strength of the Russians in all arms that the British cavalry could offer no effectual resistance. The Heavy Brigade, some 800 strong, under Lord Lucan himself, the divisional commander, did indeed make a demonstration, but without coming into actual collision with the Russians. The Light Brigade meanwhile remained in reserve under the southern slope of the Causeway Heights.

The situation is a serious one. The natural rampart to Balaklava is lost; the road from base to plateau is lost too; and the base itself at Balaklava may fall into Russian hands under the very eyes of Lord Raglan. Promptly he sends orders for two divisions to quit the plateau for the plain, and Canrobert, the French commander-in-chief, orders infantry and two regiments of *Chasseurs d'Afrique* to accompany them. These movements will, however, take time, and, until the infantry can be assembled and led down to the plain, the Russians will have a free hand.

Meanwhile, from the coign of vantage on the edge of the plateau the French and British generals and their staffs are witnesses of an imposing sight. Moving slowly up the North Valley comes a great rectangular block of Russian cavalry, which even a quick computation can assess at least at between two and three thousand men. The British cavalry division is at the moment assembled near its camping ground at the base of the heights, and the ground where they are formed up is so broken and undulating that neither body of cavalry is aware of the presence of the other. With astonishment Lord Raglan and the group alongside him, gazing down from the "gallery," see the regiments of the cavalry division sitting motionless in their saddles while this great mass of Russian horsemen is but a matter of hundreds of yards from them. Then from the Russian mass four squadrons detach themselves, climb over the hog's back, and, descending into the South Valley on the other side, move – still slowly and methodically – towards the gorge that leads to Balaklava. At the mouth of the gorge stands a small elevation – solitary and apparently unoccupied as the enemy squadrons approach, but in a moment resolving itself into a position to be reckoned with, for there leaps into life upon it a regiment of Highlanders in line. The sudden apparition of that "Thin Red Line tipped with steel" proves too much for the nerves of the Russians. They check their pace, halt, and then as a few long-range volleys ring out from the Highlanders, wheel and gallop off. The 93rd* begin to advance without orders, breaking into a double here and there, feeling baulked of their prey. But the gruff voice of old Colin Campbell, "Ninety-third! Ninety-third! Damn your eagerness!" restrains them, and the Russians get back to their main body unscathed.

Meanwhile, the main body of the Russian cavalry mass has likewise crossed the causeway and has dropped into the South Valley, heading still in its plodding way for the little harbour at Balaklava. At the same moment the heavy brigade of our cavalry division is moving leisurely on a converging route, for the same destination, quite unaware that a huge enemy cavalry force is less than a quarter of a mile away. The first intimation is the sight of lances showing over the crest of a hillock, and a second later, rank after rank of Russian horsemen. Instant action is imperative. Scarlett, the commander of the heavies, at once wheels his two leading regiments into line, and although the Russians are now little more than three hundred yards away the British squadrons are dressed by their officers with that calm and precision which only perfect discipline could ensure. The "Charge" is sounded *from the halt*, and Scarlett with his staff leads three squadrons straight towards the Russian mass, which has slowed down almost to a halt – three hundred against nigh three thousand. Hell-for-leather they go – the Greys and Inniskillings, old comrades of the great charge at Waterloo, and the watchers on the ridge can hear their battle cries, wild yells of triumph from the Inniskillings and a deep, low moan of exultation from the Greys. Into the Russians they crash, swallowed up in that vast bulk, little specks of scarlet seeping through and staining that great mass of grey. The other units of the brigade fling themselves into the fray in support. The great mass of Russian horsemen rocks and heaves and sways

---

* Now 2nd Battalion The Argyll and Sutherland Highlanders.

like some gigantic animal stricken to death. In less than five minutes all is over. The Russians break up and flee, and the British regiments, now completely mixed up, are assembled and re-formed.

Such was the Charge of the Heavy Brigade – as fine a feat of arms as had ever been performed by the British Army, and one in which superb audacity and *élan* were rewarded by a casualty list amazingly small, for less than eighty were killed and wounded. Thrilling was the sight to those watchers from the gallery above, and they held their breath in expectation waiting to see the Light Brigade take up the fight by following up in hot pursuit the Russians fleeing up the valley. But the Light Brigade never moved. One regiment indeed was seen to edge forward as if about to break into pursuit, but a solitary horseman was seen to restrain it by a peremptory gesture, and the brigade remained like wooden soldiers glued to the ground. The solitary horseman was the brigade commander, Lord Cardigan. Longing to engage in the fight he kept muttering to himself, "Damn those heavies! They have the laugh of us to-day," but his orders had been to defend the camping ground of the cavalry division, and those orders he felt he must obey to the very letter. A vain, arrogant, imperious man, Lord Cardigan felt keenly the position in which he now found himself. Although not far from sixty years of age this was his first experience of active service, and his mind had become almost petrified by forty years of peace soldiering. But his chance was soon to come.

It was now just after half-past ten. It had been an exciting morning for the spectators on the heights; for it is not often the case in war that a cavalry charge can be witnessed as if from a bench high up in an amphitheatre. The inaction of the Light Brigade had, however, come as a disconcerting anticlimax, and the sight of it remaining motionless instead of racing forward to complete the overthrow of the Russian cavalry made Raglan and his staff look at one another in dismay. "What will the French think?" was the unvoiced question which they read in one another's eyes. For Canrobert and his staff were still present – loud in their appreciation of the valour of the Heavy Brigade.

The plain below had taken on an appearance in marked contrast to that of the early morning. The North Valley was now dominated by the Russians. Viewed from the heights where stood Lord Raglan it appeared as a long, narrow horseshoe, with the open end pointing towards the watchers on the plateau. At the far end, about a mile and a half away – the arch of the horseshoe, as it were – was a large mass of mounted troops, the grey of the uniforms seeming black from the effect of distance, composed, in part, of the shattered column which had fled up the valley and had now halted and re-formed; in front could be made out twelve separate blocks, each block a Russian gun with its limber in position. Both sides of the horseshoe were held for at least half their length by Russian troops, cavalry, infantry, and guns. The right side was formed by the Causeway Heights, on which the Russians had now manned the three captured redoubts and were holding the hog's back itself round the redoubts in considerable strength. On the opposite side of the valley was a jumble of low hills, and on the slopes of several of them Russian troops could clearly be made out even with the naked eye. Briefly, the North Valley was now a regular "pocket," an advance down which would expose the attackers to artillery and musketry fire from the front and either flank.

The remainder of the day's fighting was to be marked by errors on the Allied side, and at this time a movement of the Russians on the Causeway Heights led Lord Raglan to a wrong conclusion. Looking through his glasses and seeing some stir amongst the enemy round the captured redoubts he thought that he saw indications of the abandonment of the works, and even of a retirement of the Russians from the Causeway itself. Such conclusion was entirely unwarranted. The Russians never had any idea of abandoning the redoubts. As a matter of fact they kept possession of them until almost the end of the war; and it was that retention which was to mean terrible suffering to the British troops on the heights. An extremely difficult route had now to be negotiated for the transport of supplies, and during the severe winter that was to follow it often happened that the port of Balaklava was glutted with food and warm clothing, for the conveyance of which, to the plateau above, the worn-out horses and men available were quite inadequate. At a much later stage in the war the problem was solved by the construction of a light railway, skillfully graded and engineered.

That, however, was in the distant future; and it should surely have been obvious to Lord Raglan, on this 25th October 1854, that it was most unlikely that the Russians would voluntarily abandon a captured position from which they could dominate the road that was their enemy's line of supply. Indeed, such was the importance of the capture of a portion of the Causeway Heights, that the Russians claimed the day of Balaklava as a victory; and the contention is by no means an easy one to refute.

The error of Lord Raglan and his headquarters staff was at once followed by another, which was to have immediate results. Some of the staff looking through their field-glasses at the captured redoubts declared that they could see artillery horses coming forward with lasso tackle, and at once the conclusion was formed that the Russians were about to carry off the British naval 12-pounders, which the Turks had abandoned in their flight. The thought that such a thing might happen – was indeed happening under his very eyes – profoundly disturbed Lord Raglan. It was not, from the material point of view, that the guns would be of any outstanding value to the Russians, or that their loss would be a real inconvenience to the British. From the point of view of morale, however, the matter took on an entirely different aspect. With the exception of colours, guns were then the most tangible trophies of war. If the Russians were to be able to embellish a bulletin, dealing with the capture of an important sector of the Allied position, with a statement about the capture of guns as well, it would be difficult to persuade the world (and certainly very difficult to persuade the British Cabinet) that the British army in the Crimea had not suffered a reverse. There was, too, the very real necessity of not "letting down" the British army in full view of the French. The Franco-British military alliance was a new thing. The rivalry of centuries, and the countless wars in which English and French had, as a matter of course, fought on opposing sides, were memories that could not altogether fade away. Not only to Lord Raglan, but to his officers who stood by him, it would be simply intolerable that Russians should be carrying off British guns, while French officers looked on, without a vigorous British effort made to save them.

Of those who stood near Lord Raglan and overheard – though he did not share in – the excited conversation about the removal of the guns, was a junior officer whose name was to be ever linked with the glorious tragedy that was to ensue – Captain Nolan of the 15th Hussars. Lewis Edward Nolan was no ordinary man. The son of a British officer, of Irish stock, who on retirement had accepted the post of vice-consul in Milan, then in Austrian territory, young Nolan with his two brothers had entered the Imperial service and had risen to be the senior subaltern in a regiment of Hungarian cavalry. Resigning from the Austrian service, Nolan had purchased a commission in the British Army, and was now one of the most remarkable men of his age and rank within it. He was the author of a challenging book on the achievements of cavalry which had attracted wide attention. He was a brilliant swordsman and one of the best horsemen in the army. As a linguist he was in a class by himself; for the spoke English, French, German, Hungarian and Italian with equal facility. As a passionate believer in the power of cavalry, resolutely handled and well led, Nolan, comparatively junior though he was, had achieved a wide notoriety in the army – so much so that even in his own arm he was sometimes laughingly referred to as "that madman." At the present moment he was acting as a galloper to General Airey – Lord Raglan's chief of staff.

Lord Raglan had decided that the cavalry must prevent the enemy removing "the guns." Airey pulled out his pocket-book and in pencil scribbled a few hurried lines for the cavalry divisional commander, stating Lord Raglan's wishes. Several gallopers were standing by, and the next for duty came forward to take the message, but Lord Raglan waved him aside and said briefly to Airey, "Send Nolan," although that officer was not next on the roster. Some surprise was felt by the headquarters staff at this departure from routine, but it seems to have been felt that Nolan had been selected because he was a specially daring and fearless rider. The "going" down to the plain, from the spot where stood Lord Raglan, was steep and dangerous, and only a consummate horseman could negotiate that breakneck slope with speed and certainty. And this was a case for speed.

Nolan is quickly in the saddle, and as he starts, Raglan says to him, "Tell Lord Lucan the cavalry is to attack immediately."

Nolan goes down the precipitous slope at a pace and in a

manner that make the watchers on the plateau hold their breath. No galloper in war ever bore a message more to his liking. To the cavalry enthusiast – fanatic even – that Nolan was, the day so far had been one of glorious thrill and of bitter chagrin. The charge of the Heavy Brigade had stirred him to the very soul; the inaction of the Light Brigade had almost maddened him. Now he bears an order for another cavalry attack, and to any impartial investigator of the day of Balaklava it is as certain as anything can be that the conversation Nolan had overheard about "the guns" signified to him the Russian guns at the far end of the valley.* Of one thing he is determined – if there is to be a charge he will take part in it; and his real duty to his chief, as a galloper, can take care of itself.

Slithering, scrambling, pecking, and recovering, Nolan's charger bears him safely to the plain. He jams in his spurs and gallops furiously towards Lord Lucan, who is in the saddle midway between his two brigades which are now in the North Valley, and delivers the note he has been carrying. Lord Lucan opens it at once and reads:

> "Lord Raglan wishes the cavalry to advance rapidly to the front, follow the enemy, and try to prevent the enemy carrying away the guns. Troop Horse Artillery may accompany. French cavalry is on your left. Immediate.
>
> (Sgd.) R. AIREY."

Lord Lucan looks up in bewilderment. From his position on the low ground, broken by many minor elevations, he has not, of course, the extensive range of view that Lord Raglan enjoys from the heights above – a fact which, it may be mentioned, both Raglan and Airey have completely failed to realise; still, he knows only too well that he is now in a veritable *cul-de-sac* of which the far end and the two sides are strongly held by the enemy. Where, then, is "the front"? As for guns, there is Russian artillery at the far end of the valley and on the heights on either side as well. Surely it cannot be that Lord Raglan wishes him to charge some Russian battery that may be in

---

* This is contrary to the view taken by Kinglake; but Kinglake is almost entirely concerned with the hopeless task of endeavouring to prove that there was no vagueness in Lord Raglan's expression, "the guns."

position at the far end of the North Valley. If such is the meaning of the order, then the order is a mad one. Lord Lucan was a soldier of high courage ("Yes, damn him, he's brave," was the opinion of a young officer who had been cursing his lordship for some wigging administered), but he was no reckless or vainglorious Murat. He begins, half to himself, to protest against the useless sacrifice of his division.

Nolan, quivering with impatience, cuts him short. In curt, almost peremptory tones he declares, "Lord Raglan's orders are that the cavalry shall attack immediately."

Angrily Lord Lucan retorts to Nolan, "Attack, sir! Attack what? What guns, sir?"

At once comes the reply in taunting and almost insolent tones, "*There*, my lord, is your enemy; *there* are your guns," and, as he speaks, Nolan points, not to the Causeway Heights, where are the Turkish redoubts with the captured British guns, but to the far end of the North Valley with the twelve Russian guns in position and a mass of Russian cavalry behind them.

Lord Lucan shrugs his shoulders. The last word has been said. He makes up his mind at once what to do. The Light Brigade will be sent to charge the Russian guns and he himself will follow with the heavies in support. He trots over to where Lord Cardigan is sitting in the saddle in front of the 13th Light Dragoons. Nolan moves to where his friend, Captain Morris, is with his regiment, the 17th Lancers, and asks permission to ride alongside him in the charge.

Lucan explains to Cardigan the contents of Airey's message and the action he proposes to take upon it. They are brothers-in-law and hate each other, but military punctilio is observed. Lord Cardigan brings down his sword in salute and replies, "Certainly, sir, but allow me to point out to you that the Russians have a battery in the valley in our front, and batteries and riflemen on each flank." Lord Lucan gives some sign of assent, shrugs his shoulders again, and says, "It is Lord Raglan's positive orders." Lord Cardigan salutes again and wheels his horse, muttering, "Well, here goes the last of the Brudenells," and calls for Lord George Paget of the 4th Light Dragoons, the next senior in the brigade to himself, to whom he explains briefly that the brigade is to charge the guns at the end of the valley. Cardigan proposed to charge in two lines – the

13th Light Dragoons and the 17th Lancers in front; the second line, under Lord George Paget, made up of the 4th Light Dragoons, 8th and 11th Hussars. "You are to give me your support, Lord George, your best support, mind." Lord George Paget readily promises; rather nettled, however, at the tone in which the request is conveyed.

At the last moment Lord Lucan – by an exercise of inter-ference, which does much to explain the friction between him and his brother-in-law – directed that the 11th Hussars should fall back to form a second line so that there were now three lines in all. He then enjoined upon his subordinate "to advance very steadily and quietly and to keep his men well in hand."

It does not seem that Lord Cardigan gave any explanation or instruction to any of the other four commanding officers. He merely placed himself in front of his brigade and in a quiet tone gave the orders, "The brigade will advance. Walk march. Trot"; and the regiments moved off. The brigade was at this time very weak in strength, the five regiments present totalling less than 700 of all ranks, not much more than the equivalent of a single regiment at war establishment. Lord Cardigan was now quite alone, at a distance of about two horses' lengths in advance of his two aides-de-camp, and some five horses' lengths in front of the centre of his first line.

It was indeed a case of "youth at the prow"; for it so happened that as a result of casualties, sickness, and garrison duties, not a single officer of field rank had paraded this day with either of the first line regiments, the 17th Lancers and the 13th Light Dragoons – the latter on the right. Each regiment was taken into action by a captain, Captain Oldham leading the 13th, and the 17th Lancers commanded by Captain Morris – an officer who had seen much cavalry service in the Sikh War and who, from his stocky build and immense strength, was affec-tionately known amongst his comrades by the title of the "Pocket Hercules." Lord Cardigan himself was a man well on in years, but his figure still retained the slenderness of youth. Tall, erect in the saddle, with an excellent cavalry seat, his trim figure set off by the crimson, blue, and gold of his old regiment the 11th Hussars, the Earl of Cardigan, with his high-bred features and his share of the traditional good looks of the Brudenell family, looked what he was – an English aristocrat.

He was not, however, a popular commander. Fourteen years earlier he had gained the reputation of being harsh and tyrannical. The condition of his regiment, the 11th Hussars, became almost a national scandal, and officers resigned rather than submit to Cardigan's tyranny. He was notorious for his despotism and injustice. At that time, if he appeared in a theatre he was publicly insulted: he was once hissed in a railway terminus. According to a contemporary authority Cardigan was for a time greeted wherever he went by a public disapprobation almost as marked as that which had once attended Burke and Hare.

But with all his faults – and they were many – the Earl of Cardigan had the heart of a lion. As he trotted quietly at the head of his brigade on this great day of his career, clouds of smoke began to rise at the far end of the valley – the Russian guns opening fire. Cardigan coolly took as his guiding mark the centre flash of flame with which the smoke was stabbed. And looking neither to the right nor left he held on his course with an inflexible resolution, determined to show his officers and men the straight honest road – the way down to the enemy's guns.

Perhaps fifty yards had been traversed when there took place an incident invested with a mystery which has never yet been solved. Nolan, riding alongside his friend, Captain Morris, in the front line, suddenly jammed in his spurs and like an arrow from a bow galloped furiously to the front. Morris, horrified at Nolan's impetuous action, shouted after him, "No, no, Nolan, that won't do! We have a long way to go, and we must be steady." But his words fell on deaf ears. Still galloping hard, Nolan bore to the right, actually crossing Lord Cardigan, an action which, to say the least, was a dreadful breach of military etiquette. Waving his sword Nolan turned in his saddle as if to address the brigade and shouted some words which amidst the firing were unintelligible. At that moment a Russian shell burst near Lord Cardigan; a fragment of it struck Nolan in the breast, laying bare his heart. His sword fell from his hand, but he remained erect on his charger, his right arm still stretched on high. An unearthly cry then burst from his throat. His horse swerved and galloped back through an interval of the 13th Light Dragoons and Nolan dropped from the saddle, dead.

To this day no man knows what prompted Nolan's action. A

facile explanation is that he was trying to divert the Light
Brigade from its mad venture down the valley to the objective
intended by Lord Raglan, the guns in the Turkish redoubts on
the Causeway Heights. To this there is the almost insuperable
objection that when Nolan had tauntingly replied to Lord
Lucan, "There, my lord, is your enemy; there are your guns,"
it was to the end of the valley he had pointed. And Morris's
shouted words of warning, "We have a long way to go," tell
their own tale. Morris was the last man to whom Nolan had
spoken, and it is as certain as anything can be that when Nolan
left his friend's side Morris was convinced that it was the
Russian guns at the end of the valley that were the goal of
the Light Brigade.*

The incident caused no check in the steady advance of the
brigade, which now, in addition to the sustained fire from the
twelve Russian guns in front, came under a galling cross fire
from the heights on either side. The fire had not, however, yet
become of that crushing sort that mows down half a troop in an
instant, and for some time yet the steady pace was maintained.
But to the watchers from the plateau there was visible, especially in the front line, a constant expansion and contraction
which gave that line almost the appearance of a piece of
mechanism; when a horse was killed or disabled, or deprived
of his rider, the right and left-hand man would open out, and
the next instant, when the obstacle had been cleared, they
would close in knee to knee. So frequent was this occurrence,
and of such significance was its import, that one watcher on the
plateau, in a paroxysm of admiration and of sorrow, burst into
tears. The French witnesses of that glorious descent down the
valley were torn between a generous admiration and professional criticism. C'est magnifique mais ce n'est pas la guerre. C'est
de la folie, murmured Bosquet. To Canrobert, the French
commander-in-chief, a charge by cavalry against enemy guns
in action seemed the very negation of the tactics of a modern

* Had the goal been the captured British guns, then collision with the
enemy would have taken place after about half a mile. The distance to the
Russian guns at the end of the valley was over a mile and a quarter – "a
long way to go." Morris was undoubtedly under the conviction that the
objective was the Russian battery, and it was from Nolan alone that he
could have gleaned this information.

battle. Yet, sixteen years later, Canrobert himself was to see German horsemen sabring French gunners at their guns.

Such was Lord Cardigan's coolness and such his passion for strict uniform order, that he still strove to maintain the pace merely at a rapid trot. But the lines of horsemen that followed him were consumed by the very natural desire to close with the enemy as soon as possible; and the rivalry of one regiment against another made all determined to give no appearance of a wish to lag behind. The inner squadron of the 17th Lancers was the squadron of direction, and it began to break into a canter; as its leader, Captain White, afterwards frankly expressed it, "I was anxious to get out of such a murderous fire, and into the guns, as being the best of two evils." Hurrying forward with this object he found himself in a moment alongside the briga- dier's bridle arm. But Cardigan laid his sword across the captain's breast, telling him not to force the pace and to be so good as not to ride in front of the commander of the brigade. Even in those moments of terrible and increasing peril Lord Cardigan would not for a moment brook an affront to his dignity from any officer under his command.

Long after the charge he described the thoughts that had floated through his brain during the eight minutes which elapsed from the giving the order, "The brigade will advance," till the arrival of the remnants of it at its goal. There was, in his mind, the certainty of death; and the manner of that death would be no bullet or shell splinter, but the severance of his body by a round shot from a Russian gun. This conviction was dominated and suppressed by a furious resentment – his anger at what he considered the flagrant impertinence of Captain Nolan in galloping across his front and making as if to address the brigade. "And fancy him crying out like a woman when he was hit," Lord Cardigan kept thinking. To do him justice he believed that Nolan had been merely wounded; he was unaware that the unearthly cry had been Nolan's death agony.

So on he rode, straight and erect in his saddle, giving no order, making no sign, never turning to look back at his squadrons, keeping his eyes rigidly fixed at that ever-recurring central flash of flame and riding straight down at it. But try as he would he could not control the pace as he would have wished. The impetuous squadrons now burned with a fierce impatience to rival the achievement of their comrades of the Heavy Brigade. Here and there the troopers could no longer be restrained from darting forward in front of their officers. The ceremonious advance of the three lines grew at times to an almost ungoverned onset. The racing spirit broke out, some striving to outride their comrades, some determined not to be passed. "Come on!" yelled a trooper of the 13th to his comrades, "Come on! Don't let those ————— of the 17th get in front of us." That was the spirit in which the regiments of the Light Brigade rode down the Valley of Death.

The impatient racing spirit had meanwhile spread to the lines in rear. Lord George Paget had a hard task to perform, torn as he was between the desire to keep the supporting squadrons well in hand and the memory of those words of Lord Cardigan, "Your best support, Lord George, mind." With this injunction ringing in his ears Lord George was eager to increase the pace of his 4th Light Dragoons – so much so that his regiment gradually crept up alongside the 11th Hussars and these two regiments now formed a second line, with the 8th Hussars of the original third line echeloned to the right rear. The 8th, under the iron control of its commanding officer, Colonel Shewell, maintained to the very end its cohesion and kept up that steady trot longer than the other units of the brigade; and that officer, seeing an open space to the right of the Russian guns, wisely inclined the course of his squadrons so as to come in upon them from flank and rear.

The three supporting regiments were subjected to a trial from which the first line had been exempt. Not only did they suffer their own share of casualties from that terrible inferno of fire into which the Light Brigade had plunged, but they had to pass over ground thickly strewn with dead and wounded men and horses, and to avoid every moment the maimed and wounded, both horses and men, still able to limp or crawl. A source of continual exasperation was that of riderless horses, themselves unhurt or but slightly wounded, who from instinct desperately tried to range themselves alongside the horses bearing down to the attack. Lord George Paget was especially pressed and tormented in this way. At one time as he bore along he was in the centre of a wild mob of nine riderless horses which closed in upon him and aligned themselves on either side of his charger.

Yet in all that turmoil and confusion, amid the roar of shells and the whine of bullets, while men and horses fell singly or were swept out of existence in groups, while the pace was quickening every second, there could still be heard the calm words of command from squadron leaders, "Keep back, Private Brown." "Close in to your centre." "*Do* look to your dressing." "Right squadron, right squadron, keep back." In discipline, in obedience, and in submission to authority lay the sole slight hope of safety and success; and these prevailed right to the very end.

Some eight minutes had now elapsed since the advance had begun. The lines were galloping now – but a steady gallop. Lord Cardigan, followed by the remnant of the first line, was close upon the Russian battery – so close now that he was selecting the gap through which he should make his way. At that moment there was a roar, with huge clouds of smoke and great gashes of flame as if the whole world had gone up in dissolution. It was the Russian gunners firing a salvo from all twelve guns. Most of the front line of the 13th Hussars and 17th Lancers which confronted the guns was blasted out of existence, though here and there unscathed horses and men, carried on by their eagerness and impetus, surged through the intervals between the pieces. Lord Cardigan was untouched, but so fierce was the windage from one shot that for a moment he thought he had lost a leg. His charger was blown half round by the strength of the gust, but, regaining control, Cardigan forced his mount through an open space and galloped on. He was the first man to enter the line of guns.

The scene was that of hell let loose. A thick acrid smoke hung over everything as a pall, drifting and eddying in the breeze. The Russians stuck valiantly to their guns, and those of the British troopers who had got into the battery, maddened with excitement and with their blood up – as may well be imagined – cut and thrust in the gloom at anything that seemed like a Russian soldier. As for Lord Cardigan he sped, still untouched, past limbers and tumbrels until he found himself in a comparatively open space, confronting a mass of Russian cavalry standing at the halt but eighty yards away. Such was his impetus that, before he could pull up, the distance had been reduced to twenty yards. Some Cossacks at once made for him, one of them slightly wounding him with his lance, but he quickly wheeled his charger round and dashed back again through the line of guns.

Clear of the guns, Lord Cardigan looked round him in bewilderment. He could only imagine that he was the sole mounted survivor of his brigade. His two aides had become casualties. The handful of men of the first line who had thrust through the guns had either been killed or passed out of sight to join a small residuum that had got past on one flank or another, and with splendid courage had dashed forward into the unknown. Of the second and third lines the bulk had swept round the guns, and these, too, were no longer visible. All that Lord Cardigan could see was dead men and horses lying in the track of the charge, and men, wounded or unhorsed, slowly making their way up the valley. He could make out the Heavy Brigade halted about half-way, and for a moment it flashed across his mind that at the last moment his second and third lines might have been kept back by Lord Lucan and that he had been charging the Russian guns followed by his first line alone. Remarkable this may seem; but it must be remembered that throughout the charge Lord Cardigan had never once turned his head. He had enjoined on his second-in-command, Lord George Paget, to render "your best support." His own sole duty, he conceived it, was to ride steadily at his selected mark. A commander of a cavalry charge who keeps looking over his shoulder cannot inspire the confidence of a leader who looks nowhere except at his goal. Throughout the charge Lord Cardigan never gave a single order: everything in that marvellous ride was in obedience to the implicit and unspoken "Follow me" of its leader.

So Lord Cardigan rode slowly back – most of the time at a walk – still untouched by the fire coming from the heights that bordered the valley, and rejoined the Heavy Brigade. It was characteristic of the man that, after an experience as thrilling as any soldier could ever hope to undergo, his mind was still filled with the affront he conceived had been put upon him by a junior at the beginning of the charge. He began crying out to Scarlett, the commander of the heavies, against the impropriety of Nolan's action, and how he had been grossly insulted by a junior officer. "Say no more, my lord," was Scarlett's reply, "you have nearly ridden over Captain Nolan's dead body."

In this curious manner Lord Cardigan passed out of one of the most famous cavalry charges of history. He had led the field with the utmost gallantry, coolness, and resolution, but after a glorious run he had been "thrown out." Coming as it did after the splendid example he had set his officers and men, his exit from the field was certainly of the nature of an anticlimax; and the leader who had steered an unswerving course down to the enemy's guns had, some years later, to defend his military honour by an action for libel against a scandalous imputation made in connection with this unfortunate withdrawal.

The retreat of Lord Cardigan had been unnoticed by the survivors of the brigade who, while he was slowly retiring up the valley, were heroically fighting in and behind the Russian guns. There were masses of Russian cavalry behind the battery, but they repeated the flagrant error already committed when confronting the Heavy Brigade earlier in the day, the error of receiving the attack of enemy horsemen at the halt. These mistaken tactics proved their undoing, and the extraordinary sight was witnessed of bodies of Russian cavalry driven in headlong flight by the exhausted remnants of a weak brigade – divided now into two wings, out of touch, and indeed invisible to each other – totalling not more than 230 of all ranks, of whom only about 170 were in any coherent formation. Nor did the Russian battery escape the attention of the second line. When the 4th Light Dragoons, under Lord George Paget, thundered down upon it the Russian drivers were in the act of trying to remove the guns. There was a loud "Tally-ho!" from an officer of the 4th, and in a twinkling the light dragoons were slashing at the Russian artillerymen, who like true gunners were prepared to defend their pieces to the death. The slaughter here was terrible. Kinglake has a story of one officer of the 4th who went absolutely berserk, cutting down Russian after Russian until he was besmeared with the blood of his victims. After the battle came reaction – he burst into tears and cried like a little child.

So far as can be estimated, the British cavalrymen who came through and behind the Russian guns remained some four minutes in that perilous area. Yet to such extent did they, for that brief period of time, dominate this miniature battlefield that two of the regiments (it being remembered that a "regiment" of the Light Brigade was now at most about fifty officers and men) were actually able to halt and to get into some kind of regular formation. The respite could, of course, be but of brief duration, for the Russians were recovering from their panic and coming for the dauntless survivors of the Light Brigade. Lord George Paget was in an anxious position, looking hurriedly for his chief and asking excitedly, "Where is Lord Cardigan?" Every second was of vital importance if any of the brigade were to be saved, and there was nothing now that could be done but to endeavour to seek refuge without a moment's delay. On the right, Colonel Shewell of the 8th Hussars managed to collect about seventy men of his own regiment and the 17th Lancers, and, hurrying back along the foot of the Causeway Heights, swept aside some squadrons of Russian cavalry which attempted to bar his progress. On the other side of the valley Lord George Paget with about the same number, chiefly of the 4th Light Dragoons and the 11th Hussars, actually came into collision with some Russian squadrons, but these, remaining at the halt on the flank of the retiring troopers, were brushed from their path. From one peril the shattered remnants of the Light Brigade were saved by the quick appreciation of the French. When General Morris of the French cavalry had seen, to his stupefaction, Cardigan's regiments tearing down the valley to the Russian guns, he made up his mind at once to do what he could to aid, at any rate, such survivors as might return. He sent the 4th *Chasseurs d' Afrique* to charge the guns on the heights on the north side of the valley. This charge was a brilliant affair carried out with the dash and *élan* characteristic of the French. The Russian guns were driven off, and the *Chasseurs*, at the cost of but thirty-eight casualties, had rendered an inestimable service to their British comrades in distress.

The wearied survivors of the Light Brigade were now forming up on the slopes of the Causeway facing Balaklava. The rolls were called, and of some 660 who had started, 195 mounted men answered their names. Two officers and eight mounted troopers were all that the 13th Light Dragoons could muster. In all, it seems that in officers and other ranks 113 had been killed and 134 wounded. The casualties of horses had been over 500, of which number by far the greater part had been killed. The severity of the Russian fire from front and flanks will be realised when it is remembered that the Light

Brigade was exposed to it for a space of time of but little over a quarter of an hour.

For the whole charge – the advance down the valley, the combat round the guns, and the retreat – had taken barely twenty minutes. When the men had answered to their names Lord Cardigan came forward and said, "Men, it was a mad-brained trick, but it was no fault of mine." "Never mind, my lord," shouted some men in reply, "we are ready to do it again."

The charge, of course, had been made in error. "Someone had blundered." And by a curious irony of Fate the first man killed was he who held the key of the mystery. There were recriminations, and expostulation in reply. Lord Raglan, rather ungenerously, threw the blame upon the Earl of Lucan, and actually reported to the Government that it was the latter's duty as a lieutenant-general to have refused to charge the Russian guns at the end of the valley. Lord Lucan not unnaturally replied that as a soldier he had had no option but to carry out the orders, written and verbal, conveyed to him by Captain Nolan. Lord Raglan was furious at the destruction of the Light Brigade, especially as, after all – and this was the sting – the Russians remained permanently in possession of the guns they had captured in the morning. But in a manly letter to Lord Lucan he could not suppress his admiration for this superb feat of self-sacrifice and heroism, and wrote of the Charge of the Light Brigade that it was "The finest thing ever done."

> "The knights are dust
> And their good swords are rust,
> Their souls are with the saints, we trust."

THE CANDLE THAT SHALL
NEVER BE PUT OUT

John Foxe

When Mary Tudor acceded to the throne, a period of Catholic reaction was ushered into England. The account below of the martyrdom of bishops Ridley and Latimer in 1555 is from Foxe's Book of Martyrs.

D r Ridley had a black gown such as he used to wear when he was a bishop; a tippet of velvet furred likewise about his neck, a velvet nightcap upon his head, and slippers on his feet. He walked to the stake between the mayor and an alderman.

After him came Mr Latimer in a poor Bristol frieze frock much worn, with his buttoned cap and kerchief on his head, all ready to the fire, a new long shroud hanging down to the feet; which at the first sight excited sorrow in the spectators, beholding on the one side the honour they some time had, and on the other the calamity into which they had fallen.

Dr Ridley, then looking back, saw Mr Latimer coming after, unto whom he said, "Oh, are you there?" "Yea," said Mr Latimer, "have after, as fast as I can." So he followed a pretty way off, and at length they came to the stake. Dr Ridley, first entering the place, earnestly held up both his hands, looking towards Heaven, then, shortly after seeing Mr Latimer with a cheerful look, he ran up to him and embraced him, saying, *Be of good heart, brother, for God will assuage the fury of the flames, or else strengthen us to abide it.*

He went then to the stake, and, kneeling down, prayed with

great fervour, while Mr Latimer kneeled also, and prayed as earnestly as he. After this they arose and conversed together, and while they were thus employed Dr Smith began his sermon to them upon the text, "If I yield my body to the fire to be burnt, and have not charity, I shall gain nothing thereby."

They were commanded to prepare immediately for the stake. They accordingly with all meekness obeyed. Dr Ridley made presents of small things to gentlemen standing by, divers of them pitifully weeping; happy was he who could get the least trifle for a remembrance of this good man. Mr Latimer quietly suffered his keeper to pull off his hose and his other apparel, which was very simple, and being stripped to his shroud he seemed as comely a person as one could well see.

Then Dr Ridley unlaced himself, and held up his hand and said, "O heavenly Father, I give unto thee most hearty thanks that thou hast called me to be a professor of thee, even unto death; I beseech thee, Lord God, have mercy upon this realm of England, and deliver it from all her enemies."

Then the smith took a chain of iron, and brought it about both their middles; and as he was knocking in the staple Dr Ridley took the chain in his hand, and, looking aside to the smith, said, "Good fellow, knock it in hard, for the flesh will have its course." Then his brother brought him a bag of gunpowder, and tied it about his neck. Dr Ridley asked him what it was, and he answered, Gunpowder. "Then (said he), I will take it to be sent of God; therefore I will receive it. And have you any for my brother." "Yes, sir, that I have," said he. "Then give it unto him in time (said he), lest you come too late." So his brother went and carried it to Mr Latimer.

Dr Ridley said to my lord Williams, "My lord, I must be a suitor unto your lordship in the behalf of divers poor men, and especially in the cause of my poor sister. I beseech your lordship, for Christ's sake, to be a means of grace for them. There is nothing in all the world that troubles my conscience, this only excepted. While I was in the See of London divers poor men took leases of me; now I hear that the bishop, who occupieth the same room, will not allow my grants made to them, but, contrary to all law and conscience, hath taken from them their livings. I beseech you, my lord, be a means for them; you shall do a good deed and God will reward you."

They then brought a lighted fagot and laid it at Dr Ridley's feet, upon which Mr Latimer said,

Be of good comfort, Master Ridley, and play the man; we shall this day light such a candle by God's grace in England as I trust shall never be put out.

When Dr Ridley saw the flame leaping up towards him he cried with an amazing loud voice, "Into thy hands, O Lord, I commend my spirit; Lord receive my spirit," and continued oft to repeat, "Lord, Lord receive my spirit." Mr Latimer, on the other side, cried as vehemently, "O Father of Heaven, receive my soul." After which he soon died, seemingly with little pain.

But Dr Ridley, from the ill-making of the fire (the fagots being green, and piled too high, so that the flames being kept down by the green wood, burned fiercely beneath, was put to such exquisite pain that he desired them, for God's sake, to let the fire come unto him. His brother-in-law hearing, but not very well understanding, to rid him out of his pain and not well knowing what he did, heaped fagots upon him, so that he quite covered him, which made the fire so vehement beneath that it burned all his nether parts before it touched the upper, and made him struggle under the fagots, and often desire them to let the fire come unto him, saying, "I cannot burn." Yet in all his torments he forgot not to call upon God, still having in his mouth, "Lord have mercy upon me," mingling with his cry, "Let the fire come unto me; I cannot burn."

In these pains he laboured till one of the standers-by pulled the fagots from above, and when he saw the fire flame up he wrested himself to that side, and when the fire touched the gunpowder, he was seen to stir no more, but fell down at Mr Latimer's feet.

The dreadful sight filled almost every eye with tears. Some took it grievously to see their deaths whose lives they had held so dear. Some pitied their persons, who thought their souls had no need thereof. But the sorrow of his brother, whose extreme anxiety had led him to attempt to put a speedy end to his sufferings, but who, from error and confusion, had so unhappily prolonged them, surpassed them all; and so violent was his grief that the spectators pitied him almost as much as they did the martyr.

BOMB DISPOSAL

Anonymous

The dangers of bomb disposal need little elucidation. The incident below is from World War II.

"In the blitz of 1940 I was a bomb disposal officer belonging to the Navy and attached to the Port of London. My job was to dispose of bombs which fell in the Port of London area. This wasn't very rewarding because most of the bombs fell in the water and weren't seen, so I didn't have a great deal to do, and I was feeling a little frustrated. Well, one night I was down in the basement of the Port of London Authority building which was a very safe, comfortable place during the Blitz. There was a lot of noise going on outside. The floor was heaving from time to time. The telephone rang and the call was from the air raid controller in a North London borough who said that an object had dropped in a shopping street there, and the local bomb disposal officer thought it might be a magnetic mine. He didn't know, because he'd never seen one but he wanted to know whether, if he put it on a lorry and took it away, it was likely to explode. I said I thought it was quite likely to, but it turned out in fact that he'd already done this and taken it away and it hadn't exploded, so he was lucky. Well, the next morning I went out with an officer from the Admiralty – I'll call him 'R' – who is an expert in mines, to see this thing, and there were also two other mines dropped that night which we were going to see. The first one, which this bomb disposal officer had taken away, was lying in the middle of a big common and it seemed to me an enormous thing. It was eight feet long and about two feet in diameter, thicker than a pillar-box and longer than a tall man. It was dark green and it had a huge parachute spread out behind it, not a silk one – it looked like Aertex or something of that sort. It weighed a ton, it had fifteen hundred pounds of high explosives in it, and it was full of various gadgets which you could see let into the side. This was an ordinary magnetic mine of the sort the Germans had been laying in the sea and in the estuaries and harbours of England, but during the Blitz when a lot of them were dropped, it got to be known as a land mine, although in fact it was just a perfectly ordinary magnetic mine, which went off on land if dropped on land. This officer from the Admiralty, 'R', demonstrated to us how the thing should have been dealt with. First of all, in the side, there was a little fuse which was called the bomb fuse. This fuse was supposed to set the mine off if it fell on land and not on water, and he took it out. He had some special tools. It was very stiff, but he took it out and he threw it on the ground, and about ten seconds later there was a crack and the fuse went off. He said that this demonstrated how careful one had to be dealing with these things – if you rolled the mine about a bit with the fuse in it, it was liable to go off. If the mine hit water the bomb fuse didn't function because the mine sank into the water and the pressure of the water pushed in a little pin and stopped it; but when these mines fell on land, the fuse started buzzing and it buzzed for fifteen seconds, or rather it was supposed to buzz for fifteen seconds and then go off, but some of them buzzed for a few seconds and then stuck, and so if you rolled the mine about it buzzed for the rest of the fifteen seconds and then blew up.

"As 'R' said, the important thing when dealing with these mines, if you had to move them at all before you took the fuse out, was to listen very carefully all the time, and if you heard it buzzing to run, because you might have up to fifteen seconds to get away.

"There were a lot of other gadgets in this mine which he showed us how to take out. There was an electric detonator down at the bottom of a hole in the side of the mine which was very hard to get out, since it needed a special shaped tool. Opposite it was another little hole in the mine, and he unscrewed the cover of this and there was a tremendous whoof and a spring, three feet long, shot out of it across the field. The other two of us were most alarmed as we hadn't known this was going to happen, but he said: 'Well, it's all right, you can come back, this always happens, it's part of the show.' And then finally there was a great big screwed-up cover which we eventually managed to get undone, and underneath it was a large clock made of perspex so that you could see the works, and connected to a lot of wires of different colours. This was the clock which, if the mine fell into water, started ticking, and after it had ticked for about twenty minutes turned the thing into a magnetic mine. So we took that out, and cut the wires, and then the thing was quite safe.

"Then we went off and looked at the other two. One of them had fallen on a little house while the family were having supper. They were sitting in the kitchen, and there was a tremendous uproar from the scullery, great crashings, a lot of slates falling, and so on. They had tried to get in the scullery to see what had happened, but couldn't, so they went out of the front door and round to the back door of the scullery, and then they found this mine standing up against the back of the scullery door. It was still there when we got there and the supper was still on the table.

"Well, after this demonstration I went back and I took a fuse from one of these mines with me. I worked on it and took it to bits that evening with a torpedo officer, who was working in the Port of London at that time, and we reckoned we knew pretty well how it worked. This was just as well, because in the course of that night we got another telephone call, this time from South London, to say that three large objects on parachutes had dropped in their particular area. The local Army bomb disposal officer said this was a job for the Navy because he thought they were mines, and the A.R.P. Controller wanted to know what I was going to do about it. I said that actually I wasn't suppose to deal with mines at all, but only with bombs. He said: 'Well, who does deal with mines?' I said: 'I'm afraid that the nearest people are down in Portsmouth.' He said: 'That's all very well, but I've got several thousand people evacuated round these mines, I can't wait for the people to come up from Portsmouth.' So I rang up H.M.S. *Vernon* at Portsmouth, which is the torpedo and mining school down there, and asked the duty officer whether I could go and deal with these mines. I said I thought I knew how to do it, and he reluctantly said yes. So I went and woke up the torpedo officer who'd been playing with the fuse with me, and my Chief Petty Officer, who was another torpedo-man, both of them very good with gadgets and getting difficult things unscrewed and so on. Of course we didn't have any of the proper tools for this job. (One was supposed to have nonmagnetic tools, quite apart from which most of the things were very hard to unscrew unless you had tools of the right shape.) But we got a lot of screwdrivers and, most important of all, we took a ball of string; that is the essential thing for bomb disposal.

"Well, we set off, in a car we had got from the Admiralty, and we drove through the Blitz. It was a horrible night. We drove round craters and wrecked trams and blazing gas mains past anti-aircraft batteries which were bang-banging away. We had an imperturbable driver, I was full of admiration for him, but eventually we got down into the wilds of South London and of course we got lost. We didn't know where we were, we didn't know where any of the three mines we were looking for was either. We were wandering around back streets with shrapnel coming down and not getting any closer, and it wasn't till we saw a man in a dressing-gown walking along with a suitcase that we felt we might be getting warm. So we stopped him and asked him, and he said: Oh yes, it had fallen in the garden of a house near his. So we made him come back with us and show us. We went into the back garden of this little house. This was our first mine, and we saw it lying there among the bushes, a parachute spread over the wall next door. We went up and had a look at it with our torch, and we found unfortunately that the all-important fuse was underneath, so we'd have to roll it round before we could get it out. My Chief Petty Officer and I rolled it over very, very cautiously indeed while the third member of the party kept his ear as close to it as he could and listened to see if it buzzed. It didn't. So when we'd got the fuse round to the side, we unscrewed it. But we didn't take it out because the Germans had on occasions put things under fuses in bombs so that when you took the fuse out the bomb blew up, and it was quite possible to do it in these mines as well. Having unscrewed it, when it was loose in its socket, we tied a bit of string to the top and then we retired over the garden wall into the next garden, and then over the next garden wall into the garden beyond that, and then round the corner of the house, paying out the string, and when we got there I gave a yank on the string. It seemed sort of elastic, and when I let go the string sprang back again, so we had to climb all the way back and look. Of course the string was tied up with a rose bush or something. We freed it, and then went back and had another pull, and that was all right – when we got back we found the fuse was lying on the ground. I took off the exploder and it was then quite safe. But I did just try throwing it a few yards and sure enough, it fired, it went off, so the thing was still in a fairly sensitive condition, and we were quite right to have treated it with respect.

"Well, we sat down on the mine and had a cigarette after all this, because this was really the most difficult part of the job. While sitting on the mine I noticed that my hands were covered with soot, and also that the other people's faces had a lot of soot on them, and then I realized that the mine itself was covered with soot. I think this was because it was hung outside the aircraft, underneath, and it was covered with soot as a precaution so that it didn't show up in searchlight beams or something. One always got absolutely filthy dealing with these things.

"Well, we went around South London the rest of the night and well into the following morning, looking for the other two mines. We kept on meeting people who hadn't actually seen them but thought they knew where they were, and they'd take us along somewhere and we would find nothing. Eventually we did find the next one. It was standing upright on its nose in the middle of a recreation ground. It had made a dent in the ground just deep enough to hold it up. We went up to this and laid all our tools out on the grass, which was rather long, and then of course we lost them. We couldn't find any of them again, so we had to go to a bus depot, where we broke open the emergency tool-kit and got their spanners and things out and went back and dealt with that mine. And then the final one was in a field by a gasworks in Kent. The sun was up by then, it was a sunny morning and we had a large, interested crowd which had to be held back by volunteers while we dealt with it. So by this time we'd done three mines and we had a parachute each as a souvenir, which we were very happy about, and a lot of miscellaneous explosives from these mines which we'd taken out, and we went home feeling very pleased with ourselves.

"When we got back we were summoned to the Admiralty, the Torpedoes and Mining department, and we found quite an uproar going on because it turned out that a lot of other mines had been dropped in London that night. They'd been found in roads and back gardens, hanging off trees and railway bridges and the roofs of houses, and some were standing up on their noses on the top of houses, though of course they usually just came through the roof. In fact I think about twenty per cent of the mines that were dropped didn't go off, and each one that was dropped meant the evacuation of perhaps a thousand people in some cases. The importance of these mines to the Navy was that each one of them was likely to be a perfectly good magnetic mine, with inside it a complete magnetic mine unit, which was capable of sinking a ship if the mine had been laid in the sea. So the Navy were extremely keen on getting as many of these as they could, because they had to follow the development of German magnetic mines in order to develop their counter-measures. The Navy naturally took steps to stop anybody except people whom they felt they could trust not to blow themselves up, from dealing with these mines, because they wanted the things intact. We found ourselves eventually officially accredited mine disposal officers. We used to go out every day; we were given the proper tools which we hadn't had before; we only worked in the daytime, and we weren't allowed to work at night, as we had been doing; and every morning we were sent out with a list of assignments. Mines were dropped every night and we'd be assigned a few, usually in the most remote and unheard – of parts of London. Sometimes we'd find they were quite easy, lying in playing fields or allotments, and some would be rather edgy, mines standing on their noses on the top floors of houses for instance, so that one didn't have a clear run for getting away in fifteen seconds if the thing started buzzing. However, we had no troubles at all, unlike other people. There were actually cases of people who started taking the fuses out of these mines and heard this buzzing noise and ran; it seems incredible, but they got far enough away in fifteen seconds to avoid being blown up by fifteen hundred pounds of explosive. But we had nothing particularly spectacular to deal with, again unlike other people who had to deal with mines which were welded to live rails, or inside gasometers, or hanging off the roof of the Palladium (with free tickets for life as a result). One mine we found had a rude message addressed to Mr Chamberlain chalked on the side, although Mr Chamberlain had been out of office for some months by that time. We found another one which certainly made us pause, because it had a rhyme in German on the side: something to the effect that when you think you've got it, it springs out on you. We didn't like the sound of this at all, and circled round it for quite a time before we tackled it. However, nothing particular happened.

"As a matter of fact we did do another night job, although we weren't really supposed to. This was in the Seven Sisters Road in Islington and the mine was again lying in the back garden of a house. I tied the string to the fuse and laid it out across the road, and through the house opposite, into the back garden of that, and I was just about to pull the string and get the fuse out when the string was pulled out of my hands altogether. I dashed through the house out into the road, and there I found an air raid warden, unconcernedly walking down the road with the string wrapped round his boot and the fuse of the mine rattling along the road behind him.

"We did about a dozen mines, our little team, and then we were eventually called off, because it was reckoned we'd done our quota."

COBBETT IN THE DOCK

William Cobbett

*The English writer William Cobbett (1763–1835) was an un-
compromising champion of the poor and of human decency. This
did not endear him to the powers-that-be who gave him two years in
Newgate for protesting flogging in the army. Nothing deterred, he
continued his radical writings and thus found himself at the age of
68 prosecuted by the government for sedition. Here is his defiant
speech from the dock.*

This is the second time in my life that I have been
prosecuted by an Attorney-General, and brought before
this Court. I have been writing for thirty years, and only
twice out of that long period have I been brought before this
Court. The first time was by an apostate Whig. What, indeed,
of evil have the Whigs not done? Since then, although there
have been six Attorneys-General, all Tories, and although
were I a crown lawyer I might pick out plenty of libels from
my writings, if this be a libel, yet I have never for twenty-one
years been prosecuted until this Whig Government came in.
But the Whigs were always a most tyrannical faction; they
always tried to make tyranny double tyranny; they were
always the most severe, the most grasping, the most greedy,
the most tyrannical faction whose proceedings are recorded in
history. It was they who seized what remained of the Crown
lands; it was they who took to themselves the last portion of
Church property; it was they who passed the monstrous Riot
Act; it was they also who passed the Septennial Bill. The

Government are now acquiring the credit for doing away with the rotten boroughs; but if they deserve credit for doing them away, let it be borne in mind that the Whigs created them. They established an interest in the regulation, and gave consistency and value to corruption. Then came the excise laws, which were brought in by the Whigs, and from them, too, emanated that offensive statute by which Irish men and Irish women may be transported without judge or jury. There is, indeed, no faction so severe and cruel; they do everything by force and violence; the Whigs are the Rehoboam of England; the Tories ruled us with rods, but the Whigs scourge us with scorpions! The last time I was brought before this Court, I was sent out of it to two years' imprisonment among felons, and was condemned to pay, at the expiration of the two years, a fine of £1,000 to the King, which the King took and kept. . . . In order to avoid being confined in the same cells with common felons, I was obliged to ransom myself at the rate of ten guineas per week, which I paid to the jailor, and my other expenses amounted to ten guineas a week more; so that I was obliged to pay twenty guineas a week for 104 weeks. I was carried seventy miles from my family, and shut up in jail, doubtless from the hope that I should expire from stench and mortification of mind. It pleased God, however, to bless me with health, and though deprived of liberty, by dint of sobriety and temperance, I outlived the base attempt to destroy me. What crime had I committed? For what was it that I was condemned to this horrible punishment? Simply for writing a paragraph in which I expressed the indignation I felt, and I should have been a base creature indeed if I had not expressed it. But now, military flogging excites universal indignation. If there be at present any of the jury alive who found me guilty and sentenced me to that punishment, what remorse must they not feel for their conduct when they perceive that every writer in every periodical of the present day, even including the favourite publication of the Whig Attorney-General, are now unanimous in deprecating the system of military flogging altogether! Yes, for expressing my disapprobation of that system, I was tossed into a dungeon like Daniel into the lions' den. But why am I now tossed down before this Court by the Attorney-General. What are my sins? I have called on the Government to respect the law; I have cautioned them that hard-hearted proceedings are driving the labourers to despair; that is my crime. If the Government really wish to avoid disturbances in the country, let them give us back the old laws; let them give the people the old game law, and repeal the new law; and let them do away with the other grinding laws that oppress the poor. I have read, with horror which I cannot describe, of a magistrate being accused to the Lord Chancellor of subornation of perjury; I have read of that magistrate being reinstated, and I have shuddered with horror at supposing that a poor starving labourer may be brought before such a man, and, in conjunction with another such magistrate, may be doomed to seven years' transportation for being out at night, and such a magistrate may be himself a game-preserver! This is a monstrous power, and certainly ought to be abolished. The ministry, however, will perhaps adopt the measures I have recommended, and then prosecute me for recommending them. Just so it is with Parliamentary Reform, a measure which I have been foremost in recommending for twenty years. I have pointed out, and insisted upon, the sort of reform that we must have; and they are compelled already to adopt a large part of my suggestions, and avowedly against their will. They hate me for this; they look upon it as I do, that they are married to Reform, and that I am the man who has furnished the halter in which they are led to Church. For supplying that halter, they have made this attack on me, through the Attorney-General, and will slay me if they can. The Whigs know that my intention was not bad. This is a mere pretence to inflict pecuniary ruin on me, or cause me to die of sickness in a jail; so that they may get rid of me because they can neither buy nor silence me. It is their fears which make them attack me, and it is my death they intend. In that object they will be defeated, for, thank Heaven, you stand between me and destruction. If, however, your verdict should be – which I do not anticipate – one that will consign me to death, by sending me to a loathsome dungeon, I will with my last breath pray to God to bless my country and curse the Whigs, and I bequeath my revenge to my children and the labourers of England.

(Mr Cobbett then sat down amidst loud acclamations from the spectators in the gallery, which it was with great difficulty the officers could suppress.)

The jury was unable to agree, and Cobbett was acquitted.

THE LADY OF THE LAMP

Cecil Woodham-Smith

Florence Nightingale has become a symbol of the caring ministration of the sick and wounded. Until Nightingale lit her lamp in the British soldiers' hospitals in the Crimea, nursing was a disreputable occupation talked of in the same breath as prostitution. The daughter of gentlefolk she went against her family, her class, and the whole of patriarchal Victorian society to become a nurse and then to make something like a profession out of it. Modern nursing and sanitary hospital routine owe much to her actions and her ideals as established in the Crimea, where she arrived with her assistants in November 1854.

At breakfast time the *Vectis* anchored, and during the morning Lord Stratford de Redcliffe, the British Ambassador at Constantinople, sent across Lord Napier, the Secretary of the Embassy. Lord Napier found Miss Nightingale, exhausted from the effects of prolonged sea-sickness, stretched on a sofa. Fourteen years later he recalled their first meeting: ". . . I was sent by Lord Stratford to salute and welcome you on your first arrival at Scutari . . . and found you stretched on the sofa where I believe you never lay down again. I thought then that it would be a great happiness to serve you."

The nurses were to go to the hospital at once, for wounded were expected from the Battle of Balaclava. Painted caïques, the gondola-like boats of the Bosphorus, were procured, the nurses were lowered into them with their carpet-bags and umbrellas, and the party was rowed across to Scutari.

The rain having ceased, a few fitful gleams of sunshine lit up the Asian shore, which, as it grew clearer, lost its beauty. The steep slopes to the Barrack Hospital were a sea of mud littered with refuse; there was no firm road, merely a rutted, neglected track. As the caïques approached a rickety landing stage, the nurses shrank at the sight of the bloated carcass of a large grey horse, washing backward and forward on the tide and pursued by a pack of starving dogs, who howled and fought among themselves. A few men, limping and ragged, were helping each other up the steep slope to the hospital, and groups of soldiers stood listlessly watching the dead horse and the starving dogs. A cold wind blew.

The nurses disembarked, climbed the slope, and passed through the enormous gateway of the Barrack Hospital, that gateway over which Miss Nightingale said should have been written: "Abandon hope all ye who enter here." Dr Menzies and Major Sillery, the Military Commandant, were waiting to receive them. That night Lord Stratford wrote to the Duke of Newcastle: "Miss Nightingale and her brigade of nurses are actually established at Scutari under the same roof with the gallant and suffering objects of their compassion."

From the European shore of the Bosphorus, from the magnificent house where the British Ambassador lived, the great quadrangle of the Turkish Barracks glimmered golden, magnificent as a giant's palace. At close quarters, however, romance vanished. Vast echoing corridors with floors of broken tiles and walls streaming damp, empty of any kind of furniture, stretched for miles. Miss Nightingale calculated there were four miles of beds. Everything was filthy; everything was dilapidated. The form of the building was a hollow square with towers at each corner. One side had been gutted in a fire and could not be used. The courtyard in the centre was a sea of mud littered with refuse. Within the vast ramifications of the barracks were a depot for troops, a canteen where spirits were sold, and a stable for cavalry horses. "But it is not a building, it's a town!" exclaimed a new arrival.

The vast building hid a fatal secret. Sanitary defects made it a pesthouse, and the majority of the men who died there died not of the wounds or sickness with which they arrived, but of disease they contracted as a result of being in the hospital.

When Miss Nightingale entered the Barrack Hospital on November 5, 1854, there were ominous signs of approaching disaster, but the catastrophe had not yet occurred. Food, drugs, medical necessities had already run short, the Barrack Hospital was without equipment, and in the Crimea supply was breaking down. Winter was swiftly advancing, and each week the number of sick sent to Scutari steadily increased.

There were men in the Crimea, there were men in Scutari, there were men at home in England who saw the tragedy approach. They were powerless. The system under which the health of the British Army was administered defeated them. The exactions, the imbecilities of the system killed energy and efficiency, crushed initiative, removed responsibility, and were the death of common sense.

Three departments were responsible for maintaining the health of the British Army and for the organization of its hospitals: the Commissariat, the Purveyor's Department, and the Medical Department. They were departments which during forty years of economy had been cut down nearer and still nearer the bone.

These departments had no standing. Dr Andrew Smith, Director General of the British Army Medical Service, told the Roebuck Committee that it would have been considered impertinence on his part to approach the Commander in Chief with suggestions as to the health of the army. A commissary officer did not rank as a gentleman, while the Purveyor was despised even by the commissary.

The method by which the hospitals were supplied was confused. The Commissariat were the caterers, bankers, carriers, and storekeepers of the army. They bought and delivered the standard daily rations of the men whether they were on duty or in hospital. But the Commissariat did not supply food for men too ill to eat their normal rations. At this point the Purveyor stepped in. All invalid foods, known as "medical comforts", sago, rice, milk, arrowroot, port wine, were supplied by the Purveyor. Yet he had no authority over their price, suitability, or quality, having to accept what the Commissariat sent unless he could claim the consignment was unfit for human consumption. Mr Benson Maxwell, an eminent lawyer and a member of the Hospitals Commission, declared that though he had spent some weeks in the hospitals he was completely unable to disentangle the respective duties of Commissariat and Purveyor.

Relations between the doctors and the Purveyor were even more obscure. A doctor might order a man a special diet, but it depended on the Purveyor whether the patient received it or not. Having made a requisition on the Purveyor, the doctor was powerless.

Though the system placed executive power in the hands of the Commissariat and the Purveyor, it was only a limited power. Certain goods only might be supplied. Each department had a series of "warrants" naming definite articles.

The result was the extraordinary shortages. When the sick and wounded came down to Scutari from the Crimea, they were in the majority of cases without forks, spoons, knives, or shirts. The regulations of the British Army laid down that each soldier should bring his pack into hospital with him, and his pack contained a change of clothing and utensils for eating. These articles were consequently not on the Purveyor's warrant. But most of the men who came down to Scutari had abandoned their packs after Calamita Bay, or on the march from the Alma to Balaclava, at the orders of their officers. Nevertheless, the Purveyor refused to consider any requisitions on him for these articles.

No medical officer was permitted to use his discretion. The surgeon on duty had to make as many as six different daily records of the "Diet Roll", the particulars of food and comforts to be consumed by each patient. "It must be admitted," the Roebuck Committee agreed, "that Dr Menzies, the Senior Medical Officer, had no time left for what should have been his principal duty, the proper superintendence of these hospitals."

The Barrack Hospital was the fatal fruit of the system. When the General Hospital was unexpectedly filled with cholera cases and Dr Menzies was abruptly notified that a further large number of patients were on their way, he was instructed to turn the Turkish Barracks into a hospital. The preparation and equipment of a hospital formed no part of his duties, his task being to instruct the Purveyor. How the Purveyor was to produce hospital equipment at a moment's notice, how he was to collect labour to clean the vast filthy building when no labour existed nearer than Constantinople, was not Dr Menzies' concern.

The Purveyor also knew the correct procedure. He had no authority to expend sums of money in purchasing goods in the open market, and in any case many of the articles required were not on his warrant. He requisitioned the Commissariat on the proper forms, the Commissariat wrote on the forms "None in store", and the matter was closed. The wounded arrived and were placed in the building without food, bedding, or medical attention. Having issued the instruction correctly and placed it on record, an official's duty was done.

The doctors at Scutari received the news of Miss Nightingale's appointment with disgust. They were under-staffed, overworked; it was the last straw that a youngish society lady should be foisted on them with a pack of nurses. Opinion was divided as to whether she would turn out a well-meaning, well-bred nuisance or a Government spy.

However, on November 5 Miss Nightingale and her party were welcomed into the Barrack Hospital with every appearance of flattering attention and escorted into the hospital with compliments and expressions of good will. When they saw their quarters, the picture abruptly changed. Six rooms, one of which was a kitchen and another a closet ten feet square, had been allotted to a party of forty persons. The same space had previously been allotted to three doctors, and elsewhere the same amount was occupied solely by a major. The rooms were damp, filthy, and unfurnished except for a few chairs. There were no tables; there was no food. Miss Nightingale made no comment, and the officials withdrew. It was a warning, a caution against placing reliance on the flowery promises, the resounding compliments of Lord Stratford de Redcliffe, Viscount Canning.

Lord Stratford had been British Ambassador to Constantinople three times and associated with Turkey since 1807. Physically he was extremely handsome. He lived magnificently and travelled with twenty-five servants and seventy tons of silver forks, knives, dishes, jugs, coffee and teapots, and spoons.

Miss Nightingale described him as bad-tempered, heartless, pompous, and lazy. He was not the man to interest himself in a hospital for common soldiers. In his magnificent palace on the

Bosphorus he lived for two years with, said Miss Nightingale, "the British Army perishing within sight of his windows", and during those two years he visited the hospitals only once, when she "dragged" him there for a visit of only one and a half hours.

Fourteen nurses were to sleep in one room, ten nuns in another; Miss Nightingale and Mrs Bracebridge shared the closet; Mr Bracebridge and the courier-interpreter slept in the office; the cook and her assistant went to bed in the kitchen. There was one more room upstairs, and the eight Sellonites were to sleep there. They went upstairs, and hurried back. The room was still occupied – by the dead body of a Russian general. Mr Bracebridge fetched two men to remove the corpse while the sisters waited. The room was not cleaned, and there was nothing to clean it with; it was days before they could get a broom, and meanwhile the deceased general's white hairs littered the floor. There was no furniture, no food, no means of cooking food, no beds. While the nurses and sisters unpacked, Miss Nightingale went down into the hospital and managed to procure tin basins of milkless tea. As the party drank it, she told them what she had discovered.

The hospital was totally lacking in equipment. It was hopeless to ask for furniture. There was no furniture. There was not even an operating table. There were no medical supplies. There were not even the ordinary necessities of life. For the present the nurses must use their tin basins for everything – washing, eating, and drinking.

The party had to go to bed in darkness, for the shortage of lamps and candles was acute. Sisters and nurses tried to console themselves by thinking how much greater were the sufferings of the wounded in the sick-transports. The rooms were alive with fleas, and rats scurried in the walls all night long. The spirits of all sank.

The doctors ignored Miss Nightingale. She was to be frozen out, and only one doctor would use her nurses and her supplies. She determined to wait until the doctors asked her for help. She would demonstrate that she and her party wished neither to interfere nor attract attention, that they were prepared to be completely subservient to the authority of the doctors.

It was a policy which demanded self-control. The party were to stand by, see the wounded suffer, and do nothing until officially instructed. Though Florence Nightingale could accept the hard fact that the experiments on which she had embarked could never succeed against official opposition, yet she inevitably came into conflict with her nurses.

She made them sort old linen, count packages of provisions. The cries of the men were unanswered while old linen was counted and mended – this was not what they had left England to accomplish. They blamed Miss Nightingale.

On Sunday, November 6, the ships bringing the wounded from Balaclava began to unload at Scutari. As on other occasions, the arrangements were inadequate and the men suffered frightfully.

Still Miss Nightingale would not allow her nurses to throw themselves into the work of attending on these unhappy victims. She allocated twenty-eight nurses to the Barrack Hospital and ten to the General Hospital a quarter of a mile away. All were to sleep in the Barrack Hospital, and all were to wait. No nurse was to enter a ward except at the invitation of a doctor. However piteous the state of the wounded, the doctor must give the order for attention. If the doctors did not choose to employ the nurses, then the nurses had to remain idle.

For nearly a week the party were kept shut up in their detestable quarters, making shirts, pillows, stump rests, and slings – and being observed by her penetrating eye. The time, sighed one of the English Sisters of Mercy, seemed extremely long.

"Our senior medical officer here," Miss Nightingale wrote to Sidney Herbert in January, 1855, "volunteered to say that my best nurse, Mrs Roberts, dressed wounds and fractures more skilfully than any of the dressers or assistant surgeons. But that it was not a question of efficiency, nor of the comfort of the patients, but of the 'regulations of the service'."

She was first able to get a footing in the hospital through the kitchen. To cook anything at the Barrack Hospital was practically impossible. The sole provision for cooking was thirteen Turkish coppers, each holding about 450 pints. There was only one kitchen. There were no kettles, no saucepans; the only fuel was green wood. The tea was made in the coppers in which meat had just been boiled; water was short, the coppers were not cleaned, and the tea was undrinkable.

The meat for each ward was issued to the orderly for the ward. When the orderly had the meat, he tied it up, put some distinguishing marks on it, and dropped it into the pot. Some of the articles used by the orderlies to distinguish their meat included red rags, buttons, old nails, reeking pairs of surgical scissors, and odd bits of uniform. The water did not generally boil; the fires smoked abominably. When the cook considered that sufficient time had been taken up in cooking, the orderlies threw buckets of water on the fires to put them out, and the contents of the coppers were distributed, the cook standing by to see that each man got his own joint. The joints which had been dropped in last were sometimes almost raw. The orderly then carried the meat into the ward and divided it up, usually on his bed, and never less than twenty minutes could elapse between taking it out of the pot and serving it. Not only were the dinners always cold, but the meat was issued with bone and gristle weighed in, and some men got portions which were all bone. Those who could eat meat usually tore it with their fingers – there were almost no forks, spoons, or knives. Men on a spoon diet got the water in which the meat had been cooked, as soup. There were no vegetables except, sometimes, dried peas.

The food was almost uneatable by men in good health; as a diet for cholera and dysentery cases it produced agonies. "I have never seen suffering greater," wrote one observer.

The day after Miss Nightingale arrived she began to cook "extras". She had bought arrowroot, wine and beef essences, and portable stoves in Marseilles. On the sixth of November, with the doctors' permission, she provided pails of hot arrowroot and port wine for the Balaclava survivors, and within a week the kitchen belonging to her quarters had become an extra diet kitchen, where food from her own stores was cooked. For five months this kitchen was the only means of supplying invalid food in the Barrack Hospital. She strictly observed official routine, nothing being supplied from the kitchen without a requisition signed by a doctor. No nurse was permitted to give a patient any nourishment without a doctor's written directions.

Cooking was all she had managed to accomplish when, on November 9, the situation completely changed. A flood of sick poured into Scutari on such a scale that a crisis of terrible urgency arose, and prejudices and resentments were for the moment forgotten.

It was the opening of the catastrophe. The destruction of the British Army had begun. These were the first of the stream of men suffering from dysentery, from scurvy, from starvation and exposure who were to pour down on Scutari all through the terrible winter. Over in the Crimea on the heights above Sebastopol the army was marooned, as completely as if on a lighthouse. Thousands of men possessed only what they stood up in. After the landing at Calamita Bay and after the Battle of the Alma, when the troops were riddled with cholera and the heat was intense, the men had, by their officers' orders, abandoned their packs.

Seven miles below the heights lay Balaclava, the British base. There had been one good road but the Russians had gained possession of it in the Battle of Balaclava on October 25. There remained a rough track, but it was not put into order before the winter. Men to carry out the work were non-existent. There were no tools. Above all, there was no transport. The army was still without wagons or pack animals.

Balaclava had become a nightmare of filth. Lord Raglan had been attracted by its extraordinary harbour, a landlocked lagoon, calm, clear, and almost tideless, so deep that a large vessel could anchor close inshore. No steps were taken to inspect Balaclava, a fishing village of only 500 inhabitants, before it was occupied, or to keep it in a sanitary condition. The army which marched in was stricken with cholera, and within a few days the narrow street had become a disgusting quagmire. Piles of arms and legs amputated after the Battle of Balaclava, with the sleeves and trousers still on them, had been thrown into the harbour and could be seen dimly through the water. The surface of the once translucent water was covered with brightly coloured scum, and the whole village smelled of hydrogen sulphide.

On November 5 the Russians had attacked at Inkerman, on the heights above Sebastopol. In a grim battle fought in swirling fog the British were victorious. But victory was not reassuring. The British troops were exhausted; their commanders were shaken by the revelation of Russian strength. It was evident that Sebastopol would not fall until the spring.

The British Army was going to winter on the heights before Sebastopol, and the British Army was not only totally destitute of supplies, but without the means of being able to get supplies should they ultimately arrive. Moistened by the dews of autumn, and churned by the wheels of heavy guns, the rough track from Balaclava to the camp had become impassable.

The weather changed rapidly, icy winds blew – and the troops on the heights above Sebastopol had no fuel. Every bush, every stunted tree was consumed, and the men clawed roots out of the sodden earth to gain a little warmth. As it grew colder, they had to live without shelter, without clothing, drenched by incessant driving rain, to sleep in mud, to eat hard dried peas and raw salt meat. The percentage of sickness rose and rose, and the miserable victims began to pour down on Scutari. The authorities were overwhelmed, and at last the doctors turned to Miss Nightingale. Her nurses dropped their sorting of linen and began with desperate haste to seam up great bags and stuff them with straw. These were laid down not only in the wards but in the corridors, a line of stuffed sacks on each side with just room to pass between them.

Day after day the sick poured in until the enormous building was entirely filled. The wards were full; the corridors were lined with men lying on the bare boards because the supply of bags stuffed with straw had given out. Chaos reigned. The doctors were unable even to examine each man. Sometimes men were a fortnight in the Barrack Hospital without seeing a surgeon. Yet the doctors, especially the older men, worked like lions, wrote Miss Nightingale, and were frequently on their feet for twenty-four hours at a time.

The filth became indescribable. The men in the corridors lay on unwashed rotten floors crawling with vermin. There were no pillows, no blankets; the men lay with their heads on their boots, wrapped in the blanket or greatcoat stiff with blood and filth which had been their sole covering perhaps for more than week. There were no screens or operating tables. Amputations had to be performed in the wards in full sight of the patients. One of Miss Nightingale's first acts was to procure a screen from Constantinople so that men might be spared the sight of the suffering they themselves were doomed to undergo.

She estimated that in the hospital at this time there were more than 1000 men suffering from acute diarrhœa, and only twenty chamber pots. The privies in the towers of the Barrack Hospital had been allowed to become useless; the water pipes which flushed them had been stopped up when the barracks were used for troops, and when the building was converted into a hospital they had never been unstopped. Huge wooden tubs stood in the wards and corridors for the men to use. The orderlies disliked the unpleasant task of emptying these, and they were left unemptied for twenty-four hours on end. "We have erysipelas, fever and gangrene," she wrote; ". . . the dysentery cases have died at the rate of one in two . . . the mortality of the operations is frightful . . . This is only the beginning of things." By the end of the second week in November the atmosphere in the Barrack Hospital was so frightful that the stench could be smelled outside the walls.

A change came over the men. The classification between wounded and sick was broken down. The wounded who had been well before began to catch fevers; "gradually all signs of cheerfulness disappeared, they drew their blankets over their heads and were buried in silence".

Fate had worse in store. On the night of November 14 it was noticed that the sea in the Bosphorus was running abnormally high, and there was a strange thrumming wind. Within a few days news came that the Crimea had been devastated by the worst hurricane within the memory of man. Tents were reduced to shreds, horses blown helplessly for miles, buildings destroyed, trees uprooted. The marquees which formed the regimental field hospitals vanished, and men were left half buried in mud without coverings of any kind. Most serious of all, every vessel in Balaclava harbour was destroyed, among them a large ship, the *Prince*, which had entered the harbour the previous day loaded with warm winter clothing and stores for the troops.

Winter now began in earnest with storms of sleet and winds that cut like a knife as they howled across the bleak plateau. Dysentery, diarrhœa, rheumatic fever increased by leaps and bounds. More and more shiploads of sick inundated Scutari. The men came down starved and in rags. They told the nurses to keep away because they were so filthy. "My own mother could not touch me," said one man to Sister Margaret Good-

man. By the end of November the administration of the hospital
had collapsed.

And then in the misery, the confusion, a light began to break.
Gradually it dawned on harassed doctors and overworked
officials that there was one person in Scutari who could take
action – who had the money and the authority to spend it – Miss
Nightingale.

She had a very large sum at her disposal, derived from various
sources and amounting to over £30,000, of which £7,000 had
been collected by her personally, and Constantinople was one of
the great markets of the world. During the first horrors of
November, the gathering catastrophe of December, it became
known that whatever was wanted, from a milk pudding to an
operating table, the thing to do was to go to Miss Nightingale.
Gradually, the doctors ceased to be suspicious and their jealousy disappeared.

One of her first acts was to purchase 200 hard scrubbing
brushes and sacking for washing the floors. She insisted on the
huge wooden tubs in the wards being emptied, standing quietly
and obstinately by the side of each one, sometimes for an hour at
a time, never scolding or raising her voice, until the orderlies
gave way and the tub was emptied.

By the end of December Miss Nightingale was in fact
purveying the hospital. During a period of two months she
supplied, on requisition of medical officers, about 6000 shirts,
2000 socks, and 500 pairs of drawers. She supplied nightcaps,
slippers, plates, tin cups, knives, forks, spoons in proportion.
She procured trays, tables, forms, clocks, operating tables,
scrubbers, towels, soap, and screens. She caused an entire
regiment which had only tropical clothing to be refitted with
warm clothing purchased in the markets of Constantinople
when Supply had declared such clothing unprocurable in the
time – Supply was compelled to get all its goods from England.
"I am a kind of General Dealer," she wrote to Sidney Herbert
on January 4, 1855, "in socks, shirts, knives and forks, wooden
spoons, tin baths, tables and forms, cabbages and carrots,
operating tables, towels and soap, small tooth combs, precipi-
tate for destroying lice, scissors, bed pans, and stump pillows."

Outside Sebastopol conditions grew steadily worse. The
stores lost in the hurricane were not replaced. Men, sick or

well, lay in a foot of water in the mud, covered only by a single blanket. Every root had been burned, and the men had to eat their food raw: meat stiff with salt and dried peas. There was no bread. As the percentage of sick climbed and climbed, double turns of duty were thrown on the survivors.

Men were in the trenches before Sebastopol for thirty-six hours at a stretch, never dry, never warmed, never fed. The sick were brought down to Balaclava strapped to mule-litters lent by the French – there was no British transport of any kind – naked, emaciated, and filthy. After waiting hours without food or shelter in the icy wind or driving sleet at Balaclava, they were piled on to the decks of the sick-transports and brought down to Scutari. And the catastrophe had not yet reached its height.

At the beginning of December, when the Barrack Hospital was filled to overflowing, a letter from Lord Raglan announced the arrival of a further 500 sick and wounded. It was impossible to cram any additional cases into the existing wards and corridors and Miss Nightingale pressed to have put in order the wing of the hospital which had been damaged by fire before the British occupation. It consisted of two wards and a corridor and would accommodate nearly 1000 extra cases. But the cost would be considerable, and no one in the hospital had the necessary authority to put the work in hand. Miss Nightingale took matters into her own hands. She engaged on her own responsibility 200 workmen, and paid for them partly out of her own pocket and partly out of *The Times* Fund. The wards were repaired and cleaned in time to receive the wounded.

Not only did she repair the wards; she equipped them. The Purveyor could provide nothing. One of the men described his sensation when he at last got off the filthy sick-transport and was received by Miss Nightingale and her nurses with clean bedding and warm food – "We felt we were in heaven," he said.

The affair caused a sensation. It was the first important demonstration of what men at Scutari called the "Nightingale power". Respect for the "Nightingale power" was increased when it became known that her action had been officially approved by the War Department and the money she had spent refunded to her.

But to Miss Nightingale herself these victories were only incidental. She never for a moment lost sight of the fact that the object of her mission was to prove the value of women as nurses. But, unhappily, no difficulties with doctors or purveyors were as wearing or as discouraging as her difficulties with her nurses.

"I came out, Ma'am, prepared to submit to everything, to be put on in every way. But there are some things, Ma'am, one can't submit to. There is the caps, Ma'am, that suits one face and some that suits another. And if I'd known, Ma'am, about the caps, great as was my desire to come out to nurse at Scutari, I wouldn't have come, Ma'am." Mrs Roberts from St Thomas's was worth her weight in gold. Mrs Drake from St John's House was a treasure, but most of the other hospital nurses were not fit to take care of themselves. To convince any of them, nurses or sisters, of the necessity for discipline was almost impossible. Why should a man who desperately needed stimulating food have to go without because the nurse who had the food could not give it to him until she had been authorized by a doctor? It was felt that Miss Nightingale was callous. It was said that she was determined to increase her own power and cared nothing for the sick.

Reluctance to accept her authority and obey her instructions was constant from the beginning to the end of her mission, and many of her nurses heartily disliked her.

However, she had managed to establish herself, and now her nurses were fully occupied. She had also acquired two new and loyal workers in Dr and Lady Alicia Blackwood, who had come out at their own expense after the Battle of Inkerman.

On December 14 she wrote Sidney Herbert a cheerful letter:

"What we may be considered as having effected:
(1) The kitchen for extra diets now in full action.
(2) A great deal more cleaning of wards, mops, scrubbing brushes, brooms, and combs given out by ourselves.
(3) 2000 shirts, cotton and flannel, given out and washing organized.
(4) Lying-in hospital begun.
(5) Widows and soldiers' wives relieved and attended to.
(6) A great amount of daily dressing and attention to compound fractures by the most competent of us.
(7) The supervision and stirring-up of the whole machinery generally with the concurrence of the chief medical authority.

(8) The repairing of wards for 800 wounded which would otherwise have been left uninhabitable. (And this I regard as the most important.)"

She never wrote quite so cheerfully again.

In January, 1855, the sufferings of the British Army before Sebastopol began to reach a fearful climax. Still no stores had reached the army. What had happened to them, the Roebuck Committee demanded later? Huge quantities of warm clothing, of preserved foods, of medical comforts and surgical supplies had been sent out – where did they all go? It was never discovered, but Miss Nightingale declared that stores were available all the time the men were suffering, never reaching them through the "regulations of the service". In January, 1855, when the army before Sebastopol was being ravaged by scurvy, a shipload of cabbages was thrown into the harbour at Balaclava on the ground that it was not consigned to anyone. This happened not once but several times. During November, December, and January 1854–55, when green coffee was being issued to the men, there were 173,000 rations of tea in store at Balaclava; 20,000 pounds of lime juice arrived for the troops on December 10, 1854, but none was issued until February. Why? Because no order existed for the inclusion of tea and lime juice in the daily ration.

Again, at the end of December there were blankets enough in store to have given a third one to every man. But the men lay on the muddy ground with nothing under them and nothing over them since their blankets had been lost in battle or destroyed in the hurricane, because the regulations did not entitle them to replacement.

In January, 1855, there were 12,000 men in hospital and only 11,000 in the camp before Sebastopol; and still the shiploads came pouring down. It was, Miss Nightingale wrote, "calamity unparalleled in the history of calamity".

In this emergency she became supreme. She was the rock to which everyone clung, even the purveyors. "Nursing," she wrote on January 4 to Sidney Herbert, "is the least of the functions into which I have been forced."

Her calmness, her resource, her power to take action raised

her to the position of a goddess. The men adored her. "If she were at our head," they said, "we should be in Sebastopol next week." The doctors came to be absolutely dependent on her, and a regimental officer wrote home: "Miss Nightingale now queens it with absolute power."

Sidney Herbert had asked her to write to him privately in addition to the official reports, and during her time in Scutari and the Crimea she wrote him a series of over thirty letters of enormous length, crammed with detailed and practical suggestions for the reform of the existing system. It is almost incredible that in addition to the unceasing labour she was performing, when she was living in the foul atmosphere of the Barrack Hospital incessantly harried by disputes, callers, complaints and overwhelmed with official correspondence which had to be written in her own hand, she should have found time and energy to write this long series of vast, carefully thought-out letters, many as long as a pamphlet. She never lost sight of the main issue.

"This is whether the system or no system which is found adequate in time of peace but wholly inadequate to meet the exigencies of a time of war is to be left as it is – or patched up temporarily, as you give a beggar halfpence – or made equal to the wants not diminishing but increasing of a time of awful pressure."

On January 8, at the height of the calamity, she wrote:

"I have written a plan for the systematic organization of these Hospitals, but deeming so great a change impracticable during the present heavy pressure of calamities here, I refrain from forwarding it, and substitute a sketch of a plan, by which great improvement might be made from within without abandoning the forms under which the service is carried on . . ."

Among her recommendations were the establishment of a medical school at Scutari, and finally she made an urgent plea for medical statistics.

Her facts and figures were freely used by Sidney Herbert and other members of the Cabinet, and important changes made in British Army organization during the course of the Crimean War were based on her suggestions.

In spite of the improvements in the Barrack Hospital, something was horribly wrong. The wards were cleaner, the lavatories unstopped, the food adequate, but still the mortality climbed. The disaster was about to enter its second phase. At the end of December an epidemic broke out, described variously as "Asiatic cholera" or "famine fever", similar to the cholera brought over by starving Irish immigrants after the Irish potato famine. By the middle of January the epidemic was serious – four surgeons died in three weeks, and three nurses. The officers on their rounds began to be afraid to go into the wards. They could do nothing for the unfortunates perishing within; they knocked on the door and an orderly shouted "All right, sir" from inside.

The snow ceased, and faint warmth came to the bleak plateau before Sebastopol on which the British Army was encamped. The number of men sent down by sick-transports stopped rising. The percentage of sick was still disastrously, tragically high, but it was stationary.

But in the Barrack Hospital the mortality figures continued to rise. The English were unable to bury their dead. A fatigue party could not be mustered whose strength was equal to the task of digging a pit.

In England fury succeeded fury. A great storm of rage, humiliation, and despair had been gathering through the terrible winter of 1854–55. For the first time in history, through reading the dispatches of Russell, the public had realized "with what majesty the British soldier fights". And these heroes were dead. The men who had stormed the heights at Alma, charged with the Light Brigade at Balaclava, fought the grim battle against overwhelming odds in the fog at Inkerman, had perished of hunger and neglect. Even the horses which had taken part in the Charge of the Light Brigade had starved to death.

On January 26 Mr Roebuck, Radical member for Sheffield, brought forward a motion for the appointment of a committee "to inquire into the condition of the Army before Sebastopol and the conduct of those departments of the Government whose duty it has been to minister to the wants of that Army". It was a vote of censure on the Government, and Sidney Herbert went out of office. But Miss Nightingale's position was not weakened. The new Prime Minister was her old friend and supporter, Lord Palmerston. Her reports were regularly forwarded to the Queen and studied by her. Sidney Herbert wrote to assure her that he had no intention of giving up his work for the army because he was out of office. She was still to write to him, and he would see that her reports and suggestions were forwarded to the proper quarters. He would continue to be, she wrote, "our protector in this terrible great work".

At the end of February, Lord Panmure, the new Secretary at War, sent out a Sanitary Commission to investigate the sanitary state of the building used as hospitals and of the camps both at Scutari and in the Crimea. Miss Nightingale's name did not appear, but the urgency, the clarity, the forcefulness of the instructions are unmistakably hers. "The utmost expedition must be used in starting your journey . . . On your arrival you will instantly put yourselves into communication with Lord William Paulet . . . It is important that you be deeply impressed with the necessity of not resting content with an order but that you see instantly, by yourselves or your agents, to the commencement of the work and to its superintendence day by day until it is finished." This Commission, said Miss Nightingale, "saved the British Army".

The Commissioners landed at Constantinople at the beginning of March and began work instantly. Their discoveries were hair-raising. They described the sanitary defects of the Barrack Hospital as "murderous". Beneath the magnificent structure were sewers of the worst possible construction, mere cesspools, choked, inefficient, and grossly overloaded. The whole vast building stood in a sea of decaying filth; the very walls, constructed of porous plaster, were soaked in it. Every breeze, every puff of air, blew poisonous gas through the pipes of numerous open privies into the corridors and wards where the sick were lying. The water supply was contaminated and totally insufficient. The Commissioners had the channel opened through which the water flowed, and the water supply for the greater part of the hospital was found to be passing through the decaying carcass of a horse. The courtyard and precincts of the hospital were filthy.

The Commissioners ordered them to be cleared, and during the first fortnight of this work 556 handcarts and large baskets full of rubbish were removed and twenty-four dead animals and two dead horses buried. The Commission began to flush and cleanse the sewers, to limewash the walls and free them from vermin, to tear out the wooden shelves known as Turkish divans which ran round the wards and harboured the rats for which the Barrack Hospital was notorious. The effect was instant. At last the rate of mortality began to fall. In the Crimea spring came with a rush; the bleak plateau before Sebastopol was bathed in sunlight and carpeted with crocuses and hyacinths. The road to Balaclava became passable, the men's rations improved, and the survivors of the fearful winter lost their unnatural silence and began once more to curse and swear.

The emergency was passing, and as it passed opposition to Miss Nightingale awoke again.

Miss Nightingale's mission falls into two periods. There is first the period of frightful emergency during the winter of 1854–55, when every consideration but that of averting utter catastrophe went by the board, opposition died away, and she became supreme.

But as soon as things had slightly improved, official jealousy reawoke. In the second period, from the spring of 1855 until her return to England in the summer of 1856, gratitude – except the gratitude of the troops – and admiration disappeared, and she was victimized by petty jealousies, treacheries, and misrepresentations. Throughout this second period she was miserably depressed. At the end of it she was obsessed by a sense of failure.

By the spring of 1855 she was physically exhausted. She was a slight woman who had never been robust, who was accustomed to luxury, and was now living in almost unendurable hardship. When it rained, water poured through the roof of her quarters. The food was uneatable; the allowance of water was one pint a head a day; the building was vermin-infested, the atmosphere in the hospital so foul that to visit the wards produced diarrhœa. She never went out except to hurry over the quarter of a mile of refuse-strewn mud which separated the Barrack from the General Hospital.

When a flood of sick came in, she was on her feet for twenty-four hours at a stretch. She was known to pass eight hours on her knees dressing wounds. It was her rule never to let any man who came under her observation die alone. If he was conscious, she herself stayed beside him; if he was unconscious she sometimes allowed Mrs Bracebridge to take her place. She estimated that during that winter she witnessed 2000 deathbeds. The worst cases she nursed herself. One of the nurses described accompanying her on her night rounds.

> "It seemed an endless walk . . . As we slowly passed along the silence was profound; very seldom did a moan or cry from those deeply suffering fall on our ears. A dim light burned here and there, Miss Nightingale carried her lantern which she would set down before she bent over any of the patients. I much admired her manner to the men – it was so tender and kind."

Her influence was extraordinary. She could make the men stop drinking, write home to their wives, submit to pain. "She was wonderful," said a veteran, "at cheering up anyone who was a bit low." The surgeons were amazed at her ability to strengthen men doomed to an operation. "The magic of her power over the men was felt," writes Kinglake, "in the room – the dreaded, the bloodstained room – where operations took place. There perhaps the maimed soldier, if not yet resigned to his fate, might be craving death rather than meet the knife of the surgeon, but when such a one looked and saw that the honoured Lady-in-Chief was patiently standing beside him – and with lips closely set and hands folded – decreeing herself to go through the pain of witnessing pain, he used to fall into the mood of obeying her silent command and – finding strange support in her presence – bring himself to submit and endure."

The troops worshipped her. "What a comfort it was to see her pass even," wrote a soldier. "She would speak to one, and nod and smile to as many more; but she could not do it all, you know. We lay there by hundreds; but we could kiss her shadow as it fell and lay our heads on the pillow again content." For her sake the troops gave up the bad language which has always been the privilege of the British private soldier. "Before she came," ran another letter, "there was cussing and swearing but after that it was as holy as a church."

When the war was over Miss Nightingale wrote:

". . . The tears come into my eyes as I think how, amidst scenes of loathsome disease and death, there rose above it all the innate dignity, gentleness and chivalry of the men (for never surely was chivalry so strikingly exemplified) shining in the midst of what must be considered the lowest sinks of human misery, and preventing instinctively the use of one expression which could distress a gentle-woman."

It was work hard enough to have crushed any ordinary woman; yet, she wrote, it was the least of her functions. The crushing burden was the administrative work. Her quarters were called the Tower of Babel. All day long a stream of callers thronged her stairs, asking for everything from writing paper to advice on a sick man's diet, demanding shirts, splints, bandages, port wine, stoves, and butter.

She slept in the storeroom in a bed behind a screen; in the daytime she saw callers while sitting and writing at a deal table in front of the screen. She wore a black woollen dress, white linen collar and cuffs and apron, and a white cap under a black silk handkerchief. Every time there was a pause she snatched her pen and went on writing.

It was terribly cold, and she hated cold. There was no satisfactory stove in her quarters – one had been sent out from England, but it would not draw and she used it as a table and it was piled with papers. Her breath congealed on the air; the ink froze in the well; rats scampered in the walls and peered out from the wainscoting. Hour after hour she wrote on; the staff of the hospital declared that the light in her room was never put out. She wrote for the men, described their last hours and sent home their dying messages; she told wives of their husbands' continued affection, and mothers that their sons had died holding her hand. She wrote for the nurses, many of whom had left children behind. She wrote her enormous letters to Sidney Herbert; she wrote official reports, official letters; she kept lists, filled in innumerable requisitions. Papers were piled round her in heaps; they lay on the floor, on her bed, on the chairs. Often in the morning Mrs Bracebridge found her still in her clothes on her bed, where she had flung herself down in a stupor of fatigue.

BILL NEATE VERSUS THE GAS-MAN

William Hazlitt

The fight between Bill Neate and Tom Hickman, known on account of his boasting as the "Gas-man", took place at Hungerford in England on 11 December 1821. It was done with bare-knuckles, the winner being the last man standing.

The day was fine for a December morning. The grass was wet and the ground miry, and ploughed up with multitudinous feet, except that, within the ring itself, there was a spot of virgin-green closed in and unprofaned by vulgar tread, that shone with dazzling brightness in the mid-day sun. For it was now noon, and we had an hour to wait. This is the trying time. It is then the heart sickens, as you think what the two champions are about, and how short a time will determine their fate. After the first blow is struck, there is no opportunity for nervous apprehensions; you are swallowed up in the immediate interest of the scene – but

> Between the acting of a dreadful thing
> And the first motion, all the interim is
> Like a phantasma, or a hideous dream.

I found it so as I felt the sun's rays clinging to my back, and saw the white wintry clouds sink below the verge of the horizon. "So, I thought, my fairest hopes have faded from my sight! – so will the Gas-man's glory, or that of his adversary, vanish in an hour."

The swells were parading in their white box-coats, the outer ring was cleared with some bruises on the heads and shins of the rustic assembly (for the cockneys had been distanced by the sixty-six miles); the time drew near, I had got a good stand; a bustle, a buzz, ran through the crowd, and from the opposite side entered Neate, between his second and bottle-holder. He rolled along, swathed in his loose great-coat, his knock-knees bending under his huge bulk, and, with a modest cheerful air, threw his hat into the ring.

He then just looked round, and began quietly to undress; when from the other side there was a similar rush and an opening made, and the Gas-man came forward with a conscious air of anticipated triumph, too much like the cock-of-the-walk. He strutted about more than became a hero, sucked oranges with a supercilious air, and threw away the skin with a toss of his head, and went up and looked at Neate which was an act of supererogation. The only sensible thing he did was, as he strode away from the modern Ajax, to fling out his arms, as if he wanted to try whether they would do their work that day.

By this time they had stripped, and presented a strong contrast in appearance. If Neate was like Ajax, "with Atlantean shoulders, fit to bear" the pugilistic reputation of all Bristol, Hickman might be compared to Diomed, light, vigorous, elastic, and his back glistened in the sun, as he moved about, like a panther's hide. There was now a dead pause – attention was awestruck. Who at that moment, big with a great event, did not draw his breath short – did not feel his heart throb? All was ready. They tossed up for the sun, and the Gas-man won. They were led up to the scratch – shook hands, and went at it.

In the first round every one thought it was all over. After making play for a short time, the Gas-man flew at his adversary like a tiger, struck five blows in as many seconds, three first, and then following him as he staggered back, two more, right and left, and down he fell, a mighty ruin. There was a shout, and I said, "There is no standing this." Neate seemed like a lifeless lump of flesh and bone, round which the Gas-man's blows played with the rapidity of electricity or lightning, and you imagined he would only be lifted up to be knocked down again. It was as if Hickman held a sword or a fire in that right hand of his, and directed it against an unarmed body.

They met again, and Neate seemed not cowed but particularly cautious. I saw his teeth clench together and his brows knit close against the sun. He held out both his arms at full length straight before him, like two sledge-hammers, and raised his left an inch or two higher. The Gas-man could not get over this guard – they struck mutually and fell, but without advantage on either side. It was the same in the next round; but the balance of power was thus restored – the fate of the battle was suspended. No one could tell how it would end.

This was the only moment in which opinion was divided; for, in the next, the Gas-man aiming a mortal blow at his adversary's neck, with his right hand, and failing from the length he had to reach, the other returned it with his left at full swing, planted a tremendous blow on his cheek-bone and eyebrow, and made a red ruin of that side of his face. The Gas-man went down, and there was another shout – a roar of triumph as the waves of fortune rolled tumultuously from side to side. This was a settler. Hickman got up, and "grinned a horrible ghastly smile," yet he was evidently dashed in his opinion of himself; it was the first time he had ever been so punished; all one side of his face was perfect scarlet, and his right eye was closed in dingy blackness as he advanced to the fight, less confident, but still determined. After one or two more rounds, not receiving another such remembrancer, he rallied and went at it with his former impetuosity. But in vain. His strength had been weakened, – his blows could not tell at such a distance, – he was obliged to fling himself at his adversary, and could not strike from his feet; and almost as regularly as he flew at him with his right hand, Neate warded the blow, or drew back out of its reach, and felled him with the return of his left. There was little cautious sparring – no half-hits – no tapping and trifling, none of the *petit-maîtreship* of the art – they were almost all knock-down blows – the fight was a good stand-up fight.

The wonder was the half-minute time. If there had been a minute or more allowed between each round, it would have been intelligible how they should by degrees recover strength and resolution; but to see two men smashed to the ground, smeared with gore, stunned, senseless, the breath beaten out of their bodies; and then, before you recover from the shock, to see them rise up with new strength and courage, stand steady to inflict or receive mortal offence, and rush upon each other "like two clouds over the Caspian" – this is the most astonishing thing of all – this is the high and heroic state of man!

From this time forward the event became more certain every round; and about the twelfth it seemed as if it must have been over. Hickman generally stood with his back to me; but in the scuffle, he had changed positions, and Neate just then made a tremendous lunge at him, and hit him full in the face. It was doubtful whether he would fall backwards or forwards; he hung suspended for a second or two, and then fell back, throwing his hands in the air, and with his face lifted up to the sky.

I never saw anything more terrific than his aspect just before he fell. All traces of life, of natural expression, were gone from him. His face was like a human skull, a death's head, spouting blood. The eyes were filled with blood, the nose streamed with blood, the mouth gaped blood. He was not like an actual man, but like a preternatural, spectral appearance, or like one of the figures in Dante's Inferno. Yet he fought on after this for several rounds, still striking the first desperate blow, and Neate standing on the defensive, and using the same cautious guard to the last, as if he had still all his work to do; and it was not till the Gas-man was so stunned in the seventeenth or eighteenth round, that his senses forsook him, and he could not come to time, that the battle was declared over.

Ye who despise the Fancy, do something to show as much pluck or as much self-possession as this, before you assume a superiority which you have never given a single proof of by any one action in the whole course of your lives!

When the Gas-man came to himself, the first words he uttered were, "Where am I? What is the matter?" "Nothing is the matter, Tom, – you have lost the battle, but you are the bravest man alive." And Jackson whispered to him, "I am collecting a purse for you, Tom." Vain sounds, and unheard at that moment! Neate instantly went up and shook him cordially by the hand, and seeing some old acquaintance began to flourish with his fists, calling out, "Ah, you always said I couldn't fight – What do you think now?" But all in good humour and without any appearance of arrogance; only it was evident Bill Neate was pleased that he had won the fight. When it was over, I asked

Cribb if he did not think it was a good one? He said, "Pretty well!" The carrier pigeons now mounted into the air, and one of them flew with the news of her husband's victory to the bosom of Mrs Neate. Alas, for Mrs Hickman!

THE MAN WHO BROKE
THE SOUND BARRIER

Tom Wolfe

Chuck Yeager, a former USAAF WWII "ace", was the first person to break the "sound barrier". He did so on 14 October 1947.

The plane the Air Force wanted to break the sound barrier with was called the X–I. The Bell Aircraft Corporation had built it under an Army contract. The core of the ship was a rocket of the type first developed by a young Navy inventor, Robert Truax, during the war. The fuselage was shaped like a 50-calibre bullet – an object that was known to go supersonic smoothly. Military pilots seldom drew major test assignments; they went to highly paid civilians working for the aircraft corporations. The prime pilot for the X–I was a man whom Bell regarded as the best of the breed. This man looked like a movie star. He looked like a pilot from out of *Hell's Angels*. And on top of everything else there was his name: Slick Goodlin.

The idea in testing the X–I was to nurse it carefully into the transonic zone, up to seven-tenths, eight-tenths, nine-tenths the speed of sound (.7 Mach, .8 Mach, .9 Mach) before attempting the speed of sound itself, Mach 1, even though Bell and the Army already knew the X–I had the rocket power to go to Mach 1 and beyond, if there *was* any *beyond*. The consensus of aviators and engineers, after Geoffrey de Havilland's death, was that the speed of sound was an absolute, like the firmness of the earth. The sound barrier was a farm you could buy in the

sky. So Slick Goodlin began to probe the transonic zone in the
X–I, going up to .8 Mach. Every time he came down he'd have a
riveting tale to tell. The buffeting, it was so fierce – and the
listeners, their imaginations aflame, could practically see poor
Geoffrey de Havilland disintegrating in midair. And the goddamned aerodynamics – and the listeners got a picture of a man
in ballroom pumps skidding across a sheet of ice, pursued by
bears. A controversy arose over just how much bonus Slick
Goodlin should receive for assaulting the dread Mach 1 itself.
Bonuses for contract test pilots were not unusual; but the figure
of $150,000 was now bruited about. The Army balked, and
Yeager got the job. He took it for $283 a month, or $3,396 a
year; which is to say, his regular Army captain's pay.

The only trouble they had with Yeager was in holding him
back. On his first powered flight in the X–I he immediately
executed an unauthorized zero-g roll with a full load of rocket
fuel, then stood the ship on its tail and went up to .85 Mach in a
vertical climb, also unauthorized. On subsequent flights, at
speeds between .85 Mach and .9 Mach, Yeager ran into most
known airfoil problems – loss of elevator, aileron, and rudder
control, heavy trim pressures, Dutch rolls, pitching and buffeting, the lot – yet was convinced, after edging over .9 Mach, that
this would all get better, not worse, as you reached Mach 1. The
attempt to push beyond Mach 1 – "breaking the sound barrier"
– was set for October 14, 1947. Not being an engineer, Yeager
didn't believe the "barrier" existed.

October 14 was a Tuesday. On Sunday evening, October 12,
Chuck Yeager dropped in at Pancho's, along with his wife. She
was a brunette named Glennis, whom he had met in California
while he was in training, and she was such a number, so striking,
he had the inscription "Glamorous Glennis" written on the
nose of his P–51 in Europe and, just a few weeks back, on the
X–I itself. Yeager didn't go to Pancho's and knock back a few
because two days later the big test was coming up. Nor did he
knock back a few because it was the weekend. No, he knocked
back a few because night had come and he was a pilot at Muroc.
In keeping with the military tradition of Flying & Drinking,
that was what you did, for no other reason than that the sun had
gone down. You went to Pancho's and knocked back a few and
listened to the screen doors banging and to other aviators

torturing the piano and the nation's repertoire of Familiar Favourites and to lonesome mouse-turd strangers wandering in through the banging doors and to Pancho classifying the whole bunch of them as old bastards and miserable pecker-woods. That was what you did if you were a pilot at Muroc and the sun went down.

So about eleven Yeager got the idea that it would be a hell of a kick if he and Glennis saddled up a couple of Pancho's dude-ranch horses and went for a romp, a little rat race, in the moonlight. This was in keeping with the military tradition of Flying & Drinking and Drinking & Driving, except that this was prehistoric Muroc and you rode horses. So Yeager and his wife set off on a little proficiency run at full gallop through the desert in the moonlight amid the arthritic silhouettes of the Joshua trees. Then they start racing back to the corral, with Yeager in the lead and heading for the gateway. Given the prevailing conditions, it being nighttime, at Pancho's, and his head being filled with a black sandstorm of many badly bawled songs and vulcanized oaths, he sees too late that the gate has been closed. Like many a hard-driving midnight pilot before him, he does not realize that he is not equally gifted in the control of all forms of locomotion. He and the horse hit the gate, and he goes flying off and lands on his right side. His side hurts like hell.

The next day, Monday, his side still hurts like hell. It hurts every time he moves. It hurts every time he breathes deep. It hurts every time he moves his right arm. He knows that if he goes to a doctor at Muroc or says anything to anybody even remotely connected with his superiors, he will be scrubbed from the flight on Tuesday. They might even go so far as to put some other miserable peckerwood in his place. So he gets on his motorcycle, an old junker that Pancho had given him, and rides over to see a doctor in the town of Rosamond, near where he lives. Every time the goddamned motorcycle hits a pebble in the road, his side hurts like a sonofabitch. The doctor in Rosamond informs him he has two broken ribs and he tapes them up and tells him that if he'll just keep his right arm immobilized for a couple of weeks and avoid any physical exertion or sudden movements, he should be all right.

Yeager gets up before daybreak on Tuesday morning – which

is supposed to be the day he tries to break the sound barrier –
and his ribs still hurt like a sonofabitch. He gets his wife to drive
him over to the field, and he has to keep his right arm pinned
down to his side to keep his ribs from hurting so much. At
dawn, on the day of a flight, you could hear the X–I screaming
long before you got there. The fuel for the X–I was alcohol and
liquid oxygen, oxygen converted from a gas to a liquid by
lowering its temperature to 297 degrees below zero. And when
the lox, as it was called, rolled out of the hoses and into the belly
of the X–I, it started boiling off and the X–I started steaming
and screaming like a teakettle. There's quite a crowd on hand,
by Muroc standards . . . perhaps nine or ten souls. They're still
fueling the X–I with the lox, and the beast is wailing.

The X–I looked like a fat orange swallow with white markings. But it was really just a length of pipe with four rocket
chambers in it. It had a tiny cockpit and a needle nose, two little
straight blades (only three and a half inches thick at the thickest
part) for wings, and a tail assembly set up high to avoid the
"sonic wash" from the wings. Even though his side was throbbing and his right arm felt practically useless, Yeager figured he
could grit his teeth and get through the flight – except for one
specific move he had to make. In the rocket launches, the X–I,
which held only two and a half minutes' worth of fuel, was
carried up to twenty-six thousand feet underneath a B–29. At
seven thousand feet, Yeager was to climb down a ladder from
the bomb bay of the B–29 to the open doorway of the X–I, hook
up to the oxygen system and the radio microphone and earphones, and put his crash helmet on and prepare for the launch,
which would come at twenty-five thousand feet. This helmet
was a homemade number. There had never been any such thing
as a crash helmet before, except in stunt flying. Throughout the
war pilots had used the old skin-tight leather helmet-and-
goggles. But the X–I had a way of throwing the pilot around
so violently that there was danger of getting knocked out against
the walls of the cockpit. So Yeager had bought a big leather
football helmet – there were no plastic ones at the time – and he
butchered it with a hunting knife until he carved the right kind
of holes in it, so that it would fit down over his regular flying
helmet and the earphones and the oxygen rig. Anyway, then his
flight engineer, Jack Ridley, would climb down the ladder, out

in the breeze, and shove into place the cockpit door, which had to be lowered out of the belly of the B–29 on a chain. Then Yeager had to push a handle to lock the door airtight. Since the X–I's cockpit was minute, you had to push the handle with your right hand. It took quite a shove. There was no way you could move into position to get enough leverage with your left hand.

Out in the hangar Yeager makes a few test shoves on the sly, and the pain is so incredible he realizes that there is no way a man with two broken ribs is going to get the door closed. It is time to confide in somebody, and the logical man is Jack Ridley. Ridley is not only the flight engineer but a pilot himself and a good old boy from Oklahoma to boot. He will understand about Flying & Drinking and Drinking & Driving through the goddamned Joshua trees. So Yeager takes Ridley off to the side in the tin hangar and says: Jack, I got me a little ol' problem here. Over at Pancho's the other night I sorta . . . dinged my goddamned ribs. Ridley says, Whattya mean . . . *dinged?* Yeager says, Well, I guess you might say I damned near like to . . . *broke* a coupla the sonsabitches. Whereupon Yeager sketches out the problem he foresees.

Not for nothing is Ridley the engineer on this project. He has an inspiration. He tells a janitor named Sam to cut him about nine inches off a broom handle. When nobody's looking, he slips the broomstick into the cockpit of the X–I and gives Yeager a little advice and counsel.

So with that added bit of supersonic flight gear Yeager went aloft.

At seven thousand feet he climbed down the ladder into the X–I's cockpit, clipped on his hoses and lines, and managed to pull the pumpkin football helmet over his head. Then Ridley came down the ladder and lowered the door into place. As Ridley had instructed, Yeager now took the nine inches of broomstick and slipped it between the handle and the door. This gave him just enough mechanical advantage to reach over with his left hand and whang the thing shut. So he whanged the door shut with Ridley's broomstick and was ready to fly.

At 26,000 feet the B–29 went into a shallow dive, then pulled up and released Yeager and the X–I as if it were a bomb. Like a bomb it dropped and shot forward (at the speed of the mother ship) at the same time. Yeager had been launched straight into the sun. It seemed to be no more than six feet in front of him, filling up the sky and blinding him. But he managed to get his bearings and set off the four rocket chambers one after the other. He then experienced something that became known as the ultimate sensation in flying: "booming and zooming." The surge of the rockets was so tremendous, forced him back into his seat so violently, he could hardly move his hands forward the few inches necessary to reach the controls. The X–I seemed to shoot straight up in an absolutely perpendicular trajectory, as if determined to snap the hold of gravity via the most direct route possible. In fact, he was only climbing at the 45-degree angle called for in the flight plan. At about .87 Mach the buffeting started.

On the ground the engineers could no longer see Yeager. They could only hear . . . that poker-hollow West Virginia drawl.

"Had a mild buffet there . . . jes the usual instability . . ." *Jes the usual instability?*

Then the X–I reached the speed of .96 Mach, and that incredible caint-hardlyin' aw-shuckin' drawl said:

"Say, Ridley . . . make a note here, will ya?" (*if you ain't got nothin' better to do*) ". . . elevator effectiveness *re*-gained."

Just as Yeager had predicted, as the X–I approached Mach 1, the stability improved. Yeager had his eyes pinned on the machometer. The needle reached .96, fluctuated, and went off the scale.

And on the ground they heard . . . that voice:

"Say, Ridley . . . make another note, will ya?" (*if you ain't too bored yet*) ". . . there's somethin' wrong with this ol' mach-ometer . . ." (faint chuckle) ". . . it's gone kinda screwy on me . . ."

And in that moment, on the ground, they heard a boom rock over the desert floor – just as the physicist Theodore von Kármán had predicted many years before.

Then they heard Ridley back in the B–29: "If it is, Chuck, we'll fix it. Personally I think you're seeing things."

Then they heard Yeager's poker-hollow drawl again:

"Well, I guess I am, Jack . . . And I'm still goin' upstairs like a bat."

The X–I had gone through "the sonic wall" without so much

as a bump. As the speed topped out at Mach 1.05, Yeager had
the sensation of shooting straight through the top of the sky.
The sky turned a deep purple and all at once the stars and the
moon came out – and the sun shone at the same time. He had
reached a layer of the upper atmosphere where the air was too
thin to contain reflecting dust particles. He was simply looking
out into space. As the X-I nosed over at the top of the climb,
Yeager now had seven minutes of . . . Pilot Heaven . . . ahead of
him. He was going faster than any man in history, and it was
almost silent up here, since he had exhausted his rocket fuel,
and he was so high in such a vast space that there was no
sensation of motion. He was master of the sky. His was a king's
solitude, unique and inviolate, above the dome of the world. It
would take him seven minutes to glide back down and land at
Muroc. He spent the time doing victory rolls and wing-over-
wing aerobatics while Rogers Lake and the High Sierras spun
around below.

HIS SOUL GOES MARCHING ON

E.G. Ogan

The song "John Brown's Body" is still sung, but light-heartedly and with little remembrance of the American anti-slavery campaigner whose ideals, life and hanging inspired it.

In a letter to the young son of one of his greatest friends – George Luther Stearns – John Brown, in 1857, outlined the story of the first twenty years of his amazingly eventful life. Therein he says that he "was never quarrelsome, but was excessively fond of the hardest and roughest kind of plays and could never get enough of them."

When about eleven years of age, during the war with England, he had, as he declared, "some chance to form his own boyish judgment of men and measures, and to become somewhat familiarly acquainted with some who have figured before the country since that time."

It was during the war that a circumstance occurred which caused him to become a "most determined abolitionist," and led him to declare eternal war on slavery. While staying with a well-to-do landlord, he was witness to the cruel treatment suffered by a negro boy of about his own age. The boy was poorly clothed and ill-nourished. he was frequently subjected to physical punishment, being beaten with iron shovels and many other weapons that came readily to hand. The memory of the hardships suffered by that poor negro boy was ever an inspiration to John Brown in his lifelong war on slavery.

On another occasion, some time after he had adopted the

occupation of a tanner and was living in a cabin in Hudson township, he witnessed an incident which confirmed him in his determination to do all that lay in his power to bring about the abolition of negro bondage.

Whilst in the company of his adopted brother, Levi Blakeslee, there came running to him a terror-stricken slave, who tearfully begged his help. Brown took him into his cabin, gave him food and allowed him to rest there. Towards evening the fugitive negro was terrified at hearing the clattering of horses' hooves, and his benefactor fearing that the boy was in danger of being recaptured, advised him to leave the cabin by way of the window and hide in the brush until the danger had passed.

As it turned out, the precaution proved to be unnecessary, the alarm having been caused by the return from Hudson of some neighbouring farmers. When they had passed, Brown left the cabin to search for the boy, and eventually found him almost lifeless from fear, hiding behind a log. Dealing with this incident, Brown stated, "I heard the boy's heart thumping before I reached him, and I vowed eternal enmity to slavery."

At one time it was Brown's intention to become a Congregational minister, and with this intent he returned about 1817 or 1818 from Ohio, whither his father had removed in 1805, to Connecticut to enter Amherst College. But close study affected his eyes, setting up chronic inflammation, which necessitated his relinquishing all ideas of entering the ministry.

John, therefore, decided to resume the occupation of tanner, and a year or two later was married to Dianthe Lusk, a widow. The tanning business prospered, but in spite of this, and his having erected a large house only about twelve months before, Brown decided to move on, and so he transferred his home and calling to Richmond, in Pennsylvania. In his new surroundings John went diligently about his business, building himself a substantial new tannery, and again, he prospered. Life for Brown, however, was not without its griefs, and after twelve years of happy married life his dearly loved wife died.

After that things went badly for John Brown.

Failure attended his varied activities, and in 1842 he was declared a bankrupt. Undaunted, however, by his lack of success, Brown, who had in the meantime remarried, started afresh as a breeder of sheep and cattle, winning many awards at the annual fairs at which he exhibited the animals he bred; and then, in 1844, he moved to Akron, where he returned to his original calling of a tanner, and met with considerable success.

In that year Brown associated himself with Simon Perkins in a partnership for carrying on a sheep-rearing business on an extensive scale, but although enjoying initial success there ultimately resulted a heavy financial loss, which caused the partnership to be dissolved.

By the year 1854 the resources of Brown and his family were in a precarious state, and five of his sons, therefore, resolved to seek fortune in Kansas, in which state at that time violent conflicts had begun to occur between the "free state" settlers and adherents to the pro-slavery cause. Leaving his family behind at North Elba, Brown determined the following year to join his sons in Kansas, in the hope of regaining some prosperity.

It was not long after they came to live in Kansas that John Brown and his sons became actively interested in the Free State movement. Nor did they go to any pains to disguise from the pro-slavery party their sympathy with the abolitionist move-ment; and when, shortly after their entry into Kansas, a party of Missourians, formidably armed, rode up and questioned them regarding some stray cattle, they answered that they had not seen them, and added defiantly that they were "free state, and more than that, abolitionists."

"From that moment," as young Jason Brown declared, "we were marked for destruction; before we had been in the territory a month, we found we had to go armed and to be prepared to defend our lives."

Thenceforward John Brown and his sons openly declared their sympathy with the Free Staters, and took every oppor-tunity of furthering the cause, attending meetings and engaging in other activities, while John Brown himself was elected a vice-president of the Free State Convention.

Meanwhile, they busied themselves in building their home, during which time they were constantly receiving reports of serious crimes against the Free Staters, many of whom were being put to death by the common enemy.

These spasmodic killings began towards the end of October, 1855, and one of them was later to lead to the most serious clash between the anti-slavers and the Missourians that had so far occurred. This was the treacherous shooting from behind of a young Free Stater named Charles Dow by a pro-slaver named Franklin Coleman.

The shooting arose out of a quarrel between the pair regarding the felling of timber by Coleman on Dow's settlement. As a consequence a meeting was held by the Free State settlers at which a resolution was passed protesting against the murderous attack by Coleman and calling for justice against him. On his way home from the meeting, the murdered man's friend, Jacob Branson, was suddenly seized by Sheriff Jones of Douglas County, and accused of entertaining violence and acting in a way calculated to cause a breach of the peace. Elated with their arrest, Jones and his men, some fifteen in all, celebrated their capture for the best part of two hours with a drinking bout, and on finally continuing on their way were met by a determined posse of Free Staters, who levelled their guns at them and demanded the release of their prisoner.

They succeeded in securing Branson's release without bloodshed, but their action so incensed the drunken sheriff that on his return he enlarged considerably upon the actual occurrence, declaring it to be an act of "open rebellion" on the part of Lawrence, the town from which Branson's rescuers hailed.

For their part, the inhabitants of Lawrence did not underrate the seriousness of their fellow-citizens' action, and realizing that reprisals were bound to be attempted, they hastily took precautions to organize a strong guard for the defence of the town.

Nor had they long to wait before their worst fears were realized. The pro-slavers snatched at the opportunity so providentially provided to march upon the ill-fated citizens of Lawrence. Men were hastily gathered from the surrounding districts, and to ensure an adequate force for the onslaught, an announcement was circulated throughout the border counties, calling upon everyone to march to the scene of the rebellion and put down the outlaws of Douglas County, who were committing depredations upon persons and property, burning down houses, and declaring open hostility to the law.

The outlaws, it was flagrantly misstated, numbered about one thousand, and were armed to the teeth, and every volunteer for the attacking army was urged to bring with him a rifle and ammunition. Word soon reached Lawrence of the mobilization of the pro-slavery army, and the citizens made haste to complete their preparations for the defence of the town, dispatching runners far and wide to enlist the help of all Free State supporters in Kansas.

Among those who promptly answered the call to arms were John Brown and four of his sons, Frederick, Owen, Salmon and John, but on arrival at Lawrence they discovered that Governor Shannon, in command of the Missourians, was desirous of negotiating terms with the town's defenders, fearing the consequences should he give the order for the attack. The governor requested the commander of the Free Staters to go to his camp and discuss terms, but on receiving a point-blank refusal, agreed himself to enter the town if an escort was sent for him and his safe return was ensured.

The outcome of the parley was an overwhelming success for the Kansas men, who secured the general's promise to withdraw his forces and leave themselves to manage their own affairs in future.

But the truce was not to be of long duration. Sheriff Jones, some five months later, entered Lawrence and made a further effort to secure the arrest of Branson's chief rescuer, and in this he was soon successful. But no sooner had he laid hands upon his prisoner than he was surrounded by a hostile crowd who secured the escape of the captive.

For the moment Jones submitted to defeat, but the next day, having received a refusal from several Lawrence citizens to assist him in serving a number of writs, he personally apprehended one of them, and promptly received a severe blow in the face for his pains. Three days later the sheriff, accompanied by a detachment of troops, returned to Lawrence and arrested several citizens, and had them secured in a tent. During the night, while on guard in the tent, Jones was wounded by a shot from a rifle.

Meetings were held at which the pro-slavers denounced the dastardly act and called upon the listeners to take revenge on Lawrence; and to add further fuel to the fire, reports were spread around that isolated attacks, some with fatal consequences, were being made by the Free Staters on the Missourians.

In spite of the efforts at moderation made by the governor, who counselled the pro-slavers not to give vent to the spirit of revenge, killings continued daily. For no apparent reason other than that they were declared abolitionists, men and boys received bullets in their backs, while others suffered the indignity and discomfort of being tarred and feathered.

The desire for revenge upon the citizens of Lawrence was slowly and surely being fed, the lust for blood was gradually being fired.

Soon a force of some eight hundred Southerners arrived to intimidate the citizens of Lawrence, who were inadequately armed and totally unprepared to offer resistance. Many had taken the precaution to leave their homes, and find security elsewhere. Lawrence was, in fact, at the mercy of the border ruffians, who set about their task of destruction, beginning first by an assault upon the newspaper offices, smashing the presses, scattering the type, and flinging books and paper and other contents of the offices into the river. Fired with drink and exultant with their successful onslaught on the newspaper offices, they then attacked and destroyed everything which they could lay their hands upon until the town presented a scene of utter and hopeless desolation.

John Brown and his family were not present at the destruction and pillage of Lawrence, but they had received a message post haste of the need of their support, and actually set out to lend their aid. Brown informed his wife of their journey in a letter he wrote some weeks later, in which he said:

"We were called to the relief of Lawrence, May 22, and every man (eight in all) turned out . . . On our way to Lawrence we learned that it had already been destroyed, and we encamped with John's company over night. Next day our little company left, and during the day we stopped and searched three men . . . On the second day and evening, after we left John's men, we encountered quite a number of pro-slavery men, and took them prisoners. Our prisoners were let go, but we kept some four or five horses. We were immediately after accused of murdering five men at Pottawatomie, and great efforts have since been made by Missourians and their ruffians to capture us."

That is John Brown's simple account of an incident which brought him into far greater prominence than anything else accomplished by him throughout the long struggle for abolition with the possible exception of his last great exploit.

Apparently learning that Lawrence had surrendered to the proslavers without an effort at defence, and that there was a large encampment of pro-slavers just outside the town, John Brown and his party decided to call a halt at Prairie City, and there review the situation. Up to this point Brown had been marching in the company of an armed force, part of which was under the command of his son John, but on May 23 he and a few of his followers decided to separate from the main body. The reason for this decision, according to his son Jason, was that Brown had been informed by James Townsley, one of the party, that everyone in the region was expected to be butchered by the border ruffians, and to this he had replied, "Now something *must* be done; we have got to defend our families and our neighbours as best we can. Something is going to be done *now*."

A council was summoned at which different suggestions were put forward, several demanding that radical retaliatory measures should be adopted, even to the extent of killing. Eventually it was agreed that the scene of operations should be Pottawatomie.

About midday, Brown, with his four sons, Owen, Frederick, Salmon and Oliver, and two others, Henry Thompson and Theodore Weiner, set out upon their errand of vengeance, in a wagon belonging to and driven by James Townsley.

That night, when the expedition had encamped, Brown told Townsley for the first time of his bloodthirsty errand, and when the latter, averse from taking part in such a drastic policy, stated his desire to return home with his wagon, Brown firmly refused his request.

It was not Brown's intention to give his quarry the slightest chance of effecting their escape, and for that reason he chose to strike at night when there was little or no hope of outside aid for his enemy.

At last the moment for action arrived. It was then ten o'clock. The darkness of the night was an adequate cloak under which to advance unseen to the cabin which housed their victims. Well armed with swords, cutlasses, rifles and revolvers, they proceeded cautiously across the Mosquito Creek, and soon came upon a cabin at the door of which they knocked. Instead of the door being opened, as the abolitionists expected, they were met with the unmistakable noise of a rifle being thrust through a chink in the cabin wall.

This unexpected intimation of resistance was the last thing for which they had allowed, and, as Salmon Brown relates, it caused the party to scatter precipitately. From there, however, they stealthily moved on to the next cabin, which was occupied by a family named Doyle. Here, however, at the outset another untoward incident occurred which caused them considerable apprehension and alarm.

As they approached the cabin they were met by two extremely ferocious bulldogs, and had it not been for the presence of mind of Townsley and another of the party, who promptly dispatched the fearsome animals with their swords, the ill-fated Doyle family might have taken warning in time and escaped the fearful end which awaited some of its members.

In answer to a knock, the door of the cabin was opened by Mr Doyle, upon which some of the abolitionists entered, stating, according to Mrs Doyle's account of the affair, that they were from the army. Immediately they were inside the cabin, they declared that Mr Doyle and his sons were under arrest. Mr Doyle and his two eldest sons, William and Drury, were then taken from the house and led away.

What followed is related thus by Townsley, who states that John Brown "drew his revolver and shot old man Doyle in the forehead, and Brown's two younger sons immediately fell upon the younger Doyles with their two short-edged swords."

Other accounts, however, are in conflict with Townsley's version of the executions, and these declare that John Brown himself took no active part in them.

Soon afterwards vengeance was taken in a similar way on another pro-slaver named Wilkinson, and the next victim was the notorious William Sherman.

For the time being John Brown was satisfied with the dreadful vengeance he had exacted for the razing of Lawrence, and so the party returned to join the company under John Brown, junior.

When questioned by his sons, John and Jason, as to the actual part taken by himself in the assassinations, John Brown asserted, "I did not do it, but I approved of it." He regarded the affair as absolutely necessary as a measure of self-defence and for the defence of Free Staters generally.

But John and Jason were deeply shocked at the terrible vengeance exacted by their father, and instead of joining forces with him took a separate course, fearing that they might at any moment be arrested as accomplices. They sought temporary refuge in the cabin of the Reverend Samuel Adair, and such was the mental agony suffered by John that during the night he went mad.

Meanwhile, on learning of the attack on the Doyles, a party of Missourians, under Captain Pate, set out for the Osawatomie district in search of John Brown and his compatriots, who had gone into hiding at Black Jack. Captain Pate, however, quickly hit upon the trail, but he was to meet with unexpected resistance when he finally came up with the fugitives. John Brown's party had now been reinforced by a military company under the command of Captain Shore, and with this additional strength at his command, Brown decided to stage a surprise attack on his pursuers.

The surprise was only partially successful, but after a two hours' engagement, which, however, resulted in minor casualties only, Captain Pate was compelled to surrender unconditionally.

Meanwhile, John and Jason had fallen into the hands of the Missourians, from whom they received terrible ill-treatment. With other Free State prisoners, they were chained two together, and ordered to march twenty-five miles a day, dragging their heavy shackles behind them.

Hearing of the capture of his sons, John Brown made an unsuccessful attempt to rescue them, but it was not until September 10 that John Brown junior secured his release on a general amnesty being granted to political prisoners. Jason had been liberated some time earlier.

During the week that followed the capture of Pate and his men, conflicts between John Brown's followers and the pro-slavers were frequent, and in one of them, an attack on Osawatomie by the latter party, John Brown's son Frederick met his death.

After a year of intermittent fighting against the common enemy in Kansas, during which his indomitable courage in opposing the powerful pro-slavery forces ranged against him, and his unswerving efforts to secure the abolition of slavedom had gained his cause innumerable supporters in many parts remote from the scene of actual hostilities, Brown left Kansas.

But he was by no means divorcing himself from the humane cause upon which he had set his heart. His absence was to be of a temporary character only, and his object was primarily to raise the interest of the people of the eastern states in the freedom of slaves from bondage, and also to secure funds to enable him to prosecute his campaign with even more vigour and with greater prospects of achieving ultimate success. Further, he hoped to enlist many recruits for active participation in the campaign he proposed to wage on his return to Kansas.

Many months passed before Brown, after addressing many public meetings at which he was successful in attracting both personal and financial support, returned to Kansas. But once back, he set himself to the preparation of his long-cherished objective.

Precisely when was born in the mind of John Brown the daring plan to raid the national armoury at Harper's Ferry, the little West Virginian village perched at the junction of the Potomac and Shenandoah Rivers, some sixty miles to the west of Baltimore, history does not record. As early as 1854, it is reported, he paid a visit to Colonel Woodruff, an officer who had seen active service in the war of 1812, his chief object being to enlist his active support in an attack on the arsenal as soon as it became expedient to carry out the expedition. He explained his scheme in detail, but for some reason that has never been disclosed, Brown failed to secure his adherence.

But whenever the plan originated, it is certain that many years passed, and various alternative schemes were examined, discussed and finally rejected, before the great adventure that aimed at delivering a crushing blow at slavery was eventually embarked upon. It was on June 30, 1859, that Brown, with two of his sons, Oliver and Owen, and a staunch supporter in Jeremiah Anderson, set out in high hopes and with grim determination from Chambersburg, near the southern border of Pennsylvania, for the scene of the momentous exploit in West Virginia.

To ensure against exciting the least suspicion of their true purpose in the minds of anyone with whom they might come in contact on the way, they assumed the title of "J. Smith and Sons," a company desirous of surveying suitable land for purchase, and when within about an hour's journey of Harper's Ferry, Brown entered into an agreement with the owner to rent a small farm – Kennedy Farm – on which stood two small houses, one of them little better than a cabin.

Although the farm was suitable in many ways for Brown's purpose, there was the distinct disadvantage of its being in too close proximity to the road, while another cause of apprehension was the unwelcome friendliness of the occupants of neighbouring farms, who in true southern fashion sought to make themselves agreeable to the new tenants of Kennedy Farm.

Brown and his compatriots were thereby made all too conscious of the necessity for secrecy and urgent action, but much yet remained to be done before the great attack could be launched. There were arms to be transported from across the border to the farm, and this was not finally accomplished until late in September.

Then, too, a sum of two thousand dollars which Brown had had some difficulty in raising, had almost been expended, and it became necessary to communicate with friends in Boston, from whom a further three hundred dollars was obtained.

Brown was worried, too, by the fear that someone would disclose his project to the authorities. Altogether there were not fewer than eighty people with knowledge of the objective of the gallant little force which was so eagerly awaiting the word of command, and not all of them could be relied on implicitly to safeguard the secret.

One of them, in fact, did actually disclose to John B. Floyd, the Secretary of War, the existence of the plan to attack Harper's Ferry, but it was the custom of this official to ignore all anonymous communications, and fortunately for Brown's plan he did so on this occasion.

After experiencing many alarums and excursions, preparations were at length completed. All the officers and men necessary for the great venture were assembled in the house and the cabin, and on the day of the proposed attack they remained closely confined for fear of detection by inquisitive neighbours.

At last came the hour for which they had planned. John Brown, in the cool, emotionless manner which had always made a strong appeal to, and inspired the confidence of his followers, issued the order: "Men, get on your arms; we will proceed to the Ferry."

Into the wagon which was to convey them to the scene of action, pikes, faggots, crowbars and other essential implements were loaded, while the men, eighteen in all, mustered in readiness for the fray. It was a fitting night for such a venture, dark and raw; October 16, 1859, a Sunday.

A rearguard of three was chosen to remain in charge of the arms and other supplies. One of these, perhaps foreseeing the outcome of the plan, took a pathetic farewell of his brother, who was to march with the attacking party.

As the advance guard reached the Maryland bridge they took the watchman prisoner, and a second prisoner was made on the other side of the bridge. More prisoners were soon in the hands of the attackers, including Colonel Washington, whose farm wagon was commandeered. Into this the raiders ordered the colonel's slaves, commanding them to take part in the fight for liberty. Similar scenes were enacted on the way, and at the various houses at which the attackers paid calls, consternation reigned at sight of the armed men.

One man, a night-watchman named Higgins, refused to surrender, and when he aimed a blow at Oliver Brown, was shot at and wounded. Another man, a negro who had regained his freedom, refused to respond to an order to halt, and he received a bullet through the body, from which some hours later he died.

There was by now general commotion in the village; no one appeared to know exactly how to cope with the remarkable situation. Brown and his followers were at last in possession of the engine-house and Wager House; they had achieved their object.

Brown believed that he had several hours to spare before commanding his followers to leave the arsenal, but in this he was mistaken. He had struck a resounding blow in the cause of negro liberty, and might now make a dignified retreat. But, unwisely, he decided to bide his time.

Awakened by the shooting, John Starry, a physician, went out to investigate its cause. He stood for a while watching the raiders at their work, and then, when day was breaking, he decided to saddle his horse and seek assistance from Charlestown, some eight miles distant. Here the military were hastily summoned, and while they were marching to Harper's Ferry, Brown, all unconscious of this new danger which threatened him, continued to hold the arsenal, taking prisoners all who approached.

As the morning wore on, Brown still showed no intention of making his escape, in spite of the earnest requests to do so made by Kagi, his efficient lieutenant. His indecision was to be his undoing.

Nearing midday, the Jefferson Guards were seen to be approaching. They speedily drove off Oliver Brown and some others who were guarding the Potomac bridge, and were soon in possession of the Wager House, in spite of the efforts of Brown's party to hold them off with rifle fire.

Once within the Wager House, the guards secured one of the doors, thus severing communication with Kennedy Farm and preventing the raiders from making their escape in that direction.

Dangerfield Newby, one of Brown's party who had been driven from the Potomac bridge, was shot and instantaneously killed. This was the first fatality suffered by the abolitionists.

Brown and some of his men were by this time entirely cut off from Hazlett and Anderson, who were guarding the arsenal, and from others of his force who had occupied the rifle works. He had by now realized the hopelessness of the situation; his party was outnumbered many times, and he decided therefore to dispatch one of his prisoners in company with William Thompson to effect a truce; but the effort was ineffective, the sole result being that Thompson fell into the hands of the enemy.

A further effort to bring an end to the one-sided conflict by sending out Stevens and Watson Brown with a flag of truce, proved equally abortive, and even more disastrous, for Stevens was severely wounded by gunfire and taken prisoner, while Watson Brown, although he managed with the greatest difficulty to crawl back to the engine-house, was mortally wounded.

Within the arsenal, Brown had now concentrated the remaining members of his party, together with most of the important prisoners he had captured; the rest of the prisoners were in the watch-room, and although they were entirely unguarded, none dared to take the risk of attempting escape.

One of Brown's party, the youngest of them all, made an effort to leave the arsenal and effect his escape. He was met with such a heavy fire as he attempted to get across the Potomac, that he decided to surrender. It is testimony to the savagery with which the conflict was waged that no quarter was granted to the young abolitionist, who was immediately shot, his body, when it was recovered, being found to be riddled with bullets.

The siege grew more intense as additional forces entered Harper's Ferry, but still Brown managed to resist all efforts to secure his capture, alive or dead. His son, Oliver was wounded mortally, and died in agony.

Firing ceased as night approached, and a summons to surrender was delivered to Brown; but he wished to dictate his own terms, and these were firmly refused. A further attempt to induce the raiders to surrender was also unsuccessful, and the conflicting forces settled themselves to rest, and to await the coming of dawn before resuming hostilities.

Late that night there arrived at Harper's Ferry, Brevet Colonel Robert E. Lee, then a comparatively unknown officer, but later to become famous throughout the land. He had been hastily dispatched by the government to take charge of operations against the raiders. A few hours after midnight he demanded the surrender of Brown and his remaining followers, but he also met with an obstinate refusal. Colonel Lee then gave orders to Lieutenant Green, the officer in charge of a company of marines, to storm the arsenal, and, selecting twelve of his most reliable men, and placing another twelve in reserve, he proceeded to obey orders.

It was sunrise when the attack was made. None of the marines had ever been under fire before, but they moved to the attack fearlessly, and arriving at the engine-house, proceeded to batter down the door with a heavy ladder.

A few desultory shots were fired at the attackers, who, however, suffered no casualties. Meanwhile, Brown, as Colonel Washington later declared, "was the coolest and firmest man I ever saw in defying danger and death." There was one son dead by his side, and another in terrible suffering, whose death could not be long delayed. Yet he still maintained his courage and composure, commanding his men to remain firm and sell their lives as dearly as they could.

Lieutenant Green was the first to enter the engine-room, and on Colonel Washington pointing out Brown to him, the lieutenant made a lunge with his sword which brought the abolitionist to his knees. The sword, however, met some hard obstruction, and Brown was fortunate thus to escape death.

Green then proceeded to rain blows upon Brown's head with his bent sword, which felled him and caused blood to flow. It seemed that Brown was mortally wounded, and Lieutenant Green left him where he lay.

It was only a matter of minutes before the marines were in full command of the engine-house, and the remaining raiders under arrest. Of the gallant little army that had set out with such faith and enthusiasm to assault the arsenal, all who were still alive were now in the hands of the enemy. Among them was the grievously wounded Watson Brown, who lived only a few hours longer.

And so ended the gallant, but ill-conceived and equally ill-planned attempt by the stout-hearted John Brown to strike a decisive blow at negro bondage. But what he himself had failed to achieve, his glorious failure inspired others at a later date to bring to a successful issue.

John Brown himself had to pay the penalty of his failure. Still suffering agonies from the wounds he had received, he was placed on trial for high treason in the court of Jefferson County, Virginia, just nine days after his arrest.

A plea of insanity was surprisingly made by counsel for the defence, but Brown, who had been carried into court on a couch, indignantly denied that he was insane.

The trial was not concluded until October 31, on which day at 2.15 p.m. the jury returned a verdict of guilty. Two days later, Brown was brought again into court, and was asked if he had anything to say why sentence should not be pronounced. He answered that he denied everything except what he had consistently admitted – his wish to free the slaves. He had no intention of committing murder or treason, nor had he intended to destroy property or excite to rebellion.

When Brown had concluded his address; the judge at once pronounced the death sentence, fixing the execution, which was to take place in public, for December 2, 1859.

On that day Brown was taken to the field in a wagon, seated upon his coffin. Slowly and calmly he alighted from the wagon, a placid, dignified figure. With a smile on his face, he took a last leave of those about him. At length, everything was in readiness. Moving towards the scaffold, John Brown walked firmly up the steps to the platform, a faint smile wreathing his mouth. With his pinioned hands he removed his hat, casting it down upon the scaffold by his side and, after thanking his jailer for his kindly attentions, allowed himself to be more securely pinioned and to have the cap drawn over his eyes.

Then he spoke his last words: "I am ready at any time, do not keep me waiting."

A single blow of the hatchet was then delivered by the sheriff, and the next second the great abolitionist was hanging between Heaven and earth.

> Glory glory, hallelujah,
> Glory glory, hallelujah,
> Glory glory, hallelujah,
> His soul goes marching on.

HORATIUS AT THE BRIDGE

Livy

It was in 505 BC that the Roman soldier Publius Horatius Cocles famously held the bridge over the Tiber against the army of Lars Porsena.

B y this time the Tarquins had fled to Lars Porsena, king of Clusium. There, with advice and entreaties, they besought him not to suffer them, who were descended from the Etrurians and of the same blood and name, to live in exile and poverty; and advised him not to let this practice of expelling kings to pass unpunished. Liberty, they declared, had charms enough in itself; and unless kings defended their crowns with as much vigor as the people pursued their liberty, the highest must be reduced to a level with the lowest; there would be nothing exalted, nothing distinguished above the rest; hence there must be an end of regal government, the most beautiful institution both among gods and men. Porsena, thinking it would be an honor to the Tuscans that there should be a king at Rome, especially one of the Etrurian nation, marched towards Rome with an army. Never before had such terror seized the Senate, so powerful was the state of Clusium at the time, and so great the renown of Porsena. Nor did they only dread their enemies, but even their own citizens, lest the common people, through excess of fear should, by receiving the Tarquins into the city, accept peace even though purchased with slavery. Many concessions were therefore granted to the people by the Senate during that period. Their attention, in the first place, was directed to the markets, and persons were sent, some to the Volscians, others to Cumæ, to buy up corn. The privilege of selling salt, because it was farmed at a high rate, was also taken into the hands of the government, and withdrawn from private individuals; and the people were freed from port-duties and taxes, in order that the rich, who could bear the burden, should contribute; the poor paid tax enough if they educated their children. This indulgent care of the fathers accordingly kept the whole state in such concord amid the subsequent severities of the siege and famine, that the highest as well as the lowest abhorred the name of king; nor was any individual afterwards so popular by intriguing practices as the whole Senate was by their excellent government.

Some parts of the city seemed secured by the walls, others by the River Tiber. The Sublician Bridge well-nigh afforded a passage to the enemy, had there not been one man, Horatius Cocles (fortunately Rome had on that day such a defender) who, happening to be posted on guard at the bridge, when he saw the Janiculum taken by a sudden assault and the enemy pouring down thence at full speed, and that his own party, in terror and confusion, were abandoning their arms and ranks, laying hold of them one by one, standing in their way and appealing to the faith of gods and men, he declared that their flight would avail them nothing if they deserted their post; if they passed the bridge, there would soon be more of the enemy in the Palatium and Capitol than in the Janiculum. For that reason he charged them to demolish the bridge, by sword, by fire, or by any means whatever; declaring that he would stand the shock of the enemy as far as could be done by one man. He then advanced to the first entrance of the bridge, and being easily distinguished among those who showed their backs in retreating, faced about to engage the foe hand to hand, and by his surprising bravery he terrified the enemy. Two indeed remained with him from a sense of shame: Sp. Lartius and T. Herminius, men eminent for their birth, and renowned for their gallant exploits. With them he for a short time stood the first storm of the danger, and the severest brunt of the battle. But as they who demolished the bridge called upon them to retire, he obliged them also to withdraw to a place of safety on a small portion of the bridge that was still left. Then casting his stern eyes toward the officers of the Etrurians in a threatening manner, he now challenged them singly, and then reproached them, slaves of haughty tyrants who, regardless of their own freedom, came to oppress the liberty of others. They hesitated for a time, looking round one at the other, to begin the fight; shame then put the army in motion, and a shout being raised, they hurled weapons from all sides at their single adversary; and when they all stuck in his upraised shield, and he with no less obstinacy kept possession of the bridge, they endeavored to thrust him down from it by one push, when the crash of the falling bridge was heard, and at the same time a shout of the Romans raised for joy at having completed their purpose, checked their ardor with sudden panic. Then said Cocles: "Holy Father Tiber, I pray thee, receive these arms, and this thy soldier, in thy propitious stream." Armed as he was, he leaped into the Tiber, and amid showers of darts, swam across safe to his party, having dared an act which is likely to obtain with posterity more fame than credit. The state was grateful for such valor; a statue was erected to him in the comitium, and as much land given to him as he could plow in one day. The zeal of private individuals was also conspicuous among his public honors. For amid the great scarcity, each contributed something, according to his supply, depriving himself of his own support.

DAVID AND GOLIATH

The Bible

Samuel I, Chapter 17. The paradigmatic story of how courage can triumph over brawn. An approximate date for the encounter between David the Israelite and Goliath the Philistine is 1030 BC.

Now the Philistines gathered together their armies to battle, and were gathered together at Shochoh which *belongeth* to Judah, and pitched between Shochoh and Azekah, in Ephes-dammim.

2 And Saul and the men of Israel were gathered together, and pitched by the valley of Elah, and set the battle in array against the Philistines.

3 And the Philistines stood on a mountain on the one side, and Israel stood on a mountain on the other side: and *there was* a valley between them.

4 q And there went out a champion out of the camp of the Philistines, named Goliath, of Gath, whose height *was* six cubits and a span.

5 And *he had* an helmet of brass upon his head, and he *was* armed with a coat of mail; and the weight of the coat *was* five thousand shekels of brass.

6 And *he had* greaves of brass upon his legs, and a target of brass between his shoulders.

7 And the staff of his spear *was* like a weaver's beam; and his spear's head *weighed* six hundred shekels of iron: and one bearing a shield went before him.

8 And he stood and cried unto the armies of Israel, and said

unto them. Why are ye come out to set *your* battle in array? *am* not I a Philistine, and ye servants to Saul? choose you a man for you, and let him come down to me.

9 If he be able to fight with me, and to kill me, then will we be your servants: but if I prevail against him, and kill him, then shall ye be our servants, and serve us.

10 And the Philistine said, I defy the armies of Israel this day; give me a man, that we may fight together.

11 When Saul and all Israel heard those words of the Philistine, they were dismayed, and greatly afraid.

12 q Now David *was* the son of that Ephrathite of Beth-lehem-judah, whose name *was* Jesse; and he had eight sons: and the man went among men *for* an old man in the days of Saul.

13 And the three eldest sons of Jesse went *and* followed Saul to the battle: and the names of his three sons that went to the battle *were* Eliab the firstborn, and next unto him Abinadab, and the third Shammah.

14 And David *was* the youngest: and the three eldest followed Saul.

15 But David went and returned from Saul to feed his father's sheep at Bethlehem.

16 And the Philistine drew near morning and evening, and presented himself forty days.

17 And Jesse said unto David his son. Take now for thy brethren an ephah of this parched *corn*, and these ten loaves, and run to the camp to thy brethren;

18 And carry these ten cheeses unto the captain of *their* thousand, and look how thy brethren fare, and take their pledge.

19 Now Saul, and they, and all the men of Israel, *were* in the valley of Elah, fighting with the Philistines.

20 q And David rose up early in the morning, and left the sheep with a keeper, and took, and went, as Jesse had commanded him; and he came to the trench, as the host was going forth to the fight, and shouted for the battle.

21 For Israel and the Philistines had put the battle in array, army against army.

22 And David left his carriage in the hand of the keeper of the carriage, and ran into the army, and came and saluted his brethren.

23 And as he talked with them, behold, there came up the champion, the Philistine of Gath, Goliath by name, out of the armies of the Philistines, and spake according to the same words: and David heard *them*.

24 And all the men of Israel, when they saw the man, fled from him, and were sore afraid.

25 And the men of Israel said, Have ye seen this man that is come up? surely to defy Israel is he come up: and it shall be, *that* the man who killeth him, the king will enrich him with great riches, and will give him his daughter, and make his father's house free in Israel.

26 And David spake to the men that stood by him, saying, What shall be done to the man that killeth this Philistine, and taketh away the reproach from Israel? for who *is* this uncircumcised Philistine, that he should defy the armies of the living God?

27 And the people answered him after this manner, saying. So shall it be done to the man that killeth him.

28 q And Eliab his eldest brother heard when he spake unto the men; and Eliab's anger was kindled against David, and he said, Why camest thou down hither? and with whom hast thou left those few sheep in the wilderness? I know thy pride, and the naughtiness of thine heart; for thou art come down that thou mightest see the battle.

29 And David said, What have I now done? *Is there* not a cause?

30 q And he turned from him toward another, and spake after the same manner: and the people answered him again after the former manner.

31 And when the words were heard which David spake, they rehearsed *them* before Saul: and he sent for him.

32 q And David said to Saul, Let no man's heart fail because of him; thy servant will go and fight with this Philistine.

33 And Saul said to David, Thou art not able to go against this Philistine to fight with him: for thou *art but* a youth, and he a man of war from his youth.

34 And David said unto Saul, Thy servant kept his father's sheep, and there came a lion, and a bear, and took a lamb out of the flock:

35 And I went out after him, and smote him, and delivered *it*

out of his mouth: and when he arose against me, I caught *him* by his beard, and smote him, and slew him.

36 Thy servant slew both the lion and the bear: and this uncircumcised Philistine shall be as one of them, seeing he hath defied the armies of the living God.

37 David said moreover. The LORD that delivered me out of the paw of the lion, and out of the paw of the bear, he will deliver me out of the hand of this Philistine. And Saul said unto David, Go, and the LORD be with thee.

38 q And Saul armed David with his armour, and he put an helmet of brass upon his head; also he armed him with a coat of mail.

39 And David girded his sword upon his armour, and he assayed to go; for he had not proved *it*. And David said unto Saul, I cannot go with these; for I have not proved *them*. And David put them off him.

40 And he took his staff in his hand, and chose him five smooth stones out of the brook, and put them in a shepherd's bag which he had, even in a scrip; and his sling *was* in his hand: and he drew near to the Philistine.

41 And the Philistine came on and drew near unto David; and the man that bare the shield *went* before him.

42 And when the Philistine looked about, and saw David, he disdained him: for he was *but* a youth, and ruddy, and of a fair countenance.

43 And the Philistine said unto David, *Am* I a dog, that thou comest to me with staves? And the Philistine cursed David by his gods.

44 And the Philistine said to David, Come to me, and I will give thy flesh unto the fowls of the air, and to the beasts of the field.

45 Then said David to the Philistine, Thou comest to me with a sword, and with a spear, and with a shield: but I come to thee in the name of the LORD of hosts, the God of the armies of Israel, whom thou hast defied.

46 This day will the LORD deliver thee into mine hand: and I will smite thee, and take thine head from thee; and I will give the carcases of the host of the Philistines this day unto the fowls of the air, and to the wild beasts of the earth; that all the earth may know that there is a God in Israel.

47 And all this assembly shall know that the LORD saveth not

with sword and spear: for the battle *is* the LORD's, and he will give you into our hands.

48 And it came to pass, when the Philistine arose, and came and drew nigh to meet David, that David hasted, and ran toward the army to meet the Philistine.

49 And David put his hand in his bag, and took thence a stone, and slang *it*, and smote the Philistine in his forehead, that the stone sunk into his forehead; and he fell upon his face to the earth.

50 So David prevailed over the Philistine with a sling and with a stone, and smote the Philistine, and slew him; but *there was* no sword in the hand of David.

51 Therefore David ran, and stood upon the Philistine, and took his sword, and drew it out of the sheath thereof, and slew him, and cut off his head therewith. And when the Philistines saw their champion was dead, they fled.

52 And the men of Israel and of Judah arose, and shouted, and pursued the Philistines, until thou come to the valley, and to the gates of Ekron. And the wounded of the Philistines fell down by the way to Shaaraim, even unto Gath, and unto Ekron.

53 And the children of Israel returned from chasing after the Philistines, and they spoiled their tents.

54 And David took the head of the Philistine, and brought it to Jerusalem; but he put his armour in his tent.

55 q And when Saul saw David go forth against the Philistine, he said unto Abner, the captain of the host, Abner, whose son *is* this youth? And Abner said, *As* thy soul liveth, O king, I cannot tell.

56 And the king said, Inquire thou whose son the stripling *is*.

57 And as David returned from the slaughter of the Philistine, Abner took him, and brought him before Saul with the head of the Philistine in his hand.

58 And Saul said to him, Whose son *art* thou, *thou* young man? And David answered, *I am* the son of thy servant Jesse the Bethlehemite.

NO SURRENDER

Lady Constance Lytton

Lady Constance was a prominent British "suffragette", a campaigner for the extension of the franchise to women. She was imprisoned for her beliefs and, on beginning a hunger strike in Liverpool's Walton jail in January 1910, was forcibly fed.

I was visited again by the Senior Medical Officer, who asked me how long I had been without food. I said I had eaten a buttered scone and a banana sent in by friends to the police station on Friday at about midnight. He said, "Oh, then, this is the fourth day; that is too long, I shall feed you, I must feed you at once," but he went out and nothing happened till about six o'clock in the evening, when he returned with, I think, five wardresses and the feeding apparatus. He urged me to take food voluntarily. I told him that was absolutely out of the question, that when our legislators ceased to resist enfranchising women then I should cease to resist taking food in prison. He did not examine my heart nor feel my pulse; he did not ask to do so, nor did I say anything which could possibly induce him to think I would refuse to be examined. I offered no resistance to being placed in position, but lay down voluntarily on the plank bed. Two of the wardresses took hold of my arms, one held my head and one my feet. One wardress helped to pour the food. The doctor leant on my knees as he stooped over my chest to get at my mouth. I shut my mouth and clenched my teeth. I had looked forward to this moment with so much anxiety lest my identity should be discovered beforehand, that I felt positively glad when the time had come. The sense of being overpowered by more force than I could possibly resist was complete, but I resisted nothing except with my mouth. The doctor offered me the choice of a wooden or steel gag; he explained elaborately, as he did on most subsequent occasions, that the steel gag would hurt and the wooden one not, and he urged me not to force him to use the steel gag. But I did not speak nor open my mouth, so that after playing about for a moment or two with the wooden one he finally had recourse to the steel. He seemed annoyed at my resistance and he broke into a temper as he plied my teeth with the steel implement. He found that on either side at the back I had false teeth mounted on a bridge which did not take out. The superintending wardress asked if I had any false teeth, if so, that they must be taken out; I made no answer and the process went on. He dug his instrument down on to the sham tooth, it pressed fearfully on the gum. He said if I resisted so much with my teeth, he would have to feed me through the nose. The pain of it was intense and at last I must have given way for he got the gag between my teeth, when he proceeded to turn it much more than necessary until my jaws were fastened wide apart, far more than they could go naturally. Then he put down my throat a tube which seemed to me much too wide and was something like four feet in length. The irritation of the tube was excessive. I choked the moment it touched my throat until it had got down. Then the food was poured in quickly; it made me sick a few seconds after it was down and the action of the sickness made my body and legs double up, but the wardresses instantly pressed back my head and the doctor leant on my knees. The horror of it was more than I can describe. I was sick over the doctor and wardresses, and it seemed a long time before they took the tube out. As the doctor left he gave me a slap on the cheek, not violently, but, as it were, to express his contemptuous disapproval, and he seemed to take for granted that my distress was assumed. At first it seemed such an utterly contemptible thing to have done that I could only laugh in my mind. Then suddenly I saw Jane Warton lying before me, and it seemed as if I were outside of her. She was the most despised, ignorant and helpless prisoner that I had seen. When she had served her time and was out of the prison, no one would believe anything she said, and the doctor when he had fed her by force and tortured her body, struck her on the cheek to show how he despised her! That was Jane Warton, and I had come to help her.

When the doctor had gone out of the cell, I lay quite helpless. The wardresses were kind and knelt round to comfort me, but there was nothing to be done, I could not move, and remained there in what, under different conditions, would have been an intolerable mess. I had been sick over my hair, which, though short, hung on either side of my face, all over the wall near my bed, and my clothes seemed saturated with it, but the wardresses told me they could not get me a change that night as it was too late, the office was shut. I lay quite motionless, it seemed paradise to be without the suffocating tube, without the liquid food going in and out of my body and without the gag between my teeth. Presently the wardresses all left me, they had orders to go, which were carried out with the usual promptness. Before long I heard the sounds of the forced feeding in the next cell to mine. It was almost more than I could bear, it was Elsie Howey, I was sure. When the ghastly process was over and all quiet, I tapped on the wall and called out at the top of my voice, which wasn't much just then, "No surrender," and there came the answer past any doubt in Elsie's voice, "No surrender."

HENRY V'S SPEECH AT AGINCOURT

William Shakespeare

*The year was 1415. King Henry V of England sailed to France to
claim the throne of that country, which he believed rightly his. On
25 October Henry's ten thousand Englishmen met fifty thousand
Frenchmen at Agincourt. William Shakespeare was of course not
there, but it is tempting to think that the historical Henry V must
have roused his troops with similar oratory to that below.*

Westmoreland: O that we now had here
But one ten thousand of those men in England
That do no work today!
King Henry: What's he that wishes so?
My cousin Westmoreland? No, my fair cousin.
If we are mark'd to die, we are enow
To do our country loss; and if to live,
The fewer men, the greater share of honour.
God's will! I pray thee, wish not one man more.
By Jove, I am not covetous for gold,
Nor care I who doth feed upon my cost;
It yearns me not if men my garments wear;
Such outward things dwell not in my desires;
But if it be a sin to covet honour,
I am the most offending soul alive.
No, faith, my coz, wish not a man from England.
God's peace! I would not lose so great an honour
As one man more, methinks, would share from me
For the best hope I have. O, do not wish one more!

Rather proclaim it, Westmoreland, through my host,
That he which hath no stomach to this fight,
Let him depart; his passport shall be made
And crowns for convoy put into his purse.
We would not die in that man's company
That fears his fellowship to die with us.
This day is call'd the feast of Crispian.
He that outlives this day, and comes safe home,
Will stand a tip-toe when this day is named,
And rouse him at the name of Crispian.
He that shall live this day, and see old age,
Will yearly on the vigil feast his neighbours,
And say, "To-morrow is Saint Crispian."
Then will he strip his sleeve and show his scars,
And say "These wounds I had on Crispin's day."
Old men forget; yet all shall be forgot,
But he'll remember with advantages
What feats he did that day. Then shall our names,
Familiar in his mouth as household words,
Harry the king, Bedford and Exeter,
Warwick and Talbot, Salisbury and Gloucester,
Be in their flowing cups freshly remember'd.
This story shall the good man teach his son;
And Crispin Crispian shall ne'er go by,
From this day to the ending of the world.
But we in it shall be remembered,
We few, we happy few, we band of brothers,
For he to-day that sheds his blood with me
Shall be my brother; be he ne'er so vile,
This day shall gentle his condition;
And gentlemen in England now a-bed
Shall think themselves accursed they were not here.
And hold their manhoods cheap whiles any speaks
That fought with us upon Saint Crispin's day.

THE STORMING OF CIUDAD RODRIGO

William Grattan

The storming of Ciudad Rodrigo is an example of physical courage from the classic age of blood and guts warfare, that of Napoleon Bonaparte. Ciudad Rodrigo was a fortress in Spain garrisoned by French troops. Lieutenant William Grattan of the British 88th Foot was one of the soldiers charged with its assault on the 19th of January 1812.

It was now five o'clock in the afternoon, and darkness was approaching fast, yet no order had arrived intimating that we were to take a part in the contest about to be decided. We were in this state of suspense when our attention was attracted by the sound of music; we all stood up, and pressed forward to a ridge, a little in our front, and which separated us from the cause of our movement, but it would be impossible for me to convey an adequate idea of our feelings when we beheld the 43rd Regiment, preceded by their band, going to storm the left breach; they were in the highest spirits, but without the slightest appearance of levity in their demeanour – on the contrary, there was a cast of determined severity thrown over their countenances that expressed in legible characters that they knew the sort of service they were about to perform, and had made up their minds to the issue. They had no knapsacks – their firelocks were slung over their shoulders – their shirt-collars were open, and there was an indescribable *something* about them that at one and the same moment impressed the lookers-on with admiration and awe. In passing us, each officer and soldier stepped out of the ranks for an instant, as he recognised a friend, to press his hand – many for the last time; yet, notwithstanding this animating scene, there was no shouting or huzzaing, no boisterous bravadoing, no unbecoming language; in short, every one seemed to be impressed with the seriousness of the affair entrusted to his charge, and any interchange of words was to this effect: "Well, lads, mind what you're about tonight"; or, "We'll meet in the town by and by"; and other little familiar phrases, all expressive of confidence. The regiment at length passed us, and we stood gazing after it as long as the rear platoon continued in sight: the music grew fainter every moment, until at last it died away altogether; they had no drums, and there was a melting sweetness in the sounds that touched the heart.

The first syllable uttered after this scene was, "And are we to be left behind?" The interrogatory was scarcely put, when the word "Stand to your arms!" answered it. The order was promptly obeyed, and a breathless silence prevailed when our commanding officer, in a few words, announced to us that Lord Wellington had directed our division to carry the grand breach. The soldiers listened to the communication with silent earnestness, and immediately began to disencumber themselves of their knapsacks, which were placed in order by companies and a guard set over them. Each man then began to arrange himself for the combat in such manner as his fancy or the moment would admit of – some by lowering their cartridge-boxes, others by turning theirs to the front in order that they might the more conveniently make use of them; others unclasping their stocks or opening their shirt-collars, and others oiling their bayonets; and more taking leave of their wives and children. This last was an affecting sight, but not so much so as might be expected, because the women, from long habit, were accustomed to scenes of danger, and the order for their husbands to march against the enemy was in their eyes tantamount to a victory; and as the soldier seldom returned without plunder of some sort, the painful suspense which his absence caused was made up by the gaiety which his return was certain to be productive of; or if, unfortunately, he happened to fall, his place was sure to be supplied by some one of the company to which he belonged, so that the women of our army had little cause of alarm on this head. The worst that could happen to them was the chance of being in a state of widowhood for a week.

It was by this time half-past six o'clock, the evening was piercingly cold, and the frost was crisp on the grass; there was a keenness in the air that braced our nerves at least as high as *concert pitch*. We stood quietly to our arms, and told our companies off by files, sections, and sub-divisions; the sergeants called over the rolls – not a man was absent.

It appears it was the wish of General Mackinnon to confer a mark of distinction upon the 88th Regiment, and as it was one of the last acts of his life, I shall mention it. He sent for Major Thompson, who commanded the battalion, and told him it was his wish to have the forlorn hope* of the grand breach led on by a subaltern of the 88th Regiment, adding at the same time that, in the event of his surviving, he should be recommended for a company. The Major acknowledged this mark of the General's favour, and left him folding up some letters he had been writing to his friends in England – this was about twenty minutes before the attack of the breaches. Major Thompson, having called his officers together, briefly told them the wishes of their General; he was about to proceed, when Lieutenant William Mackie (*then senior Lieutenant*) immediately stepped forward, and dropping his sword said, "Major Thompson, I am ready for that service." For once in his life poor old Thompson was affected – Mackie was his own townsman, they had fought together for many years, and when he took hold of his hand and pronounced the words, "God bless you, my boy," his eye filled, his lip quivered, and there was a faltering in his voice which was evidently perceptible to himself, for he instantly resumed his former composure, drew himself up, and gave the word, "Gentlemen, fall in," and at this moment Generals Picton and Mackinnon, accompanied by their respective staffs, made their appearance amongst us.

Long harangues are not necessary to British soldiers, and on this occasion but few words were made use of. Picton said something animating to the different regiments as he passed them, and those of my readers who recollect his deliberate and strong utterance will say with me, that his mode of speaking was

* The van of the storming party, the expression being Anglicized from the Dutch *verloren hope*, "lost party."

indeed very impressive. The address to each was nearly the same, but that delivered by him to the 88th was so characteristic of the General, and so applicable to the men he spoke to, that I shall give it word for word; it was this:

"Rangers of Connaught! it is not my intention to expend any powder this evening. We'll do this business with the could iron."

I before said the soldiers were silent – so they were, but the man who could be silent after such an address, made in such a way, and in such a place, had better have stayed at home. It may be asked what did they do? Why, what would they do, or would any one do, but give the loudest hurrah he was able.

The burst of enthusiasm caused by Picton's address to the Connaught Rangers had scarcely ceased, when the signalgun announced that the attack was to commence. Generals Picton and Mackinnon dismounted from their horses, and placing themselves at the head of the right brigade, the troops rapidly entered the trenches by sections right in front; the storming party under the command of Major Russell Manners of the 74th heading it, while the forlorn hope, commanded by Lieutenant William Mackie of the 88th, and composed of twenty volunteers from the Connaught Rangers, led the van, followed closely by the 45th, 88th, and 74th British, and the 9th and 21st Portuguese; the 77th and 83rd British, belonging to the left brigade, brought up the rear and completed the dispositions.

While these arrangements were effecting opposite the grand breach, the 5th and 94th, belonging to the left brigade of the 3rd Division, were directed to clear the ramparts and Fausse Braye wall, and the 2nd Regiment of Portuguese Caçadores, commanded by an Irish colonel of the name of O'Toole, was to escalade the curtain to the left of the lesser breach, which was attacked by the Light Division under the command of General Robert Craufurd.

It wanted ten minutes to seven o'clock when these dispositions were completed; the moon occasionally, as the clouds which overcast it passed away, shed a faint ray of light upon the battlements of the fortress, and presented to our view the glittering of the enemy's bayonets as their soldiers stood arrayed upon the ramparts and breach, awaiting our attack; yet, nevertheless, their batteries were silent, and might warrant the supposition to an unobservant spectator that the defence would be but feeble.

The two divisions got clear of the covered way at the same moment, and each advanced to the attack of their respective points with the utmost regularity. The obstacles which presented themselves to both were nearly the same, but every difficulty, no matter how great, merged into insignificance when placed in the scale of the prize about to the contested. The soldiers were full of ardour, but altogether devoid of that blustering and bravadoing which is truly unworthy of men at such a moment; and it would be difficult to convey an adequate idea of the enthusiastic bravery which animated the troops. A cloud that had for some time before obscured the moon, which was at its full, disappeared altogether, and the countenances of the soldiers were for the first time, since Picton addressed them, visible – they presented a material change. In place of that joyous animation which his fervid and impressive address called forth, a look of severity, bordering on ferocity, had taken its place; and although ferocity is by no means one of the characteristics of the British soldier, there was, most unquestionably, a savage expression in the faces of the men that I had never before witnessed. Such is the difference between the storm of a breach and fighting a pitched battle.

Once clear of the covered way, and fairly on the plain that separated it from the fortress, the enemy had a full view of all that was passing; their batteries, charged to the muzzle with case-shot, opened a murderous fire upon the columns as they advanced, but nothing could shake the intrepid bravery of the troops. The Light Division soon descended the ditch and gained, although not without a serious struggle, the top of the narrow and difficult breach allotted to them; their gallant General, Robert Craufurd, fell at the head of the 43rd, and his second in command, General Vandeleur, was severely wounded, but there were not wanting others to supply their place; yet these losses, trying as they were to the feelings of the soldiers, in no way damped their ardour, and the brave Light Division carried the left breach at the point of the bayonet. Once established upon the ramparts, they made all the dispositions necessary to ensure their own conquest, as also to render every assistance in their power to the 3rd Division in their attack. They cleared the rampart which separated the lesser from the grand breach, and relieved Picton's division from any anxiety it might have as to its safety on its left flank.

The right brigade, consisting of the 45th, 88th, and 74th, forming the van of the 3rd Division, upon reaching the ditch, to its astonishment, found Major Ridge and Colonel Campbell at the head of the 5th and 94th mounting the Fausse Braye wall. These two regiments, after having performed their task of silencing the fire of the French troops upon the ramparts, with a noble emulation resolved to precede their comrades in the attack of the grand breach. Both parties greeted each other with a cheer, only to be understood by those who have been placed in a similar situation; yet the enemy were in no way daunted by the shout raised by our soldiers – they crowded the breach, and defended it with a bravery that would have made any but troops accustomed to conquer, waver. But the "fighting division" were not the men to be easily turned from their purpose; the breach was speedily mounted, yet, nevertheless, a serious affray took place ere it was gained. A considerable mass of infantry crowned its summit, while in the rear and at each side were stationed men, so placed that they could render every assistance to their comrades at the breach without any great risk to themselves; besides this, two guns of heavy calibre, separated from the breach by a ditch of considerable depth and width, enfiladed it, and as soon as the French infantry were forced from the summit, these guns opened their fire on our troops.

The head of the column had scarcely gained the top, when a discharge of grape cleared the ranks of the three leading battalions, and caused a momentary wavering; at the same instant a frightful explosion near the gun to the left of the breach, which shook the bastion to its foundation, completed the disorder. Mackinnon, at the head of his brigade, was blown into the air. His aide-de-camp, Lieutenant Beresford of the 88th, shared the same fate, and every man on the breach at the moment of the explosion perished. This was unavoidable, because those of the advance, being either killed or wounded, were necessarily flung back upon the troops that followed close upon their footsteps, and there was not a sufficient space for the men who were ready to sustain those placed *hors de combat* to rally. For an instant all was confusion; the blaze of light caused by the explosion resembled a huge meteor, and presented to our sight the havoc which the enemy's fire had caused in our ranks; while from afar the astonished Spaniard viewed for an instant, with horror and dismay, the soldiers of the two nations grappling with each other on the top of the rugged breach which trembled beneath their feet, while the fire of the French artillery played upon our columns with irresistible fury, sweeping from the spot the living and the dead. Amongst the latter was Captain Robert Hardyman and Lieutenant Pearse of the 45th, and many more whose names I cannot recollect. Others were so stunned by the shock, or wounded by the stones which were hurled forth by the explosion, that they were insensible to their situation; of this number I was one, for being close to the magazine when it blew up, I was quite overpowered, and I owed my life to the Sergeant-Major of my regiment, Thorp, who saved me from being trampled to death by our soldiers in their advance, ere I could recover strength sufficient to move forward or protect myself.

The French, animated by this accidental success, hastened once more to the breach which they had abandoned, but the leading regiments of Picton's division, which had been disorganised for the moment by the explosion, rallied, and soon regained its summit, when another discharge from the two flank guns swept away the foremost of those battalions.

There was at this time but one officer alive upon the breach (Major Thomson, of the 74th, acting engineer); he called out to those next to him to seize the gun to the left, which had been so fatal to his companions – but this was a desperate service. The gun was completely cut off from the breach by a deep trench, and soldiers, encumbered with their firelocks, could not pass it in sufficient time to anticipate the next discharge – yet to deliberate was certain death. The French cannoniers, five in number, stood to, and served their gun with as much *sang froid* as if on a parade, and the light which their torches threw forth showed to our men the peril they would have to encounter if they dared to attack a gun so defended; but this was of no avail. Men going to storm a breach generally make up their minds that there is no great probability of their ever returning from it to tell their adventures to their friends; and whether they die at the bottom or top of it, or at the muzzle, or upon the breech of a cannon, is to them pretty nearly the same!

The first who reached the top, after the last discharge, were three of the 88th. Sergeant Pat Brazil – the brave Brazil of the Grenadier company, who saved his captain's life at Busaco – called out to his two companions, Swan and Kelly, to unscrew their bayonets and follow him; the three men passed the trench in a moment, and engaged the French cannoniers hand to hand; a terrific but short combat was the consequence. Swan was the first, and was met by the two gunners on the right of the gun, but, no way daunted, he engaged them, and plunged his bayonet into the breast of one; he was about to repeat the blow upon the other, but before he could disentangle the weapon from his bleeding adversary, the second Frenchman closed upon him, and by a *coup de sabre* severed his left arm from his body a little above the elbow; he fell from the shock, and was on the eve of being massacred, when Kelly, after having scrambled under the gun, rushed onward to succour his comrade. He bayoneted two Frenchmen on the spot, and at this instant Brazil came up; three of the five gunners lay lifeless, while Swan, resting against an ammunition chest, was bleeding to death. It was now equal numbers, two against two, but Brazil in his over-anxiety to engage was near losing his life at the onset; in making a lunge at the man next to him, his foot slipped upon the bloody platform, and he fell forward against his antagonist, but as both rolled under the gun, Brazil felt the socket of his bayonet strike hard against the buttons of the Frenchman's coat. The remaining gunner, in attempting to escape under the carriage from Kelly, was killed by some soldiers of the 5th, who just now reached the top of the breach, and seeing the serious dispute at the gun, pressed forward to the assistance of the three men of the Connaught Rangers.

While this was taking place on the left, the head of the column remounted the breach, and regardless of the cries of their wounded companions, whom they indiscriminately trampled to death, pressed forward in one irregular but heroic mass, and putting every man to death who opposed their progress, forced the enemy from the ramparts at the bayonet's point. Yet the garrison still rallied, and defended the several streets with the most unflinching bravery; nor was it until the musketry of the

Light Division was heard in the direction of the Plaza Mayor, that they gave up the contest! but from this moment all regular resistance ceased, and they fled in disorder to the Citadel. There were, nevertheless, several minor combats in the streets, and in many instances the inhabitants fired from the windows, but whether their efforts were directed against us or the French is a point that I do not feel myself competent to decide; be this as it may, many lives were lost on both sides by this circumstance, for the Spaniards, firing without much attention to regularity, killed or wounded indiscriminately all who came within their range.

During a contest of such a nature, kept up in the night, as may be supposed, much was of necessity left to the guidance of the subordinate officers, if not to the soldiers themselves. Each affray in the streets was conducted in the best manner the moment would admit of, and decided more by personal valour than discipline, and in some instances officers as well as privates had to combat with the imperial troops. In one of these encounters Lieutenant George Faris, of the 88th, by an accident so likely to occur in an affair of this kind, separated a little too far from a dozen or so of his regiment, and found himself opposed to a French soldier who, apparently, was similarly placed. It was a curious coincidence, and it would seem as if each felt that he individually was the representative of the country to which he belonged; and had the fate of the two nations hung upon the issue of the combat I am about to describe, it could not have been more heroically contested. The Frenchman fired at and wounded Faris in the thigh, and made a desperate push with his bayonet at his body, but Faris parried the thrust, and the bayonet only lodged in his leg. He saw at a glance the peril of his situation, and that nothing short of a miracle could save him; the odds against him were too great, and if he continued a scientific fight he must inevitably be vanquished. He sprang forward, and, seizing hold of the Frenchman by the collar, a struggle of a most nervous kind took place; in their mutual efforts to gain an advantage they lost their caps, and as they were men of nearly equal strength, it was doubtful what the issue would be. They were so entangled with each other their weapons were of no avail, but Faris at length disengaged himself from the grasp which held him, and he was able to use his sabre; he pushed the Frenchman from him, and ere he could recover himself he laid his head open nearly to the chin. His sword-blade, a heavy, soft, ill-made Portuguese one, was doubled up with the force of the blow, and retained some pieces of the skull and clotted hair! At this moment I reached the spot with about twenty men, composed of different regiments, all being by this time mixed *pell mell* with each other. I ran up to Faris – he was nearly exhausted, but he was safe. The French grenadier lay upon the pavement, while Faris, though tottering from fatigue, held his sword firmly in his grasp, and it was crimson to the hilt. The appearance of the two combatants was frightful! – one lying dead on the ground, the other faint from agitation and loss of blood; but the soldiers loudly applauded him, and the feeling uppermost with them was, that our man had the best of it! It was a shocking sight, but it would be rather a hazardous experiment to begin moralising at such a moment and in such a place.

THE BOY V.C.

Alistair Maclean

John ('Jack') Travers Cornwell was a mere boy of sixteen when he won the Victoria Cross for valour during the naval battle of Jutland, 1916. He served as a gunner aboard the light cruiser HMS Chester. Cornwell remains the youngest recipient ever of the V.C.

O n May 30 1916, Admiral Jellicoe, the British commander-in-chief, received information from the Admiralty that the German Battle Cruiser Squadron, under Admiral Hipper, had put to sea, and was instructed to steam out with the Grand Fleet to intercept it. Accordingly he ordered his ships to get under weigh and instructed Admiral Beatty, commander of the battle cruiser squadrons, to put out from Rosyth and steam on sixty-five miles ahead of the main body of the fleet. Both the battle and the battle cruiser fleet were to proceed in the direction of Heligoland Bight until 2 p.m. on May 31 when, if no enemy had been encountered, Beatty was to effect visual contact with Jellicoe's ships and the combined forces were to make a sweep towards the Horn's Reef before returning to their bases.

The *Chester* was attached to the Third Battle Cruiser Squadron under Admiral Hood. With her consorts she took up a position some twenty miles ahead of the main body of the Grand Fleet, and it was the task of these ships to scout ahead and report the presence of the enemy to the British flagship, *Iron Duke*.

All through the night of the 30th, the mighty armada steamed down the North Sea in the agreed direction, but nothing occurred to excite any suspicion. An occasional steamer was stopped and examined, for the British had to be on constant guard against enemy scouts disguised as trawlers or merchant ships.

Meanwhile Beatty, in a position about seventy miles south of the battle fleet, had met with no better luck. At 2 p.m. on the 31st he had still sighted no enemy, and was just about to give orders for his battle cruisers to turn north and join up with the Grand Fleet as arranged when the *Galatea*, one of his cruiser screen, announced the appearance of smoke on the horizon and set off to investigate. Twenty minutes later she signalled "Enemy in sight" and reported that she could see two cruisers bearing E.S.E. At 2.28 p.m. she opened fire, and Beatty seeing his cruiser screen engaged moved up in support. Although he did not know it at the time the enemy ships that had been sighted were the scouting cruisers attached to the German Battle Cruiser Squadron which was following them up behind, and consequently it was not long before the two battle cruiser forces came to grips.

Hipper, being inferior in gun power and ships to the British, immediately turned about and retraced his steps: coming up some fifty miles behind him was the German High Seas Fleet, and the German admiral saw a good chance of leading Beatty into a trap. By 3.45 p.m. the British ships, with their superior speed, had got within range of the German battle cruisers and Beatty ordered his squadron to form line on a course E.S.E. in order to get his guns to bear on the enemy. Seeing this, the Germans opened fire and in a few minutes the British ships were replying.

Steaming through giant columns of water and spray from each other's shell fire, both fleets hurled masses of metal across the eleven miles that separated them. The firing at first was a little erratic, but soon improved, and in the first ten minutes the Germans had scored hits both on the *Lion* and *Tiger*. At 4.00 p.m. first blood was drawn. The *Indefatigable*, the last ship in the British line, was hit by a salvo from the German ship *Von der Tann*. A burst of flame and smoke hid her completely from view, and she staggered out of the line sinking fast by the stern. A moment later a second salvo hit her; another terrible explosion rent the ship and she turned over and sank. In a few minutes all trace of this great cruiser was gone.

Twenty-six minutes later another disaster befell the British. The *Queen Mary* was struck by a salvo on her forward deck. A huge pillar of smoke ascended to the sky and she sank bow first taking with her a crew of fifty-seven officers and 1,209 men.

At 4.33 p.m. Commodore Goodenough, commanding the Second Light Cruiser Squadron in the *Southampton*, disposed some miles ahead of the battle cruisers, reported that battleships were in sight to the S.S.E., and a few minutes later the dim outlines of the German High Seas Fleet were visible. Beatty could not hope to engage such a large force with any success so, at 4.40 p.m., he gave the order for his ships to turn sixteen points to the N.W. from which direction he knew the Grand Fleet was steaming with all haste to his aid.

Meanwhile in the British battle fleet there was great excitement. The *Galatea's* signals heralding the opening of the battle cruiser action had been received in the *Iron Duke* at 2.20 p.m. Although these messages only indicated the presence of enemy light cruisers, Jellicoe ordered full steam to be raised in case of emergency, but did not increase his speed. Later reports, however, made it evident that serious action was impending, and at 2.55 p.m. he ordered his light cruisers to take up a position sixteen miles ahead and altered his course S.E. by S. At 3.30 p.m. an urgent message was received from the *Lion* informing Jellicoe that the German battle cruisers had been sighted, and a further report twenty-five minutes later told him that the action had begun.

Jellicoe at once ordered speed to be increased to twenty knots and sent the Third Battle Cruiser Squadron with the light cruisers *Chester* and *Canterbury* on in all haste to reinforce the battle cruiser fleet.

According to the Official History of the War (Naval Operations, Vol. III), "The *Invincible* in which Admiral Hood's flag was flying was then about twenty-five miles on the port bow of the *Iron Duke*, and a little ahead of station, for when at 3.15 p.m. Admiral Hood heard from the *Galatea* of the enemy's light cruisers coming northward, he had inclined to the eastward at twenty-two knots to head them off. Half an hour later, when he knew they had turned to the southward, he altered back to S. 26

E., and when the welcome order came to push ahead he was about forty-three miles from the position the *Lion* had given S. by W. of him. But as he had no margin of speed there was little hope of overtaking Admiral Beatty on that course. He had therefore altered to S.S.E. . . . and sped away at twenty-five knots."

When the order came through to push ahead young Cornwell in the *Chester*, together with the rest of the gun crew, was ordered to take up his position at the forward gun. The prospect of an early encounter with the enemy must have produced a strange mixture of emotions in him as he scanned the horizon in search of the German ships. But the sight of the other ships of his squadron, smoke pouring from their funnels, their bows cutting through the waters of the North Sea like knives, sending up huge bow waves as they rushed southwards, must have filled his heart with pride and confidence.

The squadron was steaming in line ahead with the destroyers *Shark, Christopher, Ophelia* and *Acasta* disposed ahead as a submarine screen and the *Chester* and *Canterbury* scouting five miles ahead of the destroyers. The visibility was decreasing rapidly, and by five o'clock objects could be distinguished at a distance of sixteen thousand yards in some directions, but in others at only two thousand yards.

At 5.30 p.m. the sound of gunfire was plainly heard by the *Chester* to the S.W. and she immediately turned in that direction to investigate. Six minutes later she sighted a three-funnelled light cruise on her starboard bow, accompanied by one or two destroyers. She immediately challenged but, receiving no reply closed with them. A moment or so later two more light cruisers appeared out of the mist astern of the first and the leading enemy ship opened fire on the *Chester*.

Cornwell was stationed at the forward gun. Fixed across his head and over his ears was what is known as a telepad, a sort of telephone, which was connected up with the fire control officer. Through this instrument came all the instructions for the gun crew – orders as to when and how to fire. Cornwell, as sight-setter, had a very important task to perform for upon him more than anyone else depended the accuracy of his gun's aim. When he received his orders from the gunnery officer he had to make certain adjustments to the mechanism of the gun. In front of him was a brass disc, pinned through the centre, and in some respects resembling a telephone dial. This disc was calibrated in yards, and as it was turned it raised and lowered the gun's muzzle, thus altering the range. It was essentially a job that required coolness and presence of mind. Moreover, the position in which Cornwell was obliged to stand in order to carry out his duties without interfering with the work of the gun crew, was almost entirely exposed. It was on the left hand side of the gun just by the side of the protective shield.

The visibility at the time the enemy opened fire could not have been more than eight thousand yards, i.e., about four and a half miles, which, in naval warfare, amounts almost to point blank range, and from the moment the fight began the forward turret of the *Chester* received the full force of the enemy's fire. One by one the gun crew, consisting of ten men, fell, struck by splinters of shell, until only two were left. But still young Cornwell stood calmly at his post, never flinching, ready to carry out his orders. The enemy's fourth salvo scored a direct hit and put the gun port right out of action. It also mortally wounded Cornwell.

All alone, with practically no shelter from the fierce tornado of enemy fire, he stood. All around him lay the dead and dying. He himself was torn and bleeding and faint from the pain and horror of the sights and sounds of battle. His job was done, his gun was no longer capable of firing, no orders came through the wire from the control room; they could not have been carried out even if they had, but through his mind echoed the old naval order "a gun must be kept firing so long as there is one man left who is able to crawl." So he hung on. He thought he might be needed; it was his duty to remain at his post until he dropped.

Captain Lawson of the *Chester* as soon as he realized the superiority of the force to which he was opposed, altered his course to the N.E. and towards the Third Battle Cruiser Squadron. This incident is vividly decribed by the Naval History of the War in the following words:—

The *Chester* seemed doomed, but rescue was at hand. Directly Admiral Hood heard the firing abaft his starboard beam he swung round north-west (5.37). As the German cruisers were closing to the eastward the courses quickly converged. In a few minutes our battle cruisers could see emerging from the mist the *Chester* zigzagging in a storm of shell splashes that were drenching her. A minute later her eager pursuers came suddenly into view. Immediately they saw their danger they swung round to starboard on the opposite course to Admiral Hood, but it was too late. As they passed his guns crashed into them, while the *Chester* escaped across the *Invincible's* bows, firing her last shots as she ran northward into safety. As for Admiral Boedicker, he only escaped the twelve-inch salvoes that were smothering him by recourse to his torpedoes. To avoid them Admiral Hood had to turn away, and the enemy was soon lost in the mist, but not before the *Wiesbaden* was a wreck and both the *Pillau* and *Frankfurt* badly hit.

The *Chester* then took up a station to the north-east of the Third Battle Cruiser Squadron, and at a later stage in the action joined the Second Cruiser Squadron.

During the unequal action between the *Chester* and the enemy light cruisers, which proved to belong to the German Second Scouting Group under Admiral Boedicker, the ship had suffered considerable casualties, having thirty-one killed and fifty wounded. Three guns and her fire control circuits were disabled, and she had four shell holes in her side just above the water line. But damaged as she was, she was still in fighting condition.

Cornwell had remained at his post throughout the whole action, and he was still standing there when the British battle cruisers drew off the enemy fire. When the fight was over the wounded were carried below, but it soon became apparent to the doctors that there was little hope of saving the brave young gunner's life. They bandaged his wounds, and made him as comfortable as possible, and although he must have been in terrible agony, he bore his suffering like a man and never complained.

Throughout the evening, and at intervals during the night the battle continued. The *Invincible* was struck by a salvo and sank, taking with her the gallant Admiral Hood and all but a few of her officers and men. But when the Grand Fleet came to grips with the High Seas Fleet the enemy were forced to flee. They were cut off from their ports, and twice they tried to break through the rear of the British Fleet and twice they failed. At last, under the cover of darkness they succeeded. Admiral Scheer, the German commander-in-chief had handled his fleet magnificently against superior forces, and the way that he extricated his ships from a position that looked like certain annihilation will go down in naval history as one of the greatest feats of tactics ever achieved.

On the morning of June 1, the *Chester* was ordered to proceed to the Humber and the wounded were taken off and transferred to hospital at Grimsby. Jack Cornwell was amongst them. He could still talk in whispers but was very weak and in great pain. But his cheerfulness never left him. The matron of the hospital asked him how the battle had gone and he replied in simple, sailor-like fashion, "Oh, we carried on all right." But he never mentioned the part he had played – never boasted of his heroism. Indeed, it seems that he was quite unaware of the fact that he had done anything extraordinary: all he had done was to carry out his orders to the best of his ability and anyone else, he probably thought, if he thought about it at all, would have done the same.

These words to the matron were almost the last ever spoken by Jack. Occasionally he made a whispered request that he might see his mother, and at the end, just before he died on June 2 he said to the matron: "Give mother my love, I know she is coming." He was right, his mother was coming. She had received a telegram from the Admiralty and was hurrying to her son's side. But by the time she reached the hospital it was too late.

Although Jack Cornwell's action was not spectacular and was done with little prospect of being seen, there was one keen-eyed man who witnessed this splendid example of devotion to duty. Captain Lawson, the *Chester's* commander, had noticed Cornwell's little figure at his post by the forward gun. He had noted how, with the dead and dying all round him and the enemy shells bursting thick and fast, he had never flinched. So Captain Lawson gave a full account of Jack's heroism when he made his report to his commander-in-chief, Admiral Jellicoe, who, in his official report to the Admiralty on the Battle of Jutland included the following paragraph:—

"A report from the commanding officer of the *Chester* gives a splendid instance of devotion to duty. Boy (First Class) John Travers Cornwell, of *Chester*, was mortally wounded early in the action. He nevertheless remained standing alone at a most exposed post, quietly awaiting orders till the end of the action, with the gun crew dead and wounded all around him. His age was under sixteen and a half years. I regret that he has since died, but I recommend his case for your special recognition in justice to his memory, and as an acknowledgment of the high example set by him."

This recommendation did not pass unheeded. There had been many heroes at the Battle of Jutland, but Cornwell was the only one, apart from officers, mentioned in the original despatches, and he was awarded the Victoria Cross.

In a letter to Mrs Cornwell the *Chester's* commander told her how her son met his death: it was a fine letter, and she must have been proud to know that although she had lost her son, she was the mother of such a hero. It read:—

"I know you would wish to hear of the splendid fortitude and courage shown by your boy during the action of May 31. His devotion to duty was an example to us all. The wounds which resulted in his death within a short time were received in the first few minutes of the action. He remained steady at his most exposed post, waiting for orders. His gun would not bear on the enemy: all but two of the crew of ten were killed or wounded, and he was the only one who was in such an exposed position. But he felt he might be needed, as indeed he might have been; so he stayed there, standing and waiting, under heavy fire, with just his own brave heart and God's help to support him. I cannot express to you my admiration of the son you have lost from this world. No other comfort would I attempt to give to the mother of so brave a lad but to assure her of what he was and what he did and what an example he gave. I hope to place in the boys' mess a plate with his name on and the date, and the words 'Faithful unto Death.' I hope some day you may be able to come and see it there. I have not failed to bring his name prominently before my Admiral."

The prompt award of the Victoria Cross to Jack Cornwell only partly satisfied the desire of the public to pay homage to the dead hero. His body, which had been buried privately, was exhumed and reinterred with full naval honours. The funeral took place on July 29, 1916, at Manor Park Cemetery. The coffin, covered with the Union Jack, rested on a gun carriage drawn by a team of boys from the Crystal Palace Naval Depot. Vast crowds of people lined the route, and in the carriages that followed were many famous sailors and other notabilities including Dr T J MacNamara, Financial Secretary to the Admiralty.

Six boys from the *Chester*, all of whom had themselves been in the battle, walked in the procession carrying wreaths from his old ship's company, and there were countless other floral tributes including one from the Lord Mayor of London and one from Admiral Beatty. On the latter were inscribed the simple words, "With Deep Respect."

THE DAUNT ROCK LIGHTSHIP

Patrick Howarth

Ballycotton is a small town in County Cork, Ireland. In 1936 it was the scene of one of the most daring rescues in the history of the Lifeboat Institution, a service which does not exactly want for a roll of honour.

In the first days of February 1936 there was calm weather and a grey frost. Then the wind began to blow from the southeast, the quarter which is most feared in Ballycotton. For five days the gales continued, and at times they rose to hurricane force. By Sunday, February 9, the gales had already been blowing for two days, and on that day and the next the coxswain of the lifeboat, fearing she might be driven against the breakwater, ran ropes to her to protect her.

The coxswain of the Ballycotton lifeboat at that time was Patrick Sliney. Every regular member of the crew was named either Sliney or Walsh, and Tom Sliney, the coxswain's brother, was the mechanic. Patrick Sliney was a fisherman, and the living of himself and his family depended on his boat. Shortly before midnight on Monday, February 10, his boat parted her moorings, and it seemed that she must be swept out to sea. At that time it was hardly safe even to walk through the streets of Ballycotton. Slates were flying from roofs and people trying to walk were literally spun round by gusts of wind. Down in the harbour the sea was tearing great stones out of the breakwater and hurling them about like pebbles, but all that night Coxswain Sliney and some of the other fishermen had been trying to secure their boats. About seven o'clock in the morning they succeeded in securing the coxswain's boat. Patrick Sliney had hurt his hand, but he did not consider the injury serious.

The honorary secretary of the lifeboat station was, and still is, Robert Mahony, the postmaster. His occupation is an exacting one, for there is no automatic telephone exchange in Ballycotton, and in the middle of the night he has to go downstairs and answer the telephone when it rings. He is also postman as well as postmaster, and delivers letters himself.

Mr Mahony spent most of the night of the 10th near the harbour expecting trouble, but it was not until eight o'clock in the morning, when he was at home, that a message reached him. The telephone lines linking Ballycotton with the outside world had been blown down, and the messenger had come twelve miles by car. The message was that the Daunt Rock lightship, with eight men on board, had broken from her moorings and was drifting in the direction of Ballycotton.

Mr Mahony passed on the message to Coxswain Sliney. He did not give him any orders, for he did not believe it would be possible to take the lifeboat out of the harbour.

No maroons were fired on that occasion. Coxswain Sliney did not want to alarm the people of Ballycotton, for he had already seen the look on his daughter's face when, in helping him on with his boots, she had guessed where he was going. Word was passed round quietly, and the crew assembled in the harbour.

After taking the lifeboat a mile out to sea, Coxswain Sliney made a decision which appalled those onlookers who knew the local waters. This was to take the lifeboat through a sound between two islands. By doing so he saved half a mile, and he had no means of knowing how immediate the danger of the men on board the lightship was. The seas in the sound were even worse than in the open, and after coming off the top of one sea the lifeboat fell into the trough of the next with such a thud that everyone on board believed the engines had gone through the bottom of the boat. But Tom Sliney reported to his brother that all was well; the whole crew gathered in the after cockpit, and when each sea passed over the bow Patrick Sliney carefully counted his men.

After passing through the sound the coxswain ran before the wind along the coast. Some six miles from Ballycotton the seas became even worse than before, and Coxswain Sliney decided he must put out the canvas drogue to steady the boat. To do this he eased the engines; immediately several seas struck him on the side of the head and he was half stunned. Then, as the drogue was being put out, a heavy, curling sea came over the port quarter, filled the cockpit, and knocked down every man on board. When they recovered they found that the drogue ropes had fouled, but the drogue was drawing.

The rain which had been falling turned to sleet; thick spray reduced visibility even further; and the lifeboat crew could see no sign of the lightship. The coxswain decided he must make for the lightship's usual position in the hope of finding her on the way. He went on for seven miles but saw no sign of her, and in those conditions he could not be sure of his position. He came to the conclusion that he must make for Cobh, in the hope of getting some correct information. The oil-sprays were used to calm the breakers a little, and about eleven o'clock in the morning the lifeboat reached the harbour. The position of the lightship was known there, and after trying, without success, to telephone Mr Mahony at Ballycotton, Coxswain Sliney ordered the lifeboat out again.

It was just after midday when the lifeboat found the lightship. The lightship had an anchor down and was a quarter of a mile south-west of the Daunt Rock and half a mile from the shore. Two vessels were standing by her. One was H.M. destroyer *Tenedos*, the other the S.S. *Innisfallen*. When the lifeboat arrived the steamer left.

The crew of the lightship were determined not to leave her. The lightship was some distance from her correct position and for that reason was a constant danger to navigation. But her crew could not be certain that her anchor would hold, and they asked the lifeboat to stand by. Coxswain Sliney agreed at once to do so.

For some three hours the lifeboat steamed and drifted, pitched and rolled in seas which were too bad to allow her to anchor. Then the gale eased a little for a time, and the destroyer tried to float a grass line to the lightship with a buoy attached in the hope of getting a wire cable to the lightship and taking her in tow. The lifeboat picked up the buoy and passed it to the lightship, but then the line parted. For two hours, during which they were continually swept by heavy seas, the destroyer and the lifeboat tried to effect a connexion with the lightship which would allow her to be towed away, but all their efforts failed. Darkness fell; it was impossible to approach the lightship; and as the destroyer intended to stand by all night, the lifeboat returned to Cobh. There more lines could be taken on board and the crew would be able to have their first food that day. It was half-past nine at night by the time they reached the harbour.

Some of the crew had a little sleep, but three men remained on board all the time. Then, early on the morning of Wednesday, February 12, the lifeboat put out again. When she reached the lightship the destroyer left, for the *Isolda*, a vessel belonging to the Commissioners of Irish Lights, was expected from Dublin. During the day the wind dropped a little; there was fog in place of the rain and sleet, but the sea did not seem to go down at all. All that day the lifeboat remained near at hand, only leaving the lightship from time to time to warn other vessels that the lightship was out of position and that they themselves would be in serious danger if they did not alter course. The weather forecast in the evening offered no hope of an improvement in the weather, and the lightship asked the lifeboat to stand by all night. Coxswain Sliney suggested that the time had come to take off the lightship's crew, but the captain would not agree. With the gale blowing even more strongly from the south-east the Ballycotton lifeboat stood by all that night.

When daylight came the lifeboat, which had been continuously at sea for the last twenty-four hours, had little petrol left, and it was clear that she must once more return to Cobh. She reached the harbour at nine o'clock. The last twenty-five and a half hours had been spent at sea without food; Coxswain Sliney's hand was causing him considerable pain; his son, William Sliney, the youngest member of the crew, who is to-day the lifeboat mechanic, suffered from seasickness throughout the service; the sea had caused salt-water burns; and the effects of the cold were terrible. Every man had only one immediate wish, which was for tea, and they would not even wait for it to be made in a pot. They insisted on having the tea made in their cups and drank it as it scalded their throats.

It was not until four o'clock in the afternoon that the lifeboat was able to put out again, with the prospect of having to stand by through yet another night of gales. This time the lifeboat reached the lightship at dusk. The *Isolda* had already arrived, and her captain told Coxswain Sliney that he intended to stand by all night and then try to take the lightship in tow. He had not realized what the consequences would be of a sudden change in the direction of the wind and a worsening of both sea and weather.

About eight o'clock a huge sea swept over the lightship and carried away the forward of the two red lights which had been hoisted to show that she was out of position. The wind, which had been blowing steadily from the south-east, shifted to south-south-east, and the lightship drifted farther towards the Daunt Rock. About half-past nine Coxswain Sliney took the lifeboat round the lightship's stern and had his searchlight played on her. The lightship was now only sixty yards from the rock, and if the wind shifted farther to the west she would certainly strike it. The coxswain told the captain of the *Isolda* of the dangers of the lightship's position, but the captain replied that he could do nothing. Finally he agreed that the coxswain should try to take the lightship's crew off.

Seas were now sweeping right over the lightship. She was plunging on her cable, rolling from thirty to forty degrees and burying her starboard bow in the water. She was fitted with rolling chocks, which projected more than two feet from her sides, and as she rolled these threshed the water. Because of the lightship's cable it was impossible for the lifeboat to anchor to windward and veer down on her, and Coxswain Sliney realized he could do nothing but approach her from astern and make quick runs in on her port side, each of which would give some of the crew a moment in which to jump into the lifeboat. The lightship was only 98 feet long, and if the 51-foot lifeboat, coming in at full speed, ran too far, she would go over the cable and capsize. Every time she came alongside, the lightship, with her chocks threshing the water as she plunged and rolled, might easily crash on top of the lifeboat. All these dangers were clear to Coxswain Sliney as he made his plan.

He first went ahead of the lightship and pumped oil, but it had little effect in calming the seas. Then he went astern and drove at full speed alongside. One man jumped successfully, and the lifeboat went astern. The second time she went in nobody jumped, and again she went astern. The third time five men jumped, leaving two men aboard. Then came the fourth attempt. This time the lightship sheered violently and her counter crashed on top of the lifeboat, smashing the rails and damaging the fender and deck. Nobody was hurt, but the man working the searchlight sprang clear at the last second. The lifeboat then went in a fifth time, and nobody jumped.

The lifeboat's crew now saw what was happening. The two remaining men were clinging to the rails and seemed unable to jump. Coxswain Sliney therefore had to expose some of his crew to a new danger. He sent them forward, where they might easily be swept overboard, with orders to seize the two men as the lifeboat came alongside. The orders were carried out; and the two men were seized and dragged into the lifeboat. The face of one and the legs of the other were hurt, but Tom Sliney, the mechanic, was able to give them first aid.

The lifeboat left the lightship, but the dangers to the crew were not over. One of the lightship's crew, overcome by the effects of the strain he had undergone, became hysterical. He wanted to jump overboard, and two men, themselves exhausted, had to hold him down by force. It was eleven o'clock on the night of Thursday, February 13, when the lifeboat put into Cobh harbour for the last time.

That night the crew had their first full night's sleep since the Saturday of the week before. The next day the lifeboat returned to Ballycotton in weather which had suddenly improved. She had been away from her station for seventy-six and a half hours, on service for sixty-three hours and at sea for forty-nine hours. Towards the end of the forty-nine hours Coxswain Sliney had had to carry out a feat of seamanship of the highest order and demand of his crew a response which even to men who were fresh and in good physical condition would have been exceptionally exacting. The service in which Patrick Sliney won his gold medal, his brother and the second coxswain, John Walsh, won the silver medal, and his son and two other Slineys, John and William, as well as Thomas Walsh, won the bronze medal, has had few equals and perhaps no superior in the history of the Lifeboat Institution.

THE EVACUATION OF KHAM-DUC

Philip Chinnery

*A vignette from America's Vietnam War, 1960–1975. Ten miles
from the Laotian border, Kham-Duc was a Special Forces base
which, on 12 May 1968, was overrun by NVA (North Vietnamese
Army) and accordingly evacuated. Except, by a military blunder,
three American special forces soldiers were then inserted back into
the camp. Their rescue won a Medal of Honor for pilot Colonel Joe
M. Jackson.*

A s the advancing NVA infantry took over the camp, a near-
tragedy occurred. A C-130 flown by Lieutenant Colonel Jay
Van Cleef was inexplicably instructed by the airborne control
centre to land the three-man combat control team which had
already been evacuated earlier in the day. Van Cleef protested
that the camp was almost completely evacuated, but the control
centre insisted that the team be returned and left.

Obediently Van Cleef landed his aircraft, and the three
controllers ran from the ship towards the burning camp. He
waited patiently for another two minutes for passengers expecting to be evacuated, and when none appeared he slammed
the throttles open and took off. He duly notified the control ship
that they had taken off empty, and was shocked to hear the
control ship then report to General McLaughlin that the
evacuation of Kham Duc was complete. His crew immediately
and vehemently disabused the commander and pointed out that
the camp was not evacuated, because they had, as ordered, just
deposited a combat control team in the camp. There was a

moment of stunned radio silence as the reality sank in: Kham Duc was now in enemy hands – except for three American combat controllers.

Meanwhile, Major John W. Gallagher Jr. and the other two controllers took shelter in a culvert next to the runway and started firing at the enemy in the camp with their M-16 rifles. The command post asked a C-123 to try to pick the men up, but as the aircraft touched down it came under fire from all directions. The pilot, Lieutenant Colonel Alfred J. Jeannotte Jr., could not see the team anywhere and jammed the throttles forward for take-off. Just before lift-off the crew spotted the three men, but it was now too late to stop. The C-123 took to the air and, low on fuel, turned for home. Jeannotte later received the Air Force Cross for his actions.

Technical Sergeant Mort Freedman described how he, Major Gallagher and Sergeant Jim Lundie reacted when the last Provider took off, leaving the three-man team behind. "The pilot saw no one left on the ground, so he took off. We figured no one would come back and we had two choices: either be taken prisoner, or fight it out. There was no doubt about it. We had eleven magazines among us and were going to take as many of them with us as we could."

The C-123 behind Jeannotte was being flown by Lieutenant Colonel Joe M. Jackson and Major Jesse W. Campbell. They had left Da Nang earlier in the day to haul some cargo, while Jackson went through the bi-annual check flight that is mandatory for all Air Force fliers. They had been recalled and sent to Kham Duc, arriving as the command ship requested that they make another pick-up attempt. Jesse Campbell radioed, "Roger. Going in."

Joe Jackson had been a fighter pilot for twenty years before being assigned to transport duty. He had flown 107 missions in Korea and had won the Distinguished Flying Cross. He knew that the enemy gunners would expect him to follow the same flight path as the other cargo planes and decided to call upon his fighterpilot experience and try a new tactic. At 9,000 feet, and rapidly approaching the landing area, he pointed the nose down in a steep dive. Side-slipping for maximum descent, and with power back and landing gear and flaps full down, the Provider dropped like a rock. Jackson recalls: "The book said you didn't fly transports this way, but the guy who wrote the book had never been shot at. I had two problems, the second stemming from the first. One was to avoid reaching 'blow up' speed, where the flaps, which were in full down position for the dive, are blown back up to neutral. If this happened, we would pick up even more speed, leading to problem two – the danger of overshooting the runway."

Jackson pulled back on the control column and broke the Provider's descent just above the tree-tops, a quarter of a mile from the end of the runway. He barely had time to set up a landing attitude as the aircraft settled towards the threshold. The debris-strewn runway looked like an obstacle course, with a burning helicopter blocking the way a mere 2,200 feet from the touch-down point. Jackson knew that he would have to stop in a hurry, but decided against using the reverse thrust. Reversing the engines would automatically shut off the two jets that would be needed for a minimum-run take-off. He stood on the brakes and skidded to a halt just before reaching the gutted helicopter.

The three controllers scrambled from the ditch and dived into the aircraft as the surprised enemy gunners opened fire. At the front of the aircraft Major Campbell spotted a 122mm rocket shell coming towards them, and both pilots watched in horror as it hit the ground just 25 feet in front of the nose. Luck was still on their side, however, and the deadly projectile did not explode. Jackson taxied around the shell and rammed the throttles to the firewall. "We hadn't been out of that spot ten seconds when mortars started dropping directly on it," he remembers. "That was a real thriller. I figured they just got zeroed in on us, and that the time of flight of the mortar shells was about ten seconds longer than the time we sat there taking the men aboard." Within seconds they were in the air again and one of the combat team recalled, "We were dead, and all of a sudden we were alive!"

General McLaughlin, who had witnessed the event from overhead, approved nominations for the Medal of Honor for both pilots, who landed safely back at Da Nang to discover that their C-123 had not even taken one hit! In January 1969 Colonel Jackson received the Medal of Honor in a ceremony at the White House; Major Campbell received the Air Force Cross, and the rest of the crew were awarded Silver Stars.

OBITUARY: DIGBY TATHAM-WARTER

The Daily Telegraph

Digby Tatham-Warter, the former company commander, 2nd Battalion, Parachute Regiment, who has died aged 75, was celebrated for leading a bayonet charge at Arnhem in September 1944, sporting an old bowler hat and a tattered umbrella.

During the long, bitter conflict Tatham-Warter strolled around nonchalantly during the heaviest fire. The padre (Fr Egan) recalled that, while he was trying to make his way to visit some wounded in the cellars and had taken temporary shelter from enemy fire, Tatham-Warter came up to him, and said: "Don't worry about the bullets: I've got an umbrella."

Having escorted the padre under his brolly, Tatham-Warter continued visiting the men who were holding the perimeter defences. "That thing won't do you much good," commented one of his fellow officers, to which Tatham-Warter replied: "But what if it rains?"

By that stage in the battle all hope of being relieved by the arrival of 30 Corps had vanished. The Germans were pounding the beleaguered airborne forces with heavy artillery and Tiger tanks, so that most of the houses were burning and the area was littered with dead and wounded.

But German suggestions that the parachutists should surrender received a rude response. Tatham-Warter's umbrella became a symbol of defiance, as the British, although short of ammunition, food and water, stubbornly held on to the north end of the road bridge.

Arnhem was the furthest ahead of three bridges in Holland

which the Allies needed to seize if they were going to outflank the Siegfried line. Securing the bridge by an airborne operation would enable 30 Corps to cross the Rhine and press on into Germany.

As the first V2 rocket had fallen in Britain earlier that month, speed in winning the land battle in Europe was essential. In the event, however, the parachutists were dropped unnecessarily far from the bridge, and the lightly armed Airborne Division was attacked by two German Panzer divisions whose presence in the area had not been realised: soldiers from one of them reached the bridge before the British parachutists.

Tatham-Warter and his men therefore had to fight their way to the bridge, capture the north end, try to cross it and capture the other side. This they failed to do.

At one point the back of Tatham-Warter's trouserings was whipped out by blast, giving him a vaguely scarecrow-like appearance instead of his normally immaculate turnout. Eventually he was wounded (as was the padre), and consigned to a hospital occupied by the Germans.

Although his wound was nor serious Tatham-Warter realised that he had a better chance of escape if he stayed with the stretcher cases. During the night, with his more severely wounded second-in-command (Capt A. M. Frank), he crawled out of the hospital window and reached "a very brave lone Dutch woman" who took them in and hid them. She spoke no English and was very frightened, but fed them and put them in touch with a neighbour who disguised them as house painters and sheltered them in a delivery van, from where they moved to a house.

Tatham-Warter then bicycled around the countryside, which was full of Germans, making contact with other Arnhem escapees (called evaders) and informing them of the rendezvous for an escape over the Rhine.

On one of these trips, he and his companion were overtaken by a German staff car, which skidded off the muddy road into a ditch. "As the officers seemed to be in an excitable state," he recalled, "we thought it wise to help push their car out and back on to the road. They were gracious enough to thank us for our help."

As jobbing painters, Tatham-Warter and Frank aroused no

suspicions by their presence in the home of the Wildeboer family (who owned a paint factory), although the area abounded with Gestapo, Dutch SS and collaborators. Even when four Panzer soldiers were billeted on the Wildeboers, they merely nodded and greeted each other on their comings and goings.

Eventually, with the help of the Dutch Resistance, Tatham-Warter assembled an escape party of 150, which included shot-down airmen and even two Russians. Guided by the Dutch, they found their way through the German lines, often passing within a few yards of German sentries and outposts.

Tatham-Warter suspected that the Germans deliberately failed to hear them: 30 Corps had been sending over strong fighting patrols of American parachutists temporarily under their command, and the Germans had no stomach for another bruising encounter.

In spite of Tatham-Warter's stern admonitions, he recalled that his party sounded more like a herd of buffaloes than a secret escape party. Finally, they reached the river bank where they were ferried over by British sappers from 30 Corps and met by Hugh Fraser (then in the SAS) and Airey Neave, who had been organising their escape.

Tatham-Warter was awarded the DSO after the battle.

Allison Digby Tatham-Warter was born on May 26 1917 and educated at Wellington and Sandhurst. He was destined for the Indian Army but while on the statutory year of attachment to an English regiment in India – in this case the Oxford and Bucks Light Infantry – he liked it so much that he decided to stay on. He formally transferred to the regiment in 1938.

He had ample opportunity for pig-sticking: on one occasion he killed three wild boar while hunting alone. The average weight of the boars was 150lb and their height 32in. He also took up polo – which he called "snobs' hockey" – with considerable success.

In 1939 he shot a tiger when on foot. With a few friends he had gone to the edge of the jungle to make arrangements for the reception of a tiger the next evening. As they were doing so, they suddenly noticed that one had arrived prematurely. They shinned up the nearest tree, accompanied by some equally prudent monkeys.

When the monkeys decided it was safe to descend the party followed, only to find that the tiger was once more with them. This time Tatham-Warter, who was nearest, was ready, but it was a close shave.

In 1942 the Oxford and Bucks became glider-borne. This was not exciting enough for Tatham-Warter, however, and in 1944 he joined the Parachute Regiment.

"He was lusting for action at that time," John Frost (later Major-General) recalled of Tatham-Warter, "having so far failed to get in the war. There was much of 'Prince Rupert' about Digby and he was worth a bet with anybody's money."

Tatham-Warter's striking appearance was particularly valuable when the British were fighting against impossible odds at Arnhem. For within the perimeter were soldiers from other detachments, signals, sappers and gunmen, who would not know him by sight as his own men would, but who could not fail to be inspired by his towering figure and unflagging spirit of resistance.

Brigadier (later Gen Sir Gerald) Lathbury recalled that Tatham-Warter took command of 2 Para "when the Colonel was seriously wounded and the second-in-command killed . . . he did a magnificent job, moving around the district freely and was so cool that on one occasion he arrived at the door of a house simultaneously with two German soldiers – and allowed them to stand back to let him go in first."

In 1946 Tatham-Warter emigrated to Kenya where he bought and ran two large estates at Nanyuki. An ardent naturalist, he organised and accompanied high-level safaris and was an originator of the photographic safari. He also captained the Kenya Polo team (his handicap was six), and judged at horse shows (he had won the Saddle at Sandhurst). During the Mau Mau rebellion he raised a force of mounted police which operated with great success.

In later years Tatham-Warter took up carpentry and became highly skilled at inlaid work. Fishing and sailing were his other recreations.

In Richard Attenborough's controversial film about Arnhem, *A Bridge Too Far*, the character based on Tatham-Warter was played by Christopher Good.

In 1991 Digby Tatham-Warter published his own recollections, *Dutch Courage and "Pegasus"*, which described his escape after Arnhem and paid tribute to the Dutch civilians who had helped him. He often revisited them.

He married, in 1949, Jane Boyd; they had three daughters.

March 30 1993

GEORGE WASHINGTON
AND THE CHERRY TREE

J. Berg Esenwein, Marietta Stockard, William J. Bennett

The refusal of the boy Washington to tell a lie 250 years ago is widely held up as a golden exemplar of honesty. It also, of course, took great childish courage.

When George Washington was a little boy he lived on a farm in Virginia. His father taught him to ride, and he used to take young George about the farm with him so that his son might learn how to take care of the fields and horses and cattle when he grew older.

Mr Washington had planted an orchard of fine fruit trees. There were apple trees, peach trees, pear trees, plum trees, and cherry trees. Once, a particularly fine cherry tree was sent to him from across the ocean. Mr Washington planted it on the edge of the orchard. He told everyone on the farm to watch it carefully to see that it was not broken or hurt in any way.

It grew well and one spring it was covered with white blossoms. Mr Washington was pleased to think he would soon have cherries from the little tree.

Just about this time, George was given a shiny new hatchet. George took it and went about chopping sticks, hacking into the rails of fences, and cutting whatever else he passed. At last he came to the edge of the orchard, and thinking only of how well his hatchet could cut, he chopped into the little cherry tree. The bark was soft, and it cut so easily that George chopped the tree right down, and then went on with his play.

That evening when Mr Washington came from inspecting the farm, he sent his horse to the stable and walked down to the orchard to look at his cherry tree. He stood in amazement when he saw how it was cut. Who would have dared do such a thing? He asked everyone, but no one could tell him anything about it.

Just then George passed by.

"George," his father called in an angry voice, "do you know who killed my cherry tree?

This was a tough question, and George staggered under it for a moment, but quickly recovered.

"I cannot tell a lie, father," he said. "I did it with my hatchet."

Mr Washington looked at George. The boy's face was white, but he looked straight into his father's eyes.

"Go into the house, son," said Mr Washington sternly.

George went into the library and waited for his father. He was very unhappy and very much ashamed. He knew he had been foolish and thoughtless and that his father was right to be displeased.

Soon, Mr Washington came into the room. "Come here, my boy," he said.

George went over to his father. Mr Washington looked at him long and steadily.

"Tell me, son, why did you cut the tree?"

"I was playing and I did not think—" George stammered.

"And now the tree will die. We shall never have any cherries from it. But worse than that, you have failed to take care of the tree when I asked you to do so."

George's head was bent and his cheeks were red from shame.

"I am sorry, father," he said.

Mr Washington put his hand on the boy's shoulder. "Look at me," he said. "I am sorry to have lost my cherry tree, but I am glad that you were brave enough to tell me the truth. I would rather have you truthful and brave than to have a whole orchard full of the finest cherry trees. Never forget that, my son."

George Washington never did forget. To the end of his life he was just as brave and honorable as he was that day as a little boy.

BRITAIN IS A LAND
OF UNSUNG HEROES

Robert Hardman

A newspaper article from electronic Telegraph, *5 May 1999.*

Too many civilian acts of bravery go unrecognised, according to the main organisation that honours the saving of human life.

The Royal Humane Society's major annual awards tomorrow will be presented by Princess Alexandra, but the organisation is concerned that there are many potential recipients whose heroism is unsung. Maj-Gen Christopher Tyler, secretary of the 225-year-old society, of which the Queen is patron, said: "Over the last year, we investigated 207 cases, which led to 341 people receiving awards, but we feel that there are hundreds of equally brave people whose deeds have not been recognised."

Despite the popularity of television programmes involving real emergencies, the number of nominations for saving lives is declining. Maj-Gen Tyler said: "I think that is due to the fact that the majority of reports are submitted by the emergency services and many of them are just too busy, but anyone can nominate somebody and we will examine every case."

The society's awards, which are drawn up in consultation with the Cabinet Office, salute bravery and skill in saving human life. They range from certificates of commendation, in cases which did not involve personal risk, to the Stanhope Gold Medal. This is the single award for the most conspicuous case of gallantry during the year. The winner will be announced tomorrow.

The list of the other 1997–98 medal winners includes police officers, among them Pc Ian Standerwick and Pc Steven Date, of the Avon and Somerset force. In September 1997, they answered an emergency call after a suicidal woman was seen on a ledge above the Clifton Suspension Bridge.

Pc Standerwick climbed on to the ledge but the woman began swaying as he edged towards her. He tried to grab her, losing his balance. Pc Date managed to grab him and they eventually led the woman to safety. Had she resisted, all would have fallen to their deaths. Pc Standerwick, 28, has received the society's silver medal and Pc Date, 33, bronze.

Another winner of the bronze medal is Trudi Plumb, 38, a housewife, of Burnham-on-Crouch, Essex. One night in January, she came across a car in a ditch with flames leaping from the engine. The driver was inside and unconscious.

She leaned inside to undo his seat belt and started to try to pull him out, despite a surgeon's orders not lift heavy weights after a recent cancer operation. His feet were trapped under the pedals, so she had to free them while flames ripped through the car. Despite burning the backs of her hands, she dragged the 13 stone man from the car. Seconds later the car was engulfed in flames.

Mrs Plumb said: "I didn't even think about what the doctor said about weights. I just thought I've got to do this now or he'll never get out. By the time the ambulance arrived, he would have been dead. When I told my husband what I'd done, he gave me a telling off for being so stupid. But I'd do it again. And he's coming to London with me on Thursday."

THE SPIRIT OF ST LOUIS

Charles A. Lindbergh

Today transatlantic flight is a commonplace, but when American aviator Charles A. Lindbergh took off from New York in May 1927 for Paris in a stuttering Ryan monoplane it had only been achieved once before, by the British duo Alcock and Brown in 1919. Lindbergh, however, was alone; he had to both fly and navigate himself, and stay awake for endless hours. He had no radio and knew that if he was forced to "ditch" in the Atlantic there was next to no hope of rescue.

The Eighteenth Hour

The minute hand has just passed 1:00 a.m. It's dawn, one hour after midnight . . . With this faint trace of day, the uncontrollable desire to sleep falls over me in quilted layers. I've been staving it off with difficulty during the hours of moonlight. Now it looms all but insurmountable. This is the hour I've been dreading; the hour against which I've tried to steel myself. I know it's the beginning of my greatest test. This will be the worst time of all, this early hour of the second morning – the third morning, it is, since I've slept.

I've lost command of my eyelids. When they start to close, I can't restrain them. They shut, and I shake myself, and lift them with my fingers. I stare at the instruments, wrinkle forehead muscles tense. Lids close again regardless, stick tight as though with glue. My body has revolted from the rule of its mind. Like salt in wounds, the light of day brings back my pains. Every cell of my being is on strike, sulking in protest, claiming that nothing, nothing in the world, could be worth such effort; that man's tissue was never made for such abuse. My back is stiff; my shoulders ache; my face burns; my eyes smart. It seems impossible to go on longer. All I want in life is to throw myself down flat, stretch out – and sleep.

I've struggled with the dawn often enough before, but never with such a background of fatigue. I've got to muster all my reserves, all the tricks I've learned, all remaining strength of mind, for the conflict. If I can hold in air and close to course for one more hour, the sun will be over the horizon and the battle won. Each ray of light is an ally. With each moment after sunrise, vitality will increase.

Shaking my body and stamping my feet no longer has effect. It's more fatiguing than arousing. I'll have to try something else. I push the stick forward and dive down into a high ridge of cloud, pulling up sharply after I clip through its summit. That wakes me a little, but tricks don't help for long. They're only tiring. It's better to sit still and conserve strength.

My mind strays from the cockpit and returns. My eyes close, and open, and close again. But I'm beginning to understand vaguely a new factor which has come to my assistance. It seems I'm made up of three personalities, three elements, each partly dependent and partly independent of the others. There's my body, which knows definitely that what it wants most in the world is sleep. There's my mind, constantly making decisions that my body refuses to comply with, but which itself is weakening in resolution. And there's something else, which seems to become stronger instead of weaker with fatigue, an element of spirit, a directive force that has stepped out from the background and taken control over both mind and body. It seems to guard them as a wise father guards his children; letting them venture to the point of danger, then calling them back, guiding with a firm but tolerant hand.

When my body cries out that it *must* sleep, this third element replies that it may get what rest it can from relaxation, but that sleep is not to be had. When my mind demands that my body stay alert and awake, it is informed that alertness is too much to expect under these circumstances. And when it argues excitedly that to sleep would be to fail, and crash, and drown in the ocean, it is calmly reassured, and told it's right, but that while it must not expect alertness on the body's part, it can be confident there'll be no sleep.

The Nineteenth Hour

When I leave a cloud, drowsiness advances; when I enter the next, it recedes. If I could sleep and wake refreshed, how extraordinary this world of mist would be. But now I only dimly appreciate, only partially realize. The love of flying, the beauty of sunrise, the solitude of the mid-Atlantic sky, are screened from my senses by opaque veils of sleep. All my remaining energy, all the attention I can bring to bear, must be concentrated on the task of simply passing through.

The Twentieth Hour

The nose is down, the wing low, the plane diving and turning. I've been asleep with open eyes. I'm certain they've been open, yet I have all the sensations of waking up – lack of memory of intervening time, inability to comprehend the situation for a moment, the return of understanding like blood surging through the body. I kick left rudder and pull the stick back cornerwise. My eyes jump to the altimeter. No danger; I'm at 1600 feet, a little above my chosen altitude. In a moment, I'll have the plane leveled out. But the turn-indicator leans over the left – the air speed drops – the ball rolls quickly to the side. A climbing turn in the opposite direction! My plane is getting out of control!

The realization is like an electric shock running through my body. It brings instant mental keenness. In a matter of seconds I have the *Spirit of St Louis* back in hand. But even after the needles are in place, the plane seems to be flying on its side. I know what's happening. It's the illusion you sometimes get while flying blind, the illusion that your plane is no longer in level flight, that it's spiraling, stalling, turning, that the instruments are wrong.

There's only one thing to do – shut off feeling from the mind as much as your ability permits. Let a wing stay low as far as bodily senses are concerned. Let the plane seem to maneuver as it will, dive, climb, sideslip, or bank; but keep the needles where they belong. Gradually, when the senses find that the plane is continuing on its course, that air isn't screaming through the cowlings as it would in a dive, that wings aren't trembling as they would in a stall, that there's really no pressure on the seat as there would be in a bank, they recover from their confusion and make obeisance to the mind.

As minutes pass and no new incident occurs, I fall into the state of eye-open sleep again. I fly with less anguish when my conscious mind is not awake. At times I'm not sure whether I'm dreaming through life or living through a dream. It seems I've broken down the barrier between the two, and discovered some essential relationship between living and dreaming I never recognized before. Some secret has been opened to me beyond the ordinary consciousness of man. Can I carry it with me beyond this flight, into normal life again? Or is it forbidden knowledge? Will I lose it after I land, as I've so often lost the essence of some midnight's dream?

The Twenty-second Hour

Will the fog never end? Does this storm cover the entire ocean? Except for that small, early morning plot of open sea, I've been in it or above it for nine hours. What happened to the high pressure area that was to give me a sunny sky? The only storms reported were local ones in Europe!

I remind myself again that I didn't wait for confirmation of good weather. Dr Kimball said only that stations along the coast reported clearing, and that a large high-pressure area was moving in over the North Atlantic. He didn't say there'd be no storms. The weather's no worse than I expected when I planned this flight. Why should I complain of a few blind hours in the morning? If the fog lifts by the time I strike the European coast, that's all I should ask. The flight's been as successful as I ever hoped it would be. The only thing that's seriously upset my plans is the sleepless night before I started – those extra twenty-three hours before take-off.

Of course no one thought the weather would break enough to let me start so quickly. But why did I depend on what anyone thought? Why did I take any chance? I didn't have to go to a show that evening. I didn't have to go to New York. This is the price for my amusement, and it's too high. It imperils the entire flight. If this were the first morning without sleep instead of the second, blind flying would be a different matter, and my navigation on a different plane.

The fog dissolves, and the sea appears. Flying two hundred feet higher, I wouldn't have seen it, for the overcast is just above me. There's no sun; only a pocket of clear air. Ahead, is another curtain of mist. Can I get under it this time? I push the stick forward. Waves are mountainous – even higher than before. If I fly close to their crests, maybe I can stay below the next area of fog.

I drop down until I'm flying in salt spray whipped off white-caps by the wind. I clip five feet above a breaker with my wheels, watch tossing water sweep into the trough beyond. But the fog is too thick. It crowds down between the waves themselves. It merges with their form. A gull couldn't find enough ceiling to fly above this ocean. I climb. The air's rougher than before, swirling like the sea beneath it. I open my throttle wider to hold a margin of speed and power.

Before I reach a thousand feet, waves show again, vaguely – whitecaps veiled and unveiled by low-lying scuds of fog. I nose down; but in a moment they're gone, smothered by mist. I climb.

While I'm staring at the instruments, during an unearthly age of time, both conscious and asleep, the fuselage behind me becomes filled with ghostly presences – vaguely outlined forms, transparent, moving, riding weightless with me in the plane. I feel no surprise at their coming. There's no suddenness to their appearance. Without turning my head, I see them as clearly as though in my normal field of vision. There's no limit to my sight – my skull is one great eye, seeing everywhere at once.

These phantoms speak with human voices – friendly, vapor-like shapes, without substance, able to vanish or appear at will, to pass in and out through the walls of the fuselage as though no walls were there. Now, many are crowded behind me. Now, only a few remain. First one and then another presses forward to my shoulder to speak above the engine's noise, and then draws back among the group behind. At times, voices come out of the air itself, clear yet far away, traveling through distances that can't be measured by the scale of human miles; familiar voices, conversing and advising on my flight, discussing problems of my navigation, reassuring me, giving me messages of importance unattainable in ordinary life.

The Twenty-third Hour

Sea, clouds, and sky are all stirred up together – dull gray mist, blinding white mist, patches of blue, mottling of black, a band of sunlight sprinkling diamond facets on the water. There are clouds lying on the ocean, clouds just risen from its surface, clouds floating at every level through twenty thousand feet of sky; some small, some overpowering in size – wisps, masses, layers. It's a breeding ground for mist.

I fly above, below, between the layers, as though following the interstices of a giant sponge; sometimes under a blue sky but over an ocean veiled by thick and drifting mist; sometimes brushing gray clouds with my wings while my wheels are almost rolling in the breakers' foam. It's like playing leapfrog with the weather. These cloud formations help me to stay awake. They give me something on which to fix my eyes in passing, but don't hold my stare too long. Their tremendous, changing, flashing world removes monotony from flight.

Sunlight flashes as I emerge from a cloud. My eyes are drawn to the north. My dreams are startled away. There, under my left wing, only five or six miles distant, a coastline parallels my course – purple, haze-covered hills; clumps of trees; rocky cliffs. Small, wooded islands guard the shore.

But I'm in mid-Atlantic, nearly a thousand miles from land! Half-formed thoughts rush through my mind. Are the compasses completely wrong? Am I hopelessly lost? Is it the coast of

Labrador or Greenland that I see? Have I been flying north instead of east?

It's like waking from a sound sleep in strange surroundings, in a room where you've never spent a night before. The wall-paper, the bed, the furniture, the light coming in the window, nothing is as you expected it to be.

I shake my head and look again. There can be no doubt, now, that I'm awake. But the shore line is still there. Land in mid-Atlantic! Something has gone wrong! I couldn't have been flying north, regardless of the inaccuracy of my compasses. The sun and the moon both rose on my left, and stars confirmed that my general direction was toward Europe. I know there's no land out here in mid-ocean – nothing between Greenland and Iceland to the north, and the Azores to the south. But I look down at the chart for reassurance; for my mind is no longer certain of its knowledge. To find new islands marked on it would hardly be stranger than the flight itself.

No, they must be mirages, fog islands sprung up along my route; here for an hour only to disappear, mushrooms of the sea. But so apparently real, so cruelly deceptive! *Real* clouds cover their higher hills, and pour down into their ravines. How can those bluffs and forests consist of nothing but fog? No islands of the earth could be more perfect.

The Twenty-fourth Hour

Here it's well into midday and my mind's still shirking, still refusing to meet the problems it undertook so willingly in planning for this flight. Are all those months of hard and detailed work to be wasted for lack of a few minutes of con-centrated effort? Is my character so weak that I can't pull myself together long enough to lay out a new, considered course? Has landing at Le Bourget become of so little import that I'll trade success for these useless hours of semiconscious relaxation? *No; I must, I will* become alert, and concentrate, and make decisions.

There are measures I haven't yet used – too extreme for normal times. But now it's a case of survival. Anything is justified that has effect. I strike my face sharply with my hand. It hardly feels the blow. I strike again with all the strength I have. My cheek is numb, but there's none of the sharp stinging that I counted on to wake my body. No jump of flesh, no lash on mind. It's no use. Even these methods don't work. Why try more?

But Paris is over a thousand miles away! And there's still a continent to find. I must be prepared to strike a fog-covered European coast hundreds of miles off course; and, if necessary, to fly above clouds all the hours of another night. How can I pass through such ordeals if I can't wake my mind and stir my body? But the alternative is death and failure. Can I complete this flight to Paris? Can I even reach the Irish coast? *But the alternative is death and failure! Death! For the first time in my life, I doubt my ability to endure.*

The stark concept of death has more effect than physical blow or reasoned warning. It imbues me with new power, power strong enough to communicate the emergency to my body's senses, to whip them up from their lethargy and marshall them once more – in straggling ranks, but with some semblance of order and coordination. *It's life, life, life itself at stake.* This time I'm not just saying so. *I know it.*

The Twenty-sixth Hour

Is there something alive down there under my wing? I thought I saw a dark object moving through the water. I search the surface, afraid to hope, lest I lose confidence in vision. Was it a large fish, or were my eyes deceiving me? After the fog islands and the phantoms, I no longer trust my senses. The *Spirit of St Louis* itself might fade away without causing me great surprise. But – yes, there it is again, slightly behind me now, a porpoise – the first living thing I've seen since Newfoundland. Fin and sleek, black body curve gracefully above the surface and slip down out of sight.

The ocean is as desolate as ever. Yet a complete change has taken place. I feel that I've safely recrossed the bridge to life – broken the strands which have been tugging me toward the universe beyond. Why do I find such joy, such encouragement in the sight of a porpoise? What possible bond can I have with a porpoise hundreds of miles at sea, with a strange creature I've never seen before and will never see again? What is there in that flashing glimpse of hide that means so much to me, that even makes it seem a different ocean? Is it simply that I've been looking so long, and seeing nothing? Is it an omen of land ahead? Or is there some common tie between living things that surmounts even the barrier of species?

Can it be that the porpoise was imaginary too, a part of this strange, living dream, like the fuselage's phantoms and the islands which faded into mist? Yet I know there's a difference, a dividing line that still exists between reality and apparition. The porpoise *was* real, like the water itself, like the substance of the cockpit around me, like my face which I can feel when I run my hand across it.

It's twenty-six and a half hours since I took off. That's almost twice as long as the flight between San Diego and St Louis; and that was much the longest flight I ever made. It's asking a lot of an engine to run twenty-six hours without attention. Back on the mail, we check our Liberties at the end of every trip. Are the rocker-arms on my Whirlwind still getting grease? And how long will it keep on going if one of them should freeze?

I shift arms on the stick. My left hand – being free, and apparently disconnected from my mind's control – begins aimlessly exploring the pockets of the chart bag. It pulls the maps of Europe halfway out to reassure my eyes they're there, tucks my helmet and goggles in more neatly, and fingers the shiny little first-aid kit and the dark glasses given me by that doctor on Long Island. Why have I let my eyes burn through the morning? Why have I been squinting for hours and not thought of these glasses before? I hook the wires over my ears and look out on a shaded ocean. It's as though the sky were overcast again. I don't dare use them. They're too comfortable, too pleasant. They make it seem like evening – make me want to sleep.

I slip the glasses back into their pocket, pull out the first-aid kit, and idly snap it open. It contains adhesive tape, compact bandages, and a little pair of scissors. Not enough to do much patching after a crash. Tucked into one corner are several silk-covered, glass capsules of aromatic ammonia. "For use as Smelling Salts," the labels state. What did the doctor think I could do with smelling salts over the ocean? This kit is made for a child's cut finger, or for some debutante fainting at a ball! I might as well have saved its weight on the take-off, for all the good it will be to me. I put it back in the chart bag – and then pull it out again. If smelling salts revive people who are about to faint, why won't they revive people who are about to fall asleep? Here's a weapon against sleep lying at my side unused, a weapon which has been there all through the morning's deadly hours. A whiff of one of these capsules should sharpen the dullest mind. And no eyes could sleep stinging with the vapor of ammonia.

I'll try one now. The fumes ought to clear my head and keep the compass centered. I crush a capsule between thumb and fingers. A fluid runs out, discoloring the white silk cover. I hold it cautiously, several inches from my nose. There's no odor. I move it closer, slowly, until finally it touches my nostrils. I smell nothing! My eyes don't feel the slightest sting, and no tears come to moisten their dry edges. I inhale again with no effect, and throw the capsule through the window. My mind now begins to realize how deadened my senses have become, how close I must be to the end of my reserves. And yet there may be another sleepless night ahead.

The Twenty-seventh Hour

I'm flying along dreamily when it catches my eyes, that black speck on the water two or three miles southeast. I realize it's there with the same jerk to awareness that comes when the altimeter needle drops too low in flying blind. I squeeze my lids together and look again. A boat! A small boat! Several small boats, scattered over the surface of the ocean!

Seconds pass before my mind takes in the full importance of what my eyes are seeing. Then, all feeling of drowsiness departs. I bank the *Spirit of St Louis* toward the nearest boat and nose down toward the water. I couldn't be wider awake or more keenly aware if the engine had stopped.

Fishing boats! *The coast, the European coast, can't be far away!* The ocean is behind, the flight completed. Those little vessels, those chips on the sea, are Europe. What nationality? Are they Irish, English, Scotch, or French? Can they be from

Norway, or from Spain? What fishing bank are they anchored on? How far from the coast do fishing banks extend? It's too early to reach Europe unless a gale blew behind me through the night. Thoughts press forward in confused succession. After fifteen hours of solitude, here's human life and help and safety.

The ocean is no longer a dangerous wilderness. I feel as secure as though I were circling Lambert Field back home. I could land alongside any one of those boats, and someone would throw me a rope and take me on board where there'd be a bunk I could sleep on, and warm food when I woke up.

The first boat is less than a mile ahead – I can see its masts and cabin. I can see it rocking on the water. I close the mixture control and dive down fifty feet above its bow, dropping my wing to get a better view.

But where is the crew? There's no sign of life on deck. Can all the men be out in dories? I climb higher as I circle. No, there aren't any dories. I can see for miles, and the ocean's not rough enough to hide one. Are the fishermen frightened by my plane, swooping down suddenly from the sky? Possibly they never saw a plane before. *Of course* they never saw one out so far over the ocean. Maybe they all hid below the decks when they heard the roar of my engine. Maybe they think I'm some demon from the sky, like those dragons that decorate ancient mariners' charts. But if the crews are so out of contact with the modern world that they hide from the sound of an airplane, they must come from some isolated coastal village above which airplanes never pass. And the boats look too small to have ventured far from home. I have visions of riding the top of a hurricane during the night, with a hundred-mile-an-hour wind drift. Possibly these vessels are anchored north of Ireland, or somewhere in the Bay of Biscay. Then shall I keep on going straight, or turn north, or south?

I fly over to the next boat bobbing up and down on the swells. Its deck is empty too. But as I drop my wing to circle, a man's head appears, thrust out through a cabin porthole, motionless, staring up at me. In the excitement and joy of the moment, in the rush of ideas passing through my reawakened mind, I decide to make that head withdraw from the porthole, come out of the cabin, body and all, and to point toward the Irish coast. No sooner have I made the decision than I realize its futility. Probably that fisherman can't speak English. Even if he can, he'll be too startled to understand my message, and reply. But I'm already turning into position to dive down past the boat. It won't do any harm to try. Why deprive myself of that easy satisfaction? Probably if I fly over it again, the entire crew will come on deck. I've talked to people before from a plane, flying low with throttled engine, and received the answer through some simple gesture – a nod or an outstretched arm.

I glide down within fifty feet of the cabin, close the throttle, and shout as loudly as I can, "WHICH WAY IS IRELAND?"

How extraordinary the silence is with the engine idling! I look back under the tail, watch the fisherman's face for some sign of understanding. But an instant later, all my attention is concentrated on the plane. For I realize that I've lost the "feel" of flying. I shove the throttle open, and watch the air-speed indicator while I climb and circle. As long as I keep the needle above sixty miles an hour, there's no danger of stalling. Always before, I've known instinctively just what condition my plane was in – whether it had flying speed or whether it was stalling, and how close to the edge it was riding in between. I didn't have to look at the instruments. Now, the pressure of the stick no longer imparts its message clearly to my hand. I can't tell whether air is soft or solid.

When I pass over the boat a third time, the head is still at the porthole. It hasn't moved or changed expression since it first appeared. It came as suddenly as the boats themselves. It seems as lifeless. I didn't notice before how pale it is – or am I now imagining its paleness? It looks like a severed head in that porthole, as though a guillotine had dropped behind it. I feel baffled. After all, a man who dares to show his face would hardly fear to show his body. There's something unreal about these boats. They're as weird as the night's temples, as those misty islands of Atlantis, as the fuselage's phantoms that rode behind my back.

Why don't sailors gather on the decks to watch my plane? Why don't they pay attention to my circling and shouting? What's the matter with this strange flight, where dreams become reality, and reality returns to dreams? But these aren't vessels of cloud and mist. They're tangible, made of real substance like my plane – sails furled, ropes coiled neatly on the decks, masts swaying back and forth with each new swell. Yet the only sign of crew is that single head, hanging motionless through the cabin porthole. It's like "The Rime of the Ancient Mariner" my mother used to read aloud. These boats remind me of the "painted ship upon a painted ocean".

I want to stay, to circle again and again, until that head removes itself from the porthole and the crews come out on deck. I want to see them standing and waving like normal, living people. I've passed through worlds and ages since my last contact with other men. I've been away, far away, planets and heavens away, until only a thread was left to lead me back to earth and life. I've followed that thread with swinging compasses, through lonely canyons, over pitfalls of sleep, past the lure of enchanted islands, fearing that at any moment it would break. And now I've returned to earth, returned to these boats bobbing on the ocean. I want an earthly greeting. I deserve a warmer welcome back to the fellowship of men.

Shall I fly over to another boat and try again to raise the crew? No, I'm wasting minutes of daylight and miles of fuel. There's nothing but frustration to be had by staying longer. It's best to leave. There's something about this fleet that tries my mind and spirit, and lowers confidence with every circle I make. Islands that turn to fog, I understand. Ships without crews, I do not. And that motionless head at the porthole – it's no phantom, and yet it shows no sign of life. I straighten out the *Spirit of St Louis* and fly on eastward.

The Twenty-eighth Hour

Is that a cloud on the northeastern horizon, or a strip of low fog – or – *can it possibly be land?* It looks like land, but I don't intend to be tricked by another mirage. Framed between two gray curtains of rain, not more than ten or fifteen miles away, a purplish blue band has hardened from the haze – flat below, like a water-line – curving on top, as though composed of hills or aged mountains.

I'm only sixteen hours out from Newfoundland. I allowed eighteen and a half hours to strike the Irish coast. If that's Ireland, I'm two and a half hours ahead of schedule. Can this be another, clearer image, like the islands of the morning? Is there something strange about it too, like the fishing fleet and that haunting head? Is each new illusion to become more real until reality itself is meaningless? But my mind is clear. I'm no longer half asleep. I'm awake – alert – aware. The temptation is too great. I can't hold my course any longer. The *Spirit of St Louis* banks over toward the nearest point of land.

I stare at it intently, not daring to believe my eyes, keeping hope in check to avoid another disappointment, watching the shades and contours unfold into a coast line – a coastline coming down from the north – a coast line bending toward the east – a coast line with rugged shores and rolling mountains. It's much too early to strike England, France, or Scotland. It's early to be striking Ireland; but that's the nearest land.

A fjorded coast stands out as I approach. Barren islands guard it. Inland, green fields slope up the sides of warted mountains. This *must* be Ireland. It can be no other place than Ireland. The fields are too green for Scotland; the mountains too high for Brittany or Cornwall.

Now, I'm flying above the foam-lined coast, searching for prominent features to fit the chart on my knees. I've climbed to two thousand feet so I can see the contours of the country better. The mountains are old and rounded; the farms small and stony. Rain-glistened dirt roads wind narrowly through hills and fields. Below me lies a great tapering bay; a long, bouldered island; a village. Yes, there's a place on the chart where it all fits – line of ink on line of shore – Valentia and Dingle Bay, *on the south-western coast of Ireland!*

I can hardly believe it's true. I'm almost exactly on my route, closer than I hoped to come in my wildest dreams back in San Diego. What happened to all those detours of the night around the thunderheads? Where has the swinging compass error gone? The wind above the storm clouds must have blown fiercely on my tail. In edging northward, intuition must have been more accurate than reasoned navigation.

The southern tip of Ireland! On course; over two hours ahead of schedule; the sun still well up in the sky; the weather clearing! I circle again, fearful that I'll wake to find this too a phantom, a mirage fading into mid-Atlantic mist. But there's no question about it; every detail on the chart has its counterpart below;

each major feature on the ground has its symbol on the chart. The lines correspond exactly. Nothing in that world of dreams and phantoms was like this. I spiral lower, looking down on the little village. There are boats in the harbor, wagons on the stone-fenced roads. People are running out into the streets, looking up and waving. This is earth again, the earth where I've lived and now will live once more. Here are human beings. Here's a human welcome. Not a single detail is wrong. I've never seen such beauty before – fields so green, people so human, a village so attractive, mountains and rocks so mountainous and rocklike.

THE HERO AS PRIEST

Thomas Carlyle

Carlyle wrote this appreciation of Martin Luther, the founder of Protestantism, in 1841.

Luther's birthplace was Eisleben in Saxony; he came into the world there on the 10th of November 1483. It was an accident that gave this honour to Eisleben. His parents, poor mine-labourers in a village of that region, named Mohra, had gone to the Eisleben Winter-Fair: in the tumult of this scene the Frau Luther was taken with travail, found refuge in some poor house there, and the boy she bore was named MARTIN LUTHER. Strange enough to reflect upon it. This poor Frau Luther, she had gone with her husband to make her small merchandisings; perhaps to sell the lock of yarn she had been spinning, to buy the small winter-necessaries for her narrow hut or household; in the whole world, that day, there was not a more entirely unimportant-looking pair of people than this Miner and his Wife. And yet what were all Emperors, Popes and Potentates, in comparison? There was born here, once more, a Mighty Man; whose light was to flame as the beacon over long centuries and epochs of the world; the whole world and its history was waiting for this man. It is strange, it is great. It leads us back to another Birth-hour, in a still meaner environment, Eighteen Hundred years ago, – of which it is fit that we *say* nothing, that we think only in silence; for what words are there! The Age of Miracles past? The Age of Miracles is forever here!—

I find it altogether suitable to Luther's function in this Earth.

and doubtless wisely ordered to that end by the Providence presiding over him and us and all things, that he was born poor, and brought-up poor, one of the poorest of men. He had to beg, as the school-children in those times did; singing for alms and bread, from door to door. Hardship, rigorous Necessity was the poor boy's companion; no man nor no thing would put-on a false face to flatter Martin Luther. Among things, not among the shows of things, had he to grow. A boy of rude figure, yet with weak health, with his large greedy soul, full of all faculty and sensibility, he suffered greatly. But it was his task to get acquainted with *realities*, and keep acquainted with them, at whatever cost: his task was to bring the whole world back to reality, for it had dwelt too long with semblance! A youth nursed-up in wintry whirlwinds, in desolate darkness and difficulty, that he may step-forth at last from his stormy Scandinavia, strong as a true man, as a god: a Christian Odin, – a right Thor once more, with his thunder-hammer, to smite asunder ugly enough *Fötuns* and Giant-monsters!

Perhaps the turning incident of his life, we may fancy, was that death of his friend Alexis, by lightning, at the gate of Erfurt. Luther had struggled-up through boyhood, better and worse; displaying, in spite of all hindrances, the largest intellect, eager to learn: his father judging doubtless that he might promote himself in the world, set him upon the study of Law. This was the path to rise; Luther, with little will in it either way, had consented: he was now nineteen years of age. Alexis and he had been to see the old Luther people at Mansfeldt; were got back again near Erfurt, when a thunderstorm came on; the bolt struck Alexis, he fell dead at Luther's feet. What is this Life of ours? – gone in a moment, burnt-up like a scroll, into the blank Eternity! What are all earthly preferments, Chancellorships, Kingships? They lie shrunk together – there! The Earth has opened on them; in a moment they are not, and Eternity is. Luther, struck to the heart, determined to devote himself to God and God's service alone. In spite of all dissuasions from his father and others, he became a Monk in the Augustine Convent at Erfurt.

This was probably the first light-point in the history of Luther, his purer will now first decisively uttering itself; but, for the present, it was still as one light-point in an element all of darkness. He says he was a pious monk, *ich bin ein frommer Mönch gewesen*; faithfully, painfully struggling to work-out the truth of this high act of his; but it was to little purpose. His misery had not lessened; had rather, as it were, increased into infinitude. The drudgeries he had to do, as novice in his Convent, all sorts of slave-work, were not his grievance: the deep earnest soul of the man had fallen into all manner of black scruples, dubitations; he believed himself likely to die soon, and far worse than die. One hears with a new interest for poor Luther that, at this time, he lived in terror of the unspeakable misery; fancied that he was doomed to eternal reprobation. Was it not the humble sincere nature of the man? What was he, that he should be raised to Heaven! He that had known only misery, and mean slavery: the news was too blessed to be credible. It could not become clear to him how, by fasts, vigils, formalities and mass-work, a man's soul could be saved. He fell into the blackest wretchedness; had to wander staggering as on the verge of bottomless Despair.

It must have been a most blessed discovery, that of an old Latin Bible which he found in the Erfurt Library about this time. He had never seen the Book before. It taught him another lesson than that of fasts and vigils. A brother monk too, of pious experience, was helpful. Luther learned now that a man was saved not by singing masses, but by the infinite grace of God: a more credible hypothesis. He gradually got himself founded, as on the rock. No wonder he should venerate the Bible, which had brought this blessed help to him. He prized it as the Word of the Highest must be prized by such a man. He determined to hold by that; as through life and to death he firmly did.

This, then, is his deliverance from darkness, his final triumph over darkness, what we call his conversion; for himself the most important of all epochs. That he should now grow daily in peace and clearness; that, unfolding now the great talents and virtues implanted in him, he should rise to importance in his Convent, in his country, and be found more and more useful in all honest business of life, is a natural result. He was sent on missions by his Augustine Order, as a man of talent and fidelity fit to do their business well: the Elector of Saxony, Friedrich, named the Wise, a truly wise and just prince, had cast his eye on him as a valuable person; made him Professor in his new University of

Wittenberg, Preacher too at Wittenberg; in both which capacities, as in all duties he did, this Luther, in the peaceable sphere of common life, was gaining more and more esteem with all good men.

It was in his twenty-seventh year that he first saw Rome; being sent thither, as I said, on mission from his Convent. Pope Julius the Second, and what was going-on at Rome, must have filled the mind of Luther with amazement. He had come as to the Sacred City, throne of God's Highpriest on Earth; and he found it – what we know! Many thoughts it must have given the man; many which we have no record of, which perhaps he did not himself know how to utter. This Rome, this scene of false priests, clothed not in the beauty of holiness, but in far other vesture, is *false*: but what is it to Luther? A mean man he, how shall he reform a world? That was far from his thoughts. A humble, solitary man, why should he at all meddle with the world? It was the task of quite higher men than he. His business was to guide his own footsteps wisely through the world. Let him do his own obscure duty in it well; the rest, horrible and dismal as it looks, is in God's hand, not in his.

It is curious to reflect what might have been the issue, had Roman Popery happened to pass this Luther by; to go on in its great wasteful orbit, and not come athwart his little path, and force him to assault it! Conceivable enough that, in this case, he might have held his peace about the abuses of Rome; left Providence, and God on high, to deal with them! A modest quiet man; not prompt he to attack irreverently persons in authority. His clear task, as I say, was to do his own duty; to walk wisely in this world of confused wickedness, and save his own soul alive. But the Roman Highpriesthood did come athwart him: afar off at Wittenberg he, Luther, could not get lived in honesty for it; he remonstrated, resisted, came to extremity; was struck-at, struck again, and so it came to wager of battle between them! This is worth attending to in Luther's history. Perhaps no man of so humble, peaceable a disposition ever filled the world with contention. We cannot but see that he would have loved privacy, quiet diligence in the shade; that it was against his will he ever became a notoriety. Notoriety: what would that do for him? The goal of his march through this world was the Infinite Heaven; an indubitable goal for him: in a few years, he should either have attained that, or lost it forever! We will say nothing at all, I think, of that sorrowfulest of theories, of its being some mean shopkeeper grudge, of the Augustine Monk against the Dominican, that first kindled the wrath of Luther, and produced the Protestant Reformation. We will say to the people who maintain it, if indeed any such exist now: Get first into the sphere of thought by which it is so much as possible to judge of Luther, or of any man like Luther, otherwise than distractedly; we may then begin arguing with you.

The Monk Tetzel, sent out carelessly in the way of trade, by Leo Tenth, – who merely wanted to raise a little money, and for the rest seems to have been a Pagan rather than a Christian, so far as he was anything, – arrived at Wittenberg, and drove his scandalous trade there. Luther's flock bought Indulgences; in the confessional of his Church, people pleaded to him that they had already got their sins pardoned. Luther, if he would not be found wanting at his own post, a false sluggard and coward at the very centre of the little space of ground that was his own and no other man's, had to step-forth against Indulgences, and declare aloud that *they* were a futility and sorrowful mockery, that no man's sins could be pardoned by *them*. It was the beginning of the whole Reformation. We know how it went; forward from this first public challenge of Tetzel, on the last day of October 1517, through remonstrance and argument; – spreading ever wider, rising ever higher; till it became unquenchable, and enveloped all the world. Luther's heart's-desire was to have this grief and other griefs amended; his thought was still far other than that of introducing separation in the Church, or revolting against the Pope, Father of Christendom. – The elegant Pagan Pope cared little about this Monk and his doctrines; wished, however, to have done with the noise of him: in a space of some three years, having tried various softer methods, he thought good to end it by *fire*. He dooms the Monk's writings to be burnt by the hangman, and his body to be sent bound to Rome, – probably for a similar purpose. It was the way they had ended with Huss, with Jerome, the century before. A short argument, fire. Poor Huss: he came to that Constance Council, with all imaginable promises and safe-conducts; an earnest, not rebellious kind of man: they laid him instantly in a stone dungeon "three-feet wide, six-feet high, seven-feet long;" *burnt* the true voice of him out of this world; choked it in smoke and fire. That was *not* well done!

I, for one, pardon Luther for now altogether revolting against the Pope. The elegant Pagan, by this fire-decree of his, had kindled into noble just wrath the bravest heart then living in this world. The bravest, if also one of the humblest, peaceablest; it was now kindled. These words of mine, words of truth and soberness, aiming faithfully, as human inability would allow, to promote God's truth on Earth, and save men's souls, you, God's vicegerent on earth, answer them by the hangman and fire? You will burn me and them, for answer to the God's-message they strove to bring you? *You* are not God's vicegerent; you are another's than his, I think! I take your Bull, as an emparchmented Lie, and burn *it*. You will do what you see good next: this is what I do. – It was on the 10th of December 1520, three years after the beginning of the business, that Luther, "with a great concourse of people," took this indignant step of burning the Pope's fire-decree "at the Elster-Gate of Witten-berg." Wittenberg looked on "with shoutings;" the whole world was looking on. The Pope should not have provoked that "shout"! It was the shout of the awakening of nations. The quiet German heart, modest, patient of much, had at length got more than it could bear. Formulism, Pagan Popeism, and other Falsehood and corrupt Semblance had ruled long enough: and here once more was a man found who durst tell all men that God's-world stood not on semblances but on realities; that Life was a truth, and not a lie!

At bottom, as was said above, we are to consider Luther as a Prophet Idol-breaker; a bringer-back of men to reality. It is the function of great men and teachers. Mahomet said, These idols of yours are wood; you put wax and oil on them, the flies stick on them: they are not God, I tell you, they are black wood! Luther said to the Pope, This thing of yours that you call a Pardon of Sins, it is a bit of rag-paper with ink. It *is* nothing else; it, and so much like it, is nothing else. God alone can pardon sins. Popeship, spiritual Fatherhood of God's Church, is that a vain semblance, of cloth and parchment? It is an awful fact. God's Church is not a semblance, Heaven and Hell are not semblances. I stand on this, since you drive me to it. Standing on this, I a poor German Monk am stronger than you all. I stand solitary, friendless, but on God's Truth; you with your tiaras, triple-hats, with your treasuries and armories, thunders spiritual and temporal, stand on the Devil's Lie, and are not so strong!—

The Diet of Worms, Luther's appearance there on the 17th of April 1521, may be considered as the greatest scene in Modern European History; the point, indeed, from which the whole subsequent history of civilisation takes its rise. After multiplied negotiations, disputations, it had come to this. The young Emperor Charles Fifth, with all the Princes of Germany, Papal nuncios, dignitaries spiritual and temporal, are assembled there: Luther is to appear and answer for himself, whether he will recant or not. The world's pomp and power sits there on this hand: on that, stands-up for God's Truth, one man, the poor miner Hans Luther's Son. Friends had reminded him of Huss, advised him not to go; he would not be advised. A large company of friends rode-out to meet him, with still more earnest warnings; he answered, "Were there as many Devils in Worms as there are roof-tiles, I would on." The people, on the morrow, as he went to the Hall of the Diet, crowded the windows and housetops, some of them calling out to him, in solemn words, not to recant: "Whosoever denieth me before men I" they cried to him, – as in a kind of solemn petition and adjuration. Was it not in reality our petition too, the petition of the whole world, lying in dark bondage of soul, paralysed under a black spectral Nightmare and triple-hatted Chimera, calling itself Father in God, and what not: "Free us; it rests with thee; desert us not!"

Luther did not desert us. His speech, of two hours, distinguished itself by its respectful, wise and honest tone; submissive to whatsoever could lawfully claim submission, not submissive to any more than that. His writings, he said, were partly his own, partly derived from the Word of God. As to what was his own, human infirmity entered into it; unguarded anger, blindness, many things doubtless which it were a blessing for him could he abolish altogether. But as to what stood on sound truth and the Word of God, he could not recant it. How could he? "Confute me," he concluded, "by proofs of Scripture, or else by plain just arguments: I cannot recant otherwise.

For it is neither safe nor prudent to do aught against conscience. Here stand I; I can do no other: God assist me!" – It is, as we say, the greatest moment in the Modern History of Men. English Puritanism, England and its Parliaments, Americas, and vast work these two centuries; French Revolution, Europe and its work everywhere at present: the germ of it all lay there: had Luther in that moment done other, it had all been otherwise! The European World was asking him: Am I to sink ever lower into falsehood, stagnant putrescence, loathsome accursed death; or, with whatever paroxysm, to cast the falsehoods out of me, and be cured and live?—

RORKE'S DRIFT

F.E. Whitton

Britain's highest medal for military gallantry, the Victoria Cross, was awarded to no less than nine soldiers at Rorke's Drift, more than for any other single engagement.

The lonely little Swedish mission station, which stood on a rocky terrace on the Natal side of the Buffalo River, hardly knew itself in those early days of January 1879. It had had greatness thrust upon it. About a quarter of a mile away there was a drift, or ford, over the river, by which Zululand could be entered, known to this day as Rorke's Drift. Four columns acting from the circumference of the country were to penetrate into Zululand and make for the royal Kraal at Ulundi, and, of these columns, that known as Number 3 – with which was the commander-in-chief, Lord Chelmsford, himself – was to cross the Buffalo River and enter the enemy's country at this drift of which we have just spoken.

The actual ford was supplemented by huge ferry-boats, or ponts, of a size sufficient to carry over a large Cape waggon or a company of infantry at a time; and to protect these and also some stores that were to be collected at the spot, as well as a hospital which was to be formed there, a small garrison was to be dropped when the Centre Column entered Zululand. The little mission station lent itself admirably for the purpose of a hospital and a commissariat store, and had, therefore, been requisitioned when the Column came up from Natal early in January 1879.

A large outhouse, some eighty by twenty feet, which the Swedish missionary, the Rev. Mr Witt, had used as a church, was turned into a store for mealies and boxes of biscuits, as well as for ammunition; while the other building, the house where Mr Witt lived with his wife and three children, was converted into a hospital. The dwelling-house was sixty feet by eighteen in size, and both buildings were constructed of brick and were thatched. Behind the mission station – to the south – were steep and lofty mountains through which ran the rough road to Helpmakaar, in Natal. In front – that is to say, looking in the direction of the river – was a fine orchard, and between this and the houses, which were about thirty yards apart, ran a natural step or ledge of rock three to four feet high, so that the buildings stood that height above the ground in the orchard – or "garden" as it was usually called. Between the garden and this platform there was first the waggon-track – the word "road" is apt to convey a wrong impression – leading to the drift, and then, between this track and the rocky terrace was a strip, some twenty yards wide, of bush, which had not been cut down. On the other, or southern, side of the buildings were a cook-house and two ditches with ovens – running at right angles to each other – the bank of each being two feet high, while beyond that again were the tents of the garrison of the post. The enumeration of these details may be wearisome, but, before the African sun had swiftly set on the 22nd of January 1879, thatch and rock, cook-house and bush, were all to mean life or death to assailant or defender, to white man or to Zulu.

The actual garrison of the post consisted of "B" Company of the 2nd Battalion 24th Regiment* under Lieutenant Gonville Bromhead, and a detachment – about equal to a company – of the Natal Native Contingent under a colonial officer with the temporary rank of captain. Further, in addition to some half-dozen details, there were thirty-three N.C.O.'s and men sick in the hospital. Bromhead and the colonial captain were not, however, the only officers stationed at Rorke's Drift. A sub-altern of sappers – John Chard by name – was there in charge of the ponts. Then there was the medical officer in charge of the hospital, Surgeon Reynolds of the Army Medical Department.

* Later The South Wales Borderers.

There were also three commissariat officers – civilians in those days – and a missionary, the Rev. George Smith, who was acting as chaplain to the troops. Occasionally at the post was the staff officer in charge of this section of the line of communications, Major Spalding of the 104th Regiment, D.A.Q.M.G. As Rorke's Drift was on the Zulu border, it follows that it was at the moment the most advanced post of this line. To the south the nearest troops were two companies of the 1st Battalion of the 24th Regiment back at Helpmakaar, ten miles away.

It was a glorious day of South African summer, but although the little post was now free from the hustle and worry caused by the passage of the Column across the river some days earlier, there was yet an atmosphere of tension and of strain. At dawn there had ridden in from the Zulu side of the river a young subaltern of the 95th who was in charge of 100 ox-waggons with the Column. He had been sent back at midnight with a message from Lord Chelmsford to hurry up a column of native rein-forcements under Colonel Durnford, R.E. He told how the Column had gone into camp under the far side of a hill, nine miles away, called Isandhlwana, and that "a big fight was expected." It had been a jumpy ride back in inky darkness, along a rough track intersected by steep dongas and through country that was known to be swarming with Zulus – especially for a twenty-year-old subaltern. But this young subaltern had the heart of a lion. His name was Horace Smith-Dorrien.

Having borrowed eleven rounds of revolver ammunition from "Gonny" Bromhead, young Smith-Dorrien recrossed the river about half-past six and galloped off towards Isandhl-wana. Then, after breakfast, Chard obtained leave from Major Spalding to ride out to that place himself and ascertain if there were any fresh orders which would affect the service of the ponts of which he was in charge. Chard returned shortly before noon with the information that large bodies of Zulus had been reported working round the left of the camp at Isandhlwana, and he said that he thought it just possible they might be intending to ignore that camp and to "make a dash at the drift." This was exciting news, but no one seems to have imagined for a moment that the post could be in any real danger. After all, the Column at Isandhlwana – about 4000 strong, although more than half of these were natives, and very

unreliable natives at that – with a battery of six 7-pounders, was
only nine miles away from the drift, and Lord Chelmsford
would hardly allow the Zulus to move unmolested against his
advanced base. And if a battle then developed, who could doubt
the result? There seemed, therefore, nothing to worry about,
and it is certain that no steps of any kind were taken to place the
post in a state of defence. Indeed, the Rev. Mr Witt, the
Swedish missionary, who was still there, with the Rev. George
Smith and Surgeon Reynolds, went up to the top of a neighbouring hill "to see the fun" on the other side of the river,
which, in the extraordinary clearness of the South African
atmosphere, was quite feasible even with glasses of moderate
power.

At lunch-time, however, it seems to have been decided that a
reinforcement of the post might be desirable. A company of the
1st 24th ought to have arrived from Helpmakaar two days
before, but for some reason it had not yet reached Rorke's
Drift. Major Spalding, in supreme command of this section of
the line of communications, decided to ride back himself and
bring the belated company with him to the post. At two o'clock,
therefore, he rode off, and before leaving told Lieutenant Chard
that, during his – Spalding's – absence, he would be in command of the post. So far as the two regular subalterns were
concerned this was in order, for Chard was senior to Bromhead.
But there was also another combatant officer present, of the
Natal Native Contingent, with the rank of "Captain." As,
however, both Chard and Bromhead were regular soldiers of
more than eleven years' service apiece, and the captain had
obtained his temporary commission merely a short time before,
on the raising of the Native Contingent, Major Spalding did not
worry himself about any titular claim to command which the
colonial officer might have preferred. It was just as well.

After Major Spalding's departure Chard rode down to the
drift, where he busied himself with matters concerning the
ponts which were his special charge. All was quiet at the river,
but about 3.15 P.M. he was startled to see two mounted white
men riding hell-for-leather on the Zulu side, heading towards
the drift. In response to their shouts one of the ferry-boats was
sent across, and the horsemen proved to be an officer and
trooper of a mounted irregular corps belonging to the Column.

The officer, Lieutenant Adendorff, had a terrible tale to relate. The camp at Isandhlwana had been attacked that morning by 10,000 Zulus, and, of the white troops there in camp, only a handful had escaped. It appeared that before dawn Lord Chelmsford had gone out with half the Column to make a reconnaissance in force and to select a new camping ground. There had been left behind at Isandhlwana some 1800 officers and men, including six companies of the 24th Regiment,* and about noon the Zulus, who had been reported earlier in overwhelming strength, advanced upon the camp in the form of an immense semicircle, with the "horns" gradually closing in. The camp was in no way whatever prepared for defence. The tents were all standing. Not a waggon had been laagered; not a sod had been turned; not one stone had been placed upon another to form a breastwork. There had been, however, no question of surprise. The country was open, and for hours the Zulus had been observed by the outposts. But the outposts were too far out and too scattered, and when they were driven in upon the main body the situation became critical. The native contingent immediately broke and fled. The 7-pounders continued gallantly in action, and the companies of the 24th, as the Zulus closed upon them, met the attack with a steady and disciplined fire. Then the terrible thing had happened. The firing slackened, died away, and then ceased altogether. Ammunition had run out. Yet there had been no real lack of ammunition. There was all the reserve supply of the Column – hundreds of boxes of it.† But, when the cry for "More ammunition" was raised, the screw-drivers wherewith to open the boxes could not be found; or, if found, the boxes could not be got at, for many of them were strapped on the backs of mules which were plunging or bolting in terror. The Zulus had suffered enormous losses, but now, encouraged by the cessation of the rifle fire, they had rushed within assegai range, and what followed had been a massacre. Standing in groups, often back to back, the officers and men of the 24th, as well as the few white irregulars, had been killed almost to a man. A few white men, provided with horses, at the last moment dashed after the fleeing natives, but

---

* 5 companies 1st Battalion; 1 company 2nd Battalion.

† 400,000 rounds. It was packed in the regulation wooden boxes, the lid of each box being fastened by nine screws.

the horns of the Zulu *impi* had closed. As to what had happened to the detachment which had gone out with Lord Chelmsford it was impossible to say. By half-past one all was over at Isandhlwana. No sign whatever had been seen of Lord Chelmsford or of his force. Meanwhile thousands of Zulus were advancing rapidly towards Rorke's Drift.

Chard had been little over an hour in command at Rorke's Drift. Well might he have been dismayed by this terrible news, and any suspicion that the tidings had been exaggerated was discounted by the receipt of a note from Bromhead to say that a mounted infantryman had just come in with an urgent message, and to beg Chard to come up at once and take command. Chard instantly gave orders to pack up such stores as were at the drift and to bring them up to the post in the waggon. Of the two men who had crossed the river the trooper was sent off with the news to Helpmakaar, while the officer pluckily asked to be allowed to stay and help in the defence of the post.

Chard then galloped up to the post, where he found Bromhead feverishly engaged in loopholing the commissariat store and the hospital, and in connecting the two buildings by walls of mealie-bags supplemented by two waggons that were in the camp. Bromhead gave Chard the note – brought in by the mounted infantryman – in which it was stated that Zulus were advancing in force against Rorke's Drift and that the post there was to be strengthened and held at all costs. But in all orders it may happen that circumstances may have completely changed since the order was issued. The instructions to strengthen and hold the post at Rorke's Drift had been given before the force at Isandhlwana was attacked, and when it was even believed that the Zulus might pass by that place in their eagerness – as Chard himself had surmised – "to have a dash at the drift." It was one thing to hold on to Rorke's Drift when the whole of Number 3 Column was in being and but a few hours' march away: it was quite another to try and hold it with a mere handful of men now that half that Column had been massacred and the other half might well have been massacred too. Besides, since the note had been written, the strength of the Zulus had been enormously increased. It was known, at the outbreak of hostilities, that a proportion of them possessed rifles and guns, but now their complete victory at Isandhlwana had yielded them at least fifteen hundred more firearms and a practically unlimited supply of ammunition. In circumstances so startlingly altered prudence might well have recommended a short withdrawal from Rorke's Drift to some suitable defensive position in rear, where, at any rate, a good field of fire might be obtained, and where union with the company coming up from Helpmakaar might more certainly be effected.

But there was another point to be considered. If the detachment which had gone out under Lord Chelmsford from the camp at Isandhlwana could manage to fight its way back, then it was imperative that the stores at Rorke's Drift should be preserved. For, by the disaster, all the transport, all the supplies and all the reserve ammunition of the Column had been lost, and at that very moment the detachment might be fighting its way towards the river, short of ammunition and in desperate need of food. To fall back to a defensive position in rear, although it might mean the safety of the garrison, would infallibly mean that the stores would immediately fall into Zulu hands.

At all cost, therefore, even though the circumstances had since morning so dramatically changed, it was imperative to defend the post. Chard held a hurried consultation with Bromhead and with Mr Dalton of the commissariat, who was doing splendid work. It was decided that it was useless to try to hold the drift as well as the post. The two were more than a quarter of a mile apart; and, besides, there were other fords in the vicinity which would certainly be known to the advancing Zulus. Every man, therefore, must be concentrated at, or immediately round, the post itself. Chard accordingly galloped down again to the drift to hurry up the guard there of one sergeant and six men. On his arrival, the sergeant and the ferryman – a civilian – instantly volunteered to moor the ponts in the centre of the river and with a few men to defend the crossing with these improvised monitors. But Chard did not feel warranted in accepting an offer which would have meant a terrible risk to the men concerned, though he was cheered by the spirit in which it was made, and felt that it augured well for the fight which must now be at hand.

Back again to the post galloped Chard. He was not letting the grass grow under his feet, for little more than a quarter of an hour had elapsed since he had seen the two horsemen galloping to the drift with the news of the terrible disaster at Isandhlwana. It was now exactly half-past three, and shortly afterwards what seemed to be a welcome reinforcement arrived. This was an officer with about a hundred native horsemen of Durnford's force who had escaped from the massacre. The officer asked Chard for orders, and was requested to send a detachment to observe the drifts and ponts, to throw out outposts in the direction of the enemy and to check his advance as much as possible; when forced to retire, the natives were to fall back on the post and to assist in its defence. Meanwhile the work of putting the place in a state of defence was proceeding with great activity. The tents had already been struck. The windows and doors of the hospital were blocked up with mattresses and tables, and loopholes were constructed in the walls of both this building and the storehouse. The wall of mealie-bags was raised to a height of four feet, and continued so that a large rectangle was formed of which the ends were filled by the hospital and store respectively. Of the sick in hospital many were able to turn out to play their part in the defence; an attempt was made to remove the serious cases to some place of safety, but when the two ox-waggons were brought up news had come in that the Zulus had been sighted. So the two waggons were incorporated in the southern wall of mealies joining the hospital and the store. The water-cart in the meantime had been hastily filled and brought within the enclosure.

Every man was ordered to his post, and events now moved quickly. The Swedish missionary and his companions returned with the news that large numbers of Zulus had crossed the river by a drift about a mile away and were moving so as to take the post in reverse. In five minutes they would probably be close at hand. Mr Witt then rode off to try to reach his wife and family, who had been sent back to a farm when the mission station had been taken over by the military.

About a quarter past four the sound of firing was heard behind the hills to the south, and just then the officer of Durnford's horsemen galloped in reporting the enemy close at hand, but reporting also that his men would not stand and were making off towards Helpmakaar. Chard looked in the direction in which the officer pointed, and there they were, about a hundred of them, galloping from the field. The sight was too much for the detachment of the Natal Native Contingent at the post. They, too, made off, and their officer, mounting his horse, galloped away likewise. By this defection the total number within the post was now reduced to, all told, 8 officers and 131 other ranks, of which latter number 33 were hospital patients. Of the figure 131 other ranks the 24th Regiment accounted for 110. Save for four or five natives in the hospital the defence of the post was now entirely in the keeping of white men.

Although possibly Chard and Bromhead were well rid of the fainthearts, it was now only too clear that the line of defence was too extended for the small number of men who remained. Chard, however, was equal to the emergency. There were wooden boxes full of biscuit in the store, and with these a retrenchment was at once begun connecting the two parallel walls of mealie-bags at the storehouse end of the enclosure, so that what was virtually an inner work might be thus provided. Feverishly every man that could be spared worked at the task, but, before the wall was two boxes high, a murmur of "Here they come," from the southern wall of mealie-bags, sent every man hurrying to his allotted post.

Pouring over the right shoulder of the hill behind the mission station there appeared a dense mass of five to six hundred Zulus. On they came at the run, deploying as they advanced, making straight for the southern wall of mealie-bags which filled the gap between the storehouse and the hospital. The attack was met with a steady and well-sustained fire; but although the old 577 Martini-Henry was a real man-stopper, and although Zulu after Zulu was knocked over, the survivors with rare courage got to within fifty yards of the wall. Here, however, they came under a terrible cross fire from the wall of mealie-bags and the loopholes of the storehouse, and the onrush was definitely stayed. Some of the Zulus at once took cover behind the cookhouse and in the trenches where the field ovens were situated, and from this cover kept up a harassing fire. The bulk, however, swerved to their left, and, passing round the hospital, made a desperate attempt to rush the mealie-bags at the north-west corner of the enclosure. But the attempt was repulsed, and the baffled Zulus, now edging eastwards, found cover in the piece of bush and below the rocky terrace on which the northern breastwork of mealie-bags had been erected.

The post was, therefore, threatened from both front and rear. But this was not the worst. The Zulus hitherto engaged were but the advanced guard. Thousands more could be made out lining a ledge of rocks and some caves overlooking the post four hundred yards to the southward. This main body for some minutes kept up a brisk fire which seriously inconvenienced the defenders of the post. Mr Dalton, one of the commissariat officers, who had done splendid work in preparing the defences and had been continually moving along the breastwork encouraging the men, was now wounded. Unable to use his rifle any longer – though he continued to direct the fire of the men near him – he handed it to his storekeeper, Byrne, who, however, was almost immediately shot dead.

Meanwhile many of the main body of the Zulus had rushed forward from the rocks and caves behind, and, bearing well to the left, had passed the hospital, where they changed direction to the right, with the result that the northern face of the post was now in great peril. The garden on the farther side of the waggon track was soon occupied by a large body, and, taking advantage of some cover from view there afforded, the Zulus prepared to storm the northern breastwork. With a wild rush they crossed the track and the belt of bush, and, scrambling up the rocky terrace, actually held one side of the breastwork while the men of the 24th held the other. Maddened with desire to kill the white men, the Zulus made several desperate attempts to swarm over the parapet, but every attempt was splendidly met and repulsed with the bayonet. Many Zulus actually grasped the bayonets of the defenders, and in two instances wrenched them from the rifles, but they were instantly shot down. One Zulu standing on the parapet fired at Corporal Schiess, of the Natal Native Contingent, the charge blowing the corporal's hat off. Schiess instantly jumped on to the parapet, bayoneted the Zulu, regained his place, bayoneted another, and then climbed once more upon the sacks and bayoneted a third. The corporal was nominally a hospital patient, and, in addition, had been seriously wounded in the foot some time earlier in the engagement.

But the steadfast courage of the thin line of heaving, thrusting, sweating soldiers of the 24th who held that northern wall of mealie-bags could but delay the inevitable. A hand-to-hand fight in which the white men were enormously outnumbered could have but one end, and it was only a question of time before the corn-sacks would be torn from the breastwork and a wave of Zulus with their stabbing assegais would surge in among the defenders. Nor was this all. In addition to the hand-to-hand combat in front, the defenders were still being fired upon heavily from the rocks and caves four hundred yards in rear. Although that fire had at first been wild and ill-directed it had now become much more serious, and within a few minutes five of the defenders had been killed by bullets from the rear. The company from Helpmakaar could not be expected for some hours, and it was most unlikely that it could force its way through the thousands of Zulus between it and the drift.

In these circumstances Lieutenant Chard gave the order for all the men who were holding the ramparts of mealie-bags to retire behind the entrenchment of biscuit boxes at the eastern end of the enclosure. But now the grave drawback of the position became at once apparent. The hospital at the other end was isolated. The post now resembled a sailing ship attacked by pirates' boats, the majority of the crew driven from the waist of the vessel to the poop, leaving the forecastle and its defenders completely cut off. The hospital building was now the forecastle; but the position was really worse than this; for in a forecastle the door would have opened on to the main-deck, whereas from the hospital there was no egress on that side save by a small window high above the ground.

All this time the Zulus had been trying desperately to set fire to the thatched roof of the hospital, and scores of them leaped over the walls of mealie-bags in their eagerness to get to the inner side of the building. Scores of them were mown down by volleys at a few yards' range from the rampart of biscuit boxes, but others took their place, yelling out their war-cry of *Usutu! Usutu!* Foiled in their attempt to fire the roof from the enclosure the Zulus redoubled their efforts at the farther end, where at any rate they were not exposed to those terrible volleys from the retrenchment. Soon they succeeded in their work, and, to the horror of the defenders of the eastern end of the post, a cloud of smoke rose from the hospital roof.

There were gallant deeds done at Rorke's Drift that day. But for courage and devotion to duty nothing can exceed the conduct of the half-dozen privates of the 24th Regiment left as the garrison of the doomed building. No officer, no non-commissioned officer, was there to command and encourage them. The roof of the building was in flames; the place was filled with smoke; within it were at least a dozen patients too ill or too seriously incapacitated to take their place in the fight; the building with its separate and improvised wards was most unsuited for defence. In one of the farther rooms two privates and a couple of patients held the door for more than an hour until their ammunition was expended, and then continued to guard the portal with their bayonets. With a fierce rush a band of Zulus at length forced an entrance, and Private Joseph Williams was seized by them, dragged outside and butchered before the eyes of his three companions. The surviving private and the two patients were now cut off in the farthest room of the hospital, but, while the Zulus were busy dispatching their victim, the white men succeeded in making a hole in the partition with an axe and escaping into another room. Here they were joined by another private of the 24th, Henry Hooke by name; and he and John Williams, one keeping off the Zulus with a bayonet and the other smashing holes into the adjoining room, relieved each other every few minutes. One patient ventured through one of the openings thus cut, but was immediately seized by Zulus and dragged away; the others, however, managed to scramble through the little window overlooking the enclosure, and, running the gauntlet of the enemy's fire, most of them got safely within the retrenchment.

In another ward two privates of the 24th defended their post until six out of seven of the patients had been removed. The seventh was a sergeant who was ill with fever and delirious. One of the privates went back to try to carry him out, but the room was now full of Zulus and the sergeant had been killed. The last patients to escape were the more serious cases, and these had great difficulty in climbing up to the little window. Once through, they had to fall to the ground, and, being unable to walk, had to crawl to the retrenchment under the Zulu fire. A few patients dashed out upon the verandah on the north side of the hospital and endeavoured to cross the whole length of the enclosure to gain the retrenchment, but two or three were assegaied in the attempt.

From behind their low rampart of biscuit boxes but thirty yards away the defenders of the retrenchment had witnessed with heartfelt sorrow the tragedy enacted under their eyes. But their own position was also one of the utmost peril. Flushed with their success at the hospital end, the Zulus were straining every nerve to fire the thatch of the storehouse roof. Chard's inventive mind was again equal to the emergency. There were in the retrenchment two large piles of mealie sacks, and by his orders these were hurriedly formed, under heavy fire, into an oblong and lofty redoubt from which a second and elevated tier of fire was obtained, and within which the wounded were dragged for safety. So long as daylight lasted the redoubt immensely strengthened the defence; but in South Africa darkness comes swiftly, and soon the retrenchment and storehouse were completely surrounded. Several times the Zulus attempted to rush the position, and although every attempt was most gallantly repulsed, the defenders were forced back into the kraal at the eastern end of the retrenchment.

The Zulus were now to pay for their successful effort of firing the hospital roof. The burning thatch flared up, illuminating the scene for hundreds of yards around, and the light thus given was of priceless service to the defenders. At about 10 P.M., however, the fire had burnt itself out, and in the darkness that ensued the Zulu attacks were again renewed. But the indomitable and steadfast courage of the 24th never failed. The men behaved with the greatest coolness. Not a single shot was wasted, and there was always the bayonet to do the work when the Zulus tried to force their way over the low perimeter of the kraal.

It was not until midnight that the rushes and heavy fire of the Zulus began to slacken. But there was little rest for the defenders, now exhausted by eight hours' ceaseless fighting; for until nearly dawn a desultory fire was kept up from the caves and rocky ledge in rear, and from the bush and garden in front. At last, however, some respite came, and about 4 A.M., for the first time in twelve hours, the firing died away.

Shortly afterwards the first streak of dawn appeared and the little garrison was heartened by the sight of dead Zulus piled up in heaps round the walls of mealie-bags and especially in front of the hospital; and cheered still more by the sight of the enemy retiring round the shoulder of the hill from which they had approached on the previous afternoon. Chard and Bromhead decided to send out some patrols to search the immediate vicinity of the post. These soon returned with about one hundred rifles and guns and some four hundred assegais left by the enemy on the field.

Meanwhile those left within the post were strengthening the defences of the place. But while the thatch was being removed from the storehouse roof a large body of Zulus suddenly appeared again on the hills to the south-west. The work upon the defences was instantly stopped and every man was ordered to his post. Chard scribbled a hasty note to Major Spalding begging him to bring help without a moment's delay, and this he sent off by a friendly Kaffir who had taken refuge in the post at dawn. The Zulus came on in the same formation and with the same determination as before, and the garrison steeled itself for another contest against the same desperate odds. Suddenly, however, there was a check in the enemy's advance. The Zulu line seemed to waver; and then, slowly retiring, it disappeared behind the shoulder of the hill whence it had emerged.

We must go back to the previous morning and transport ourselves to the camp of No. 3 Column at Isandhlwana, nine miles across the river. Before dawn Lord Chelmsford had taken half the Column with him as a reconnaissance in force and to select a further camping ground. Some brisk skirmishing with bodies of Zulus had taken place in the forenoon, and, while thus engaged, Lord Chelmsford had received more than one message to say that the camp at Isandhlwana was in imminent danger of attack by large enemy forces. These messages had been treated as merely alarmist; and when Lord Chelmsford – galloping to a hill-top – had seen with his glasses the tents at Isandhlwana still standing and men in red uniform moving about he had been completely reassured. Finally, however, messages of such grave import had been received that Lord Chelmsford had decided to march his force back to Isandhlwana, and, while *en route*, the terrible truth had been revealed. An officer was met who had ridden back to Isandhlwana to make some arrangements about rations for his men; while riding unconscious of danger into the camp, with its "men moving about in red coats," he had been fired on; and almost too late had discovered that the redcoats were Zulus dressed in the tunics of the 24th.*

It was pitch dark when Lord Chelmsford's force stumbled into the deserted camp. The silence of the tomb reigned everywhere. Patrols moving cautiously about came upon grisly evidence of disaster. Overturned waggons, looted stores and piles of mutilated corpses told their tale. There was nothing that could possibly be done but hold on for the night and make for Rorke's Drift at dawn. As the dispirited Column wended its way to the river in the early hours of the 23rd a large force of Zulus was seen to the north about a mile away moving in the opposite direction. Each column silently held its course. The Zulus – they were those who had been attacking the drift and had seen the approach of Lord Chelmsford's force – had learnt that every fight was not to be an Isandhlwana. In Lord Chelmsford's force the men were exhausted with the marching and fighting of the last twenty-four hours; they were without food; all the reserve ammunition had been lost; and the men had but fifty rounds apiece. And so, right arm to right arm, the two columns, Zulu and British, like ships that pass in the night, held each upon its way.

As the British force topped a rise a pillar of smoke could be seen rising from the drift. Too late! The news was whispered down the Column and the men plodded dejectedly on, their hearts sinking at the thought of another charnel-house they were soon to find. Suddenly there is excitement at the head of the Column, and there is hurried talk among the men that figures have been described on the roof of one of the buildings at the drift, vigorously waving to the Column. A fierce roar of cheering bursts from the throats of those tired, hungry and exhausted men. A section of mounted infantry gallops down to the drift, crosses the river, and in a few moments is among the survivors of as gallant a defence as the annals of the British Army have ever known.

*   *   *

* At Isandhlwana were 21 officers and 581 other ranks of the 24th. All the officers and 578 other ranks were killed.

Of the 139 officers and other ranks engaged, 15 were killed and 12 wounded, two of the latter dying later of their hurts. The attacking Zulu force consisted of two regiments – the Undi and Udkloko – in all a total of nearly four thousand warriors. Of these, 371 lay dead around the little post at Rorke's Drift.

SPREADING THE WORD

John Wesley

Wesley was the founder of Methodism, an evangelical offshoot of the Anglican Church. To spread the new word, Wesley spent 51 years preaching, in the process walking upwards of 250,000 miles. On much of his life's journey, he met with abuse, ridicule and physical assault.

*F*riday, March 19, 1742. I rode once more to Pensford, at the earnest request of several serious people. The place where they desired me to preach was a little green spot near the town. But I had no sooner begun, than a great company of rabble, hired (as we afterwards found) for that purpose, came furiously upon us, bringing a bull which they had been baiting and now drove in among the people. But the beast was wiser than his drivers, and continually ran either on one side of us or the other, while we quietly sang praise to God and prayer for about an hour. The poor wretches finding themselves disappointed, at length seized upon the bull, now weak and tired after being so long torn and beaten both by dogs and men, and by main strength partly dragged and partly thrust him in among the people. When they had forced their way to the little table on which I stood, they strove several times to throw it down by thrusting the helpless beast against it, who of himself stirred no more than a log of wood. I once or twice put aside his head with my hand, that the blood might not drop upon my clothes, intending to go on as soon as the hurry should be a little over. But the table falling down, some of our friends caught me in their arms and carried me right away on their shoulders, while the rabble wreaked their vengeance on the table which they tore bit from bit. We went a little way off, where I finished my discourse without any noise or interruption.

Wednesday, October 18, 1749. I rode, at the desire of John Bennet, to Rochdale, in Lancashire. As soon as ever we entered the town, we found the streets lined on both sides with multitudes of people, shouting, cursing, blaspheming and gnashing upon us with their teeth. Perceiving it would not be practicable to preach abroad, I went into a large room, open to the street and called aloud "Let the wicked forsake his way, and the unrighteous man his thoughts." . . . None opposed or interrupted; and there was a very remarkable change in the behaviour of the people as we afterwards went through the town.

We came to Bolton about five in the evening. We had no sooner entered the main street than we perceived the lions at Rochdale were lambs in comparison of those at Bolton. Such rage and bitterness I scarce ever saw before in any creatures that bore the form of men. They followed us in full cry to the house where we went and, as soon as we were gone in, took possession of all the avenues to it, and filled the street from one end to the other . . . When the first stone came among us through the window, I expected a shower to follow, and the rather because they had now procured a bell to call their whole forces together; but they did not design to carry on the attack at a distance. Presently one ran up and told us the mob had bursted into the house; he added that they had got J[ohn] B[ennet] in the midst of them. They had; and he laid hold on the opportunity to tell them of "the terrors of the Lord".

Meantime D[avid] T[aylor] engaged another part of them with smoother and softer words. Believing the time was now come, I walked down into the thickest of them. They had now filled all the rooms below. I called for a chair. The winds were hushed and all was calm and still. My heart was filled with love, my eyes with tears, and my mouth with arguments. They were ashamed that they were melted down, they devoured every word.

THE HEROES OF EYAM

Paul Chadburn

This half-forgotten epic from the England of 1665 reminds us that heroism can be the prerogative of a whole civilian community. It also reminds us that courage is strengthened by conviction. In 1665 the villagers of Eyam in Derbyshire were visited by the bubonic plague. Rather than fleeing (and so probably spreading the plague) they chose another way.

August, 1665, and in the Derbyshire Peak village of Eyam great merrymaking. For it is the day of the wake, combined church and harvest festival. More than usual gaiety and more people from neighbouring villages and hamlets than in previous years. The times are prosperous. Below ground, the lead mines on which the community lives are being busily exploited; above ground, rich pastures are ripening to harvest. The little village, nestling in a fold half-way up the hills, is all jollification, young people dancing on the green, old folks sitting outside the inns, children – and the families are large in these days – laughing, chattering, whipping their tops and bowling their hoops along the streets.

There is George Vicars, the tailor, young enough yet to enjoy a fling with his landlady, the widow Cooper. Here, sitting over his ale, is farmer Mortins, his greyhound curled at his feet; here, too, is Merril, come from lonely Hollin's House, his residence, to enjoy the life and company. The widow Kempe has walked over from Shepherds Flats. Her young family and the Mortins's children are playing together. From the neighbouring village of

Riley have come the numerous members of the Hancock and the Talbot families. With the three hundred and fifty inhabitants of Eyam intermingle their relatives, sweethearts, friends from all the district round.

Here it is at this annual wake that romances start, to be consummated, if all goes well, the year succeeding at the altar of Eyam church.

One of these romances is even now beginning; the housewives comment complacently upon it, as well they may – for it brings together two of the most handsome young people in the neighbourhood, the beautiful Emmot Sydall and Master Rowland, of Middleton Dale, a mile south-east of Eyam.

One other, especially, is noticeable in that gay gathering. Remarkable, as he paces among the gay throng, for two things – his great size and his coarse, boisterous ways. It is the village Samson, Marshall Howe. His son is with him, hardly less powerfully built than he. They are inseparable.

Standing rather aloof, watching the country dances, is the man who has the spiritual charge of Eyam, William Mompesson, the rector, a frail-looking man of middle height, with a sensitive, scholarly face. He has been little more than a year in this parish. Only twenty-seven, not long from Oxford, and with the memories still vivid in his mind of a chaplaincy with Sir George Savile and of the fashionable world his patron moved amongst, he looks on these simple villagers with a touch of urbane scorn for rustic manners. There is something faintly condescending, faintly bored in his expression, as if to say: "What have I, ambitious and intelligent, to do with this backward community, lost to the world, obscure below a lonely peak?"

But, looking at his companion, the expression vanishes from Mompesson's face; for by his side, her arm linked through his, is a woman not only exceptionally beautiful, but with such gentleness in her face and such a charm and grace of manner as are seldom combined in one person. It is his wife, Catherine. A little girl of three and her brother, one year older, stand shyly attached to their mother's skirts, awed by the rough gambols of their village contemporaries, at the same time itching to join in with them.

One other man of marked breeding looks on. He, too, wears

the sober clothing of a minister. It is Thomas Stanley, the dissenting clergyman, once rector of Eyam, who has stayed on here, an outcast of the Oath of Conformity he would not take.

Such was the scene in Eyam in August of the year 1665, in a village isolated from urban life to an extent scarcely imaginable by modern minds. Twenty years of civil war, Scottish invasion, revolution, retribution; twenty years of tumult, change violence, of persecution, poverty and fear: years of catastrophe that had shaken London to its foundations, had left the village outposts high and dry, untouched, unmoved, unchanged. The Restoration, five years ago, had sometimes brought new vicars there, and that was all.

So with the crowning horror that had smitten Londoners the year before, the terrible visitation of bubonic plague. True, this had spread into the South and Midlands, all over the east coast, southwards into Surrey, Kent, but Eyam was a hundred and fifty miles northwards. Eyam was safe.

Yet even then, at that village wake, death – death in its most horrible apparel – the putrid, blackened, token-flecked plague corpse, was treading invisible its horrible counter-dance to the harvest hays. Of all these people there assembled to celebrate the festivities of life and fruition, a half were already marked for sudden, tortured destruction.

A few days afterwards, a servant of George Vicars, the tailor, opened a parcel that had arrived addressed to his master. It contained wares of the trade – various cloths. They had come from London. On taking them out, the servant found they were damp. So he put them to dry before the kitchen range. The steam rose from them as they hung before the fire. And with that steam, death. Death, latent in the cloth, exhaled, warmed to frightful virulence, reared and struck. The servant died in a few hours, marked all over his body with the ringed deathprick of the plague, the fatal "tokens"; every internal organ of his body distorted by poison.

But the first Eyam death was merciful compared with what was to come. This victim died swiftly. He died only once. Many of his followers underground – some into the tomb, more into the pits when death had outpaced the sexton – died a thousand times, in children, relatives and friends; when these were gone, in fears.

That month five other parishioners died. The plague had come to Eyam. Immediately this was known there happened on a small scale what, on a scale that has besmirched history, had already occurred in London. The wealthier inhabitants of Eyam fled. The two clergymen stayed: Mompesson, the new rector; Stanley, the old one.

The situation that was to develop in Eyam, an epical situation, contained a peculiar dramatic element. It had been noticeable in London, during the plague of the previous year, that proportionately more dissenting ministers than orthodox ones had stayed in the infected city, coming out into the open and appropriating pulpits craven conforming clergymen had vacated. These men had taken the opportunity to prove their faith. Mompesson, in Eyam, was on his mettle, for Stanley, the Nonconformist, was there to shame him if he flinched.

Mompesson stood up to the challenge, and if more is known of his heroic ministrations than of those of his colleague, this is because Mompesson was orthodox and orthodoxy was in sore need of heroes in those plague times.

Eyam's rector was married. At the outbreak of the plague, his wife implored him to leave the parish. There were the two little children to be considered. Mompesson refused to go. "You leave with the children," he replied, "but it is my duty to stay in Eyam." His wife was worthy of him. The two little ones were sent away to safety, but Catherine Mompesson stayed at her husband's side.

From the kitchen of the tailor's house, where it had diffused through the room, the plague virus floated, hovered and fell upon the village of Eyam; it sent its invisible tendrils creeping this way and that; it buried into and impregnated the soil. Silently it struck household after household. The next month, October, the number of victims quadrupled – twenty-three deaths from plague were marked in the parish register. Where one of the family was taken, the rest generally followed. There was no combating it; for Eyam was without a doctor, without science. Concoctions were brewed of roots of herbs, simples of all kinds; talismans were worn. All useless. There seemed only one thing to do – to fly and scatter over the countryside, for each family to fend for itself, to stay with relatives in neighbouring villages, or at lodgings taken in the towns. They prepared to make off and leave Eyam a desolate, poisoned village.

That was the resolution of the flock; but it was not the will of the two pastors. Whether they first acted separately or in concert, by which the decision was first made, we do not know. It does not greatly matter. What does matter is, both came to realize that for many of the villagers there could now be no escape, for they must be smitten without knowing it. They would succumb after they had left Eyam, but, what was even more dreadful, they would communicate the plague wherever they went, spreading death about a district that, save for the village or doom, was free of it. There were about three hundred and fifty dwellers in that village; but who could estimate how many thousands they might infect outside it?

It was then that the young rector, he who had been slightly scornful of his parish before, who had stood aloof, conscious of a barrier dividing his cultured and fastidious mind from the unlettered stock of the Peak, it was then Mompesson found himself and his mission. At the same time that he saw the duty binding him, the rector, to his parishioners, he clearly understood the grim duty that bound the inhabitants to their village.

The task before the ministers now was to persuade the terrified people to remain in their doomed village. They appealed to the honour of the parishioners, to the duty they owed humanity, to the dignity inherent in man by which he will suffer martyrdom for a worthy cause. How would they be accountable to God, who worked His designs in terrible ways for inscrutable purposes, if, knowing the certain effect of flight, they yet persisted in this destructive urge?

How many impassioned exhortations were needed to convince the people records do not tell. But that one or both of the ministers must have been inspired with more than ordinary eloquence to overcome impulses than which there are no stronger – love of life, fear of lurking death in confined spaces – is certain. Much may have been effected by the appeal to individual choice. In London the same method of confining the sick and sound together had been officially enforced. A household with one stricken member was locked there in the poisoned dwelling until forty days had elapsed without fresh infection. Guards were below the windows, fires were burning in the street, and on the blighted doors the red plague cross and the legend: "Lord have mercy upon us!"

Because, in London, there had been no question of voluntary sacrifice, the people had not submitted. They had cheated the authorities and made their escapes in divers ways – some not notifying plague in their house, leaving the doomed inmates to die and themselves carrying the virus far and wide; some breaking and burrowing out like nailed-in rats.

There had been no persuading the London poor to their death – only dragooning them to it, and that with results more direful to the populace by far than properly organized segregation of suspects would have been.

The inhabitants of Eyam were free to choose. If, in the light of modern science, the alternatives put before them – likely annihilation of the few of Eyam or certain death among the many of Derbyshire – were not exhaustive and exclusive of other possibilities, the lesson of Eyam remains, and the eternal truth – that men will sacrifice themselves, nay, their wives and their families, for a cause they believe to be good; forced, they will succumb to all the instincts of the animal.

The villagers of Eyam remained. Of its own free will the community resolved to isolate itself. A boundary was drawn half a mile round Eyam, a line marked out by various landmarks – rocks, brooks, coppices and the like. Beyond this, no Eyam inhabitant was to go – none ever did go. Within this bourne, from outside, any "foreigner" came at his risk. It was indeed the bourne from which few travellers, very few, could hope to return.

There commenced the historic siege of Eyam – strange, inverted siege, where the enemy must at all costs be kept, not out, but *in*. From outside, relief did come – by Mompesson's arrangement with the Earl of Devonshire, living nearby at Chatsworth, stores were sent out and left beside the boundary line – inside there was no respite from the silent enemy. The hopes that winter's onset would furnish an ally in biting and purifying cold were dashed by the December toll. After November's sudden drop in plague mortality – a drop from twenty-three deaths to seven – the Christmas month showed the dread foe resurgent – nine deaths. By then, altogether, forty-five plague-stricken villagers had been put in the church-

yard, their tombs a melancholy prognostic for awed parishioners filing to Christmas service. How many more of them, they
must have asked themselves, would lie underground when
summer's return touched the branches of the churchyard limes
into verdant life?

The villagers, men, women, children, puffed pipes interminably, inhaling with the smoke a faint hope that tobacco would
keep the virus at bay. They took copious draughts of herb tea.
Some fled the village and, still inside the half-mile radius, built
themselves huts and lived in isolation from their fellows. Vain
measure, for the plague was in the very earth, seething up as the
warm sun struck upon it.

There was nothing to do but wait, wait and pray. Little
distraction from dread was afforded by tending the sick, for
these for the most part died quickly. The most that could be
done for many was closing their eyes. The plague often left its
victims staring horribly.

The street of the village in plague time was like a vista deep in
Dante's hells; re-echoing with raging cries of the agonized
victims or sounding with the wailings of mothers bereaved.
Corpses – coffins there was no time to make – were daily
trundled away. Sometimes you would hear a sudden commotion in a house as of a violent struggle, then doors would slam
and there would issue into the street, half-clothed, or naked
even, a victim driven mad by the racking headpains of the
plague, dashing his skull against walls, falling stupefied beside
the way.

Or a man, a moment before perfectly active, would suddenly
become comatose and, sitting on a doorstep, fall into the
dreaded sleep, prelude to plague death.

You would see mothers darting into the street to drag off a
child from its playmates, vainly hoping to snatch it away from a
contamination that was everywhere. One villager, talking to
another, might be the first to see that his friend was stricken,
notice a bubonic swelling behind the ear, or the "token" on his
cheek. Stare and convey the sentence in his face.

So passed the winter in Eyam, month after month adding to
the plague mortality – forty-five, fifty, fifty-eight, sixty-four,
seventy-three, seventy-seven. And now June had come: a leafy,
lovers' month that the poor people of Eyam dreaded more than

all the winter ones together. The finer the weather the fiercer the plague.

There were nineteen deaths in June. By now there was no more burying in the churchyard, and in the church no services for the quick or the dead. Lest proximity in worship should spread contagion, the congregation left their consecrated building for the open air. Services were held in a grassy dell under the vaulting of the sky, the worshippers scattered apart from one another, the preacher, for his pulpit, standing in the natural arch of a rock, known to this day as Cucklett Church. There Mompesson, frail and resolute amidst the June riot of unheeding nature, instilled hope and courage into the sad hearts of the people. Perhaps never before, never since, has there been a congregation who, together, singly, so needed consolation. There cannot have been one worshipper there who had not during the last half-year lost friends, relations, or family. For in that little village community the greater part was inter-related and each was well known to all.

London held Hell's Carnival amidst the plague-eroded structures of religion and morality. Eyam was upstayed by its two preachers. The fierce passions and warped instincts, the gossip and slander, brutality and lust and greed that are often so highly concentrated in village communities were supplanted in Eyam – and many villagers must have thought divinely punished there – by the far more dreadful ravages of the plague.

If they had not had this religious conviction, those doomed villagers could never have been induced to immure themselves in a village that was to all intents and purposes a plague-house.

One character there was, though, whose coarse, nervous fibre was as resistant to the horror as his iron constitution had been to the thong itself of the plague. This was that village Samson mentioned before, boisterous, devil-may-care Marshall Howe. He was the man who now undertook the grim work of bearing off the plague victims and heaving them into the pits. He had no fear of infection, first because he had no fear of anything, and second, because he had himself been one of the first the plague had attacked and believed, erroneously, that this made him immune. He would enter the house of death, carry off the victim, joke and guffaw as he passed along the street with his ghastly burden, and, when he returned – perhaps for more – to scare those who needed no scaring, he recounted how he saw Old Nick grinning on the ivied rock as he returned from burying this or that villager in the dell. He boasted how, with his wages – the household relics of the dead he buried – he had "pinners and napkins enough to kindle his pipe with while he lived." Long afterwards this man was a legend in Eyam, and mothers bothered by fractious children would threaten them with Marshall Howe as with a bogy man.

But to Marshall Howe came a saddening and a sobering blow. For one day, on returning home from his macabre business, he found his only son, inheritor of Howe's huge frame and iron constitution, at grips with the invisible enemy. Despite all the father's care, despite his magnificent physique, the son succumbed. From the time when the gigantic corpse-carrier buried his own son in the pits, that last ministration was performed by Marshall Howe with proper awe.

Still the deaths from plague rose as the summer advanced – July fifty-six deaths, August seventy-seven. The plague was at its height. One year had passed since the ironic festivities at Eyam.

What had become now of that ardent couple who had danced together on the green, Emmot Sydall and her lover Rowland? A tragedy that still lingers in legend had separated them. After the outbreak of the plague, Rowland, who lived a mile away from Eyam, had constantly visited his betrothed and her family, her father, mother and four young sisters. The two planned to marry at next year's wake, hoping with desperate hope that the pestilent cloud would then have lifted from Eyam. Then came June and the terrible increase in plague mortality; then came the action of Stanley and Mompesson, encircling the village with a half-mile radius, cutting it off from the outside world. The boundary line passed between Middleton Dale, where Rowland lived, and the cottage home of Emmot Sydall. The lovers could not meet. Rowland, so legend relates, used to climb to a height that overlooked the forbidden plague village. There he would scan the street for a far sight of his Emmot. He did not see her. It was many months before he trod the familiar path to the Sydalls' cottage again; the plague had yet a long course to run, slaying, sundering, annihilating entire families, before Rowland, on the threshold of her dwelling, was to know the answer to his torturing question: Dead is she, too, or is there a God in heaven?

What of those others who had danced on Eyam's green? What of the Mortins family, the Kempe family, whose children had played so happily together? In a lonely hut on the hillside, Mortins is living still, living with no other company than four cows and his greyhound – with these and the ghosts of his dead family. His children, playing with those of the widow Kempe, had brought the plague into Mortins's homestead, Shepherds Flats. One by one his family had been taken, till there remained only his wife and one other child still unborn. Then his wife was infected; the pains and the fever brought on premature labour. No woman help was available and Mortins himself assisted at the birth; Mortins himself immediately afterwards performed the last rites on the last two of his family. Then he went away to the hillside, a hermit with his memories.

Merril still lives, though severed from all intercourse with his fellows. Tradition tells his only companion is a cock.

At Riley, the Talbot and Hancock families, so prolific in children, have been wiped out – their graves are to be seen today – all exterminated except one, as if the demon of plague had wished to inscribe his exploit there on one living memory. Mrs. Hancock lost her husband, her children, and with her own hands buried them. She saw all her neighbours, the Talbots, transformed in those few lethal months from healthy to madly suffering human beings, from that to corpses.

These specific cases are among the few recorded ones of the plague at Eyam. Many that must have been as terrible have left no mark in history. There is one other tragedy, though, that cannot be omitted. All through these months Mompesson and Catherine his wife, absorbed in consoling the sick and the bereaved, had thought little of their own danger. One precaution Mrs Mompesson had taken: she had made an incision in her husband's leg and, keeping it open, had hoped in this way to preserve a vent for the pestilence's escape should it ever visit Mompesson.

One day she saw issuing from the wound a greenish ichor. Supposing this to be the plague leaving her husband's body, she congratulated him joyfully, without one fear for herself, who, if that green issue were indeed the plague, was now almost certainly marked as the enemy's next victim.

Mompesson himself was not convinced. He believed the issue was an ointment he had used as dressing. That incident did not make him believe his wife was doomed. Shortly afterwards he received an intimation that did make him tremble for her. Towards the middle of August, when the plague darts were striking down victims daily, he was walking with his wife through the fields behind the rectory. The day was so still and bright, there seemed such a benign spirit in nature that Catherine Mompesson was more cheerful than usual, as though she had received a hint of the plague's approaching cessation, of a calm that must succeed its fiercest rage. "How sweet the air smells," she said, filling her lungs deep.

Mompesson started, then looked away. He did not wish his wife to see the apprehension on his face. For that seemingly innocent remark of hers, expressing her brave gratitude for God's smallest blessing in the time of his most terrible visitation, even that remark betrayed infection – there was plague in his wife's nostrils. For the rector knew what she did not know – it had been a common observation that "the plague smells sweet, like ripe apples."

When he had mastered his emotion, Mompesson examined his wife's features for any confirmation of his dreadful surmise. There was no taint upon her flesh, she was beautiful as ever, with that ethereal quality one could not associate with the hideous physical distortions of the plague. But, looking at her, he could not but remember that this very fairylike frailty was itself partly due to another disease. His wife had for some time suffered from consumption, an ally – how refined an ally – to the brute plague.

On getting home, the worst happened. Catherine discovered death's fingerprints on her skin. She begged her husband not to nurse her, at all costs to keep himself whole for his supreme duty of consoling and fortifying the few remaining souls of his parish. But this Mompesson would not do. He stayed with his wife to the end, watching the plague's loathsome transformation of body's beauty into a twisted and discoloured corpse.

He buried her; in his wrought state with the one consolation that he must soon follow her through the same nightmare portal.

In this belief, he wrote two letters, one to his little children, recording his grief at their mother's tragic death, setting on record her rare moral excellence and devotion; the other to his former patron, Sir George Savile, such a letter as might have been penned by one of the last few survivors of a doomed ship and sent drifting in a bottle to add its page to the history of human tragedy. He wrote that scarcely one-sixth of the villagers remained, that there was little likelihood now of anyone's escape.

But in this surmise Mompesson was wrong. Even as he wrote, the virulence had passed its murderous meridian. There had been seventy-two victims in August, September's death-roll showed twenty-four – a terrible enough percentage, considering the decimated population.

October's record showed fourteen deaths. And then, after the eleventh day of that month, with but a scattering of human beings left to slay, the plague stayed its hand in Eyam. There is no death recorded after October 11.

For many days the villagers remained in a dazed condition, fearing to hope. They continued trudging across to the half-mile limit, stopping on the Eyam side of that well that is still called Mompesson's Well, bearing away their provisions, casting payment into the water for disinfection. If they met a purveyor on the far side, "No," they would answer the query, "not yet – not another death – we are in God's hands – the Lord have mercy on us!"

The change from fear to hope, the last look behind before setting their wills to living afresh that old life they had known before the lethal interlude that death had played them, is expressed for the villagers of Eyam in the third extant letter of their rector:

"The condition of this place has been so sad that I persuade myself it did exceed all history and example. Our town has become a Golgotha, the place of a skull. My ears have never heard such doleful lamentations – my nose never smelled such horrid smells, and my eyes never beheld such ghastly spectacles. Here have been seventy-six families visited within my parish, out of which two hundred and fifty-nine persons died. Now (blessed be God) all our fears are over, for none have died of the plague since the eleventh of October, and the pest houses have been long empty. During this dreadful visitation I have not had the least symptom of disease, nor had I ever better health. My man had the distemper, and upon the appearance of the tumor I gave him some chemical anti-dotes, which operated, and after the rising broke he was very well. My maid continued in health, which was a blessing; for had she quailed, I should have been ill-set to have washed and gotten my provisions."

A tale is told in Eyam of how one of the hermits of the epidemic, Merril of Hollin's House, was apprised of the pla-gue's cessation. One day, soon after October 11, the cock – his sole companion – left him and made its way back to the village. Taking this as an omen, and recalling Noah's dove, Merril took his courage in his hands and entered the village he had left a year before, missing many there he had known then, but finding, indeed, that the plague had gone.

About the same time another exile returned. Rowland, who for months had been chafing in Middleton Dale, hoping against hope, wondering if rumours he had heard were true, at last crossed the boundary and approached the native village of Emmot Sydall. Eyam was unrecognizable. Much familiar to Rowland in the old jaunty days of his courtship had gone. The street was quiet, almost deserted. In the faces of the few loiterers there was a look it was not good for any man to see, a look that told of experiences that could not come again, of nerves inured to horror, of deadened sensibilities that would never fully vibrate again to sorrow or gladness. To add to the melancholy effect, these people were scarcely clothed. They wore the barest necessaries of decent covering. Everything else had been burnt to destroy infection. Looking in at cottage windows, he saw bare rooms, all but essential furnishing de-stroyed. The few children he saw were unfamiliar to him. They were others of the same name he had known, carefree, sportive children. These poor creatures were scared-eyed, prematurely old. Of the dogs that had frisked round him as he strode toward the Sydalls' home, of the basking cats that had blinked lazily from the window-ledges, he noticed none. All destroyed as possible plague-carriers. Instead, ravages of rats, mice, rabbits.

Much there was that Rowland found depleted, everything, in fact, save the riot of vermin and there, under the brilliant foliage of the lime trees, the swelled churchyard earth, teeming with Eyam's recent dead. If he stopped to look for her name there, he did not find it. But knowing what he did of the charnel pits, he would not have hoped overmuch from that omission.

Rowland opened the wicket of the Sydalls' home, pushed through the rank confusion of weed and garden shrub. No one answered his knock. At his touch the door groaned open on its rusty hinges. He saw the familiar dresser in the kitchen, the crockery on which he had so often shared his meals with the family, ranged there in the old order. On the table, in the disorder of a meal not cleared away, were other dishes. Approaching, he found the plates and the spoons quite clean. Yes, a meal had been eaten there; but long ago – and it had been finished by rats. Someone had died in that house alone. Weeks since. There was no need to look at the table, to search through the house; weeds were pushing through the tiles of the floor.

The plague had killed all the Sydalls. The last left had been the mother and Emmot. Then Emmot sickened. The ring Rowland had given her was not on her finger when the plague-sexton bore her away to the pits. That her mother had slipped from her hand rather than let the yet unrepentant carrier filch it for his fee. Vain hope, for next came the mother's turn, and the plague, vicariously, by its macabre minister, stole away even this, the symbol of a troth it had already robbed of fulfilment on this earth.

So ended Eyam's heroic resistance to the unseen enemy. God knows what consolation the villagers took from their ultimate victory, from the thought that they had kept that ravening pestilence in, gripped it to their bosoms, wrestled with the demon of death to stop it desolating Derbyshire from end to end; their destitution, so many deaths among their nearest and dearest, must have checked all exultation of duty nobly carried through.

Whether or not Mompesson's and Stanley's order was scientifically the best, the heroism of the two ministers and the people of Eyam will live for ever among the epics of the world.

FACING THE END

R.F. Scott

It has become fashionable to mock the ambition and amateurism of the British explorer R.F. Scott, and his doomed attempt on the South Pole in 1910. But few have ever faced death with such gallantry as Scott and his companions, particularly the self-sacrificing Titus Oates, as Scott's diary of the expedition's last days recounts so movingly.

Friday, March 16, or Saturday 17 Lost track of dates, but think the last correct. Tragedy all along the line. At lunch, the day before yesterday, poor Titus Oates said he couldn't go on; he proposed we should leave him in his sleeping-bag. That we could not do, and we induced him to come on, on the afternoon march. In spite of its awful nature for him he struggled on and we made a few miles. At night he was worse and we knew the end had come.

Should this be found I want these facts recorded. Oates' last thoughts were of his Mother, but immediately before he took pride in thinking that his regiment would be pleased with the bold way in which he met his death. We can testify to his bravery. He has borne intense suffering for weeks without complaint, and to the very last was able and willing to discuss outside subjects. He did not – would not – give up hope till the very end. He was a brave soul. This was the end. He slept through the night before last, hoping not to wake; but he woke in the morning – yesterday. It was blowing a blizzard. He said, "I am just going outside and may be some time." He went out into the blizzard and we have not seen him since.

I take this opportunity of saying that we have stuck to our sick companions to the last. In case of Edgar Evans, when absolutely out of food and he lay insensible, the safety of the remainder seemed to demand his abandonment, but Providence mercifully removed him at this critical moment. He died a natural death, and we did not leave him till two hours after his death. We knew that poor Oates was walking to his death, but though we tried to dissuade him, we knew it was the act of a brave man and an English gentleman. We all hope to meet the end with a similar spirit, and assuredly the end is not far.

I can only write at lunch and then only occasionally. The cold is intense, –40° at midday. My companions are unendingly cheerful, but we are all on the verge of serious frostbites, and though we constantly talk of fetching through, I don't think any one of us believes it in his heart.

We are cold on the march now, and at all times except meals. Yesterday we had to lie up for a blizzard and to-day we move dreadfully slowly. We are at No. 14 pony camp, only two pony marches from One Ton Depôt. We leave here our theodolite, a camera, and Oates' sleeping-bags. Diaries, etc., and geological specimens carried at Wilson's special request, will be found with us or on our sledge.

Sunday, March 18 To-day, lunch, we are 21 miles from the depôt. Ill fortune presses, but better may come. We have had more wind and drift from ahead yesterday; had to stop marching; wind N.W., force 4, temp. –35°. No human being could face it, and we are worn out *nearly*.

My right foot has gone, nearly all the toes – two days ago I was proud possessor of best feet. These are the steps of my downfall. Like an ass I mixed a small spoonful of curry powder with my melted pemmican – it gave me violent indigestion. I lay awake and in pain all night; woke and felt done on the march; foot went and I didn't know it. A very small measure of neglect and I have a foot which is not pleasant to contemplate. Bowers takes first place in condition, but there is not much to choose after all. The others are still confident of getting through – or pretend to be – I don't know! We have the last *half* fill of oil in our primus and a very small quantity of spirit – this alone between us and thirst. The wind is fair for the moment, and that is perhaps a fact to help. The mileage would have seemed ridiculously small on our outward journey.

Monday, March 19 Lunch. We camped with difficulty last night and were dreadfully cold till after our supper of cold pemmican and biscuit and a half a pannikin of cocoa cooked over the spirit. Then, contrary to expectation, we got warm and all slept well. To-day we started in the usual dragging manner. Sledge dreadfully heavy. We are 15½ miles from the depôt and ought to get there in three days. What progress! We have two days' food, but barely a day's fuel. All our feet are getting bad – Wilson's best, my right foot worse, left all right. There is no chance to nurse one's feet till we can get hot food into us. Amputation is the least I can hope for now, but will the trouble spread? That is the serious question. The weather doesn't give us a chance – the wind from N. to N.W. and –40° temp to-day.

Wednesday, March 21 Got within 11 miles of depôt Monday night; had to lie up all yesterday in severe blizzard. To-day forlorn hope, Wilson and Bowers going to depôt for fuel.

22 and 23 Blizzard bad as ever – Wilson and Bowers unable to start – to-morrow last chance – no fuel and only one or two [rations] of food left – must be near the end. Have decided it shall be natural – we shall march for the depôt with or without our effects and die in our tracks.

Thursday March 29 Since the 21st we have had a continuous gale from W.S.W. and S.W. We had fuel to make two cups of tea apiece and bare food for two days on the 20th. Every day we have been ready to start for our depôt 11 *miles* away, but outside the door of the tent it remains a scene of whirling drift. I do not think we can hope for any better things now. We shall stick it out to the end, but we are getting weaker, of course, and the end cannot be far.

    It seems a pity, but I do not think I can write more.

R. Scott.

Last entry. For God's sake look after our people.

MAN-EATER

Colonel Jim Corbett

Colonel Corbett was an an Anglo-Indian soldier, naturalist and big-game hunter. His speciality, so to speak, was killing tigers which preyed on the peasant villages of darkest India: the man-eaters. The difficulty of hunting the "man-eater" below was only exacerbated by a painful abcess affecting Corbett's head at the time.

I had wounded the tigress on 7 April, and it was now the 10th. As a general rule a tiger is not considered to be dangerous – that is, liable to charge at sight – twenty-four hours after being wounded. A lot depends on the nature of the wound, however, and on the temper of the wounded individual. Twenty-four hours after receiving a light flesh wound a tiger usually moves away on being approached, whereas a tiger with a painful body-wound might continue to be dangerous for several days. I did not know the nature of the wound the tigress was suffering from, and as she had made no attempt to attack me the previous day I believed I could now ignore the fact that she was wounded and look upon her only as a man-eater, and a very hungry man-eater at that, for she had eaten nothing since killing the woman whom she had shared with the cubs.

Where the tigress had crossed the stream there was a channel, three feet wide and two feet deep, washed out by rain-water. Up this channel, which was bordered by dense brushwood, the tigress had gone. Following her tracks I came to a cattle path. Here she had left the channel and gone along the path to the right. Three hundred yards along was a tree with heavy foliage and under this tree the tigress had lain all night. Her wound had troubled her and she had tossed about, but on the leaves on which she had been lying there was neither blood nor any discharge from her wound. From this point on I followed her fresh tracks, taking every precaution not to walk into an ambush. By evening I had tracked her for several miles along cattle paths, water channels, and game tracks, without having set eyes on so much as the tip of her tail. At sunset I collected my men, and as we returned to camp they told me they had been able to follow the movements of the tigress through the jungle by the animals and birds that had called at her, but that they too had seen nothing of her.

When hunting unwounded man-eating tigers the greatest danger, when walking into the wind, is of an attack from behind, and to a lesser extent from either side. When the wind is from behind, the danger is from either side. In the same way, if the wind is blowing from the right the danger is from the left and from behind, and if blowing from the left the danger is from the right and from behind. In none of these cases is there any appreciable danger of an attack from in front, for in my experience all unwounded tigers, whether man-eaters or not, are disinclined to make a head-on attack. Under normal conditions man-eating tigers limit the range of their attack to the distance they can spring, and for this reason they are more difficult to cope with than wounded tigers, who invariably launch an attack from a little distance, maybe only ten or twenty yards, but possibly as much as a hundred yards. This means that whereas the former have to be dealt with in a matter of split seconds, the latter give one time to raise a rifle and align the sights. In either case it means rapid shooting and a fervent prayer that an ounce or two of lead will stop a few hundred pounds of muscle and bone.

In the case of the tigress I was hunting, I knew that her wound would not admit of her springing and that if I kept out of her reach I would be comparatively safe. The possibility that she had recovered from her wound in the four days that had elapsed since I had last seen her had, however, to be taken into account. When therefore I started out alone on the morning of 11 April to take up the tracks where I had left them the previous evening, I resolved to keep clear of any rock, bush, tree, or other object behind which the tigress might be lying up in wait for me.

She had been moving the previous evening in the direction of the Tanakpur road. I again found where she had spent the night, this time on a soft bed of dry grass, and from this point I followed her fresh tracks. Avoiding dense cover – possibly because she could not move through it silently – she was keeping to water channels and game tracks and it became apparent that she was not moving about aimlessly but was looking for something to kill and eat. Presently, in one of these water channels she found and killed a few-weeks-old *kakar*. She had come on the young deer as it was lying asleep in the sun on a bed of sand, and had eaten every scrap of it, rejecting nothing but the tiny hooves. I was now only a minute or two behind her, and knowing that the morsel would have done no more than whet her appetite, I redoubled my precautions. In places the channels and game tracks to which the tigress was keeping twisted and turned and ran through dense cover or past rocks. Had my condition been normal I would have followed on her footsteps and possibly been able to catch up with her, but unfortunately I was far from normal. The swelling on my head, face, and neck, had now increased to such proportions that I was no longer able to move my head up or down or from side to side, and my left eye was closed. However, I still had one good eye, fortunately my right one, and I could still hear a little.

During the whole of that day I followed the tigress without seeing her and without, I believe, her seeing me. Where she had gone along water channels, game tracks, or cattle paths that ran through dense cover I skirted round the cover and picked up her pug-marks on the far side. Not knowing the ground was a very great handicap, for not only did it necessitate walking more miles than I need have done, but it also prevented my antici-pating the movements of the tigress and ambushing her. When I finally gave up the chase for the day, the tigress was moving up the valley in the direction of the village.

Back in camp I realized that the "bad time" I had foreseen and dreaded was approaching. Electric shocks were stabbing through the enormous abscess, and the hammer blows were increasing in intensity. Sleepless nights and a diet of tea had made a coward of me, and I could not face the prospect of sitting on my bed through another long night, racked with pain and waiting for something, I knew not what, to happen. I had come to Talla Des to try to rid the hill people of the terror that menaced them and to tide over my bad time, and all that I had accomplished so far was to make their condition worse. Deprived of the ability to secure her natural prey, the tigress, who in eight years had only killed a hundred and fifty people would now, unless she recovered from her wound, look to her easiest prey – human beings – to provide her with most of the food she needed. There was therefore an account to be settled between the tigress and myself, and that night was as suitable a time as any to settle it.

Calling for a cup of tea – made hill-fashion with milk – which served me as dinner, I drank it while standing in the moonlight. Then, calling my eight men together, I instructed them to wait for me in the village until the following evening, and if I did not return by then to pack up my things and start early the next morning for Naini Tal. Having done this I picked up my rifle from where I put it on my bed, and headed down the valley. My men, all of whom had been with me for years, said not a word either to ask me where I was going or to try to dissuade me from going. They just stood silent in a group and watched me walk away. Maybe the glint I saw on their cheeks was only imagination, or maybe it was only the reflection of the moon. Anyway, when I looked back not a man had moved. They were just standing in a group as I had left them . . .

One of the advantages of making detailed mental maps of ground covered is that finding the way back to any given spot presents no difficulty. Picking up the pug-marks of my quarry where I had left them, I resumed my tracking, which was now only possible on game tracks and on cattle paths, to which the tigress was, fortunately, keeping. *Sambhar* and *kakar* had now come out on to the open glades, some to feed and others for protection, and though I could not pin-point their alarm calls they let me know when the tigress was on the move and gave me a rough idea of the direction in which she was moving.

On a narrow, winding cattle path running through dense cover I left the pug-marks of the tigress and worked round through scattered brushwood to try to pick them up on the far

side. The way round was longer than I had anticipated, and I
eventually came out on an open stretch of ground with short
grass and dotted about with big oak trees. Here I came to a halt
in the shadow of a big tree. Presently, by a movement of this
shadow, I realized that the tree above me was tenanted by a
troop of *langurs*. I had covered a lot of ground during the
eighteen hours I had been on my feet that day, and here now
was a safe place for me to rest awhile, for the *langurs* above
would give warning of danger. Sitting with my back against the
tree and facing the cover round which I had skirted, I had been
resting for half an hour when an old *langur* gave his alarm call;
the tigress had come out into the open and the *langur* had caught
sight of her. Presently I, too, caught sight of the tigress just as
she started to lie down. She was a hundred yards to my right and
ten yards from the cover, and she lay down broadside on to me
with her head turned looking up at the calling *langur*.

I have had a lot of practice in night shooting, for during the
winter months I assisted our tenants at Kaladhungi to protect
their crops against marauding animals such as pig and deer. On
a clear moonlight night I can usually count on hitting an animal
up to a range of about a hundred yards. Like most people who
have taught themselves to shoot, I keep both eyes open when
shooting. This enables me to keep the target in view with one
eye, while aligning the sights of the rifle with the other. At any
other time I would have waited for the tigress to stand up and
then fired at her, but unfortunately my left eye was now closed
and a hundred yards was too far to risk a shot with only one eye.
On the two previous nights the tigress had lain in the one spot
and had possibly slept most of the night, and she might do the
same now. If she lay right down on her side – she was now lying
on her stomach with her head up – and went to sleep I could
either go back to the cattle path on which I had left her pug-
marks and follow her tracks to the edge of the cover and get to
within ten yards of her, or I could creep up to her over the open
ground until I got close enough to make sure of my shot.
Anyway, for the present I could do nothing but sit perfectly
still until the tigress made up her mind what she was going to
do.

For a long time, possibly half an hour or a little longer, the
tigress lay in the one position, occasionally moving her head

from side to side, while the old *langur* in a sleepy voice continued to give his alarm call. Finally she got to her feet and very slowly and very painfully started to walk away to my right. Directly in the line in which she was going there was an open ravine ten to fifteen feet deep and twenty to twenty-five yards wide, which I had crossed lower down when coming to the spot where I now was. When the tigress had increased the distance between us to a hundred and fifty yards, and the chances of her seeing me had decreased, I started to follow her. Slipping from tree to tree, and moving a little faster than she, I reduced her lead to fifty yards by the time she reached the edge of the ravine. She was now in range, but was standing in shadow, and her tail end was a very small mark to fire at. For a long and anxious minute she stood in the one position and then, having made up her mind to cross the ravine, very gently went over the edge.

As the tigress disappeared from view I bent down and ran forward on silent feet. Bending my head down and running was a very stupid mistake for me to have made, and I had only run a few yards when I was overcome by vertigo. Near me were two oak saplings, a few feet apart and with interlaced branches. Laying down my rifle I climbed up the saplings to a height of ten or twelve feet. Here I found a branch to sit on, another for my feet, and yet other small branches for me to rest against. Crossing my arms on the branches in front of me, I laid my head on them, and at that moment the abscess burst, not into my brain as I feared it would, but out through my nose and left ear.

"No greater happiness can man know, than the sudden cessation of great pain", was said by someone who had suffered and suffered greatly, and who knew the happiness of sudden relief. It was round about midnight when relief came to me, and the grey light was just beginning to show in the east when I raised my head from my crossed arms. Cramp in my legs resulting from my having sat on a thin branch for four hours had roused me, and for a little while I did not know where I was or what had happened to me. Realization was not long in coming. The great swelling on my head, face, and neck had gone and with it had gone the pain. I could now move my head as I liked, my left eye was open, and I could swallow without discomfort. I had lost an opportunity of shooting the tigress, but what did that matter now, for I was over my bad time and no matter where or how far the tigress went I would follow her, and sooner or later I would surely get another chance.

When I last saw the tigress she was heading in the direction of the village. Swinging down from the saplings, up which I had climbed with such difficulty, I retrieved my rifle and headed in the same direction. At the stream I stopped and washed and cleaned myself and my clothes as best I could. My men had not spent the night in the village as I had instructed them to, but had sat round a fire near my tent keeping a kettle of water on the boil. As, dripping with water, they saw me coming towards them they sprang up with a glad cry of "Sahib! Sahib! You have come back, and you are well." "Yes", I answered, "I have come back, and I am now well." When an Indian gives his loyalty, he gives it unstintingly and without counting the cost. When we arrived at Talla Kote the headman put two rooms at the disposal of my men, for it was dangerous to sleep anywhere except behind locked doors. On this my bad night, and fully alive to the danger, my men had sat out in the open in case they could be of any help to me, and to keep a kettle on the boil for my tea – if I should return. I cannot remember if I drank the tea, but I can remember my shoes being drawn off by willing hands, and a rug spread over me as I lay down on my bed.

Hours and hours of peaceful sleep, and then a dream. Someone was urgently calling me, and someone was as urgently saying I must not be disturbed. Over and over again the dream was repeated with slight variations, but with no less urgency, until the words penetrated through the fog of sleep and became a reality. "You *must* wake him or he will be very angry." And the rejoinder, "We will *not* wake him for he is very tired." Ganga Ram was the last speaker, so I called out and told him to bring the man to me. In a minute my tent was besieged by an excited throng of men and boys all eager to tell me that the man-eater had just killed six goats on the far side of the village. While pulling on my shoes I looked over the throng and on seeing Dungar Singh, the lad who was with me when I shot the cubs, I asked him if he knew where the goats had been killed and if he could take me to the spot. "Yes, yes," he answered eagerly, "I know where they were killed and I can take you there." Telling the headman to keep the crowd back, I armed myself with my

.275 rifle and, accompanied by Dungar Singh, set off through the village.

On the way down the hill the lad had told me that round about midday a large flock of goats in charge of ten or fifteen boys was feeding in the hollow, when a tiger – which they suspected was the man-eater – suddenly appeared among them and struck down six goats. On seeing the tiger the boys started yelling and were joined by some men collecting firewood near by. In the general confusion of goats dashing about and human beings yelling, the tiger moved off and no one appeared to have seen in which direction it went Grabbing hold of three dead goats the men and boys dashed back to the village to give me the news, leaving three goats with broken backs in the hollow.

That the killer of the goats was the wounded man-eater there could be no question, for when I last saw her the previous night she was going straight towards the village. Further, my men told me that an hour or so before my return to camp a *kakar* had barked near the stream, a hundred yards from where they were sitting, and thinking that the animal had barked on seeing me they had built up the fire. It was fortunate that they had done so, for I later found the pug-marks of the tigress where she had skirted round the fire and had then gone through the village, obviously with the object of securing a human victim. Having failed in her quest she had evidently taken cover near the village, and at the first opportunity of securing food had struck down the goats. This she had done in a matter of seconds, while suffering from a wound that had made her limp badly.

As I was not familiar with the ground, I asked Dungar Singh in which direction he thought the tigress had gone. Pointing down the valley he said she had probably gone in that direction, for there was heavy jungle farther down. While I was questioning him about this jungle, with the idea of going down and looking for the tigress, a *kalege* pheasant started chattering. On hearing this the lad turned round and looked up the hill, giving me an indication of the direction in which the bird was calling. To our left the hill went up steeply, and growing on it were a few bushes and stunted trees. I knew the tigress would not have attempted to climb this hill, and on seeing me looking at it Dungar Singh said the pheasant was not calling on the hill but in a ravine round the shoulder of it. As we were not within sight of the pheasant, there was only one thing that could have alarmed it, and that was the tigress. Telling Dungar Singh to leave me and run back to the village as fast as he could go, I covered his retreat with my rifle until I considered he was clear of the danger zone and then turned round to look for a suitable place in which to sit.

The only trees in this part of the valley were enormous pines which, as they had no branches for thirty or forty feet, it would be quite impossible to climb. So of necessity I would have to sit on the ground. This would be all right during daylight, but if the tigress delayed her return until nightfall, and preferred human flesh to mutton, I would need a lot of luck to carry me through the hour or two of darkness before the moon rose.

On the low ridge running from left to right on the near side of the hollow was a big flat rock. Near it was another and smaller one. By sitting on this smaller rock I found I could shelter behind the bigger, exposing only my head to the side from which I expected the tigress to come. So here I decided to sit. In front of me was a hollow some forty yards in width with a twenty-foot-high bank on the far side. Above this bank was a ten- to twenty-yard-wide flat stretch of ground sloping down to the right. Beyond this the hill went up steeply. The three goats in the hollow, which were alive when the boys and men ran away, were now dead. When striking them down the tigress had ripped the skin on the back of one of them.

The *kalege* pheasant had now stopped chattering, and I speculated as to whether it had called at the tigress as she was going up the ravine after the lad and I had arrived or whether it had called on seeing the tigress coming back. In the one case it would mean a long wait for me, and in the other a short one. I had taken up my position at 2 p.m., and half an hour later a pair of blue Himalayan magpies came up the valley. These beautiful birds, which do a lot of destruction in the nesting season among tits and other small birds, have an uncanny instinct for finding in a jungle anything that is dead. I heard the magpies long before I saw them, for they are very vocal. On catching sight of the goats they stopped chattering and very cautiously approached. After several false alarms they alighted on the goat with the ripped back and started to feed. For some time a king vulture had been quartering the sky, and now, on seeing the magpies on the goat, he came sailing down and landed as lightly as a feather on the dead branch of a pine tree. These king vultures with their white shirt-fronts, black coats, and red heads and legs, are always the first of the vultures to find a kill. Being smaller than other vultures it is essential for them to be first at the table, for when the others arrive they have to take a back seat.

I welcomed the vulture's coming, for he would provide me with information I lacked. From his perch high up on the pine tree he had an extensive view, and if he came down and joined the magpies it would mean that the tigress had gone, whereas if he remained where he was it would mean that she was lying up somewhere close by. For the next half hour the scene remained unchanged – the magpies continued to feed, and the vulture sat on the dead branch – and then the sun was blotted out by heavy rain-clouds. Shortly after, the *kalege* pheasant started chattering again and the magpies flew screaming down the valley. The tigress was coming, and here, sooner than I had expected, was the chance of shooting her that I had lost the previous night when overcome by vertigo.

A few light bushes on the shoulder of the hill partly obstructed my view in the direction of the ravine, and presently through these bushes I saw the tigress. She was coming, very slowly, along the flat bit of ground above the twenty-foot-high bank and was looking straight towards me. With only head exposed and my soft hat pulled down to my eyes, I knew she would not notice me if I made no movement. So, with the rifle resting on the flat rock, I sat perfectly still. When she had come opposite to me the tigress sat down, with the bole of a big pine tree directly between us. I could see her head on one side of the tree and her tail and part of her hindquarters on the other. Here she sat for minutes, snapping at the flies that, attracted by her wound, were tormenting her . . .

The people of Talla Des had suffered and suffered grievously from the tigress, and for the suffering she had inflicted she was now paying in full. To put her out of her misery I several times aligned the sights of my rifle on her head, but the light, owing to the heavy clouds, was not good enough for me to make sure of hitting a comparatively small object at sixty yards.

Eventually the tigress stood up, took three steps and then

stood broadside on to me, looking down at the goats. With my elbows resting on the flat rock I took careful aim at the spot where I thought her heart would be, pressed the trigger, and saw a spurt of dust go up on the hill on the far side of her. On seeing the dust the thought flashed through my mind that not only had I missed the tigress's heart, but that I had missed the whole animal. And yet, after my careful aim, that could not be. What undoubtedly had happened was that my bullet had gone clean through her without meeting any resistance. At my shot the tigress sprang forward, raced over the flat ground like a very frightened but unwounded animal, and before I could get in another shot disappeared from view.

Mad with myself for not having killed the tigress when she had given me such a good shot, I was determined now that she would not escape from me. Jumping down from the rock, I sprinted across the hollow, up the twenty-foot bank and along the flat ground until I came to the spot where the tigress had disappeared. Here I found there was a steep forty-foot drop down a loose shale scree. Down this the tigress had gone in great bounds. Afraid to do the same for fear of spraining my ankles, I sat down on my heels and tobogganed to the bottom. At the foot of the scree was a well-used footpath, along which I felt sure the tigress had gone, though the surface was too hard to show pug-marks. To the right of the path was a boulder-strewn stream, the one that Dungar Singh and I had crossed farther up, and flanking the stream was a steep grassy hill. To the left of the path was a hill with a few pine trees growing on it. The path for some distance was straight, and I had run along it for fifty or more yards when I heard a *ghooral* give its alarm sneeze. There was only one place where the *ghooral* could be and that was on the grassy hill to my right. Thinking that the tigress had possibly crossed the stream and gone up this hill, I pulled up to see if I could see her. As I did so, I thought I heard men shouting. Turning round I looked up in the direction of the village and saw a crowd of men standing on the saddle of the hill. On seeing me look round they shouted again and waved me on, *on*, straight along the path. In a moment I was on the run again, and on turning a corner found fresh blood on the path.

The skin of animals is loose. When an animal that is standing still is hit in the body by a bullet and it dashes away at full speed, the hole made in the skin does not coincide with the hole in the flesh, with the result that, as long as the animal is running at speed, little if any blood flows from the wound. When, however, the animal slows down and the two holes come closer together, blood flows and continues to flow more freely the slower the animal goes. When there is any uncertainty as to whether an animal that has been fired at has been hit or not, the point can be very easily cleared up by going to the exact spot where the animal was when fired at, and looking for cut hairs. These will indicate that the animal was hit, whereas the absence of such hairs will show that it was clean missed.

After going round the corner the tigress had slowed down, but she was still running, as I could see from the blood splashes, and in order to catch up with her I put on a spurt. I had not gone very far when I came to a spur jutting out from the hill on my left. Here the path bent back at a very acute angle, and not being able to stop myself, and there being nothing for me to seize hold of on the hillside, I went over the edge of the narrow path, all standing. Ten to fifteen feet below was a small rhododendron sapling, and below the sapling a sheer drop into a dark and evil-looking ravine where the stream, turning at right angles, had cut away the toe of the hill. As I passed the sapling with my heels cutting furrows in the soft earth, I gripped it under my right arm. The sapling, fortunately, was not uprooted, and though it bent it did not break. Easing myself round very gently, I started to kick footholds in the soft loamy hill-face which had a luxuriant growth of maidenhair fern.

The opportunity of catching up with the tigress had gone, but I now had a well-defined blood-trail to follow, so there was no longer any need for me to hurry. The footpath which at first had run north now ran west along the north face of a steep and well-wooded hill. When I had gone for another two hundred yards along the path, I came to flat ground on a shoulder of the hill. This was the limit I would have expected a tiger shot through the body to have travelled, so I approached the flat ground, on which there was a heavy growth of bracken and scattered bushes, very cautiously.

A tiger that has made up its mind to avenge an injury is the most terrifying animal to be met with in an Indian jungle. The tigress had a very recent injury to avenge and she had demonstrated – by striking down six goats and by springing and dashing away when I fired at her – that the leg wound she had received five days before was no handicap to rapid movement. I felt sure, therefore, that as soon as she became aware that I was following her and she considered that I was within her reach, she would launch an all-out attack on me, which I would possibly have to meet with a single bullet. Drawing back the bolt of the rifle, I examined the cartridge very carefully, and satisfied that it was one of a fresh lot I had recently got from Manton in Calcutta, I replaced it in the chamber, put back the bolt, and threw off the safety catch.

The path ran through the bracken, which was waist high and which met over it. The blood trail led along the path into the bracken, and the tigress might be lying up on the path or on the right or the left-hand side of it. So I approached the bracken foot by foot and looking straight ahead for, on these occasions, it is unwise to keep turning the head. When I was within three yards of the bracken I saw a movement a yard from the path on the right. It was the tigress gathering herself together for a spring. Wounded and starving though she was, she was game to fight it out. Her spring, however, was never launched, for, as she rose, my first bullet raked her from end to end, and the second bullet broke her neck.

Days of pain and strain on an empty stomach left me now trembling in every limb, and I had great difficulty in reaching the spot where the path bent back at an acute angle and where, but for the chance dropping of a rhododendron seed, I would have ended my life on the rocks below.

The entire population of the village, plus my own men, were gathered on the saddle of the hill and on either side of it, and I had hardly raised my hat to wave when, shouting at the tops of their voices, the men and boys came swarming down. My six Garhwalis were the first to arrive. Congratulations over, the tigress was lashed to a pole and six of the proudest Garhwalis in Kumaon carried the Talla Des man-eater in triumph to Talla Kote village. Here the tigress was laid down on a bed of straw for the women and children to see, while I went back to my tent for my first solid meal in many weeks. An hour later with a crowd of people round me I skinned the tigress.

DOLLEY MADISON RESCUES THE NATIONAL TREASURE

Dolley Madison

It is now all but forgotten, but between 1812 and 1815 Britain and America were at war. Towards the end of the campaign, the British marched on Washington DC which caused government officials to pack up and pack off historic documents and national treasures. Unfortunately, the portrait of George Washington in the dining room of the White House refused to leave the wall as the redcoats approached. It would have been a bruising humiliation for it to fall into British hands. Dolley Madison, wife of the fourth president, saved the day. And even managed to pen a letter about the episode as gun and cannon sounded around her.

Tuesday, August 23, 1814

Dear Sister:

My husband left me yesterday morning to join General Winder. He inquired anxiously whether I had courage or firmness to remain in the President's house until his return on the morrow, or succeeding day, and on my assurance that I had no fear but for him, and the success of our army, he left, beseeching me to take care of myself, and of the Cabinet papers, public and private. I have since received two dispatches from him, written with a pencil. The last is alarming, because he desires I should be ready at a moment's warning to enter my carriage, and leave the city; that the enemy seemed stronger than had at first been reported, and it might happen that they would reach the city with the intention of destroying it. I am accordingly ready; I have pressed as many Cabinet papers into trunks as to fill one carriage; our private property must be sacrificed, as it is impossible to procure wagons for its transportation.

I am determined not to go myself until I see Mr Madison safe, so that he can accompany me, as I hear of much hostility toward him. Disaffection stalks around us. My friends and acquaintances are all gone, even Colonel C. with his hundred, who were stationed as a guard in this enclosure. French John [a faithful servant], with his usual activity and resolution, offers to spike the cannon at the gate, and lay a train of powder, which would blow up the British, should they enter the house. To this last proposition I positively object, without being able to make him understand why all advantages in war may not be taken.

Wednesday morning, twelve o'clock. Since sunrise I have been turning my spy-glass in every direction, and watching with unwearied anxiety, hoping to discover the approach of my dear husband and his friends; but, alas! I can descry only groups of military, wandering in all directions, as if there was a lack of arms, or of spirit to fight for their own fireside.

Three o'clock. Will you believe it, my sister? we have had a battle, or skirmish, near Bladensburg, and here I am still, within sound of the cannon! Mr Madison comes not. May God protect us! Two messengers, covered with dust, come to bid me fly; but here I mean to wait for him . . . At this late hour a wagon has been procured, and I have had it filled with plate and the most valuable portable articles, belonging to the house. Whether it will reach its destination, the "Bank of Maryland," or fall into the hands of British soldiery, events must determine. Our kind friend, Mr Carroll, has come to hasten my departure, and in a very bad humor with me, because I insist on waiting until the large picture of General Washington is secured, and it requires to be unscrewed from the wall. This process was found too tedious for these perilous moments; I have

ordered the frame to be broken, and the canvas taken out.
It is done! and the precious portrait placed in the hands of
two gentlemen of New York, for safekeeping. And now,
dear sister, I must leave this house, or the retreating army
will make me a prisoner of it by filling up the road I am
directed to take. When I shall again write to you, or where
I shall be tomorrow, I cannot tell!

Dolley

ON TRIAL

Lillian Hellman

The internal politics of the USA in the early 1950s were conditioned by the fears of the Cold War with the USSR. A witch-hunt led by Senator McCarthy attacked citizens suspected of left-wing views, many of whom were "blacklisted", prevented from working. A particular target for the attentions of McCarthyism was the entertainment industry; playwright Lillian Hellman was only one of many writers and artists to be asked to appear before Congress's House Un-American Activities Committee to admit their political belief and "name names" of other suspected Communists. Hellman appeared before the House Un-American Activities Committee on 21 May 1952. Her self-deprecating account of trial before that modern witch-hunt should not disguise her courage in being one of the those who refused to "name names".

The Committee room was almost empty except for a few elderly, small-faced ladies sitting in the rear. They looked as if they were permanent residents and, since they occasionally spoke to each other, it was not too long a guess that they came as an organized group or club. Clerks came in and out, put papers on the rostrum, and disappeared. I said maybe we had come too early, but Joe [Rauh, Hellman's lawyer] said no, it was better that I get used to the room.

Then, I think to make the wait better for me, he said, "Well, I can tell you now that in the early days of seeing you, I was scared that what happened to my friend might happen to me."

He stopped to tell Pollitt [Rauh's assistant] that he didn't understand about the press – not one newspaperman had appeared.

I said; "What happened to your friend?"

"He represented a Hollywood writer who told him that he would under no circumstances be a friendly witness. That was why my friend took the case. So they get here, in the same seats we are, sure of his client, and within ten minutes the writer is one of the friendliest witnesses the Committee has had the pleasure of. He throws in every name he can think of, including his college roommate, childhood friend."

I said, "No, that won't happen and for more solid reasons than your honour or even mine. I told you I can't make quick changes."

Joe told Pollitt that he thought he understood about no press and the half-empty room: the Committee had kept our appearance as quiet as they could. Joe said, "That means they're frightened of us. I don't know whether that's good or bad, but we want the press here and I don't know how to get them."

He didn't have to know. The room suddenly began to fill up behind me and the press people began to push toward their section and were still piling in when Representative Wood began to pound his gavel. I hadn't seen the Committee come in, don't think I had realized that they were to sit on a raised platform, the government having learned from the stage, or maybe the other way around. I was glad I hadn't seen them come in – they made a gloomy picture. Through the noise of the gavel I heard one of the ladies in the rear cough very loudly. She was to cough all through the hearing. Later I heard one of her friends say loudly, "Irma, take your good cough drops."

The opening questions were standard: what was my name, where was I born, what was my occupation, what were the titles of my plays. It didn't take long to get to what really interested them: my time in Hollywood, which studios had I worked for, what periods of what years, with some mysterious emphasis on 1937. (My time in Spain, I thought, but I was wrong.)

Had I met a writer called Martin Berkeley? (I had never, still have never, met Martin Berkeley, although Hammett* told me

---

* Dashiell Hammett. The detective story writer, author of such private eye classics as *The Maltese Falcon*, was Hellman's long-time partner.

later that I had once sat at a lunch table of sixteen or seventeen people with him in the old Metro-Goldwyn-Mayer commissary.) I said I must refuse to answer that question. Mr Tavenner said he'd like to ask me again whether I had stated I was abroad in the summer of 1937. I said yes, explained that I had been in New York for several weeks before going to Europe, and got myself ready for what I knew was coming: Martin Berkeley, one of the Committee's most lavish witnesses on the subject of Hollywood, was now going to be put to work. Mr Tavenner read Berkeley's testimony. Perhaps he is worth quoting, the small details are nicely formed, even about his "old friend Hammett", who had no more than a bowing acquaintance with him.

MR TAVENNER: . . . I would like you to tell the committee when and where the Hollywood section of the Communist Party was first organized.

MR BERKELEY: Well, sir, by a very strange coincidence the section was organized in my house . . . In June of 1937, the middle of June, the meeting was held in my house. My house was picked because I had a large living room and ample parking facilities . . . And it was a pretty good meeting. We were honoured by the presence of many functionaries from downtown, and the spirit was swell . . . Well, in addition to Jerome and the others I have mentioned before, and there is no sense in me going over the list again and again . . . Also present was Harry Carlisle, who is now in the process of being deported, for which I am very grateful. He was an English subject. After Stanley Lawrence had stolen what funds there were from the party out here, and to make amends had gone to Spain and gotten himself killed, they sent Harry Carlisle here to conduct Marxist classes . . . Also at the meeting was Donald Ogden Stewart. His name is spelled Donald Ogden S-t-e-w-a-r-t. Dorothy Parker, also a writer. Her husband Allen Campbell, C-a-m-p-b-e-l-l; my old friend Dashiell Hammett, who is now in jail in New York for his activities; that very excellent playwright, Lillian Hellman . . .

And so on.

When this nonsense was finished, Mr Tavenner asked me if it

was true. I said that I wanted to refer to the letter I had sent, I would like the Committee to reconsider my offer in the letter.

MR TAVENNER: In other words, you are asking the committee not to ask you any questions regarding the participation of other persons in the Communist Party activities?

I said I hadn't said that.

Mr Wood said that in order to clarify the record Mr Tavenner should put into the record the correspondence between me and the Committee. Mr Tavenner did just that, and when he had finished Rauh sprang to his feet, picked up a stack of mimeographed copies of my letter, and handed them out to the press section. I was puzzled by this – I hadn't noticed he had the copies – but I did notice that Rauh was looking happy.

Mr Tavenner was upset, far more than the printed words of my hearing show. Rauh said that Tavenner himself had put the letters in the record, and thus he thought passing out copies was proper. The polite words of each as they read on the page were not polite as spoken. I am convinced that in this section of the testimony, as in several other sections – certainly in Hammett's later testimony before the Senate Internal Security Subcommittee – either the court stenographer missed some of what was said and filled it in later, or the documents were, in part, edited. Having read many examples of the work of court stenographers, I have never once seen a completely accurate report.

Mr Wood told Mr Tavenner that the Committee could not be "placed in the attitude of trading with the witnesses as to what they will testify to" and that thus he thought both letters should be read aloud.

Mr Tavenner did just this, and there was talk I couldn't hear, a kind of rustle, from the press section. Then Mr Tavenner asked me if I had attended the meeting described by Berkeley, and one of the hardest things I ever did in my life was to swallow the words, "I don't know him, and a little investigation into the time and place would have proved to you that I could not have been at the meeting he talks about." Instead, I said that I must refuse to answer the question. The "must" in that sentence annoyed Mr Wood – it was to annoy him again and again – and he corrected me: "You might refuse to answer, the question is asked, do you refuse?"

But Wood's correction of me, the irritation in his voice, was making me nervous, and I began to move my right hand as if I had a tic, unexpected, and couldn't stop it. I told myself that if a word irritated him, the insults would begin to come very soon. So I sat up straight, made my left hand hold my right hand, and hoped it would work. But I felt the sweat on my face and arms and knew that something was going to happen to me, something out of control, and I turned to Joe, remembering the suggested toilet intermission. But the clock said we had only been there sixteen minutes, and if it was going to come, the bad time, I had better hang on for a while.

Was I a member of the Communist Party, had I been, what year had I stopped being? How could I harm such people as Martin Berkeley by admitting I had known them, and so on. At times I couldn't follow the reasoning, at times I understood full well that in refusing to answer questions about membership in the Party I had, of course, trapped myself into a seeming admission that I once had been.

But in the middle of one of the questions about my past, something so remarkable happened that I am to this day convinced that the unknown gentleman who spoke had a great deal to do with the rest of my life. A voice from the press gallery had been for at least three or four minutes louder than the other voices. (By this time, I think, the press had finished reading my letter to the Committee and were discussing it.) The loud voice had been answered by a less loud voice, but no words could be distinguished. Suddenly a clear voice said, "Thank God somebody finally had the guts to do it."

It is never wise to say that something is the best minute of your life, you must be forgetting, but I still think that unknown voice made the words that helped to save me. (I had been sure that not only did the elderly ladies in the room disapprove of me, but the press would be antagonistic.) Wood rapped his gavel and said angrily, "If that occurs again, I will clear the press from these chambers."

"You do that, sir," said the same voice.

Mr Wood spoke to somebody over his shoulder and the somebody moved around to the press section, but that is all that happened. To this day I don't know the name of the man who spoke, but for months later, almost every day I would say to myself, I wish I could tell him that I had really wanted to say to Mr Wood: "There is no Communist menace in this country and you know it. You have made cowards into liars, an ugly business, and you made me write a letter in which I acknowledged your power. I should have gone into your Committee room, given my name and address, and walked out." Many people have said they liked what I did, but I don't much, and if I hadn't worried about rats in jail, and such . . . Ah, the bravery you tell yourself was possible when it's all over, the bravery of the staircase.

In the Committee room I heard Mr Wood say, "Mr Walter does not desire to ask the witness any further questions. Is there any reason why this witness should not be excused from further attendance before the Committee?"

Mr Tavenner said, "No, sir."

My hearing was over an hour and seven minutes after it began. I don't think I understood that it was over, but Joe was whispering so loudly and so happily that I jumped from the noise in my ear.

He said, "*Get up. Get up.* Get out of here immediately. Pollitt will take you. Don't stop for any reason, to answer any questions from anybody. Don't run, but walk as fast as you can and just shake your head and keep moving if anybody comes near you."

Some years later Hellman asked Rauh why she was not prosecuted by the Committee:

He said, "There were three things they wanted. One, names which you wouldn't give. Two, a smear by accusing you of being a 'Fifth Amendment Communist'. They couldn't do that because in your letter you offered to testify about yourself. And three, a prosecution which they couldn't do because they forced us into taking the Fifth Amendment. They had sense enough to see that they were in a bad spot. We beat them, that's all."

THE SHOW MUST GO ON

Giles Playfair

The English 19th-century actor Edmund Kean, arguably the greatest interpreter of Shakespeare's villains, was cited in a divorce case by a London alderman. A high moral fervour was whipped up, which led to mob protests during Kean's performances in Drury Lane.

*T*he Times was enraged when it learned that its victim intended to brave the storm of popular fury which it had been at such pains to create. "Mr Kean is not merely an adulterer," it wrote in a leading article; "he is an adulterer anxious to show himself before the public with all the disgrace of the verdict of guilty about his neck, because that very disgrace is calculated to excite the sympathies of the profligate, and to fill the theatre with all that numerous class of morbidly curious idlers who flock to a play or an execution to see how a man looks when he is hanged, or deserves to be hanged . . . When every person who can read knows that his offence is aggravated by the most shocking circumstances of indecency, brutality, obscenity, perfidy, and hypocrisy – we do say that the public . . . ought not to be insulted by his immediate obtrusion before them, as a candidate for their applause. Let him hide himself for a reasonable time; his immediate appearance is as great an outrage to decency, as if he were to walk naked through the streets at mid-day."

The results of this kind of publicity were inevitable. On the night of the 24th of January, Drury Lane was besieged by a seething, hysterical mass of humanity who, in truth, had the lust to view an execution, not the desire to see a play. Outside, the theatre was patrolled by a detachment of police from Bow Street, who had been given stern instructions by their chief that they were not to enter the building unless an actual riot broke out. Inside, the auditorium was jammed full half an hour before the curtain rose, and a kind of suppressed pandemonium had already been let loose. When Edmund made his entrance, a wild shout went up, like the battle-cry of some barbarian army on the march.

For three hours and more it continued unabated. But the curtain was not lowered. The show went on. Edmund and his fellow-actors played their parts, though scarcely a line that they uttered could be heard above the general din.

. . . When Edmund was on the stage neither his supporters nor his opponents let him alone for an instant. And when he was off, a series of side-shows took place. Private brawls broke out in the pit and in the boxes, hats were thrown in the air, dirty handkerchiefs were waved, missiles were hurled across the auditorium, and placards with lewd inscriptions were raised on high. Then Edmund re-entered and the persecution began.

He himself was apparently unmoved. He tried once or twice to address the house, but in vain. And so, heedless of the showers of orange peel which fell around him and the maniacal shouts which drowned his utterance, he played his part to the bitter end.

No one who saw him that night could have doubted his courage. Throughout a terrible ordeal he had not flinched. Perhaps the hostile newspapers which reported the proceedings the next morning with gleeful indignation, felt satisfied that the experience must have unnerved him and that he would not come back any more. But they were wrong. On the 28th of January *The Times* was forced to announce: "That obscene little personage (Mr Kean) is, we see, to make another appearance this evening . . . His real friends and supporters, who have hitherto upheld him, because they thought his frailties over-balanced by his talents, must now desert him, when they see him dead even to the lowest degree of shame which distin-guishes human from animal nature. We suspect that he will scarcely find adequate consolation among his 'Wolves' (a club of Kean's admirers) and – we need not add the alliterative adjunct."

He appeared as Othello; and he had to contend with another prolonged exhibition of mass hysteria which was no less humiliating than the one which he had already suffered. In fact, Othello gave his audience an even better chance for coarse enjoyment at his expense than Richard II had done. Many of the lines which he was obliged to speak were greedily interpreted as references to his own morals. And, of course, during the scenes with Desdemona there were shrieks of disgusted delight.

. . . (At the end of the play) Edmund was received with mingled cheers and hisses, but this time he was allowed to speak. He addressed the house briefly and under stress of obvious emotion. He disclaimed any intention of justifying his private conduct, though he suggested that he had been victimised. "I stand before you," he said, "as the representative of Shakespeare's heroes . . . If this is the work of a hostile press, I shall endeavour with firmness to withstand it; but if it proceeds from your verdict and decision, I will at once bow to it, and shall retire with deep regret and with a grateful sense of all the favours which your patronage has hitherto conferred on me."

After that speech the issue was really settled. In spite of the frantic efforts of his enemies, Edmund had neither retreated nor begged for mercy. The odds had appeared to be overwhelmingly against him, but heroically he had refused to yield, and it was obvious that now he would never do so.

HECKLING NIXON

Ron Kovic

Kovic, a paralysed Vietnam veteran, gate-crashed the 1972 Re-
publican Convention to make an anti-war protest. To do so, he had
to quell two of humanity's great fears: speaking in public and
making a fool of oneself. Kovic's story was later filmed by Holly-
wood as Born on the Fourth of the July *starring Tom Cruise.*

It was the night of Nixon's acceptance speech and now I was
on my own deep in his territory, all alone in my wheelchair in
a sweat-soaked marine utility jacket covered with medals from
the war. A TV producer I knew from the Coast had gotten me
past the guards at the entrance with his press pass. My eyes
were still smarting from teargas. Outside the chain metal fence
around the Convention Center my friends were being clubbed
and arrested, herded into wagons. The crowds were thick all
around me, people dressed as if they were going to a banquet,
men in expensive summer suits and women in light elegant
dresses. Every once in a while someone would look at me as if I
didn't belong there. But I had come almost three thousand
miles for this meeting with the president and nothing was going
to prevent it from taking place.

I worked my way slowly and carefully into the huge hall,
moving down one of the side aisles. "Excuse me, excuse me," I
said to delegates as I pushed past them farther and farther to the
front of the hall toward the speakers' podium.

I had gotten only halfway toward where I wanted to be when
I was stopped by one of the convention security marshals.

"Where are you going?" he said. He grabbed hold of the back of my chair, I made believe I hadn't heard him and kept turning my wheels, but his grip on the chair was too tight and now two other security men had joined him.

"What's the matter?" I said. "Can't a disabled veteran who fought for his country sit up front?"

The three men looked at each other for a moment and one of them said, "I'm afraid not. You're not allowed up front with the delegates." I had gotten as far as I had on sheer bluff alone and now they were telling me I could go no farther. "You'll have to go to the back of the convention hall, son. Let's go," said the guard who was holding my chair.

In a move of desperation I swung around facing all three of them, shouting as loud as I could so Walter Cronkite and the CBS camera crew that was just above me could hear me and maybe even focus their cameras in for the six o'clock news. "I'm a Vietnam veteran and I fought in the war! Did you fight in the war?"

One of the guards looked away.

"Yeah, that's what I thought," I said. "I bet none of you fought in the war and you guys are trying to throw me out of the convention. I've got just as much right to be up front here as any of these delegates. I fought for that right and I was born on the Fourth of July."

I was really shouting now and another officer came over. I think he might have been in charge of the hall. He told me I could stay where I was if I was quiet and didn't move up any farther. I agreed with the compromise. I locked my brakes and looked for other veterans in the tremendous crowd. As far as I could tell, I was the only one who had made it in.

People had begun to sit down all around me. They all had Four More Years buttons and I was surprised to see how many of them were young. I began speaking to them, telling them about the Last Patrol and why veterans from all over the United States had taken the time and effort to travel thousands of miles to the Republican National Convention. "I'm a disabled veteran!" I shouted. "I served two tours of duty in Vietnam and while on my second tour of duty up in the DMZ I was wounded and paralyzed from the chest down." I told them I would be that way for the rest of my life. Then I began to talk about the hospitals and how they treated the returning veterans like animals, how I, many nights in the Bronx, had lain in my own shit for hours waiting for an aide. "And they never come," I said. "They never come because that man that's going to accept the nomination tonight has been lying to all of us and spending the money on war that should be spent on healing and helping the wounded. That's the biggest lie and hypocrisy of all – that we had to go over there and fight and get crippled and come home to a government and leaders who could care less about the same boys they sent over."

I kept shouting and speaking, looking for some kind of reaction from the crowd. No one seemed to want to even look at me.

"Is it too real for you to look at? Is this wheelchair too much for you to take? The man who will accept the nomination tonight is a liar!" I shouted again and again, until finally one of the security men came back and told me to be quiet or they would have to take me to the back of the hall.

I told him that if they tried to move me or touch my chair there would be a fight and hell to pay right there in front of Walter Cronkite and the national television networks. I told him if he wanted to wrestle me and beat me to the floor of the convention hall in front of all those cameras he could.

By then a couple of newsmen, including Roger Mudd from CBS, had worked their way through the security barricades and begun to ask me questions.

"Why are you here tonight?" Roger Mudd asked me. "But don't start talking until I get the camera here," he shouted.

It was too good to be true. In a few seconds Roger Mudd and I would be going on live all over the country. I would be doing what I had come here for, showing the whole nation what the war was all about. The camera began to roll, and I began to explain why I and the others had come, that the war was wrong and it had to stop immediately. "I'm a Vietnam veteran," I said. "I gave America my all and the leaders of this government threw me and the others away to rot in their V.A. hospitals. What's happening in Vietnam is a crime against humanity, and I just want the American people to know that we have come all the way across this country, sleeping on the ground and in the rain, to let the American people see for themselves the men who fought their war and have come to oppose it. If you can't believe the veteran who fought the war and was wounded in the war, who can you believe?"

"Thank you," said Roger Mudd, visibly moved by what I had said. "This is Roger Mudd," he said, "down on the convention floor with Ron Kovic, a disabled veteran protesting President Nixon's policy in Vietnam." . . .

Suddenly a roar went up in the convention hall, louder than anything I had ever heard in my life. It started off as a rumble, then gained in intensity until it sounded like a tremendous thunderbolt. "Four more years, four more years," the crowd roared over and over again. The fat woman next to me was jumping up and down and dancing in the aisle. It was the greatest ovation the president of the United States had ever received and he loved it. I held the sides of my wheelchair to keep my hands from shaking. After what seemed forever, the roar finally began to die down.

This was the moment I had come three thousand miles for, this was it, all the pain and the rage, all the trials and the death of the war and what had been done to me and a generation of Americans by all the men who had lied to us and tricked us, by the man who stood before us in the convention hall that night, while men who had fought for their country were being gassed and beaten in the street outside the hall. I thought of Bobby who sat next to me and the months we had spent in the hospital in the Bronx. It was all hitting me at once, all those years, all that destruction, all that sorrow.

President Nixon began to speak and all three of us took a deep breath and shouted at the top of our lungs, "Stop the bombing, stop the war, stop the bombing, stop the war," as loud and as hard as we could, looking directly at Nixon. The security agents immediately threw up their arms, trying to hide us from the cameras and the president. "Stop the bombing, stop the bombing," I screamed. For an instant Cronkite looked down, then turned his head away. They're not going to show it, I thought. They're going to try and hide us like they did in the hospitals. Hundreds of people around us began to clap and shout "Four more years," trying to drown out our protest. They all seemed very angry and shouted at us to stop. We continued shouting, interrupting Nixon again and again until Secret Service agents grabbed our chairs from behind and began pulling us backward as fast as they could out of the convention hall. "Take it easy," Bobby said to me. "Don't fight back."

I wanted to take a swing and fight right there in the middle of the convention hall in front of the president and the whole country. "So this is how they treat their wounded veterans!" I screamed.

A short guy with a big Four More Years button ran up to me and spat in my face. "Traitor!" he screamed, as he was yanked back by police. Pandemonium was breaking out all around us and the Secret Service men kept pulling us out backward.

"I served two tours of duty in Vietnam!" I screamed to one newsman. "I gave three-quarters of my body for America. And what do I get? Spit in the face!" I kept screaming until we hit the side entrance where the agents pushed us outside and shut the doors, locking them with chains and padlocks so reporters wouldn't be able to follow us out for interviews.

All three of us sat holding onto each other shaking. We had done it. It had been the biggest moment of our lives, we had shouted down the president of the United States and disrupted his acceptance speech. What more was there left to do but go home?

I sat in my chair still shaking and began to cry.

SIR WALTER SCOTT
AND HIS CREDITORS

Sir Walter Scott

A wildly successful writer of historical novels, Scott's finances went awry when he decided to dabble as a publisher. In 1826 his publishing enterprise broke down and Scott was left owing one hundred and twenty thousand pounds to his creditors. He did not run, he did not plead bankruptcy but instead with heroic endeavour worked to pay off every penny, turning out novels at dizzying speed. He died in harness in 1832. A year or two later the debt was fully extinguished.

December 18, 1825. The general knowledge that an author must write for his bread, at least for improving his pittance, degrades him and his productions in the public eye. He falls into the second-rate rank of estimation:

> While the harness sore galls, and the spurs his side goad,
> The high-mettled racer's a hack on the road.

It is a bitter thought; but if tears start at it, let them flow. My heart clings to the place I have created – there is scarce a tree on it that does not owe its being to me.

What a life mine has been! – half-educated, almost wholly neglected, or left to myself; stuffing my head with most non-sensical trash, and under-valued by most of my contemporaries for a time; getting forward, and held a bold and clever fellow, contrary to the opinion of all who thought me a mere dreamer; broken-hearted for two years; my heart handsomely pieced again – but the crack will remain till my dying day. Rich and poor four or five times; once on the verge of ruin, yet opened a new source of wealth almost overflowing. Now to be broken in my pitch of pride, and nearly winged (unless good news should come) because London chooses to be in an uproar, and in the tumult of bulls and bears, a poor inoffensive lion like myself is pushed to the wall. But what is to be the end of it? God knows; and so ends the catechism.

Nobody in the end can lose a penny by me – that is one comfort. Men will think pride has had a fall. Let them indulge their own pride in thinking that my fall will make them higher, or seem so at least. I have the satisfaction to recollect that my prosperity has been of advantage to many, and to hope that some at least will forgive my transient wealth on account of the innocence of my intentions, and my real wish to do good to the poor. Sad hearts, too, at Darnick, and in the cottages of Abbotsford. I have half resolved never to see the place again. How could I tread my hall with such a diminished crest? – how live a poor indebted man, where I was once the wealthy, the honoured? I was to have gone there on Saturday in joy and prosperity to receive my friends. My dogs will wait for me in vain. It is foolish – but the thoughts of parting from these dumb creatures has moved me more than any of the painful reflections I have put down. Poor things! I must get them kind masters! There may be yet those who, loving me, may love my dog, because it has been mine. I must end these gloomy forebodings, or I shall lose the tone of mind with which men should meet distress. I find my dogs' feet on my knees – I hear them whining and seeking me everywhere. This is nonsense, but it is what they would do could they know how things may be. An odd thought strikes me – When I die, will the journal of these days be taken out of the ebony cabinet at Abbotsford, and read with wonder, that the well-seeming Baronet should ever have experienced the risk of such a hitch? – or will it be found in some obscure lodging-house, where the decayed son of Chivalry had hung up his scutcheon, and where one or two old friends will look grave, and whisper to each other, "Poor gentleman" – "a well-meaning man" – "nobody's enemy but his own" –

"thought his parts would never wear out" – "family poorly left"
– "pity he took that foolish title." Who can answer this question?

December 26. My God! what poor creatures we are! After all
my fair proposals yesterday, I was seized with a most violent
pain in the right kidney and parts adjacent, which forced me
instantly to go to bed and send for Clarkson. He came, inquired,
and pronounced the complaint to be gravel augmented by bile. I
was in great agony till about two o'clock, but awoke with the
pain gone. I got up, had a fire in my dressing closet, and had
Dalgleish to shave me – two trifles, which I only mention,
because they are contrary to my hardy and independent personal habits. But although a man cannot be a hero to his valet, his
valet in sickness becomes of great use to him. I cannot expect
that the first will be the last visit of this cruel complaint: but
"shall we receive good at the hand of God, and not receive
evil?"

January 22nd. I feel neither dishonoured nor broken down by
the bad – now really bad – news I have received. I have walked
my last on the domains I have planted – sate the last time in the
halls I have built. But death would have taken them from me if
misfortune had spared them. My poor people whom I loved so
well! – There is just another die to turn up against me in this run
of ill-luck; *i.e.* if I should break my magic wand in the fall from
this elephant, and lose my popularity with my fortune. Then
Woodstock and "Bony" may both go to the paper-maker, and I
may take to smoking cigars and drinking grog, or turn devotee,
and intoxicate the brain another way. In prospect of absolute
ruin, I wonder if they would let me leave the Court of Session. I
would like, methinks, to go abroad,

And lay my bones far from the Tweed.

But I find my eyes moistening, and that will not do. I will not
yield without a fight for it. It is odd, when I set myself to work
doggedly, as Dr Johnson would say, I am exactly the same man
as I ever was – neither low-spirited nor distrait. In prosperous
times I have sometimes felt my fancy and powers of language
flag, but adversity is to me at least a tonic and bracer; the

fountain is awakened from its inmost recesses, as if the spirit of affliction had troubled it in his passage.

Poor Mr Pole the harper [who taught Scott's daughters] sent to offer me £500 or £600, probably his all. There is much good in the world, after all.

January 23. Slept ill, not having been abroad these eight days – *splendida bilis*. Then a dead sleep in the morning, and when the awakening comes, a strong feeling how well I could dispense with it for once and for ever. This passes away, however, as better and more dutiful thoughts arise in my mind. I know not if my imagination has flagged – probably it has; but at least my powers of labour have not diminished during the last melancholy week. On Monday and Tuesday my exertions were suspended. Since Wednesday inclusive, I have written thirty-eight of my close MS. pages, of which seventy make a volume of the usual Novel size.

January 24. I went to the Court for the first time today, and, like the man with the large nose, thought everybody was thinking of me and my mishaps. Many were, undoubtedly, and all rather regrettingly; some obviously affected. It is singular to see the difference of men's manner whilst they strive to be kind or civil in their way of addressing me. Some smiled as they wished me good-day, as if to say, "Think nothing about it, my lad; it is quite out of our thoughts." Others greeted me with the usual affected gravity which one sees and despises at a funeral. The best-bred – all, I believe, meaning equally well – just shook hands and went on. A foolish puff in the papers, calling on men and gods to assist a popular author, who having choused the public of many thousands, had not the sense to keep wealth when he had it. If I am hard pressed, and measures used against me, I must use all means of legal defence, and subscribe myself bankrupt in a petition for sequestration. It is the course one should, at any rate, have advised a client to take. But for this I would, in a Court of Honour, deserve to lose my spurs. No, – if they permit me, I will be their vassal for life, and dig in the mine of my imagination to find diamonds (or what may sell for such) to make good my engagements, not to enrich myself. And this from no reluctance to be called the Insolvent, which I probably am, but because I will not put out of the power of my creditors the resources, mental or literary, which yet remain to me.

May 26. Dull, drooping, cheerless, has this day been. I cared not carrying my own gloom to the girls, and so sate in my own room, dawdling with old papers, which awakened as many stings as if they had been the nest of fifty scorpions. Then the solitude seemed so absolute – my poor Charlotte* would have been in the room half a score of times to see if the fire burned, and to ask a hundred kind questions. Well, that is over – and if it cannot be forgotten, must be remembered with patience.

Christmas, 1827. My reflections in entering my own gate to-day were of a very different and more pleasing cast than those with which I left this place about six weeks ago. I was then in doubt whether I should fly my country, or become avowedly bankrupt, and surrender up my library and household furniture, with the liferent of my estate, to sale. A man of the world will say I had better done so. No doubt had I taken this course at once, I might have employed the money I have made since the insolvency of Constable and Robinson's houses in compounding my debts. But I could not have slept sound, as I now can under the comfortable impression of receiving the thanks of my creditors, and the conscious feeling of discharging my duty as a man of honour and honesty. I see before me a long, tedious, and dark path, but it leads to stainless reputation. If I die in the harrows, as is very likely, I shall die with honour; if I achieve my task, I shall have the thanks of all concerned, and the approbation of my own conscience. And so, I think, I can fairly face the return of Christmas-Day.

* His wife, who died earlier in the month.

THE BLOCKING OF ZEEBRUGGE

Sir Archibald Hurd

This story of naval and marine daring is from the First World War, when the Belgian port of Zeebrugge was in German hands.

Situated on the Belgian coast, some twelve miles apart, and facing a little to the west of north, Zeebrugge was in reality but a sea-gate of the inland port of Bruges – the latter being the station to which the enemy destroyers and submarines were sent in parts from the German workshops; where they were assembled; and whence, by canal, they proceeded to sea by way of Zeebrugge and Ostend. Of these two exits, Zeebrugge, the northernmost, was considerably the nearer to Bruges and the more important – Zeebrugge being eight, while Ostend was eleven miles distant from their common base – and to receive an adequate impression of what was subsequently achieved there it is necessary to bear in mind its salient features.

Unlike Ostend, apart from its harbour, it possessed no civic importance, merely consisting of a few streets of houses clustering about its railway station, locks, wharves, and storehouses, its sandy roadstead being guarded from the sea by an immensely powerful crescentic Mole. It was into this roadstead, that the Bruges canal opened between heavy timbered breakwaters, having first passed through a sea-lock, some half a mile higher up. Between the two lighthouses, each about twenty feet above high-water level, that stood upon the ends of these breakwaters, the canal was 200 yards wide, narrowing to a width, in the lock itself, of less than seventy feet.

Leading from the canal entrance to the tip of the Mole, on which stood a third lighthouse, and so out to sea, was a curved channel, about three-quarters of a mile long, kept clear by continual dredging; and this was protected both by a string of armed barges and by a system of nets on its shoreward side. It was in its great sea-wall, however, some eighty yards broad and more than a mile long, that Zeebrugge's chief strength resided; and this had been utilized, since the German occupation, to the utmost extent. Upon the seaward end of it, near the lighthouse, a battery of 6-inch guns had been mounted, other batteries and machine-guns being stationed at various points throughout its length. With a parapet along its outer side, some sixteen feet higher than the level of the rest of the Mole, it not only carried a railway-line but contained a sea-plane shed, and shelters for stores and *personnel*. It was connected with the shore by a light wood and steel viaduct – a pilework structure, allowing for the passage of the through-current necessary to prevent silting.

Emplaced upon the shore, on either side of this, were further batteries of heavy guns; while, to the north of the canal en-trance, and at a point almost opposite to the tip of the Mole, was the Goeben Fort, containing yet other guns covering both the Mole and the harbour. Under the lee of the parapet were dug-outs for the defenders, while, under the lee of the Mole itself, was a similar shelter for the enemy's submarines and destroyers. Nor did this exhaust the harbour's defences, since it was further protected not only by minefields, but by natural shoals, always difficult to navigate, and infinitely more so in the absence of beacons.

Even to a greater extent was this last a feature of Ostend, though here the whole problem was somewhat simpler, there being no Mole, and therefore no necessity – though equally no opportunity – for a subsidiary attack. Covered, of course, from the shore by guns of all calibres – and here it should be remembered that there were 225 of these between Nieuport and the Dutch frontier – the single object in this case was to gain the entrance, before the block ships should be discovered by the enemy, and sunk by his gunners where their presence would do no harm. Since for complete success, however, it was necessary to seal both places, and, if possible, to do so simultaneously, it will readily be seen that, in the words of Sir Eric Geddes – the successor, as First Lord of the Admiralty, to Mr Balfour and Sir Edward Carson – it was, "a particularly intricate operation which had to be worked strictly to timetable." It was also one that, for several months before, required the most arduous and secret toil.

Begun in 1917 while Sir John Jellicoe was still First Sea Lord, the plan ultimately adopted – there had been several previous ones, dropped for military reasons – was devised by Vice-Admiral Roger Keyes, then head of the Plans Division at the Admiralty. From the first it was realized, of course, by all concerned that the element of surprise would be the determining factor; and it was therefore decided that the attempt to block the harbours should take place at night. It was also clear that, under modern conditions of star-shells and searchlights, an extensive use would have to be made of the recent art of throwing out smokescreens; and fortunately, in Commander Brock, Admiral Keyes had at his disposal just the man to supply this need. A Wing-Commander in the Royal Naval Air Service, in private life Commander Brock was a partner in a well-known firm of firework makers; and his inventive ability had already been fruitful in more than one direction. A first-rate pilot and excellent shot, Commander Brock was a typical English sportsman; and his subsequent death during the operations, for whose success he had been so largely responsible, was a loss of the gravest description both to the Navy and the empire.

The next consideration was the choosing of the block-ships and for these the following vessels were at last selected – the *Sirius* and *Brilliant* to be sunk at Ostend, and the *Thetis*, *Iphigenia*, and *Intrepid* to seal the canal entrance at Zeebrugge. These were all old cruisers, and they were to be filled with cement, which when submerged would turn into concrete, fuses being so placed that they could be sunk by explosion as soon as they had reached the desired position; and it was arranged that motor-launches should accompany them in order to rescue their crews.

So far these general arrangements were applicable to both places; but, as regarded Zeebrugge, it was decided to make a diversion in the shape of a subsidiary attack on the Mole, in which men were to be landed and to do as much damage as possible. Such an attack, it was thought, would help to draw the enemy's attention from the main effort, which was to be the sinking of the block-ships, and, apart from this, would have valuable results both material and moral. For this secondary operation, three other vessels were especially selected and fitted out – two Liverpool ferry boats, the *Iris* and *Daffodil*, obtained by Captain Grant, not without some difficulty, owing to the natural reluctance of the Liverpool authorities and the impossibility of divulging the object for which they were wanted – and the old cruiser *Vindictive*. This latter vessel had been designed as a "ram" ship more than twenty years before, displacing about 5,000 tons and capable of a speed of some twenty knots. She had no armour-belt, but her bow was covered with plates, two inches thick and extending fourteen feet aft, while her deck was also protected by hardened plates, covered with nickel steel, from a half to two inches thick. Originally undergunned, she had subsequently been provided with ten 6-inch guns and eight 12-pounders.

This was the vessel chosen to convey the bulk of the landing party, and, for many weeks, under the supervision of Commander E. O. B. S. Osborne, the carpenters and engineers were hard at work upon her. An additional high deck, carrying thirteen brows or gangways, was fitted upon her port side; pom-poms and machine-guns were placed in her fighting-top; and she was provided with three howitzers and some Stokes mortars. A special flame-throwing cabin, fitted with speaking tubes, was built beside the bridge, and another on the port quarter.

It was thus to be the task of the *Vindictive* and her consorts to lay themselves alongside the Mole, land storming and demolition parties, and protect these by a barrage as they advanced down the Mole; and, in order to make this attack more effective, yet a third operation was designed. This was to cut off the Mole from the mainland, thus isolating its defenders and preventing the arrival of reinforcements; and, in order to do so, it was decided to blow up the viaduct by means of an old submarine charged with high explosives. Meanwhile the whole attempt was to be supported from out at sea by a continuous bombardment from a squadron of monitors; sea-planes and aeroplanes, weather permitting, were to render further assistance; and flotillas of destroyers were to shepherd the whole force and to hold the flanks against possible attack.

This then was the plan of campaign, one of the most daring ever conceived, and all the more so in face of the difficulty of keeping it concealed from the enemy during the long period of preparation – a difficulty enhanced in that it was not only necessary to inform each man of his particular *rôle*, but of the particular objectives of each attack and the general outline of the whole scheme. That was unavoidable since it was more than likely that, during any one of the component actions, every officer might be killed or wounded and the men themselves become responsible. Nor was it possible, even approximately, to fix a date for the enterprise, since this could only be carried out under particular conditions of wind and weather. Thus the night must be dark and the sea calm; the arrival on the other side must be at high water; and there must above all things be a following wind, since, without this, the smoke screens would be useless. Twice, when all was ready, these conditions seemed to have come, and twice, after a start had been made, the expedition had to return; and it was not until April 22nd, 1918, that the final embarkation took place.

By this time Vice-Admiral Keyes had succeeded Vice-Admiral Bacon in command of the Dover Patrol; and he was therefore in personal charge of the great adventure that he had initiated and planned with such care. Every man under him was not only a volunteer fully aware of what he was about to face, but a picked man, selected and judged by as high a standard, perhaps, as the world could have provided. Flying his own flag on the destroyer *Warwick*, Admiral Keyes had entrusted the *Vindictive* to acting Captain A. F. B. Carpenter, the *Iris* and the *Daffodil* being in the hands respectively of Commander Valentine Gibbs and Lieutenant Harold Campbell. The marines, consisting of three companies of the Royal Marine Light Infantry and a hundred men of the Royal Marine Artillery, had been drawn from the Grand Fleet, the Chatham, Portsmouth, and Devonport Depots, and were commanded by Lieutenant-Colonel Bertram Elliot. The three block-ships that were to be sunk at Zeebrugge, the *Thetis*, *Intrepid*, and *Iphigenia*, were in charge of Commander Ralph S. Sneyd, Lieutenant Stuart Bonham-Carter, and Lieutenant E. W. Billyard-Leake; while the old submarine *C3* that was to blow up the viaduct was commanded by Lieutenant R. D. Sandford. In control of the motor-launches, allotted to the attack on Zeeb-rugge, was Admiral Keyes' flag-captain, Captain R. Collins, those at Ostend being directed by Commander Hamilton Benn, M. P. – the operations at the latter place being in charge of Commodore Hubert Lynes. Also acting in support, was a large body of coastal motor-boats under Lieutenant A. E. P. Well-man, and a flotilla of destroyers under Captain Wilfred Tom-kinson, the general surveying of the whole field of attack – including the fixing of targets and firing-points – being in the skilful hands of Commander H. P. Douglas and Lieutenant-Commander F. E. B. Haselfoot.

Included among the monitors were the *Erebus* and *Terror*, each mounting 15-inch guns, to operate at Zeebrugge; and the *Prince Eugene*, *General Crauford*, and *Lord Clive*, carrying 12-inch guns, and the *Marshal Soult*, carrying 15-inch guns, to assist at Ostend. To the old *Vindictive* Admiral Keyes had presented a horseshoe that had been nailed for luck to her centre funnel; and, to the whole fleet, on its way across, he signalled the message, "St. George for England." Few who received that message expected to return unscathed, and in the block-ships none; but it is safe to say that, in the words of Nelson, they would not have been elsewhere that night for thousands.

Such then were the forces that, on this still dark night, safely arrived at their first rendezvous and then parted on their perilous ways, some to Zeebrugge and some to Ostend. It was at a point about fifteen miles from the Belgian coast that the two parties separated; and, since it is impossible to follow them both at once, let us confine ourselves at first to the former. Theirs was the more complicated, though, as it afterwards proved, the more swiftly achieved task, the first to arrive on the scene of action, almost at the stroke of midnight, being the old cruiser *Vindictive* with her two stout little attendants. These she had been towing as far as the rendezvous; but, at this point, she had cast them off, and they were now following her, under their own steam, to assist in berthing her and to land their own parties. Ahead of them the small craft had been laying their smoke-screens, the north-east wind rolling these shorewards, while already the monitors could be heard at work bombarding the coast defences with their big guns. Accustomed as he was to such visitations, this had not aroused in the enemy any particular alarm; and it was not until the *Vindictive* and the two ferry-boats were within 400 yards of the Mole that the off-shore wind caused the smoke-screen to lift somewhat and left them exposed to the enemy. By this time the marines and bluejackets, ready to spring ashore, were mustered on the lower and main decks; while Colonel Elliot, Major Cordner, and Captain Chater, who were to lead the marines, and Captain Halahan, who was in charge of the bluejackets, were waiting on the high false deck.

It was a crucial moment, for there could be no mistaking now what was the *Vindictive*'s intention. The enemy's star-shells, soaring into the sky, broke into a baleful and crimson light; while his searchlights, that had been wavering through the darkness, instantly sprang together and fastened upon the three vessels. This, as Captain Carpenter afterwards confessed, induced "an extraordinarily naked feeling," and then, from every gun that could be brought to bear, both from the Mole and the coast, there burst upon her such a fire as, given another few minutes, must inevitably have sunk her. Beneath it Colonel Elliot, Major Cordner, and Captain Halahan, all fell slain; while Captain Carpenter himself had the narrowest escape from destruction. His cap – he had left his best one at home – was two or three times over pierced by bullets, as was the case of his binoculars, slung by straps over his back; while, during the further course of the action, both his searchlight and smoke-goggles were smashed.

The surprise had so far succeeded, however, that, within less than five minutes, the *Vindictive*'s bow was against the side of the Mole, and all but her upper works consequently protected from the severest of the enemy's fire. Safe – or comparatively so – as regarded her water-line, she was nevertheless still a point-blank target; her funnels were riddled over and over again, the one carrying the horse-shoe suffering least; the signal-room was smashed and the bridge blown to pieces, just as Commander Carpenter entered the flame-throwing cabin; and this in its turn, drawing the enemy's fire, was soon twisted and splintered in all directions. It was now raining; explosion followed explosion till the whole air quaked as if in torment; and meanwhile a new and unforeseen danger had just made itself apparent. Till the harbour was approached, the sea had been calm, but now a ground-swell was causing a "scend" against the Mole, adding tenfold not only to the difficulties of landing, but of maintaining the *Vindictive* at her berth. In this emergency, it was the little *Daffodil* that rose to and saved the situation. Her primary duty, although she carried a landing party, had been to push the *Vindictive* in until the latter had been secured; but, as matters were, she had to hold her against the Mole throughout the whole hour and a quarter of her stay there. Even so, the improvised gangways that had been thrust out from the false deck were now some four feet up in the air and now crashing down from the top of the parapet; and it was across these brows, splintering under their feet, and in the face of a fire that baffled description, that the marines and bluejackets had to scramble ashore with their Lewis guns, hand-grenades, and bayonets.

Under such conditions, once a man fell, there was but little hope of his regaining his feet; and it was only a lucky chance that saved one of the officers from being thus trodden to death. This was Lieutenant H. T. C. Walker, who, with an arm blown away, had stumbled and fallen on the upper deck, the eager storming parties, sweeping over him until he was happily discovered and dragged free. Let it be said at once that Lieutenant Walker bore no malice, and waved them good luck with his remaining arm. The command of the marines had now devolved upon Major Weller; and, of the 300 or so who followed him ashore, more than half were soon to be casualties. But the landing was made good; the awkward drop from the parapet was successfully negotiated thanks to the special scaling-ladders; the barrage was put down; and they were soon at hand-to-hand grips with such of the German defenders as stayed to face them. Many of these were in the dug-out under the parapets, but, seeing that to remain there was only to be bayoneted, they made a rush for some of their own destroyers that were hugging the lee of the Mole. But few reached these, however, thanks to the vigour of the marines and the fire of the machine-guns from the *Vindictive*'s top, while one of the destroyers was damaged by hand-grenades and by shells lobbed over the Mole from the *Vindictive*'s mortars.

Meanwhile the *Vindictive* was still the object of a fire that was rapidly dismantling all of her that was visible. A shell in her fighting-top killed every man at the guns there except Sergeant

Finch of the Royal Marine Artillery, who was badly wounded, but who extricated himself from a pile of corpses, and worked his gun for a while single-handed. Another shell, bursting forward, put the whole of a howitzer crew out of action, and yet a third, finding the same place, destroyed the crew that followed.

Fierce as was the ordeal through which the *Vindictive* was passing, however, that of the *Iris* was even more so. Unprotected, as was her fellow the *Daffodil*, boring against the side of the larger *Vindictive*, the *Iris*, with her landing-party, was trying to make good her berth lower down the Mole, ahead of Captain Carpenter. Unfortunately the grapnels with which she had been provided proved to be ineffective owing to the "scend," and, with the little boat tossing up and down, and under the fiercest fire, two of the officers, Lieutenant-Commander Bradford and Lieutenant Hawkins, climbed ashore to try and make them fast. Both were killed before they succeeded, toppling into the water between the Mole and the ship, while, a little later, a couple of shells burst aboard with disastrous results. One of these, piercing the deck, exploded among a party of marines, waiting for the gangways to be thrust out, killing forty-nine and wounding seven; while another, wrecking the ward-room, killed four officers and twenty-six men. Her Captain, Commander Gibbs, had both his legs blown away, and died in a few hours, the *Iris* having been forced meanwhile to change her position, and take up another astern of the *Vindictive*.

Before this happened, however, every man aboard her, as aboard the *Vindictive, Daffodil*, and upon the Mole, had been thrilled to the bone by the gigantic explosion that had blown up the viaduct lower down. With a deafening roar and a gush of flame leaping up hundreds of yards into the night, Lieutenant Sandford had told them the good tidings of his success with the old submarine. Creeping towards the viaduct, with his little crew on deck, he had made straight for an aperture between the steel-covered piles, and to the blank amazement and apparent paralysis of the Germans crowded upon the viaduct, had rammed in the submarine up to her conning-tower before lighting the fuse that was to start the explosion.

Before himself doing this, he had put off a boat, his men

needing no orders to tumble into her, followed by their commander, as soon as the fuse was fired, with the one idea of getting away as far as possible. As luck would have it, the boat's propeller fouled, and they had to rely for safety upon two oars only, pulling, as Lieutenant Sandford afterwards described it, as hard as men ever pulled before. Raked by machine-gun fire and with shells plunging all round them, most of them, including Lieutenant Sandford, were wounded; but they were finally borne to safety by an attendant picket-boat under his brother, Lieutenant-Commander F. Sandford.

That had taken place about fifteen minutes after the *Vindictive* and her consorts had reached their berths, and a few minutes before the block-ships, with *Thetis* leading, had rounded the light-house at the tip of the Mole. In order to assist these to find their bearings, an employee of Commander Brock, who had never before been to sea, had for some time been firing rockets from the after cabin of the *Vindictive*; and presently they came in sight, exposed as the *Vindictive* had been, by the partial blowing back of their smoke screen. Steaming straight ahead for their objectives, they were therefore opposed by the intensest fire; and the spirit in which they proceeded is well illustrated by what had just taken place on board the *Intrepid*, It had been previously arranged that, for the final stage of their journey, the crews of the block-ships should be reduced to a minimum; but, when the moment came to disembark the extra men, those on the *Intrepid*, so anxious were they to remain, actually hid themselves away. Many of them did in fact succeed in remaining, and sailed with their comrades into the canal.

The first to draw the enemy's fire, the *Thetis*, had the misfortune, having cleared the armed barges, to foul the nets – bursting through the gate and carrying this with her, but with her propellers gathering in the meshes and rendering her helpless. Heavily shelled, she was soon in a sinking condition, and Commander Sneyd was obliged to blow her charges, but not before he had given the line, with the most deliberate coolness, to the two following block-ships – Lieutenant Littleton, in a motor-launch, then rescuing the crew.

Following the *Thetis* came the *Intrepid*, with all her guns in full action, and Lieutenant Bonham-Carter pushed her right into the canal up to a point actually behind some of the German batteries. Here he ran her nose into the western bank, ordered his crew away, and blew her up, the engineer remaining down below in order to be able to report results. These being satisfactory, and every one having left, Lieutenant Bonham-Carter committed himself to a Carley float – a kind of lifebuoy that, on contact with the water, automatically ignited a calcium flare. Illuminated by this, the *Intrepid*'s commander found himself the target of a machine-gun on the bank, and, but for the smoke still pouring from the *Intrepid*, he would probably have been killed before the launch could rescue him.

Meanwhile the *Iphigenia*, close behind, had been equally successful under more difficult conditions. With the *Intrepid*'s smoke blowing back upon her, she had found it exceedingly hard to keep her course, and had rammed a dredger with a barge moored to it, pushing the latter before her when she broke free. Lieutenant Billyard-Leake, however, was able to reach his objective – the eastern bank of the canal entrance – and here he sank her in good position, with her engines still working to keep her in place. Both vessels were thus left lying well across the canal, as aeroplane photographs afterwards confirmed; and thanks to the persistent courage of Lieutenant Percy Dean, the crews of both block-ships were safely removed.

With the accompanying motor-launch unhappily sunk as she was going in, Lieutenant Dean, under fire from all sides, often at a range of but a few feet, embarked in *Motor-Launch 282* no less than 101 officers and men. He then started for home, but, learning that there was an officer still in the water, at once returned and rescued him, three men being shot at his side as he handled his little vessel. Making a second start, just as he cleared the canal entrance, his steering-gear broke down; and he had to manœuvre by means of his engines, hugging the side of the Mole to keep out of range of the guns. Reaching the harbour mouth he then, by a stroke of luck, found himself alongside the destroyer *Warwick*, who was thus able to take on board and complete the rescue of the block-ships' crews.

It was now nearly one o'clock on the morning of the 23rd; the main objects of the attack had been secured; and Captain Carpenter, watching the course of events, decided that it was time to recall his landing-parties. It had been arranged to do so with the *Vindictive*'s siren, but this, like so much of her gear, was no longer serviceable; and it was necessary to have recourse to the *Daffodil*'s little hooter, so feebly opposed to the roar of the guns. Throughout the whole operation, humble as her part had been, the *Daffodil* had been performing yeoman's service, and, but for the fine seamanship of Lieutenant Harold Campbell, and the efforts of her engine-room staff, it would have been quite impossible to re-embark the marines and bluejackets from the Mole. In the normal way her boilers developed some 80-lbs steam-pressure per inch; but, for the work of holding the *Vindictive* against the side of the Mole, it was necessary throughout to maintain double this pressure. All picked men, under Artificer-Engineer Sutton, the stokers held to their task in the ablest fashion; and, in ignorance of what was happening all about them, and to the muffled accompaniment of bursting shells, they worked themselves out, stripped to their vests and trousers, to the last point of exhaustion.

Nor did their colleagues on board the *Vindictive* fall in any degree short of the same high standard, as becomes clear from the account afterwards given by one of her stokers, Alfred Dingle. "My pigeon," he said, "was in the boiler-room of the *Vindictive*, which left with the other craft at two o'clock on Tuesday afternoon. We were in charge of Chief Artificer-Engineer Campbell, who was formerly a merchant-service engineer and must have been specially selected for the job. He is a splendid fellow. At the start he told us what we were in for, and that before we had finished we should have to feed the fires like mad. 'This ship was built at Chatham twenty years ago,' he said, 'and her speed is 19 knots, but if you don't get 21 knots out of her when it is wanted, well – it's up to you to do it anyway.' We cheered, and he told us, when we got the order, to get at it for all we were worth, and take no notice of anybody. We were all strong fellows, the whole thirteen of us . . . The *Vindictive* was got to Zeebrugge; it was just before midnight when we got alongside the Mole. We had gas-masks on then, and were stoking furiously all the time, with the artificer-engineer backing us up, and joking and keeping us in the best of spirits. Nobody could have been down-hearted while he was there. There is no need to say it was awful; you know something from the accounts in the papers, although no written accounts could make you understand what it was really like . . . Well, there we were, bump, bump, bump against the Mole for I don't know how long, and all the time the shells shrieking and crashing, rockets going up, and a din that was too awful for words, added to which were the cries and shrieks of wounded officers and men . . . Several times Captain Carpenter came below and told us how things were going on. That was splendid of him, I think. He was full of enthusiasm, and cheered us up wonderfully. He was the same with the seamen and men on deck . . . I can't help admiring the marines. They were a splendid lot of chaps, most of them seasoned men, whilst the bluejackets (who were just as good) were generally quite young men. The marines were bursting to get at the fight and were chafing under the delay all the time . . . While we were alongside I was stoking and took off my gas-mask, as it was so much in the way. It was a silly thing to do, but I couldn't get on with the work with it on. Suddenly I smelt gas. I don't know whether it came from an ordinary shell, but I know it was not from the smoke screen, and you ought to have seen me nip round for the helmet. I forgot where I put it for the moment, and there was I running round with my hand clapped on my mouth till I found it. In the boiler-room our exciting time was after the worst was over on shore. All of a sudden the telegraph rang down, 'Full speed ahead,' and then there was a commotion. The artificer-engineer shouted 'Now for it; don't forget what you have to do – 21 knots, if she never does it again.' In a minute or two the engines were going full pelt. Somebody came down and said we were still hitched on to the Mole, but Campbell said he didn't care if we towed the Mole back with us; nothing was going to stop him. As a matter of fact, we pulled away great chunks of the masonry with the grappling irons, and brought some of it back with us. Eventually we got clear of the Mole, and there was terrific firing up above. Mr Campbell was urging us on all the time, and we were shoving in the coal like madmen. We were all singing. One of the chaps started with 'I want to go home,' and this eventually developed into a verse, and I don't think we stopped singing it for three and a half hours – pretty nearly all the time we were coming back. In the other parts of the ship there wasn't much singing, for all the killed and wounded men we could get hold of had been brought on board, and were being attended to by the doctors and sick bay men. I don't know if we did the 21 knots, but we got jolly near it, and everybody worked like a Trojan, and was quite exhausted when it was all over. When we were off Dover the Engineer-Commander came down into the boiler-room and asked Artificer-Engineer Campbell, 'What have you got to say about your men?' He replied, 'I'm not going to say anything for them or anything against them; but if I was going to hell to-morrow night I would have the same men with me.' "

Not until the Mole had been cleared of every man that could possibly be removed did the *Vindictive* break away, turning in a half-circle and belching flames from every pore of her broken funnels. That was perhaps her worst moment, for now she was exposed to every angry and awakened battery; her lower decks were already a shambles; and many of her navigating staff were killed or helpless. But her luck held; the enemy's shells fell short; and soon she was comparatively safe in the undispersed smoke-trails, with the glorious consciousness that she had indeed earned the Admiral's "Well done, *Vindictive*."

ZOLA AND THE DREYFUS CASE

Frederick Laws

It was perhaps inevitable that the novelist Emile Zola would involve himself in the Dreyfus Case which so exercised France in the 1890s (and continues to do so till this day). Dreyfus, a French Jewish Army officer had been unjustly convicted of passing national secrets to a foreign power. The smell of anti-Semitism wafted heavy over the affair. Although not political, Zola had – as proved by novels such as Germinal *and* La Terre – *a passionate desire for truth and an equally passionate dislike of hypocrisy. In espousing the cause of Dreyfus, Zola set himself at odds with almost the entire French nation.*

I t was while Zola was in Rome working on his book [*Rome*] in that city that the Dreyfus affair began. Like most other people Zola assumed that Dreyfus was guilty and went on with his work. Captain Dreyfus was sent to Devil's Island in 1895 and Zola finished *Rome* and began on *Paris*. His only contact with the affair was in writing an article defending the Jews from some of the fantastic attacks which were being made on them by newspapers with clerical support who were using them as an object of hatred for political reasons.

The whole truth about the Dreyfus affair may never be known. Facts were falsified for reasons of State, documents were destroyed, new documents were forged, vital witnesses disappeared, and partisan feeling tortured the truth in innumerable ways. Anti-Semitism had been growing for some time. Newspapers, publicists and politicians of the Fascist type fanned the flame.

A document which could only have come from the War
Office was found by a spy in the German Embassy. Captain
Dreyfus, the only Jew in the War Office, was accused of treason,
apparently on the evidence of handwriting alone. There was
immense public indignation; he was degraded and sent to
Devil's Island. He asserted his innocence constantly, and his
family fought for a retrial. Then a year later Colonel Picquart,
the new head of the Intelligence Department of the War Office,
found evidence which incriminated a certain Colonel Esterhazy
and pointed to the innocence of Dreyfus. Esterhazy was tried by
secret court martial and acquitted. An important piece of
evidence in his favour was an unconvincing "liberating document" about a treasonable Captain D—, which had been
handed to Esterhazy by a veiled lady in the presence of two
witnesses. Colonel Picquart was removed to a Colonial post and
later put in prison on an obscure charge. It was alleged that at
Esterhazy's trial Picquart and other witnesses were under
military discipline prevented from telling all they knew.

The scandal spread; many influential people were convinced
that Esterhazy was guilty and that the War Office was refusing
to admit that it had been wrong about Dreyfus. Anti-Semitic
disturbances in the streets of Paris continued, and it was said
that a new enquiry into the Dreyfus affair would endanger the
army and the republic. Zola had friends who were sure of
Dreyfus's innocence and they persuaded him to leave his
semi-retirement and look into the affair.

Zola disliked the unscientific "racial theory" of the anti-
Semitic party. He had no illusions about the wisdom of the high
command. He believed the clerical party to be utterly unscru-
pulous. He knew that organized society has not infrequently
made an innocent man the scapegoat for its own follies or
crimes. And he was profoundly suspicious of the motives of
the crowds shouting in the streets. Besides the story of Dreyfus
contained so much that did not ring true. It was a cheap
feuilleton – a newspaper novelette – and Zola hated cheap
feuilletons. To begin with, there was something altogether
too convenient, too neat, too melodramatic in the story that a
traitor to France should be found in the only Jew in the War
Office just at a time when extremists were demanding that Jews
should be removed from positions of trust in the State. And

then that business of the accusation: Dreyfus was asked to write something containing the words of the treasonable document in a room full of mirrors. There was too much of the romantic detective unveiling wickedness with picturesque tricks about those mirrors. Then there was the evidence of Dreyfus's jailer. The jailer had been favourably impressed by the bearing of his prisoner, and he told a very queer story about the military prosecutor visiting the prison at night and wanting to scare a confession out of Dreyfus by suddenly flashing a lantern in his face when he was sleeping.

The behaviour of Dreyfus, assuming him guilty, was curious too. Witnesses of his degradation said that when the drums rolled and his decorations were ripped from his uniform he cried out: "I am innocent. Long live France." A guilty man would hardly have the courage or the imagination to act such a part. The secrecy of the trial of Esterhazy and the removal of Picquart were suspicious enough, but that wretched veiled lady with her so convenient liberating document was the last straw. She was preposterous. It was like the story of Marie Antoinette's necklace, it was like comic opera, it was impossible. It was as bad as Zola's early feuilleton which had to end half-way through. The master of the realistic novel rejected as unconvincing the story which authority had concocted and which the mob accepted, and set out to force a little realism down the throats of a number of generals of the French army.

Zola began his campaign. He had a great example before him – the example of Voltaire who gave up three years of his life to establish the innocence of a Protestant who had been broken on the wheel on the false accusation produced by fanatical Catholics that he had murdered his son to prevent him abjuring Protestantism. He began by demanding an investigation in three newspaper articles in *Figaro*. Then the editor had to refuse to print more. Next he published a pamphlet *A Letter to Youth*. It was addressed to the young men shouting in the streets. He became unpopular. He was hissed even when walking in the funeral procession of his friend Daudet. Again in a pamphlet *A Letter to France* he warned his country of the dangers of dictatorship and clericalism. But it was in vain. The trial of Esterhazy went its curious way. Picquart had been imprisoned. It was clear that no ordinary legal methods could revive the question of the innocence or guilt of Dreyfus. So he decided to use the revolutionary method of forcing himself into court by committing a libel. He wrote his famous letter to the President of the Republic, *I Accuse*, and it was published in *L'Aurore* on January 13, 1898.

The stinging rhetoric of that letter was masterly. It could not be ignored. "A council of war has dared to acquit an Esterhazy in obedience to orders. This is a final blow at all truth, at all justice. It has been done, France bears this stain upon her cheek. Since they have dared, I will dare also. It is my duty to speak; I will not be an accomplice. My nights would be haunted by the spirit of an innocent man suffering in a far country the most frightful tortures for a crime which he did not commit. . . . Dreyfus knows several languages – a crime; no compromising documents were found on his premises – a crime; he sometimes visits the country of his birth – a crime; he is industrious and wants to know everything – a crime; he does not get confused – a crime; he gets confused – a crime. . . . It is a question of the sword, the master that may be given us, tomorrow perhaps. And to kiss devoutly the hilt of the sword, the fetish – no!" Zola tried to make certain of forcing a prosecution. He accused the Minister of War – of having an inferior intelligence. He accused General de Boisdeffre, the Chief of Staff – of yielding to his passionate clericalism. He accused General Gonse – of having an accommodating conscience.

But the authorities were cautious. There were riots in which the windows of *L'Aurore* and of Zola's house were broken, but when, after three days, Zola was finally charged with defamation of character he found that the indictment was carefully limited to those passages in his letter which dealt only with the Esterhazy trial. All the references to Dreyfus were ignored. His elaborate insults to the individuals who were behind the Dreyfus trial were swallowed. He had been presented with writs by the handwriting experts who exonerated Esterhazy, but it was clear that the authorities whose hand he had wanted to force were determined that the case of Dreyfus should remain a thing judged. Zola and the manager of *L'Aurore* protested vigorously against this piece-meal treatment of the letter, and accused the military authorities of using legal trickery in order to keep Dreyfus in his prison on Devil's Island, but their protests were ineffective.

The trial of Zola began early in February, before a jury of Parisian tradesmen. A seedsman, a linen draper, a wine merchant, and a slater were amongst the twelve whose duty was to examine the justice of Zola's charges against the court martial who freed Esterhazy. The honesty of the jury could be relied on, but every conceivable form of legal and illegal pressure was brought to bear on them. Their names and addresses were published by anti-Jewish papers, their doors were chalked with threats of what would happen to them if Zola were acquitted, and in the Chamber of Deputies a powerful politician announced that he was confident that they would do their patriotic duty. Patriotism seemed to mean that the army chiefs must be vindicated right or wrong and Zola publicly shamed. The cry that the country was in danger went up. It appeared that if Zola were acquitted the Germans would march on Paris the next day. To remain completely unbiased those twelve tradesmen would have had to be supermen. It is greatly to the credit of the independence of judgment of the French bourgeois and artisan that when their vote was taken, five of the twelve stood out for Zola. But the great question was not whether Zola and the manager of *L'Aurore* should be fined or not, it was whether the truth about Dreyfus and Esterhazy could be brought out in open court.

Against the full reopening of the case the public prosecutor and the judge stood firm. Zola was to be tried on so many phrases of a libellous letter and nothing outside those carefully selected phrases would be mentioned in court if it could possibly be prevented. Again and again Zola's brilliant young counsel put damaging questions to witnesses whom the judge allowed to remain silent. Irrelevant oratory was permitted to the prosecution and the defence was silenced whenever it mentioned the trial of Dreyfus. The innocence of Dreyfus was the major point at issue, but a rigid legal ruling placed it theoretically outside the scope of the court.

The moment the trial began it became clear what Zola and his advocate Labori had to fight against. The President of the Court, Delegorgue, a weak man with a short temper went through the list of witnesses called by the defence. One after another he read the names of generals and accusers of Dreyfus who had answered the summons of the court with arrogant excuses. General Billot wrote that the keeper of the seals had given him permission not to appear in court. General de Boisdeffre, General Mercier, and General de Pellieux pleaded their military duties and the certainty that their evidence could add nothing to the information of the court. The prosecutor of Dreyfus, Colonel du Paty de Clam, wrote that his military superiors had excused his attendance. M. le Commandant Esterhazy could not attend the first session of the court.

Amongst uproar from the public part of the court and against opposition from Delegorgue, Labori maintained the power of the civil court of law over every French citizen, and demanded that these insolent apologies should be refused and that the generals should be forced to come and testify. Mademoiselle de Comminges, who was believed to be the famous veiled lady, and Madame de Boulancy, who had received damagingly unpatriotic letters from Esterhazy, had both sent in doctors' certificates of illness. Labori had foreseen this and had ready a legal document insisting that the court should send its own doctor to decide just how dangerous the unfortunate illnesses of these ladies really were.

Madame Dreyfus took the stand. She wished to testify to her belief in the good faith of Zola, and to tell the story of how her husband's prosecutor, du Paty de Clam, had forced her and her family into silence at the time of the arrest with vague threats and vaguer promises. But Delegorgue could not see what that could have to do with the case. He would not let Madame Dreyfus speak. Angrily Zola leapt to his feet: "I ask to be allowed here the liberty that is accorded thieves and murderers. They can defend themselves, summon witnesses, and ask them questions, but every day I am insulted in the street, they break my carriage windows, they roll me in the mud and an unclean press treats me as a bandit. I have a right to prove my good faith, my honesty and my honour."

The Judge: "Do you know Article 52 of the law of 1881?"
Zola: "I do not know the law and at this moment I do not want to know it. I appeal to the probity of the jurors. I make them judges of my position, and I entrust myself to them."

He had made a bad tactical blunder in speaking contemptuously of the law, and had given his enemies a weapon against him. Next day he apologized, "I am not an orator. I am a writer. I do not revolt against the great conception of law, I submit to it completely, and from it I expect justice. My revolt was against all these legal quibbles raised against me, against the way in which I am being prosecuted, against the limitation of the complaint to fifteen lines taken from my long letter of accusation; and these things I declare unworthy of justice."

The defence continued and evidence piled up against Esterhazy in spite of the monotonous ruling of Delegorgue—"The question will not be put." When Colonel Picquart gave his evidence about the guilt of Esterhazy and the conspiracy of silence of the generals, his superior officer came forward and, interrupting, gave him the lie direct. And the president of the court did not interfere. Casimir Perrier, an ex-President of the Republic, rebuked the generals with the quiet words, "I am a simple citizen and at the service of the courts of my country." In spite of everything Zola was winning.

On the third day of the trial the body of the court was filled with officers in uniform. The military witnesses with their friend Esterhazy had arrived. But they were determined upon giving as little evidence as possible. To almost every question put by Labori General de Boisdeffre began his reply with the words: "Professional secrecy does not permit me. . . ." Another witness made his refrain: "I cannot repeat what happened behind closed doors in the trial of Commandant Esterhazy." To howls of applause General Gonse threatened to resign his post if Zola were acquitted. General de Pellieux evaded the issue by prophesying war if the honour of the army were besmirched. Esterhazy unwillingly went into the witness box, and after a hypocritical protest against being put on trial twice, stood silent with his back turned to Labori. However, silence could not save him. For a whole hour Labori put question after question to the silent spy. At the end of that hour his treachery had been categorically exposed.

The handwriting experts who condemned Dreyfus stood up again, and repeated their belief that because the handwriting of the fatal paper did not resemble that of the Jew on Devil's Island, it was clear that he had cleverly disguised his hand.

Generals pledged their honour that new documents, which for reasons of state they did not produce, had been found which fixed the guilt on Dreyfus. The forgery in which the phrase "That beast D—"occurred was published in the newspapers with "D—" expanded into "Dreyfus." It was useless for Jaurès, one of the few Socialists in the French Parliament, to proclaim the greatness of Zola: "They pursue in him the man who maintained the rational and scientific explanation of miracles, they persecute in him the man who predicted in *Germinal* the springing up of the wretched workers from the depths of suffering to the sunlight." The soldiers in court howled Jaurès down, and the Attorney-General rose to pour abuse on Zola and to demand a "patriotic" verdict.

Again Zola was allowed to speak. Soberly he attacked the political pressure brought to bear on justice. He demolished the legend of the Jewish syndicate who were supposed to have bribed all the witnesses for the defence. "And it is upon this poisoned bread that an unclean Press has been feeding our nation for months, and we should not be astonished at the spectacle of a disastrous crisis; for when stupidity and lies are sown at such a rate a crop of madness is sure to be harvested . . ."

He appealed to the jury. "I know you, I know who you are. You are the heart and mind of Paris, of my great Paris, where I was born, which I love with an infinite tenderness, which I have studied and written about for forty years.

"Do I look like a liar and a traitor? Why then should I act as I do? I have behind me neither political ambition nor sectarian passions. I am a free writer, who has given his life to toil, who tomorrow will again take his place in the ranks and resume his interrupted task.

". . . The question now is whether France is still the France of the rights of man, the France which gave liberty to the world and which ought to give it justice."

And finally, quivering with passion, he cried:

"I swear that Dreyfus is innocent." For two long sessions, harried by interruptions, Lábori pleaded eloquently for justice. But by a majority of seven to five Zola was found guilty. Sadly the novelist stood and gazed at the mob. "These people are cannibals," he said. He was condemned to a year in jail and a fine of three thousand francs, and with him Perrenx who bore the responsibility for printing *I Accuse* was given four months and a similar fine of three thousand francs. Zola left the court with his head high. Here are the words of a witness of the scene: "He was awkward, he was short sighted, he held his umbrella clumsily under his arm, he had the gestures and bearing of a student. But when he descended one by one the steps of the palace of justice, amid cries of hatred, shouts of death, under an archway of lifted sticks, it was like a king going down the great staircase of a palace under an archway of naked swords . . . It was the greatest thing I have ever seen in my life."

The army and injustice seemed to have triumphed. The men who had supported Zola were thrown out of office and humiliated. Colonel Picquart was arrested again, and the incident was closed. But the Press of Europe and America reached a very different verdict from that of the seven Paris tradesmen. The English papers were unanimously for Zola. Tolstoi wrote his sympathy, and even so unpolitical a writer as Mark Twain was angry: "I am filled with the deepest respect and the most boundless admiration for him. Ecclesiastical and military courts made up of cowards, hypocrites and time servers can be produced by the million every year and there could still be some to spare. It takes five centuries to produce a Joan of Arc or a Zola."

Zola himself "returned to his interrupted task," and worked on his set of four novels known as the "Gospels." They were to present "a new ethic and a new morality" and were to be entitled *Fruitfulness, Labour, Truth*, and *Justice*. Unfortunately for the military conspiracy Zola had been summoned to court not by the Esterhazy court martial whom he was supposed to have libelled but by an individual, and his conviction was quashed by an honest court of appeal. Zola was then charged by the court martial on an even shorter passage chosen from *I Accuse*.

The Dreyfus case gathered speed. Madame Dreyfus asked for her legal right to go to live on Devil's Island with her husband. That right was refused on the grounds that she might help him to escape. As a precautionary measure Dreyfus was put in irons – a piece of pointless cruelty. In an election anti-Semitic members were returned to Parliament in great numbers. A member of the War Office who was suspected of forging some of the documents which condemned Dreyfus was found hanged, and it was announced that he had committed suicide. Zola saw that there could be no wisdom in fighting the same case again, and was judged by default. He was ready to go to prison for a year, but Labori and his friends convinced him that he could carry on the fight outside the prison. Rapidly he fled to England. Living under false names he worked at his novels, wrote pamphlet after pamphlet on the theme "Truth is on the march and nothing will stop her," and waited for news from France. He had lost nearly a half of the normal income which came to him through the sale of his books, and when the courts distrained upon his goods to pay the fines recorded against him, he was very nearly a poor man again.

In France journalistic abuse of Zola grew more and more intense. It was said that a copy of the original Dreyfus document had been found with notes in the margin in the handwriting of William II, the German emperor. In the hope of killing the affair once and for all, the authorities stirred it up again, and during a new official inquiry two of the hundred documents added to the Dreyfus dossier were proved to be forgeries. One continuous document was supposed to have been torn in two and pasted together afterwards. The second piece was found to have been written on slightly different coloured notepaper from the first. The forger, a certain Colonel Henry, broke down under cross-examination. The Press of the Right raved about "the liberating sword" and cried "Death to the intellectuals." The suppression of freedom of speech was proposed. Colonel Henry "cut his throat" in prison. It was unprecedented for a prisoner to be allowed an open razor. Colonel Picquart was set free, and began libel actions against his calumniators. Esterhazy took flight and fled to England. Madame Dreyfus formally appealed for a revision of her husband's sentence. And the appeal could not be denied. The Court of Appeal decided on a new trial. Zola returned to France. The Court of Appeal annulled the sentence of Dreyfus leaving the way open for a new trial. An attempt by an anti-Semitic mob to carry out a *coup d'état* was a pitiful failure.

On June 5, 1899, after four years of living hell, Dreyfus was set free. But his enemies were not satisfied. At his second trial at Rennes, the advocate Labori was shot at as he entered the court.

Zola stayed away from Rennes to avoid prejudicing the trial. Still justice was not done. New forgeries were produced, fresh documents hinted at, and General Mercier swore that war was imminent. Again Dreyfus was condemned, only to be pardoned after ten days by the President of the Republic.

France had for two years now been split into two bitterly angry parties. In Zola's words, "All former political parties have now collapsed and there remain but two camps – that of the reactionary forces of the past, and that of the men bent on enquiry, truth and righteousness." This may sound rhetorical to English ears but in the light of history, it is a sober statement of the truth. France had been in danger of the overthrow of the rights of the citizen. She had come very near to a military dictatorship. Freedom of speech and the reign of law had been threatened. But for *I Accuse* and the obstinacy of Zola, suppression would almost certainly have been the fate of the parties of the Left who now had gathered strength to fight social injustice. Zola's novels – in particular *Germinal* about the miners, and *The Earth* about the peasants – gave fuel to the growing fire of socialism. His action in the Dreyfus affair saved the freedom for which the French Revolution was fought. He wrote once, "The novel is the great weapon of this epoch," and now the first three of his openly propagandist "Gospels" *Fruitfulness Labour*, and *Truth* were ready as weapons for the men who wished to build a new France.

Dreyfus was pardoned but France was still in an uproar. Zola was still to be re-tried, Picquart was in the midst of several lawsuits, some of the perjured generals and their subordinates were still at their posts, and there was to be an International Exhibition in 1900. Visitors must not be frightened away by rioting and political up-heavals. Parliament passed an Act of Amnesty for everything which had been done in the Dreyfus affair. Conspirator and innocent victim were pardoned in the same breath. Obstinately Zola protested, "Parliament is saying that there are no more judges . . . They are befouling us by placing us on a par with ruffians."

It was his last protest. In September, 1902, he was found dead in his room stifled by fumes caused by a defective chimney. Even on the report of his death the clerical papers published foul libels upon him. But he was buried with military honours, and as the procession passed by, workers cried out "Germinal, Germinal." His last "Gospel," *Justice*, was never finished. Full justice was only done to Dreyfus two years after his death. But his work was completed. When his ashes were placed in the Panthéon amongst the greatest of his country's dead, Anatole France spoke:

"And Zola deserved well of his country by refusing to despair of justice in France. We must not pity him for having suffered and endured. Let us rather envy him: he honoured his country and the world by immense literary work and by a great deed. Let us rather envy him; his destiny and his heart gave him the grandest fate: in him at one moment was set the conscience of mankind."

"J'ACCUSE . . ."

Emile Zola

The text of Zola's famous address to President Faure, as published in L'Aurore *in January 1898.*

To President Félix Faure of France

Mr President,

Permit me, I beg you, in return for the gracious favours you once accorded me, to be concerned with regard to your just glory and to tell you that your record, so fair and fortunate thus far, is now threatened with the most shameful, the most ineffaceable blot.

You escaped safe and sane from the basest calumnies; you conquered all hearts. You seem radiant in the glory of a patriotic celebration . . . and are preparing to preside over the solemn triumph of our Universal Exposition, which is to crown our great century of work, truth and liberty. But what a clod of mud is flung upon your name – I was about to say your reign – through this abominable Dreyfus affair. A court martial has but recently, by order, dared to acquit one Esterhazy – a supreme slap at all truth, all justice! And it is done; France has this brand upon her visage; history will relate that it was during your administration that such a social crime could be committed.

Since, they have dared, I too shall dare. I shall tell the truth because I pledged myself to tell it if justice, regularly empowered, did not do so, fully, unmitigatedly. My duty is to speak; I have no wish to be an accomplice. My nights would be haunted by the spectre of the innocent being, expiating under the most frightful torture, a crime he never committed.

And it is to you, Mr President, that I shall out this truth, with the force of my revolt as an honest man. To your honour, I am convinced that you are ignorant of the crime. And to whom, then, shall I denounce the malignant rabble of true culprits, if not to you, the highest magistrate in the country? . . .

I accuse Colonel du Paty de Clam of having been the diabolical agent of the judicial error, unconsciously, I prefer to believe, and of having continued to defend his deadly work during the past three years through the most absurd and revolting machinations.

I accuse General Mercier of having made himself an accomplice in one of the greatest crimes of history, probably through weak-mindedness.

I accuse General Billot of having had in his hands the decisive proofs of the innocence of Dreyfus and of having concealed them, and of having rendered himself guilty of the crime of lèse humanity and lèse justice, out of political motives and to save the face of the General Staff.

I accuse General Boisdeffre and General Gonse of being accomplices in the same crime, the former no doubt through religious prejudice, the latter out of *esprit de corps*.

I accuse General de Pellieux and Major Ravary of having made a scoundrelly inquest, I mean an inquest of the most monstrous partiality, the complete report of which composes for us an imperishable monument of naïve effrontery.

I accuse the three handwriting experts, MM. Belhomme, Varinard and Couard, of having made lying and fraudulent reports, unless a medical examination will certify them to be deficient of sight and judgment.

I accuse the War Office of having led a vile campaign in the press, particularly in *l'Éclair* and *l'Écho de Paris*, in order to misdirect public opinion and cover up its sins.

I accuse, lastly, the first court martial of having violated all human right in condemning a prisoner on testimony kept secret from him, and I accuse the second court martial of having covered up this illegality by order, committing in turn the judicial crime of acquitting a guilty man with full knowledge of his guilt.

In making these accusations I am aware that I render myself liable to articles 30 and 31 of Libel Laws of 29 July 1881, which punish acts of defamation. I expose myself voluntarily.

As to the men I accuse, I do not know them, I have never seen them, I feel neither resentment nor hatred against them. For me they are only entities, emblems of social malfeasance. The action I take here is simply a revolutionary step designed to hasten the explosion of truth and justice.

I have one passion only, for light, in the name of humanity which has borne so much and has a right to happiness. My burning protest is only the cry of my soul. Let them dare, then, to carry me to the court of appeals, and let there be an inquest in the full light of the day!

I am waiting.

Mr President, I beg you to accept the assurances of my deepest respect.

Emile Zola

MORAL FIBRE IN BOMBER COMMAND

Max Hastings

An historian's examination of the workings of courage (and of fear) among the RAF's bomber crews in World War II. From Hasting's Bomber Command, *1979.*

Throughout the war, morale on British bomber stations held up astonishingly well, although there were isolated collapses on certain squadrons at certain periods – for example, during the heavy losses of the Battle of Berlin. Morale never became a major problem, as it did on some 8th Air Force stations during the terrible losses of 1943 and early 1944. An RAF doctor seconded to study aircrew spirit at one American station reported in dismay: "Aircrew are heard openly saying that they don't intend to fly to Berlin again or do any more difficult sorties. This is not considered a disgrace or dishonourable." Partly the Americans found the appalling business of watching each other die on daylight sorties more harrowing than the anonymity of night operations. Partly also, they were far from their homes, and many did not feel the personal commitment to the war that was possible for Englishmen.

But most of the crews of Bomber Command fought an unending battle with fear for most of their tours, and some of them lost it. Even today, the Judge-Advocate General of the Forces is implacably unhelpful on inquiries relating to the problems of disciplinary courts martial and "LMF" – lacking moral fibre – cases among wartime aircrew. I believe that around one man in seven was lost to operational aircrew at some point between OTU and completing his tour for morale or medical causes, merely because among a hundred aircrew whom I have interviewed myself, almost all lost one member of their crew at some time, for some reason. Few of these cases would be classified by any but the most bigoted as simple "cowardice," for by now the Moran principle that courage is not an absolute human characteristic, but expendable capital every man possesses in varying quantity, has been widely recognized. But in 1943 most men relieved of operational duty for medical or moral reasons were treated by the RAF with considerable harshness. There was great fear at the top of the service that if an honourable path existed to escape operations, many men would take it. "LMF could go through a squadron like wildfire if it was unchecked," says one of the most distinguished post-war leaders of the RAF, who in 1943 was commanding a bomber station. "I made certain that every case before me was punished by court martial, and where applicable by an exemplary prison sentence, whatever the psychiatrists were saying."

Command was enraged when stories emerged at courts martial of doctors in Glasgow or Manchester who for five pounds would brief a man on the symptoms necessary to get him taken off operations: insomnia, waking screaming in his quarters, bedwetting, headaches, nightmares. Station medical officers became notoriously unsympathetic to aircrew with any but the most obvious symptoms of illness. The Air Staff were in a constant dilemma about the general management of aircrew, who were intensively trained to fly their aircraft, yet for little else. Regular officers were exasperated by the appearance and off-duty behaviour of many temporary officers and NCOs. In their turn, the relentless pursuit of career opportunities by some regular airmen even in the midst of war did not escape the scornful notice of aircrew, especially when this took the form of officers burying themselves in Flying Training Command or in staff jobs rather than flying with operational squadrons.

The Air Ministry considered that morale and disciplinary problems were closely linked. In a 1943 report which attacked the practice of holding All Ranks dances at bomber stations, which noted that Harris's men had the highest rate of venereal disease in the RAF and No. 6 Group's Canadians a rate five times higher than anyone else's, the Inspector-General of the RAF noted with displeasure:

> Aircrew are becoming more and more divorced from their legitimate leaders, and their officers are forgetting, if they ever learnt them, their responsibilities to their men. Aircrew personnel must be disabused of the idea that their sole responsibility is to fly . . . and to do this, their leisure hours must be more freely devoted to training and hard work.

The Air Ministry never lost its conviction that gentlemen made the best aircrew, and a remarkable staff memorandum of late 1942 expressed concern about the growing proportion of Colonials in Bomber Command and suggested: "There are indications in a number of directions that we are not getting a reasonable percentage of the young men of the middle and upper classes, who are the backbone of this country, when they leave the public schools."

When Ferris Newton was interviewed for a commission, the group captain had already noted without enthusiasm that he owned a pub, and inquired whether it catered to the coach trade. Yet the Commonwealth aircrew, especially, believed that it was their very intimacy with their crews, their indifference to rank, that often made them such strong teams in the air. An Australian from 50 Squadron cited the example of a distinguished young English ex-public school pilot who was killed in 1943. This boy, he said, was a classic example of an officer who never achieved complete cohesion with his crew, who won obedience only by the rings on his sleeves and not by force of personality: "He simply wouldn't have known how to go out screwing with his gunners in Lincoln on a Saturday night." In his memoirs Harris argues that the English made the best aircrew, because they had the strongest sense of discipline. It was a difference of tradition.

To the men on the stations, the RAF's attitude to their problems often seemed savagely unsympathetic. One day on a cross-country exercise before they began operations, the bomb-aimer of Lindaas's crew at 76 Squadron fell through the forward hatch of the aircraft, which had somehow come loose. The rest of the crew thought at first that he had fallen out completely. Only after several seconds did they realize that he was clinging desperately beneath the aircraft. Only after several more seconds of struggle did they get the dinghy rope around him, and haul him back into the fuselage. When he returned to the ground, he said flatly that he would never fly again. He was pronounced LMF, and vanished from the station. Normally in such cases, an NCO was stripped of his stripes, which had been awarded in recognition of his aircrew status, and posted to ground duties. Only in incontrovertible cases of "cowardice in the face of the enemy," as at one 5 Group station where one night three members of a crew left their aircraft as it taxied to take-off, was the matter referred to court martial. A further cause of resentment against Permanent Commissioned Officers was that if they wished to escape operations, they could almost invariably arrange a quiet transfer to non-operational duties, because the service was reluctant to instigate the court martial that was always necessary in their case, to strip them of rank.

It was very rare for a case to be open and shut. The navigator of a Whitley in 1941 ran amok and had to be laid out with the pilot's torch over Germany. The man disappeared overnight from the squadron – normal procedure throughout the war, to avoid the risk that he might contaminate others. But the pilot recounting this experience added: "Don't draw the obvious conclusion. The next time I saw the man's name, he was navigating for one of the Dambusting crews." Many men had temporary moral collapses in the midst of operational tours. The most fortunate, who were sensitively treated, were sent for a spell at the RAF convalescent home at Matlock in Derbyshire. A post-war medical report argues that many such men sincerely wanted to be rehabilitated and return to operations to save their own self-respect, while genuine LMF cases proved on close study to be men who should never have survived the aircrew selection process.

But the decisive factor in the morale of bomber aircrew, like that of all fighting men, was leadership. At first, it is difficult to understand what impact a leader can have, when in battle his men are flying with only their own crews over Germany, far out of sight and command. Yet a post-war 8 Group medical report stated emphatically: "The morale of a squadron was almost always in direct proportion to the quality of leadership shown by the squadron commanders, and the fluctuations in this respect were most remarkable." A good CO's crews pressed home attacks with more determination; suffered at least marginally lower losses; perhaps above all, had a low "Early Return" rate. Guy Gibson, the leader of the Dambusters, was one kind of legendary Bomber Command CO. Not a cerebral man, he represented the apogee of the pre-war English public schoolboy, the perpetual team captain, of unshakeable courage and dedication to duty, impatient of those who could not meet his exceptional standards. "He was the kind of boy who would have been head prefect in any school," said Sir Ralph Cochrane, his commander in 5 Group.

For the first four months of 1943, 76 Squadron was commanded by Leonard Cheshire, another of the great British bomber pilots of the war, of a quite different mould from Gibson, but even more remarkable. Cheshire, the son of a distinguished lawyer, read law at Oxford, then joined the RAF shortly before the outbreak of war. In 1940 he began flying Whitleys over Germany. By 1943, with two brilliant tours already behind him, he was a 26-year-old wing-commander. There was a mystical air about him, as if he somehow inhabited another planet from those around him, yet without affection or pretension. "Chesh is crackers," some people on the squadrons said freely in the days before this deceptively gentle, mild man became famous. They were all the more bewildered when he married and brought back from America in 1942 an actress fifteen years older than himself.

Yet Leonard Cheshire contributed perhaps more than any other single pilot to the legend of Bomber Command. He performed extraordinary feats of courage, studied the techniques of bombing with intense perception and intelligence, and later pioneered the finest precision marking of the war as leader of 617 Squadron. At 76 Squadron there was a joke about Cheshire, that "the moment he walks into a bar, you can see him starting to work out how much explosive it would need to knock it down." He was possibly not a natural flying genius in an aircraft like Micky Martin, but, by absolute dedication to his craft, he made himself a master. He flew almost every day. If he had been on leave and was due to operate that night, he went up for two hours in the morning to restore his sense of absolute intimacy with his aircraft. He believed that to survive over Germany it was necessary to develop an auto-pilot within himself, which could fly the aircraft quite instinctively, leaving all his concentration free for the target and the enemy. As far back as 1941 he wrote a paper on marking techniques. He had always been an advocate of extreme low-level bombing.

Cheshire himself wrote, "I loved flying and was a good pilot, because I threw myself heart and soul into the job. I found the dangers of battle exciting and exhilarating, so that war came easily to me." Most of those he commanded knew themselves to be frailer flesh, and he dedicated himself to teaching them everything that he knew. He never forgot that Lofty, his own first pilot on Whitleys, had taught him to know every detail of his aircraft, and he was determined to show others likewise. He lectured 76's crews on Economical Cruising Heights, Escape and Evasion techniques, and methods of improving night vision. They knew that he was devoted to their interests. On a trip to Nuremberg they were detailed to cross the French coast at 2,000 feet. He simply told Group that he would not send them at that height. It would be 200 feet or 20,000. He made his point.

A CO who flew the most dangerous trips himself contributed immensely to morale – some officers were derisively christened "François" for their habit of picking the easy French targets when they flew. Cheshire did not have his own crew – only Jock Hill, his wireless operator. Instead, he flew as "Second Dickey" with the new and nervous. Perhaps the chief reason that "Chesh" inspired such loyalty and respect was that he took the trouble to know and recognize every single man at Linton. It was no mean feat, learning five hundred or more faces which changed every week. Yet the ground crews chorused: "We are Cheshire cats!" because the CO spent so much of his day driving round the hangars and dispersals chatting to them and remembering exactly who had sciatica. It was the same with the aircrew. A young wireless operator, who had arrived at Linton the previous day, was climbing into the truck for the dispersals when he felt Cheshire's arm round his shoulder. "Good luck, Wilson." All the way to the aircraft, the W/Op pondered in bewildered delight: "How the hell did the CO know my name?" They knew that when Cheshire flew, it was always the most difficult and dangerous operations. He would ask them to do nothing that he had not done himself. It was Cheshire who noticed that very few Halifax pilots were coming home on three engines. He took up an aircraft to discover why. He found that if a Halifax stalled after losing an engine it went into an uncontrollable spin. After a terrifying minute falling out of the sky, Cheshire was skillful and lucky enough to be able to recover the aircraft and land, and report on the problem, which he was convinced was caused by a fault in the rudder design.

Handley Page, the manufacturers, then enraged him by refusing to interrupt production to make a modification. Only when a Polish test-pilot had been killed making further investigations into the problem which Cheshire had exposed was the change at last made. His imagination and courage became part of the folklore of Bomber Command. He left 76 Squadron in April 1943 and later took command of 617, the Dambusters squadron. By the end of the war, with his Victoria Cross, three Distinguished Service Orders, Distinguished Flying Cross and fantastic total of completed operations, he had become a legend.

Cheshire left the squadron in April, to be succeeded by Wing-Commander Don Smith, a regular officer who came to Linton with a log-book which had been endorsed "exceptional" in every category of airmanship throughout his service career. Smith had flown fifty-eight successful operations in the Middle East while commanding two Blenheim squadrons in Aden in 1940 and 1941. He now began an eventful tour at 76 Squadron, flying the maximum twenty trips, sixteen on German targets. One July night, he and his crew were on the way home from Mont Beliard when

unexpected things began to happen. The two starboard engines cut out within five seconds of each other and Red muttered something about "fifteen gallons left." Steve looked at Pete, and Pete looked at Steve, and the one thought uppermost in the minds of both of them was just how many seconds the port engines were going to last out. Steve opened the hatch, and Pete went through with no trouble at all . . . They were somewhat shaken by the factory chimneys of Scunthorpe 200 feet below, but fortunately came to earth in the last field before the houses at the edge of the town. Instead of the motley array of pikes and pitchforks, which they were expecting, they were greeted on arrival by a deputation of Scunthorpe ladies in negligés, all very solicitous and all bearing cups of tea. Inside the aircraft, Red was having a pitched battle with the skipper, who refused to put on his chute and who in any case could not safely leave the controls even had he wanted to. So the skipper neatly hopped a couple of hedges and made another of his renowned belly-landings, this time in a potato field. He and "Dirts" Ashton went off to search for ham and eggs (and found them), leaving an equally hungry engineer to guard the remains of our third aircraft . . . We never found out just what started it all, but Red, at any rate, was exonerated.

Don Smith remained at Holme until the end of December, when he was awarded a DSO to add to the DFC he had won in May with 76 Squadron, and the Mention in Dispatches awarded to him for operations in the Middle East. He was then posted to instruct at an Operational Training Unit.

Yet whatever the quality of leadership and morale on a squadron, there was seldom any Hollywood-type enthusiasm for take-off on a bomber operation. One summer evening at Holme, 76 Squadron's crews were scattered at the dispersals, waiting miserably for start-up time before going to Berlin, the most hated target in Germany. The weather forecast was terrible, and the CO had been driving round the pans chatting to crews in an effort to raise spirits. Then, suddenly, a red Very light arched into the sky, signalling a "wash out." All over the airfield a great surge of cheering and whistle-blowing erupted.

A 76 Squadron pilot who later completed a second tour on Mosquitoes said that his colleagues on the light bombers "simply could never understand how awful being on heavies was." Some men simply found the strain intolerable. There were pilots who found themselves persistently suffering from "mag drop," so easily achieved by running up an engine with the magnetos switched off, oiling up the plugs. After two or three such incidents preventing take-off, the squadron CO usually intervened. One of the aircrew at 76 Squadron returned from every operation to face persecution from his wife and his mother, both of whom lived locally. "Haven't you done enough?" the wife asked insistently, often in the hearing of other aircrew. "Can't you ever think of me?" In the end the man asked to be taken off operations, and was pronounced LMF.

A 76 Squadron wireless operator completed six operations with one of the Norwegian crews before reporting sick with ear trouble. He came up before the CO for a lecture on the need for highly trained and experienced aircrew to continue flying, and was given a few days to consider his position. At a second interview, he told the CO he had thought over what had been said, but he wanted a rest. He felt that having volunteered "in" for aircrew duties, he could also volunteer "out." He was reduced to the ranks, stripped of his flying brevet, posted to the depot at Chessington which dealt with such cases, and spent the rest of the war on ground duties. So did Alf Kirkham's rear gunner:

> After our first few trips together, which were very rough indeed [wrote Kirkham], he simply did not like the odds. He decided that he wanted to live, and told me that nothing anyone could do to him would be worse than carrying on with operations. He was determined to see the war out, and as far as I know he was successful.

Marginal LMF suspects, along with disciplinary cases who had broken up the sergeants' mess, had been discovered using high-octane fuel in their cars, or involved in "avoidable flying accidents," were sent to the "Aircrew Refresher Centres" at Sheffield, Brighton or Bournemouth. In reality these centres were open-arrest detention barracks, where they spent a few weeks doing PT and attending lectures before being sent back to their stations, or in extreme cases posted to the depot as "unfit for further aircrew duties." They were then offered a choice of transferring to the British army, or going to the coal mines. By 1943 the "Refresher Centres" were handling thousands of aircrew. One 76 Squadron rear gunner went from Sheffield to the Parachute Regiment, and survived the war. His crew were killed over Kassel in October.

F/Lt Denis Hornsey joined 76 Squadron in the autumn of

1943. He was among very many men who spent their war in Bomber Command fighting fear and dread of inadequacy, without ever finally succumbing. At the end of the war Hornsey wrote an almost masochistically honest and hitherto unpublished account of his experiences and feelings. At thirty-three, he was rather older than most aircrew and suffered from poor eyesight – he wore corrected goggles on operations – and almost chronic minor ailments throughout the war. He hated the bureaucracy and lack of privacy in service life, and was completely without confidence in his own ability as a pilot. After flying some Whitley operations in 1941, he was returned to OTU for further training, and his crew was split up. He then spent a relatively happy year as a staff pilot at a navigation school. He felt that he was an adequate flier of single or twin-engined aircraft, and repeatedly requested a transfer to an operational station where he could fly one or the other. But by 1943 it was heavy-aircraft pilots who were needed. Everybody wanted to fly Mosquitoes. Hornsey was posted to Halifaxes. He knew that he was by now being accompanied from station to station by a file of unsatisfactory reports. He began his tour at 76 Squadron with two "Early Returns," which made him more miserable than ever. Fear of being considered LMF haunted him almost as much as the fear of operations.

> Each operation, in my experience, was a worse strain than the last, and I felt sure that I was not far wrong in supposing that every pilot found it the same. It was true that it was possible to get used to the strain, but this did not alter the fact that the tension of each trip was "banked" and carried forward in part to increase the tension of the next. If this were not so, the authorities would not have thought it necessary to restrict a tour to thirty trips.

There were men who were stronger than Hornsey, even men who enjoyed operational flying, but his conscious frailty was far closer to that of the average pilot than the nerveless brilliance of a Martin or Cheshire. The day after 76 Squadron lost four aircraft over Kassel and George Dunn's crew completed their tour, Hornsey recorded a conversation in the mess:

"What chance has a man got at this rate?" one pilot asked plaintively. "Damn it all, I don't care how brave a chap is, he likes to think he has a *chance*. This is plain murder."

"Better tell that to Harris," someone else suggested.

"You needn't worry," I said, "you represent just fourteen bombloads to him. That's economics, you know."

As it transpired, operations were cancelled at the eleventh hour, when we were all dressed up in our kit ready to fly. It was too late then to go out, so I went to the camp cinema and saw "Gun for Hire," a mediocre film portraying what I would have once thought was the dangerous life of a gangster. Now, by contrast, it seemed tame.

That night, I found it difficult to settle down. There was much going on inside my mind that I wanted to express. I felt lonely and miserable, apprehensive and resigned, yet rebellious at the thought of being just a mere cog in a machine with no say in how that machine was used.

But I was getting used to such attacks, which I learned to expect at least once in the course of a day, as soon as I found myself at a loose end. As I could now recognize, without fear of it adding to my mental discomfort, they merely signified an onset of operational jitters. So composing myself as best I could, I went to sleep as quickly as I could.

Hornsey's tragedy was that he was acutely imaginative. He pressed the Air Ministry for the introduction of parachutes that could be worn at all times by bomber aircrew, so many of whom never had the chance to put them on after the aircraft was hit. He made his crew practise "Abandon aircraft" and "Ditching" drill intensively, and protested violently when he found the remaining armour plate being stripped from his Halifax on Group orders, to increase bombload.

The men who fared best were those who did not allow themselves to think at all. Many crews argued that emotional entanglements were madness, whether inside or outside marriage. They diverted a man from the absolute single-mindedness he needed to survive over Germany. When a pilot was seen brooding over a girl in the mess, he was widely regarded as a candidate for "the chop list." Hornsey, with a wife and baby daughter, was giving only part of his attention and very little of his heart to 76 Squadron.

Cheshire argued emphatically that what most men considered a premonition of their own death – of which there were innumerable instances in Bomber Command – was in reality defeatism. A man who believed that he was doomed would collapse or bale out when his aircraft was hit, whereas in Cheshire's view if you could survive the initial fearsome shock of finding your aircraft damaged, you had a chance. Yet by the autumn of 1943, many men on 76 Squadron were talking freely of their own fate. One much-liked officer came fresh from a long stint as an instructor to be a flight commander. "You'd better tell me about this business, chaps," he said modestly in the mess. "I've been away on the prairies too long." After a few operations, he concluded readily that he had no chance of survival. "What are you doing for Christmas, Stuart?" somebody asked him in the mess one day. "Oh, I shan't be alive for Christmas," he said wistfully, and was gone within a week, leaving a wife and three children.

"The line between the living and the dead was very thin," wrote Hornsey. "If you live on the brink of death yourself, it is as if those who have gone have merely caught an earlier train to the same destination. And whatever that destination is, you will be sharing it soon, since you will almost certainly be catching the next one."

On the night of 3 November 1943, Hornsey's was one of two 76 Squadron aircraft shot down on the way to Düsseldorf. He was on his eighteenth trip with Bomber Command. It is pleasant to record that he survived and made a successful escape across France to England, for which he was awarded a DFC perhaps better deserved and more hardly earned than the Air Ministry ever knew.

MISSION TO LEIPZIG

Bert Stiles

Stiles was a USAAF co-pilot on B-17s flying out of East Anglia. Below is his account of a mission to Leipzig in 1944. After completing his tour of 35 bomber missions, he elected to remain in Europe and fly fighters. He was killed flying a P-51 Mustang in late 1944.

Leipzig

The crews scheduled for that haul were waked up around 0300 hours. There was plenty of bitching about that.

I was so tired I felt drunk.

They told us there'd be eggs for breakfast, but there was just bacon without eggs. There was plenty of bitching about that too.

In the equipment hut I heard somebody say, "Today I'm catching up on my sack time."

Some other gunner said, "I slept most of the way to Augsburg yesterday."

Nobody said anything about the Luftwaffe. Leipzig is in there deep, but plenty of gunners bitched about taking extra ammunition. Plenty of gunners didn't take any.

Beach was flying his last mission with Langford's crew.

"We're the last of Lieutenant Newton's gang," he said wanly.

"And I'll be the very last," I said. "Take it easy today."

We had an easy ride in. I didn't feel sleepy. I just felt dazed.

There was soft fuzz over a thin solid overcast going in, but inside Germany the clouds broke up. There was haze under the cumulus and the ground showed pale green through the holes.

"We're way back," Green said.

The group was tucked in nicely, the low squadron was up close, and Langford was doing a pretty job of flying high.

The lead and high groups of our wing looked nice too. But our group, the low, was way back and below. Our wing was the tail end, with most of the 8th up ahead.

The wing had S-ed out and called our group leader to catch up. He didn't.

If I didn't listen to the engine roar it was quiet up there. The sky was a soft sterile blue. Somehow we didn't belong there.

There was death all over the sky, the quiet threat of death, the anesthesia of cold sunlight filled the cockpit.

The lady named Death is a whore . . . Luck is a lady . . . and so is Death . . . I don't know why. And there's no telling who they'll go for. Sometimes it's a quiet, gentle, intelligent guy. The Lady Luck strings along with him for a while, and then she hands him over to the lady named Death. Sometimes a guy comes along who can laugh in their faces. The hell with luck, and the hell with death . . . And maybe they go for it . . . and maybe they don't.

There's no way to tell. If you could become part of the sky you might know . . . because they're always out there. The lady of Luck has a lovely face you can never quite see, and her eyes are the night itself, and her hair is probably dark and very lovely . . . but she doesn't give a damn.

And the lady named Death is sometimes lovely too, and sometimes she's a screaming horrible bitch . . . and sometimes she's a quiet one, with soft hands that rest gently on top of yours on the throttles.

The wing leader called up, "We're starting our climb now." We only had a half hour or so until target time.

He hadn't listened. The lead and high groups were already far above us. We were back there alone.

We never caught up after that.

"I don't like this," Green said.

"Tuck it in," somebody said over VHF. "Bandits in the target area."

I was tense and drawn taut. The sky was cold and beautifully aloof.

Green was on interphone and I was on VHF, listening for anything from the lead ship.

I heard a gun open up.

Testing, I decided.

I saw some black puffs and a couple of bright bursts.

Jesus, we're in the flak already, I thought.

Then the guns opened up. Every gun on the ship opened up. A black Focke-Wulf slid under our wing, and rolled over low.

I flipped over on interphone and fear was hot in my throat and cold in my stomach.

"Here they come." It was Mock, I think, cool and easy, like in a church. Then his guns fired steadily.

The air was nothing but black polka dots and firecrackers from the 20-millimeters.

"Keep your eye on 'em, keep 'em out there . . ." It was Mock and Bossert.

"Got the one at seven . . ." Bossert of Mock. Steady.

They came through again, coming through from the tail.

I saw two Forts blow up out at four o'clock. Some other group.

A trio of gray ones whipped past under the wing and rolled away at two o'clock. Black crosses on gray wings . . . 109s.

A night-fighter Focke-Wulf moved up almost in formation with us, right outside the window, throwing shells into somebody up ahead. Somebody powdered him.

One came around at ten o'clock . . . and the nose guns opened up on him. He rolled over and fell away . . . maybe there was smoke . . .

The instruments were fine. Green looked okay. My breath was in short gasps.

"Better give me everything," Green said. Steady voice.

I jacked-up the RPM up to the hilt.

They were queuing up again back at four and six and eight. A hundred of them . . . maybe two hundred . . . getting set to come through again . . . fifteen or twenty abreast . . .

. . . I looked up at the other wing-ship. The whole stabilizer was gone. I could see blue sky through there . . . but the rudder still worked . . . still flapped . . . then his wing flared up . . . he fell off to the right.

We were flying off Langford, but he was gone . . . sagging off low at three o'clock. Green slid us in under the lead squadron. Langford was in a dive . . . four or five planes were after him . . . coming in . . . letting them have it . . . swinging out . . . and coming in again . . . Beach was in that ball . . . poor goddamn Beach . . . .

"Here they come!"

"Four o'clock level."

"Take that one at six."

All the guns were going again.

There wasn't any hope at all . . . just waiting for it . . . just sitting there hunched up . . . jerking around to check the right side . . . jerking back to check the instruments . . . everything okay . . . just waiting for it . . .

They came through six times, I guess . . . maybe five . . . maybe seven . . . queuing up back there . . . coming in . . . throwing those 20s in there.

. . . we were hit . . .

. . . the whole low squadron was gone . . . blown up . . . burned up . . . shot to hell . . . one guy got out of that.

. . . we were the only ones left in the high . . . tucked in under the lead. The lead squadron was okay . . . we snuggled up almost under the tail guns. They were firing steadily . . . the shell cases were dropping down and going through the cowling . . . smashing against the plexiglass . . . chipping away at the windshields . . . coming steady . . . coming all the time . . . then his guns must have burned out . . .

. . . there were a few 51s back there . . . four against a hundred . . . maybe eight . . .

"Don't shoot that 51," Mock again, cool as hell . . .

I punched the wheel forward. A burning plane was nosing over us.

Green nodded, kept on flying . . .

The guns were going . . . not all of them any more . . . some of them were out . . . burned out . . . maybe.

And then it was over. They went away.

We closed up and dropped our bombs.

Six out of twelve gone.

We turned off the target, waiting for them . . . knowing they'd be back . . . cold . . . waiting for them . . .

There was a flow to it . . . we were moving . . . we were always moving . . . sliding along through the dead sky . . .

I flicked back to VHF.

No bandits called off.

Then, I heard, ". . . is my wing on fire? . . . will you check to see if my wing is on fire? . . ."

He gave his call sign. It was the lead ship.

We were right underneath. We pulled up even closer.

"You're okay," I broke the safety wire on the transmitter. "You're okay . . . baby . . . your wing is okay. No smoke . . . no flame . . . stay in there, baby."

It was more of a prayer.

". . . I'm bailing out my crew . . ."

I couldn't see any flame. I wasn't sure it was the same plane. But they were pulling out to the side.

All my buddies. Maurie . . . Uggie . . .

I told Green. "We better get back to the main group . . . we better get back there fast . . ."

We banked over. I saw the rear door come off and flip away end over end in the slipstream. Then the front door, then something else . . . maybe a guy doing a delayed jump. It didn't look like a guy very much.

It must have been set up on automatic pilot. It flew along out there for half an hour. If they jumped they were delayed jumps.

Maybe they made it.

We found a place under the wing lead.

I reached over and touched Green. What a guy. Then I felt the control column. Good airplane . . . still flying . . . still living . . .

Everybody was talking.

Nobody knew what anybody said.

There was a sort of beautiful dazed wonder in the air . . . . . . still here. . . . Still living . . . still breathing.

And then it came through . . . the thought of all those guys . . . those good guys . . . cooked and smashed and down there somewhere, dead or chopped up or headed for some Stalag.

We were never in that formation. We were all alone, trailing low.

From the day you first get in a 17 they say formation flying is the secret.

They tell you over and over. Keep those planes tucked in and you'll come home.

The ride home was easy. They never came back.

The sky was a soft unbelievable blue. The land was green, never so green.

When we got away from the Continent we began to come apart. Green took off his mask.

There weren't any words, but we tried to say them.

"Jesus, you're here," I said.

"I'm awfully proud of them," he said quietly.

Bradley came down out of the turret. His face was nothing but teeth. I mussed up his hair, and he beat on me.

The interphone was jammed.

". . . all I could do was pray . . . and keep praying." McAvoy had to stay in the radio room the whole time, seeing nothing, doing nothing . . .

"You can be the chaplain," Mock said. His voice just the same, only he was laughing a little now.

". . . if they say go tomorrow . . . I'll hand in my wings . . . I'll hand in every other goddamn thing . . . but I won't fly tomorrow . . ." Tolbert was positive.

. . . if Langford went down . . . that meant Fletch . . . Fletch and Johnny O'Leary and Beach . . .

. . . and all the others . . . Maurie had long black eyelashes, and sort of Persian's eyes . . . sort of the walking symbol of sex . . . and what a guy . . . maybe he made it . . . maybe he got out . . .

It was low tide. The clouds were under us again, almost solid, and then I saw a beach through a hole . . . white sand and England.

There was never anywhere as beautiful as that.

We were home.

Green made a sweet landing. We opened up the side windows and looked around. Everything looked different. There was too much light, too much green . . . just too much . . .

We were home . . .

They sent us out to get knocked off and we came home.

And then we taxied past E-East.

"Jesus, that's Langford," I grabbed Green.

It was. Even from there we could see they were shot to hell.

Their tail was all shot up . . . one wing was ripped and chopped away.

Green swung around into place, and I cut the engines.

. . . we were home . . .

There were empty spaces where ships were supposed to be, where they'd be again in a day, as soon as ATC could fly them down.

We started to talk to people. There were all kinds of people. Jerry, a crew chief, came up and asked us about the guys on the other wing. We told him. Blown up.

. . . honest to God . . . we were really home . . .

The 20-millimeter hit our wing . . . blew up inside . . . blew away part of the top of number two gas tank . . . blew hell out of everything inside there . . . puffed out the leading edge . . . blew out an inspection panel.

We didn't even lose any gas.

We didn't even blow up.

I stood back by the tail and looked at the hole. I could feel the ground, and I wanted to take my shoes off. Every time I breathed, I knew it.

I could look out into the sky over the hangar and say thank you to the lady of the luck. She stayed.

I was all ripped apart. Part of me was dead, and part of me was wild, ready to take off, and part of me was just shaky and twisted and useless.

Maybe I told it a thousand times.

I could listen to myself. I could talk, and start my voice going, and step back and listen to it.

I went down to Thompson's room, and he listened. He listened a couple of times.

It was a pretty quiet place. Eight ships out of a group is a quiet day at any base.

Colonel Terry just got married. Thompson didn't know about it. I went back to my room and sat across the room from Langford and kept telling myself it was him.

"When I saw you there were at least eight of them," I said. "Just coming in, and pulling out, and coming in." I showed him with my hands.

Then Fletch came in.

Then I thought about Beach.

Beach got three at least. He shot up every shell he had, and got three.

He came over after interrogation.

"I guess they can't kill us Denver guys," he said. He didn't believe it either. He was all through.

"Jesus," I said, "I sure thought they had you."

Green came in with O'Leary.

"I knew you were down," O'Leary said. "I told everyone."

Green smiled. He looked okay, "We're on pass," he said quietly. "Let's get out of here."

I wanted to touch him again. I wanted to tell him I was glad I was on his crew, and it was the best goddamn crew I'd ever heard of, but I didn't say anything, and he didn't either.

I got out my typewriter and started a letter to my folks.

And then it came in again . . . all those guys . . . all those good guys . . . shot to hell . . . or captured . . . or hiding there waiting for it.

. . . waiting for it . . .

Then I came all apart, and cried like a little kid. . . . I could watch myself, and hear myself, and I couldn't do a goddamn thing.

. . . just pieces of a guy . . . pieces of bertstiles all over the room . . . maybe some of the pieces were still over there.

And then it was all right. I went in and washed my face. Green was calling up about trains, standing there in his shorts.

"I think the boys need a rest," he said. "You going in?"

"I'll meet you in London at high noon," I said. "Lobby of the Regent Palace."

"Okay," he said. "Get a good night's sleep."

"Meet you there," I said.

But I didn't.

They sent me to the Flak House. There was an opening, and the squadron sent me.

THE DEATH OF SOCRATES

Plato

The philosopher Socrates was found guilty by the Athenian state on a jumped up charge of "corrupting the minds of the youth" (he'd developed a humanistic, rather than a theocratic, ethics). When Socrates contemptuously refused to pay a fine, and thus admit guilt, he was sentenced to death in 399 BC by the drinking of hemlock.

Crito made a sign to the servant, who was standing by; and he went out, and after some time returned with the jailer carrying the cup of poison. Socrates said: My good friend, you are an expert in these matters; what must I do? The man answered: You have only to walk about until your legs are heavy, and then to lie down, and the poison will act. At the same time he handed the cup to Socrates, who very cheerfully and without the least tremor or change of colour or feature, glancing upwards and looking the man full in the face, Echecrates, as his manner was, took the cup and said: What about making a libation out of this cup? May I, or not? The man answered: We only prepare, Socrates, just so much as we think enough. I understand, he said: but I may and must ask the gods to prosper my journey from this to the other world – even so – and so be it according to my prayer. Then raising the cup to his lips, quite readily and cheerfully he drank of the poison. Till then most of us had been able to control our sorrow; but now when we saw him drinking, and saw too that he had finished the draught, we could do it no longer, and in spite of myself my own tears were flowing fast; so that I covered my face and wept, not for him, but at the thought of my own calamity in having to part from such a friend. Nor was I the first; for Crito, when he found himself unable to restrain his tears, had got up, and I followed; and at that moment Apollodorus, who had been in tears all the time, broke out in a loud and passionate cry which made cowards of us all. Socrates alone retained his calmness: What are you doing, you strange people? he said. I sent away the women mainly in order that they might not strike this false note, for I have been told that a man should die in peace. Be quiet then, and have patience. When we heard his words we were ashamed, and checked our tears; and he walked about until, as he said, his legs began to fail, and then he lay on his back, according to the directions, and the man who gave him the poison now and then looked at his feet and legs; and after a while he pressed his foot hard, and asked him if he could feel; and he said, No; and then his leg, and so upwards and upwards, and showed us that he was cold and stiff. Then he felt them again, and said: When the poison reaches the heart, that will be the end. He was beginning to grow cold about the groin, when he uncovered his face, for he had covered himself up, and said: Crito, I owe a cock to Asclepius; will you remember to pay the debt? The debt shall be paid, said Crito; is there anything else? There was no answer to this question; but in a minute or two a movement was heard, and the attendants uncovered him; his eyes were set, and Crito closed his eyes and mouth.

Such was the end, Echecrates, of our friend; of whom I may truly say, that of all the men of his time whom I have known, he was the wisest and justest and best.

THE CRUCIFIXION OF CHRIST

The Bible

The Crucifixion of Christ occurred c. AD 30. During his brief life, the courage of Christ was tested many times but the Crucifixion has a greater hold on the world's imagination than, say the Temptations in the Wilderness, because of the pain Christ faced on the cross. It was perhaps the ultimate physical test of courage. The cowardice of Peter in the passion, in denying Christ three times when accused of being a follower, only makes Jesus' behaviour more heroic. From 'The Gospel According to John'

Chapter 18

W hen Jesus had spoken these words, he went forth with his disciples over the brook Cedron, where was a garden, into the which he entered, and his disciples.

2 And Judas also, which betrayed him, knew the place: for Jesus oft-times resorted thither with his disciples.

3 Judas then, having received a band *of men* and officers from the chief priests and Pharisees, cometh thither with lanterns and torches and weapons.

4 Jesus therefore, knowing all things that should come upon him, went forth, and said unto them, Whom seek ye?

5 They answered him, Jesus of Nazareth. Jesus saith unto them. I am *he*. And Judas also, which betrayed him, stood with them.

6 As soon then as he had said unto them, I am *he*, they went backward, and fell to the ground.

7 Then asked he them again, Whom seek ye? And they said, Jesus of Nazareth.

8 Jesus answered, I have told you that I am *he*: if therefore ye seek me, let these go their way:

9 That the saying might be fulfilled, which he spake, Of them which thou gavest me have I lost none.

10 Then Simon Peter having a sword drew it, and smote the high priest's servant, and cut off his right ear. The servant's name was Malchus.

11 Then said Jesus unto Peter, Put up thy sword into the sheath: the cup which my Father hath given me, shall I not drink it?

12 Then the band and the captain and officers of the Jews took Jesus, and bound him.

13 And led him away to Annas first; for he was father in law to Caiaphas, which was the high priest that same year.

14 Now Caiaphas was he, which gave counsel to the Jews, that it was expedient that one man should die for the people.

15 q And Simon Peter followed Jesus, and so *did* another disciple: that disciple was known unto the high priest, and went in with Jesus into the palace of the high priest.

16 But Peter stood at the door without. Then went out that other disciple, which was known unto the high priest, and spake unto her that kept the door, and brought in Peter.

17 Then saith the damsel that kept the door unto Peter, Art not thou also *one* of this man's disciples? He saith, I am not.

18 And the servants and officers stood there, who had made a fire of coals; for it was cold: and they warmed themselves: and Peter stood with them, and warmed himself.

19 q The high priest then asked Jesus of his disciples, and of his doctrine.

20 Jesus answered him, I spake openly to the world; I ever taught in the synagogue, and in the temple, whither the Jews always resort; and in secret have I said nothing.

21 Why askest thou me? ask them which heard me, what I have said unto them: behold, they know what I said.

22 And when he had thus spoken, one of the officers which stood by struck Jesus with the palm of his hand, saying, Answerest thou the high priest so?

23 Jesus answered him, if I have spoken evil, bear witness of the evil: but if well, why smitest thou me?

24 Now Annas had sent him bound unto Caiaphas the high priest.

25 And Simon Peter stood and warmed himself. They said therefore unto him. Art not thou also *one* of his disciples? He denied *it*, and said, I am not.

26 One of the servants of the high priest, being *his* kinsman whose ear Peter cut off, saith, Did not I see thee in the garden with him?

27 Peter then denied again: and immediately the cock crew.

28 q Then led they Jesus from Caiaphas unto the hall of judgment: and it was early; and they themselves went not into the judgment hall, lest they should be defiled; but that they might eat the passover.

29 Pilate then went out unto them, and said, What accusation bring ye against this man?

30 They answered and said unto him. If he were not a malefactor, we would not have delivered him up unto thee.

31 Then said Pilate unto them, Take ye him, and judge him according to your law. The Jews therefore said unto him. It is not lawful for us to put any man to death:

32 That the saying of Jesus might be fulfilled, which he spake, signifying what death he should die.

33 Then Pilate entered into the judgment hall again, and called Jesus, and said unto him, Art thou the King of the Jews?

34 Jesus answered him, Sayest thou this thing of thyself, or did others tell it thee of me?

35 Pilate answered, Am I a Jew? Thine own nation and the chief priests have delivered thee unto me: what hast thou done?

36 Jesus answered, My kingdom is not of this world: if my kingdom were of this world, then would my servants fight, that I should not be delivered to the Jews: but now is my kingdom not from hence.

37 Pilate therefore said unto him, Art thou a king then? Jesus answered, Thou sayest that I am a king. To this end was I born, and for this cause came I into the world, that I should bear witness unto the truth. Every one that is of the truth heareth my voice.

38 Pilate saith unto him. What is truth? And when he had said

this, he went out again unto the Jews, and saith unto them, I find in him no fault *at all*.

39 But ye have a custom, that I should release unto you one at the passover: will ye therefore that I release unto you the King of the Jews?

40 Then cried they all again, saying, Not this man, but Barabbas. Now Barabbas was a robber.

Chapter 19

THEN Pilate therefore took Jesus, and scourged *him*.

2 And the soldiers plaited a crown of thorns, and put *it* on his head, and they put on him a purple robe.

3 And said, Hail, King of the Jews! and they smote him with their hands.

4 Pilate therefore went forth again, and saith unto them, Behold, I bring him forth to you, that ye may know that I find no fault in him.

5 Then came Jesus forth, wearing the crown of thorns, and the purple robe. And *Pilate*, saith unto them. Behold the man!

6 When the chief priests therefore and officers saw him, they cried out, saying, Crucify *him*, crucify *him*. Pilate saith unto them, Take ye him, and crucify *him*: for I find no fault in him.

7 The Jews answered him, We have a law, and by our law he ought to die, because he made himself the Son of God.

8 q When Pilate therefore heard that saying, he was the more afraid;

9 And went again into the judgment hall, and saith unto Jesus, Whence art thou? But Jesus gave him no answer.

10 Then saith Pilate unto him, Speakest thou not unto me? Knowest thou not that I have power to crucify thee, and have power to release thee?

11 Jesus answered. Thou couldest have no power *at all* against me, except it were given thee from above: therefore he that delivered me unto thee hath the greater sin.

12 And from thenceforth Pilate sought to release him: but the Jews cried out, saying, If thou let this man go, thou art not Cæsar's friend: whosoever maketh himself a king speaketh against Cæsar.

13 q When Pilate therefore heard that saying, he brought Jesus forth, and sat down in the judgment seat in a place that *is* called the Pavement, but in the Hebrew, Gabbatha.

14 And it was the preparation of the passover, and about the sixth hour: and he saith unto the Jews, Behold your King!

15 But they cried out, Away with *him*, away with *him*, crucify him. Pilate saith unto them, Shall I crucify your King? The chief priests answered, We have no king but Cæsar.

16 Then delivered he him therefore unto them to be crucified. And they took Jesus, and led *him* away.

17 And he bearing his cross went forth into a place called *the place* of a skull, which is called in the Hebrew Golgotha:

18 Where they crucified him, and two other with him, on either side one, and Jesus in the midst.

19 q And Pilate wrote a title, and put *it* on the cross. And the writing was, JESUS OF NAZARETH THE KING OF THE JEWS.

20 This title then read many of the Jews: for the place where Jesus was crucified was nigh to the city: and it was written in Hebrew, *and* Greek, *and* Latin.

21 Then said the chief priests of the Jews to Pilate, Write not, The King of the Jews; but that he said, I am King of the Jews.

22 Pilate answered. What I have written I have written.

23 q Then the soldiers, when they had crucified Jesus, took his garments, and made four parts, to every soldier a part; and also *his* coat: now the coat was without seam, woven from the top throughout.

24 They said therefore among themselves, Let us not rend it, but cast lots for it, whose it shall be: that the scripture might be fulfilled, which saith. They parted my raiment among them, and for my vesture they did cast lots. These things therefore the soldiers did.

25 q Now there stood by the cross of Jesus his mother, and his mother's sister, Mary the *wife* of Cleophas, and Mary Magdalene.

26 When Jesus therefore saw his mother, and the disciple standing by, whom he loved, he saith unto his mother, Woman, behold thy son!

27 Then saith he to the disciple, Behold thy mother! And from that hour that disciple took her unto his own *home*.

28 q After this, Jesus knowing that all things were now accomplished, that the scripture might be fulfilled, saith, I thirst.

29 Now there was set a vessel full of vinegar: and they filled a sponge with vinegar, and put *it* upon hyssop, and put *it to* his mouth.

30 When Jesus therefore had received the vinegar, he said, It is finished: and he bowed his head, and gave up the ghost.

31 The Jews therefore, because it was the preparation, that the bodies should not remain upon the cross on the sabbath day, (for that sabbath day was an high day,) besought Pilate that their legs might be broken, and *that* they might be taken away.

32 Then came the soldiers, and brake the legs of the first, and of the other which was crucified with him.

33 But when they came to Jesus, and saw that he was dead already, they brake not his legs:

34 But one of the soldiers with a spear pierced his side, and forthwith came there out blood and water.

35 And he that saw *it* bare record, and his record is true: and he knoweth that he saith true, that ye might believe.

36 For these things were done, that the scripture should be fulfilled, A bone of him shall not be broken.

37 And again another scripture saith, They shall look on him whom they pierced.

38 q And after this Joseph of Arimathæa, being a disciple of Jesus, but secretly for fear of the Jews, besought Pilate that he might take away the body of Jesus: and Pilate gave *him* leave. He came therefore, and took the body of Jesus.

39 And there came also Nicodemus, which at the first came to Jesus by night, and brought a mixture of myrrh and aloes, about an hundred pound *weight*.

40 Then took they the body of Jesus, and wound it in linen clothes with the spices, as the manner of the Jews is to bury.

41 Now in the place where he was crucified there was a garden; and in the garden a new sepulchre, wherein was never man yet laid.

42 There laid they Jesus therefore because of the Jews' preparation *day*; for the sepulchre was nigh at hand.

THE BOAT JOURNEY

Ernest Shackleton

In 1914 the veteran British polar explorer Ernest Shackleton set off to transverse the entire wastes of Antarctica. Things went wrong from the start. The expedition's ship, Endurance, *was frozen solid in the Weddell Sea before being crushed to splinters. Shackleton and his crew escaped onto the ice floes which, when carried into warmer waters, cracked and shrunk. The ice was abandoned for three lifeboats which eventually made landfall on Elephant Island in the South Shetlands. This was no salvation, however, for Elephant Island was uninhabited and barren. To secure relief, Shackleton decided that a small group of men – led by himself – should undertake a boat journey to South Georgia, 800 miles away across the most savage sea on Earth. Their vessel, the* James Caird, *was a 23 foot-long lifeboat.*

A boat journey in search of relief was necessary and must not be delayed. That conclusion was forced upon me. The nearest port where assistance could certainly be secured was Port Stanley, in the Falkland Islands, 540 miles away, but we could scarcely hope to beat up against the prevailing north-westerly wind in a frail and weakened boat with a small sail area. South Georgia was over 800 miles away, but lay in the area of the west winds, and I could count upon finding whalers at any of the whaling stations on the east coast. A boat party might make the voyage and be back with relief within a month, provided that the sea was clear of ice and the boat survive the great seas. It was not difficult to decide that South Georgia must be the objective, and I proceeded to plan ways and means. The hazards of a boat journey across 800 miles of stormy sub-Antarctic ocean were obvious, but I calculated that at worst the venture would add nothing to the risks of the men left on the island. There would be fewer mouths to feed during the winter and the boat would not require to take more than one month's provisions for six men, for if we did not make South Georgia in that time we were sure to go under. A consideration that had weight with me was that there was no chance at all of any search being made for us on Elephant Island.

The case required to be argued in some detail, since all hands knew that the perils of the proposed journey were extreme. The risk was justified solely by our urgent need of assistance. The ocean south of Cape Horn in the middle of May is known to be the most tempestuous storm-swept area of water in the world. The weather then is unsettled, the skies are dull and overcast, and the gales are almost unceasing. We had to face these conditions in a small and weatherbeaten boat, already strained by the work of the months that had passed. Worsley and Wild realized that the attempt must be made, and they both asked to be allowed to accompany me on the voyage. I told Wild at once that he would have to stay behind. I relied upon him to hold the party together while I was away and to make the best of his way to Deception Island with the men in the spring in the event of our failure to bring help. Worsley I would take with me, for I had a very high opinion of his accuracy and quickness as a navigator, and especially in the snapping and working out of positions in difficult circumstances – an opinion that was only enhanced during the actual journey. Four other men would be required, and I decided to call for volunteers, although, as a matter of fact, I pretty well knew which of the people I would select. Crean I proposed to leave on the island as a right-hand man for Wild, but he begged so hard to be allowed to come in the boat that, after consultation with Wild, I promised to take him. I called the men together, explained my plan, and asked for volunteers. Many came forward at once. Some were not fit enough for the work that would have to be done, and others would not have been much use in the boat since they were not seasoned sailors, though the experiences of recent months entitled them to some consideration as seafaring men. McIlroy and Macklin were both anxious to go but realized that their duty lay on the island with the sick men. They suggested that I should take Blackborrow in order that he might have shelter and warmth as quickly as possible, but I had to veto this idea. It would be hard enough for fit men to live in the boat. Indeed, I did not see how a sick man, lying helpless in the bottom of the boat, could possibly survive in the heavy weather we were sure to encounter. I finally selected McNeish, McCarthy, and Vincent in addition to Worsley and Crean. The crew seemed a strong one, and as I looked at the men I felt confidence increasing.

The decision made, I walked through the blizzard with Worsley and Wild to examine the *James Caird*. The 23-ft. boat had never looked big; she appeared to have shrunk in some mysterious way when I viewed her in the light of our new undertaking. She was an ordinary ship's whaler, fairly strong, but showing signs of the strains she had endured since the crushing of the *Endurance*. Where she was holed in leaving the pack was, fortunately, about the water line and easily patched. Standing beside her, we glanced at the fringe of the storm-swept, tumultuous sea that formed our path. Clearly, our voyage would be a big adventure. I called the carpenter and asked him if he could do anything to make the boat more seaworthy. He first inquired if he was to go with me, and seemed quite pleased when I said "Yes." He was over fifty years of age and not altogether fit, but he had a good knowledge of sailing boats and was very quick. McCarthy said that he could contrive some sort of covering for the *James Caird* if he might use the lids of the cases and the four sledge runners that we had lashed inside the boat for use in the event of a landing on Graham Island at Wilhelmina Bay. This bay, at one time the goal of our desire, had been left behind in the course of our drift, but we had retained the runners. The carpenter proposed to complete the covering with some of our canvas, and he set about making his plans at once.

Noon had passed and the gale was more severe than ever. We could not proceed with our preparations that day. The tents were suffering in the wind and the sea was rising. We made our way to the snow slope at the shoreward end of the spit, with the intention of digging a hole in the snow large enough to provide shelter for the party. I had an idea that Wild and his men might camp there during my absence, since it seemed impossible that the tents could hold together for many more days against the attacks of the wind; but an examination of the spot indicated that any hole we could dig probably would be filled quickly by the drift. At dark, about 5 p.m., we all turned in, after a supper consisting of a pannikin of hot milk, one of our precious biscuits, and a cold penguin leg each.

The gale was stronger than ever on the following morning (April 20). No work could be done. Blizzard and snow, snow and blizzard, sudden lulls and fierce returns. During the lulls we could see on the far horizon to the northeast bergs of all shapes and sizes driving along before the gale, and the sinister appearance of the swift moving masses made us thankful indeed that, instead of battling with the storm amid the ice, we were required only to face the drift from the glaciers and the inland heights. The gusts might throw us off our feet, but at least we fell on solid ground and not on the rocking floes. Two seals came up on the beach that day, one of them within ten yards of my tent. So urgent was our need of food and blubber that I called all hands and organized a line of beaters instead of simply walking up to the seal and hitting it on the nose. We were prepared to fall upon this seal *en masse* if it attempted to escape. The kill was made with a pick handle, and in a few minutes five days' food and six days' fuel were stowed in a place of safety among the boulders above highwater mark. During this day the cook, who had worked well on the floe and throughout the boat journey, suddenly collapsed. I happened to be at the galley at the moment and saw him fall. I pulled him down the slope to his tent and pushed him into its shelter with orders to his tentmates to keep him in his sleeping bag until I allowed him to come out or the doctors said he was fit enough. Then I took out to replace the cook one of the men who had expressed a desire to lie down and die. The task of keeping the galley fire alight was both difficult and strenuous, and it took his thoughts away from the chances of immediate dissolution. In fact, I found him a little later gravely concerned over the drying of a naturally not overclean pair of socks which were hung up in close proximity to our evening milk. Occupation had brought his thoughts back to the ordinary cares of life.

There was a lull in the bad weather on April 21, and the carpenter started to collect material for the decking of the *James Caird*. He fitted the mast of the *Stancomb Wills* fore and aft inside the *James Caird* as a hog-back and thus strengthened the keel with the object of preventing our boat "hogging" – that is, buckling in heavy seas. He had not sufficient wood to provide a deck, but by using the sledge runners and box lids he made a framework extending from the forecastle aft to a well. It was a patched-up affair, but it provided a base for a canvas covering. We had a bolt of canvas frozen stiff, and this material had to be cut and then thawed out over the blubber stove, foot by foot, in order that it might be sewn into the form of a cover. When it had been nailed and screwed into position it certainly gave an appearance of safety to the boat, though I had an uneasy feeling that it bore a strong likeness to stage scenery, which may look like a granite wall and is in fact nothing better than canvas and lath. As events proved, the covering served its purpose well. We certainly could not have lived through the voyage without it.

Another fierce gale was blowing on April 22, interfering with our preparations for the voyage. The cooker from No. 5 tent came adrift in a gust, and, although it was chased to the water's edge, it disappeared for good. Blackborrow's feet were giving him much pain, and McIlroy and Macklin thought it would be necessary for them to operate soon. They were under the impression then that they had no chloroform, but they found some subsequently in the medicine chest after we had left. Some cases of stores left on a rock off the spit on the day of our arrival were retrieved during this day. We were setting aside stores for the boat journey and choosing the essential equipment from the scanty stock at our disposal. Two ten-gallon casks had to be filled with water melted down from ice collected at the foot of the glacier. This was a rather slow business. The blubber stove was kept going all night, and the watchmen emptied the water into the casks from the pot in which the ice was melted. A working party started to dig a hole in the snow slope about forty feet above sea level with the object of providing a site for a camp. They made fairly good progress at first, but the snow drifted down unceasingly from the inland ice, and in the end the party had to give up the project.

The weather was fine on April 23, and we hurried forward

our preparations. It was on this day I decided finally that the crew for the *James Caird* should consist of Worsley, Crean, McNeish, McCarthy, Vincent, and myself. A storm came on about noon, with driving snow and heavy squalls. Occasionally the air would clear for a few minutes, and we could see a line of pack ice, five miles out, driving across from west to east. This sight increased my anxiety to get away quickly. Winter was advancing, and soon the pack might close completely round the island and stay our departure for days or even for weeks. I did not think that ice would remain around Elephant Island continuously during the winter, since the strong winds and fast currents would keep it in motion. We had noticed ice and bergs going past at the rate of four or five knots. A certain amount of ice was held up about the end of our spit, but the sea was clear where the boat would have to be launched.

Worsley, Wild, and I climbed to the summit of the seaward rocks and examined the ice from a better vantage point than the beach offered. The belt of pack outside appeared to be sufficiently broken for our purposes, and I decided that, unless the conditions forbade it, we would make a start in the *James Caird* on the following morning. Obviously the pack might close at any time. This decision made, I spent the rest of the day looking over the boat, gear, and stores, and discussing plans with Worsley and Wild.

Our last night on the solid ground of Elephant Island was cold and uncomfortable. We turned out at dawn and had breakfast. Then we launched the *Stancomb Wills* and loaded her with stores, gear, and ballast, which would be transferred to the *James Caird* when the heavier boat had been launched. The ballast consisted of bags made from blankets and filled with sand, making a total weight of about 1000 lb. In addition we had gathered a number of round boulders and about 250 lb. of ice, which would supplement our two casks of water.

The stores taken in the *James Caird*, which would last six men for one month, were as follows:

30 boxes of matches.
6½ gallons paraffin.
1 tin methylated spirit.
10 boxes of flamers.

1 box of blue lights.
2 Primus stoves with spare parts and prickers.
1 Nansen aluminium cooker.
6 sleeping bags.
A few spare socks.
A few candles and some blubber oil in an oil bag.

Food:
3 cases sledging rations = 300 rations.
2 cases nut food = 200 rations.
2 cases biscuits = 600 biscuits.
1 case lump sugar.
30 packets of Trumilk.
1 tin of Bovril cubes.
1 tin of Cerebos salt.
36 gallons of water.
112 lb. of ice.

Instruments:
Sextant.   Sea anchor.
Binoculars.   Charts.
Prismatic compass.   Aneroid.

The swell was slight when the *Stancomb Wills* was launched and the boat got under way without any difficulty; but half an hour later, when we were pulling down the *James Caird*, the swell increased suddenly. Apparently the movement of the ice outside had made an opening and allowed the sea to run in without being blanketed by the line of pack. The swell made things difficult. Many of us got wet to the waist while dragging the boat out – a serious matter in that climate. When the *James Caird* was afloat in the surf she nearly capsized among the rocks before we could get her clear, and Vincent and the carpenter, who were on the deck, were thrown into the water. This was really bad luck, for the two men would have small chance of drying their clothes after we had got under way. Hurley, who had the eye of the professional photographer for "incidents," secured a picture of the upset, and I firmly believe that he would have liked the two unfortunate men to remain in the water until he could get a "snap" at close quarters; but we hauled them out immediately, regardless of his feelings.

The *James Caird* was soon clear of the breakers. We used all the available ropes as a long painter to prevent her drifting away to the northeast, and then the *Stancomb Wills* came alongside, transferred her load, and went back to the shore for more. As she was being beached this time the sea took her stern and half filled her with water. She had to be turned over and emptied before the return journey could be made. Every member of the crew of the *Stancomb Wills* was wet to the skin. The water casks were towed behind the *Stancomb Wills* on this second journey, and the swell, which was increasing rapidly, drove the boat on to the rocks, where one of the casks was slightly stove in. This accident proved later to be a serious one, since some sea water had entered the cask and the contents were now brackish.

By midday the *James Caird* was ready for the voyage. Vincent and the carpenter had secured some dry clothes by exchange with members of the shore party (I heard afterwards that it was a full fortnight before the soaked garments were finally dried), and the boat's crew was standing by waiting for the order to cast off. A moderate westerly breeze was blowing. I went ashore in the *Stancomb Wills* and had a last word with Wild, who was remaining in full command, with directions as to his course of action in the event of our failure to bring relief, but I practically left the whole situation and scope of action and decision to his own judgment, secure in the knowledge that he would act wisely. I told him that I trusted the party to him and said good-bye to the men. then we pushed off for the last time, and within a few minutes I was aboard the *James Caird*. The crew of the *Stancomb Wills* shook hands with us as the boats bumped together and offered us the last good wishes. Then, setting our jib, we cut the painter and moved away to the northeast. The men who were staying behind made a pathetic little group on the beach, with the grim heights of the island behind them and the sea seething at their feet, but they waved to us and gave three hearty cheers. There was hope in their hearts and they trusted us to bring the help that they needed.

I had all sails set, and the *James Caird* quickly dipped the beach and its line of dark figures. The westerly wind took us rapidly to the line of pack, and as we entered it I stood up with my arm around the mast, directing the steering, so as to avoid the great lumps of ice that were flung about in the heave of the sea. The pack thickened and we were forced to turn almost due east, running before the wind towards a gap I had seen in the morning from the high ground. I could not see the gap now, but we had come out on its bearing and I was prepared to find that it had been influenced by the easterly drift. At four o'clock in the afternoon we found the channel, much narrower than it had seemed in the morning but still navigable. Dropping sail, we rowed through without touching the ice anywhere, and by 5:30 p.m. we were clear of the pack with open water before us. We passed one more piece of ice in the darkness an hour later, but the pack lay behind, and with a fair wind swelling the sails we steered our little craft through the night, our hopes centered on our distant goal. The swell was very heavy now, and when the time came for our first evening meal we found great difficulty in keeping the Primus lamp alight and preventing the hoosh splashing out of the pot. Three men were needed to attend to the cooking, one man holding the lamp and two men guarding the aluminum cooking pot, which had to be lifted clear of the Primus whenever the movement of the boat threatened to cause a disaster. Then the lamp had to be protected from water, for sprays were coming over the bows and our flimsy decking was by no means watertight. All these operations were conducted in the confined space under the decking, where the men lay or knelt and adjusted themselves as best they could to the angles of our cases and ballast. It was uncomfortable, but we found consolation in the reflection that without the decking we could not have used the cooker at all.

The tale of the next sixteen days is one of supreme strife amid heaving waters. The sub-Antarctic Ocean lived up to its evil winter reputation. I decided to run north for at least two days while the wind held and so get into warmer weather before turning to the east and laying a course for South Georgia. We took two-hourly spells at the tiller. The men who were not on watch crawled into the sodden sleeping bags and tried to forget their troubles for a period; but there was no comfort in the boat. The bags and cases seemed to be alive in the unfailing knack of presenting their most uncomfortable angles to our rest-seeking bodies. A man might imagine for a moment that he had found a position of ease, but always discovered quickly that some unyielding point was impinging on muscle or bone. The first night aboard the boat was one of acute discomfort for us all, and we were heartily glad when the dawn came and we could set about the preparation of a hot breakfast.

This record of the voyage to South Georgia is based upon scanty notes made day by day. The notes dealt usually with the bare facts of distances, positions, and weather, but our memories retained the incidents of the passing days in a period never to be forgotten. By running north for the first two days I hoped to get warmer weather and also to avoid lines of pack that might be extending beyond the main body. We needed all the advantage that we could obtain from the higher latitude for sailing on the great circle, but we had to be cautious regarding possible ice streams. Cramped in our narrow quarters and continually wet by the spray, we suffered severely from cold throughout the journey. We fought the seas and the winds and at the same time had a daily struggle to keep ourselves alive. At times we were in dire peril. Generally we were upheld by the knowledge that we were making progress towards the land where we would be, but there were days and nights when we lay hove to, drifting across the storm-whitened seas and watching, with eyes interested rather than apprehensive, the uprearing masses of water, flung to and fro by Nature in the pride of her strength. Deep seemed the valleys when we lay between the reeling seas. High were the hills when we perched momentarily on the tops of giant combers. Nearly always there were gales. So small was our boat and so great were the seas that often our sail flapped idly in the calm between the crests of two waves. Then we would climb the next slope and catch the full fury of the gale where the wool-like whiteness of the breaking water surged around us. We had our moments of laughter – rare, it is true, but hearty enough. Even when cracked lips and swollen mouths checked the outward and visible signs of amusement we could see a joke of the primitive kind. Man's sense of humor is always most easily stirred by the petty misfortunes of his neighbors, and I shall never forget Worsley's efforts on one occasion to place the hot aluminum stand on top of the Primus stove after it had fallen off in an extra-heavy roll. With his frostbitten fingers he picked it up, dropped it, picked it up again, and toyed with it gingerly as though it were some fragile article of lady's wear. We laughed, or rather gurgled with laughter.

The wind came up strong and worked into a gale from the northwest on the third day out. We stood away to the east. The increasing seas discovered the weaknesses of our decking. The continuous blows shifted the box lids and sledge runners so that the canvas sagged down and accumulated water. Then icy trickles, distinct from the driving sprays, poured fore and aft into the boat. The nails that the carpenter had extracted from cases at Elephant Island and used to fasten down the battens were too short to make firm the decking. We did what we could to secure it, but our means were very limited, and the water continued to enter the boat at a dozen points. Much baling was necessary, and nothing that we could do prevented our gear from becoming sodden. The searching runnels from the canvas were really more unpleasant than the sudden definite douches of the sprays. Lying under the thwarts during watches below, we tried vainly to avoid them. There were no dry places in the boat, and at last we simply covered our heads with our Burberrys and endured the all-pervading water. The baling was work for the watch. Real rest we had none. The perpetual motion of the boat made repose impossible; we were cold, sore, and anxious. We moved on hands and knees in the semidarkness of the day under the decking. The darkness was complete by 6 p.m., and not until 7 a.m. of the following day could we see one another under the thwarts. We had a few scraps of candle, and they were preserved carefully in order that we might have light at mealtimes. There was one fairly dry spot in the boat, under the solid original decking at the bows, and we managed to protect some of our biscuit from the salt water; but I do not think any of us got the taste of salt out of our mouths during the voyage.

The difficulty of movement in the boat would have had its humorous side if it had not involved us in so many aches and pains. We had to crawl under the thwarts in order to move along the boat, and our knees suffered considerably. When a watch turned out it was necessary for me to direct each man by name when and where to move, since if all hands had crawled about at the same time the result would have been dire confusion and many bruises. Then there was the trim of the boat to be considered. The order of the watch was four hours on and four hours off, three men to the watch. One man had the tiller ropes, the second man attended to the sail, and the third baled for all he was worth. Sometimes when the water in the boat had been reduced to reasonable proportions, our pump could be used. This pump, which Hurley had made from the Flinders bar case of our ship's standard compass, was quite effective, though its capacity was not large. The man who was attending the sail could pump into the big outer cooker, which was lifted and emptied overboard when filled. We had a device by which the water could go direct from the pump into the sea through a hole in the gunwale, but this hole had to be blocked at an early stage of the voyage, since we found that it admitted water when the boat rolled.

While a new watch was shivering in the wind and spray, the men who had been relieved groped hurriedly among the soaked sleeping bags and tried to steal a little of the warmth created by the last occupants; but it was not always possible for us to find even this comfort when we went off watch. The boulders that we had taken aboard for ballast had to be shifted continually in order to trim the boat and give access to the pump, which became choked with hairs from the moulting sleeping bags and finneskoe. The four reindeer-skin sleeping bags shed their hair freely owing to the continuous wetting, and soon became quite bald in appearance. The moving of the boulders was weary and painful work. We came to know every one of the stones by sight and touch, and I have vivid memories of their angular peculiarities even today. They might have been of considerable interest as geological specimens to a scientific man under happier conditions. As ballast they were useful. As weights to be moved about in cramped quarters they were simply appalling. They spared no portion of our poor bodies. Another of our troubles, worth mention here, was the chafing of our legs by our wet clothes, which had not been changed now for seven months. The insides of our thighs were rubbed raw, and the one tube of Hazeline cream in our medicine chest did not go far in alleviating our pain, which was increased by the bite of the salt water. We thought at the time that we never slept. The fact was that we would doze off uncomfortably, to be aroused quickly by some new ache or another call to effort. My own share of the general unpleasantness was accentuated by a finely developed bout of sciatica. I had become possessor of this originally on the floe several months earlier.

Our meals were regular in spite of the gales. Attention to this point was essential, since the conditions of the voyage made increasing calls upon our vitality. Breakfast, at 8 a.m., consisted of a pannikin of hot hoosh made from Bovril sledging ration, two biscuits, and some lumps of sugar. Lunch came at 1 p.m., and comprised Bovril sledging ration, eaten raw, and a pannikin of hot milk for each man. Tea, at 5 p.m., had the same menu. Then during the night we had a hot drink, generally of milk. The meals were the bright beacons in those cold and stormy days. The glow of warmth and comfort produced by the food and drink made optimists of us all. We had two tins of Virol, which we were keeping for an emergency; but, finding ourselves in need of an oil lamp to eke out our supply of candles, we emptied one of the tins in the manner that most appealed to us, and fitted it with a wick made by shredding a bit of canvas. When this lamp was filled with oil it gave a certain amount of light, though it was easily blown out, and was of great assistance to us at night. We were fairly well off as regarded fuel, since we had $6\frac{1}{2}$ gallons of petroleum.

A severe southwesterly gale on the fourth day out forced us to heave to. I would have liked to have run before the wind, but the sea was very high and the *James Caird* was in danger of broaching to and swamping. The delay was vexatious, since up to that time we had been making sixty or seventy miles a day; good going with our limited sail area. We hove to under double-reefed mainsail and our little jigger, and waited for the gale to blow itself out. During that afternoon we saw bits of wreckage, the remains probably of some unfortunate vessel that had failed to weather the strong gales south of Cape Horn. The weather conditions did not improve, and on the fifth day out the gale was so fierce that we were compelled to take in the double-reefed mainsail and hoist our small jib instead. We put out a sea anchor to keep the *James Caird*'s head up to the sea. This anchor consisted of a triangular canvas bag fastened to the end of the painter and allowed to stream out from the bows. The boat was high enough to catch the wind, and, as she drifted to leeward, the drag of the anchor kept her head to windward. Thus our boat took most of the seas more or less end on. Even then the crests of the waves often would curl right over us and we shipped a great deal of water, which necessitated unceasing baling and pumping. Looking out abeam, we would see a hollow like a tunnel formed as the crest of a big wave toppled over on to the swelling body of water. A thousand times it appeared as though the *James Caird* must be engulfed; but the boat lived. The southwesterly gale had its birthplace above the Antarctic Continent, and its freezing breath lowered the temperature far towards zero. The sprays froze upon the boat and gave bows, sides, and decking a heavy coat of mail. This accumulation of ice reduced the buoyancy of the boat, and to that extent was an added peril; but it possessed a notable advantage from one point of view. The water ceased to drop and trickle from the canvas, and the spray came in solely at the well in the after part of the boat. We could not allow the load of ice to grow beyond a certain point, and in turns we crawled about the decking forward, chipping and picking at it with the available tools.

When daylight came on the morning of the sixth day out we saw and felt that the *James Caird* had lost her resiliency. She was not rising to the oncoming seas. The weight of the ice that had formed in her and upon her during the night was having its effect, and she was becoming more like a log than a boat. The situation called for immediate action. We first broke away the spare oars, which were encased in ice and frozen to the sides of the boat, and threw them overboard. We retained two oars for use when we got inshore. Two of the fur sleeping bags went over the side; they were thoroughly wet weighing probably 40 lb. each, and they had frozen stiff during the night. Three men constituted the watch below, and when a man went down it was better to turn into the wet bag just vacated by another man than to thaw out a frozen bag with the heat of his unfortunate body. We now had four bags, three in use and one for emergency use in case a member of the party should break down permanently. The reduction of weight relieved the boat to some extent, and vigorous chipping and scraping did more. We had to be very careful not to put axe or knife through the frozen canvas of the decking as we crawled over it, but gradually we got rid of a lot of ice. The *James Caird* lifted to the endless waves as though she lived again.

About 11 a.m. the boat suddenly fell off into the trough of the sea. The painter had parted and the sea anchor had gone. This was serious. The *James Caird* went away to leeward, and we had no chance at all of recovering the anchor and our valuable rope, which had been our only means of keeping the boat's head up to the seas without the risk of hoisting sail in a gale. Now we had to set the sail and trust to its holding. While the *James Caird* rolled heavily in the trough, we beat the frozen canvas until the bulk of the ice had cracked off it and then hoisted it. The frozen gear worked protestingly, but after a struggle our little craft came up to the wind again, and we breathed more freely. Skin frostbites were troubling us, and we had developed large blisters on our fingers and hands. I shall always carry the scar of one of these frostbites on my left hand, which became badly inflamed after the skin had burst and the cold had bitten deeply.

We held the boat up to the gale during that day, enduring as best we could discomforts that amounted to pain. The boat tossed interminably on the big waves under grey, threatening skies. Our thoughts did not embrace much more than the necessities of the hour. Every surge of the sea was an enemy to be watched and circumvented. We ate our scanty meals, treated our frostbites, and hoped for the improved conditions that the morrow might bring. Night fell early, and in the lagging hours of darkness we were cheered by a change for the better in the weather. The wind dropped, the snow squalls became less frequent, and the sea moderated. When the morning of the seventh day dawned there was not much wind. We shook the reef out of the sail and laid our course once more for South Georgia. The sun came out bright and clear, and presently Worsley got a snap for longitude. We hoped that the sky would remain clear until noon, so that we could get the latitude. We had been six days out without an observation, and our dead reckoning naturally was uncertain. The boat must have presented a strange appearance that morning. All hands basked in the sun. We hung our sleeping bags to the mast and spread our socks and other gear all over the deck. Some of the ice had melted off the *James Caird* in the early morning after the gale began to slacken, and dry patches were appearing in the decking. Porpoises came blowing round the boat, and Cape pigeons wheeled and swooped within a few feet of us. These little black-

and-white birds have an air of friendliness that is not possessed by the great circling albatross. They had looked grey against the swaying sea during the storm as they darted about over our heads and uttered their plaintive cries. The albatrosses, of the black or sooty variety, had watched with hard, bright eyes, and seemed to have a quite impersonal interest in our struggle to keep afloat amid the battering seas. In addition to the Cape pigeons an occasional stormy petrel flashed overhead. Then there was a small bird, unknown to me, that appeared always to be in a fussy, bustling state, quite out of keeping with the surroundings. It irritated me. It had practically no tail, and it flitted about vaguely as though in search of the lost member. I used to find myself wishing it would find its tail and have done with the silly fluttering.

We reveled in the warmth of the sun that day. Life was not so bad, after all. We felt we were well on our way. Our gear was drying, and we could have a hot meal in comparative comfort. The swell was still heavy, but it was not breaking and the boat rode easily. At noon Worsley balanced himself on the gunwale and clung with one hand to the stay of the mainmast while he got a snap of the sun. The result was more than encouraging. We had done over 380 miles and were getting on for halfway to South Georgia. It looked as though we were going to get through.

The wind freshened to a good stiff breeze during the afternoon, and the *James Caird* made satisfactory progress. I had not realized until the sunlight came how small our boat really was. There was some influence in the light and warmth, some hint of happier days, that made us revive memories of other voyages, when we had stout decks beneath our feet, unlimited food at our command, and pleasant cabins for our ease. Now we clung to a battered little boat, "alone, alone, all, all alone, alone on a wide, wide sea." So low in the water were we that each succeeding swell cut off our view of the skyline. We were a tiny speck in the vast vista of the sea – the ocean that is open to all and merciful to none, that threatens even when it seems to yield, and that is pitiless always to weakness. For a moment the consciousness of the forces arrayed against us would be almost overwhelming. Then hope and confidence would rise again as our boat rose to a wave and tossed aside the crest in a sparkling shower like the play of prismatic colors at the foot of a waterfall. My double-barreled gun and some cartridges had been stowed aboard the boat as an emergency precaution against a shortage of food, but we were not disposed to destroy our little neighbors, the Cape pigeons, even for the sake of fresh meat. We might have shot an albatross, but the wandering king of the ocean aroused in us something of the feeling that inspired, too late, the Ancient Mariner. So the gun remained among the stores and sleeping bags in the narrow quarters beneath our leaking deck, and the birds followed us unmolested.

The eighth, ninth, and tenth days of the voyage had few features worthy of special note. The wind blew hard during those days, and the strain of navigating the boat was unceasing, but always we made some advance towards our goal. No bergs showed on our horizon, and we knew that we were clear of the ice fields. Each day brought its little round of troubles, but also compensation in the form of food and growing hope. We felt that we were going to succeed. The odds against us had been great, but we were winning through. We still suffered severely from the cold, for, though the temperature was rising, our vitality was declining owing to shortage of food, exposure, and the necessity of maintaining our cramped positions day and night. I found that it was now absolutely necessary to prepare hot milk for all hands during the night, in order to sustain life till dawn. This meant lighting the Primus lamp in the darkness and involved an increased drain on our small store of matches. It was the rule that one match must serve when the Primus was being lit. We had no lamp for the compass and during the early days of the voyage we would strike a match when the steersman wanted to see the course at night; but later the necessity for strict economy impressed itself upon us, and the practice of striking matches at night was stopped. We had one watertight tin of matches. I had stowed away in a pocket, in readiness for a sunny day, a lens from one of the telescopes, but this was of no use during the voyage. The sun seldom shone upon us. The glass of the compass got broken one night, and we contrived to mend it with adhesive tape from the medicine-chest. One of the memories that comes to me from those days is of Crean singing at the tiller. He always sang while he was steering, and nobody ever discovered what the song was. It was devoid of tune and as monotonous as the chanting of a Buddhist monk at his prayers; yet somehow it was cheerful. In moments of inspiration Crean would attempt "The Wearing of the Green."

On the tenth night Worsley could not straighten his body after his spell at the tiller. He was thoroughly cramped, and we had to drag him beneath the decking and massage him before he could unbend himself and get into a sleeping bag. A hard northwesterly gale came up on the eleventh day (May 5) and shifted to the southwest in the late afternoon. The sky was overcast and occasional snow squalls added to the discomfort produced by a tremendous cross-sea – the worst, I thought, that we had experienced. At midnight I was at the tiller and suddenly noticed a line of clear sky between the south and southwest. I called to the other men that the sky was clearing, and then a moment later I realized that what I had seen was not a rift in the clouds but the white crest of an enormous wave. During twenty-six years' experience of the ocean in all its moods I had not encountered a wave so gigantic. It was a mighty upheaval of the ocean, a thing quite apart from the big white-capped seas that had been our tireless enemies for many days. I shouted, "For God's sake, hold on! It's got us!" Then came a moment of suspense that seemed drawn out into hours. White surged the foam of the breaking sea around us. We felt our boat lifted and flung forward like a cork in breaking surf. We were in a seething chaos of tortured water; but somehow the boat lived through it, half full of water, sagging to the dead weight and shuddering under the blow. We baled with the energy of men fighting for life, flinging the water over the sides with every receptacle that came to our hands, and after ten minutes of uncertainty we felt the boat renew her life beneath us. She floated again and ceased to lurch drunkenly as though dazed by the attack of the sea. Earnestly we hoped that never again would we encounter such a wave.

The conditions in the boat, uncomfortable before, had been made worse by the deluge of water. All our gear was thoroughly wet again. Our cooking stove had been floating about in the bottom of the boat, and portions of our last hoosh seemed to have permeated everything. Not until 3 a.m., when we were all chilled almost to the limit of endurance, did we manage to get

the stove alight and make ourselves hot drinks. The carpenter
was suffering particularly, but he showed grit and spirit. Vincent had for the past week ceased to be an active member of the
crew, and I could not easily account for his collapse. Physically
he was one of the strongest men in the boat. He was a young
man, he had served on North Sea trawlers, and he should have
been able to bear hardships better than McCarthy, who, not so
strong, was always happy.

The weather was better on the following day (May 6), and we
got a glimpse of the sun. Worsley's observation showed that we
were not more than a hundred miles from the north-west corner
of South Georgia. Two more days with a favorable wind and we
would sight the promised land. I hoped that there would be no
delay, for our supply of water was running very low. The hot
drink at night was essential, but I decided that the daily
allowance of water must be cut down to half a pint per man.
The lumps of ice we had taken aboard had gone long ago. We
were dependent upon the water we had brought from Elephant
Island, and our thirst was increased by the fact that we were
now using the brackish water in the breaker that had been
slightly stove in the surf when the boat was being loaded. Some
sea water had entered at that time.

Thirst took possession of us. I dared not permit the allowance
of water to be increased since an unfavourable wind might drive
us away from the island and lengthen our voyage by many days.
Lack of water is always the most severe privation that men can
be condemned to endure, and we found, as during our earlier
boat voyage, that the salt water in our clothing and the salt spray
that lashed our faces made our thirst grow quickly to a burning
pain. I had to be very firm in refusing to allow any one to
anticipate the morrow's allowance, which I was sometimes
begged to do. We did the necessary work duly and hoped for
the land. I had altered the course to the east so as to make sure of
our striking the island, which would have been impossible to
regain if we had run past the northern end. The course was laid
on our scrap of chart for a point some thirty miles down the
coast. That day and the following day passed for us in a sort of
nightmare. Our mouths were dry and our tongues were swollen.
The wind was still strong and the heavy sea forced us to
nagivate carefully, but any thought of our peril from the waves

was buried beneath the consciousness of our raging thirst. The bright moments were those when we each received our one mug of hot milk during the long, bitter watches of the night. Things were bad for us in those days, but the end was coming. The morning of May 8 broke thick and stormy, with squalls from the northwest. We searched the waters ahead for a sign of land, and though we could see nothing more than had met our eyes for many days, we were cheered by a sense that the goal was near at hand. About ten o'clock that morning we passed a little bit of kelp, a glad signal of the proximity of land. An hour later we saw two shags sitting on a big mass of kelp, and knew then that we must be within ten or fifteen miles of the shore. These birds are as sure an indication of the proximity of land as a light-house is, for they never venture far to sea. We gazed ahead with increasing eagerness, and at 12:30 p.m., through a rift in the clouds, McCarthy caught a glimpse of the black cliffs of South Georgia, just fourteen days after our departure from Elephant Island. It was a glad moment. Thirst-ridden, chilled, and weak as we were, happiness irradiated us. The job was nearly done.

We stood in towards the shore to look for a landing place, and presently we could see the green tussock grass on the ledges above the surf-beaten rocks. Ahead of us and to the south, blind rollers showed the presence of uncharted reefs along the coast. Here and there the hungry rocks were close to the surface, and over them the great waves broke, swirling viciously and spouting thirty and forty feet into the air. The rocky coast appeared to descend sheer to the sea. Our need of water and rest was well nigh desperate, but to have attempted a landing at that time would have been suicidal. Night was drawing near, and the weather indications were not favorable. There was nothing for it but to haul off till the following morning, so we stood away on the starboard tack until we had made what appeared to be a safe offing. Then we hove to in the high westerly swell. The hours passed slowly as we waited the dawn, which would herald, we fondly hoped, the last stage of our journey. Our thirst was a torment and we could scarcely touch our food; the cold seemed to strike right through our weakened bodies. At 5 a.m. the wind shifted to the northwest and quickly increased to one of the worst hurricanes any of us had ever experienced. A great cross-sea was running, and the wind simply shrieked as it tore the tops off the waves and converted the whole seascape into a haze of driving spray. Down into valleys, up to tossing heights, straining until her seams opened, swung our little boat, brave still but laboring heavily. We knew that the wind and set of the sea was driving us ashore, but we could do nothing. The dawn showed us a storm-torn ocean, and the morning passed without bringing us a sight of the land; but at 1 p.m., through a rift in the flying mists, we got a glimpse of the huge crags of the island and realized that our position had become desperate. We were on a dead lee shore, and we could gauge our approach to the unseen cliffs by the roar of the breakers against the sheer walls of rock. I ordered the double-reefed mainsail to be set in the hope that we might claw off, and this attempt increased the strain upon the boat. The *James Caird* was bumping heavily, and the water was pouring in everywhere. Our thirst was forgotten in the realization of our imminent danger, as we baled unceasingly, and adjusted our weights from time to time; occasional glimpses showed that the shore was nearer. I knew that Annewkow Island lay to the south of us, but our small and badly marked chart showed uncertain reefs in the passage between the island and the mainland, and I dared not trust it, though as a last resort we could try to lie under the lee of the island. The afternoon wore away as we edged down the coast, with the thunder of the breakers in our ears. The approach of evening found us still some distance from Annewkow Island, and, dimly in the twilight, we could see a snow-capped mountain looming above us. The chance of surviving the night, with the driving gale and the implacable sea forcing us on to the lee shore, seemed small. I think most of us had a feeling that the end was very near. Just after 6 p.m., in the dark, as the boat was in the yeasty backwash from the seas flung from this ironbound coast, then, just when things looked their worst, they changed for the best. I have marveled often at the thin line that divides success from failure and the sudden turn that leads from apparently certain disaster to comparative safety. The wind suddenly shifted, and we were free once more to make an offing. Almost as soon as the gale eased, the pin that locked the mast to the thwart fell out. It must have been on the point of doing this throughout the hurricane; and if it had gone nothing could have saved us; the mast would have snapped like a carrot. Our backstays had carried away once before when iced up and were not too strongly fastened now. We were thankful indeed for the mercy that had held that pin in its place throughout the hurricane.

We stood off shore again, tired almost to the point of apathy. Our water had long been finished. The last was about a pint of hairy liquid, which we strained through a bit of gauze from the medicine chest. The pangs of thirst attacked us with redoubled intensity, and I felt that we must make a landing on the following day at almost any hazard. The night wore on. We were very tired. We longed for day. When at last the dawn came on the morning of May 10 there was practically no wind, but a high cross-sea was running. We made slow progress towards the shore. About 8 a.m. the wind backed to the northwest and threatened another blow. We had sighted in the meantime a big indentation which I thought must be King Haakon Bay, and I decided that we must land there. We set the bows of the boat towards the bay and ran before the freshening gale. Soon we had angry reefs on either side. Great glaciers came down to the sea and offered no landing place. The sea spouted on the reefs and thundered against the shore. About noon we sighted a line of jagged reef, like blackened teeth, that seemed to bar the entrance to the bay. Inside, comparatively smooth water stretched eight or nine miles to the head of the bay. A gap in the reef appeared, and we made for it. But the fates had another rebuff for us. The wind shifted and blew from the east right out of the bay. We could see the way through the reef, but we could not approach it directly. That afternoon we bore up, tacking five times in the strong wind. The last tack enabled us to get through, and at last we were in the wide mouth of the bay. Dusk was approaching. A small cove, with a boulder-strewn beach guarded by a reef, made a break in the cliffs on the south side of the bay, and we turned in that direction. I stood in the bows directing the steering as we ran through the kelp and made the passage of the reef. The entrance was so narrow that we had to take in the oars, and the swell was piling itself right over the reef into the cove; but in a minute or two we were inside, and in the gathering darkness the *James Caird* ran in on a swell and touched the beach. I sprang ashore with the short painter and held on when the boat went out with the backward surge. When the *James Caird* came in again three of the men got ashore, and they held the painter while I climbed some rocks with another line. A slip on the wet rocks twenty feet up nearly closed my part of the story just at the moment when we were achieving safety. A jagged piece of rock held me and at the same time bruised me sorely. However, I made fast the line, and in a few minutes we were all safe on the beach, with the boat floating in the surging water just off the shore. We heard a gurgling sound that was sweet music in our ears, and, peering around, found a stream of fresh water almost at our feet. A moment later we were down on our knees drinking the pure, ice-cold water in long draughts that put new life into us. It was a splendid moment.

After this landing, Shackleton and two companions crossed mountains and glaciers to reach the whaling station at Stromness Bay. Despite their exhaustion, they managed the crossing in three days (a record which has never been beaten). Eventually, all of the men of Shackleton's expedition were rescued alive.

THE GENERAL SAYS "NUTS"

Russell F. Weighley

*A vignette from the Battle of the Bulge, 1944, when a German
counter-offensive entrapped contingents of American troops.*

It is not surprising that the enemy detected in the westerly
battles a scarcity of American infantry grievous enough to
warrant a surrender demand. About noon on December 22, four
Germans under a flag of truce entered the lines of Company F
of the 327th. A major, a captain, and two enlisted men, they
described themselves as "parlementaires". The commander of
the 327th could not immediately be found, so it was the
regimental operations officer who received from the Germans
a written note from "The German Commander", which he
delivered to division headquarters. The note referred to the
progress of German spearheads farther west toward the Meuse
as evidence of the futility of holding out at Bastogne, which
adds perspective to the importance of the battles concurrently
being fought by the 2nd and 3rd Armored and 84th Infantry
Divisions in front of the Meuse crossings. Thus suggesting that
the German tide was irresistible anyway, the note demanded the
surrender of the encircled town within two hours, on pain of
annihilation of "the U.S.A. troops in and near Bastogne".

[Brigadier-General Anthony C.] McAuliffe received this
demand just as he was about to leave headquarters to congratulate the defenders of a roadblock who had given an especially
good account of themselves. He dropped the message on the
floor, said "Nuts", and left.

When he returned his staff reminded him of the message, and for the first time he gave it serious enough thought to ask what he should say in reply. His G-3 suggested, "That first remark of yours would be hard to beat."

"What did I say?" asked McAuliffe, and he was told. So the formal reply, typed on bond paper and delivered to the officer parlementaires at the F Company command post by Colonel Joseph H. Harper of the 327th, read:

To the German Commander:
Nuts!
The American Commander

Harper naturally found the parlementaires uncertain about the translation. He also found them apparently assuming their surrender demand would be met. Settling at first for advising them that the reply was decidedly not affirmative, by the time he had escorted the German officers back to the Company F outpost line, where they picked up the two enlisted men, Harper had pondered long enough on what he took to be their arrogance to send them off with: "If you don't understand what 'Nuts' means, in plain English it is the same as 'Go to hell'. I will tell you something else – if you continue to attack, we will kill every goddamn German that tries to break into this city."

ALONE

Douglas Mawson

*In September 1912 the Australian explorer Mawson set off, with
two companions, to explore Antarctica's King George V Land.
Three months later, Metz and Ninnis were dead and Mawson was
left all alone on the ice, exhausted with supplies a hundred miles
away. As the writer Hugh Kingsmill noted in his book on* Courage
*it might be objected that Mawson's subsequent endeavour displayed
only the the instinct for self-preservation; in fact, a less courageous
man would simply have lain down and given up. For as Gloucester
says in Shakespeare's* King Lear, *"No further, sir, a man may rot
even here".*

[J anuary 8] Outside the bowl of chaos was brimming with
drift-snow and as I lay in the sleeping-bag beside my dead
companion I wondered how, in such conditions, I would
manage to break and pitch camp single-handed. There appeared to be little hope of reaching the Hut, still one hundred
miles away. It was easy to sleep in the bag, and the weather was
cruel outside. But inaction is hard to bear and I braced myself
together determined to put up a good fight.

Failing to reach the Hut it would be something done if I
managed to get to some prominent point likely to catch the eye
of a search-party, where a cairn might be erected and our diaries
cached. So I commenced to modify the sledge and camping gear
to meet fresh requirements.

The sky remained clouded, but the wind fell off to a calm
which lasted several hours. I took the opportunity to set to work

on the sledge, sawing it in halves with a pocket tool and discarding the rear section. A mast was made out of one of the rails no longer required, and a spar was cut from the other. Finally, the load was cut down to a minimum by the elimination of all but the barest necessities, the abandoned articles including, sad to relate, all that remained of the exposed photographic films.

Late that evening, the 8th, I took the body of Mertz, still toggled up in his bag, outside the tent, piled snow blocks around it and raised a rough cross made of the two discarded halves of the sledge runners.

On January 9 the weather was overcast and fairly thick drift was flying in a gale of wind, reaching about fifty miles an hour. As certain matters still required attention and my chances of re-erecting the tent were rather doubtful . . . the start was delayed.

Part of the time that day was occupied with cutting up a waterproof clothes-bag and Mertz's burberry jacket and sewing them together to form a sail. Before retiring to rest in the evening I read through the burial service and put the finishing touches on the grave.

January 10 arrived in a turmoil of wind and thick drift. The start was still further delayed. I spent part of the time in reckoning up the food remaining and in cooking the rest of the dog meat, this latter operation serving the good object of lightening the load, in that the kerosene for the purpose was consumed there and then and had not to be dragged forward for subsequent use. Late in the afternoon the wind fell and the sun peered amongst the clouds just as I was in the middle of a long job riveting and lashing the broken shovel.

The next day, January 11, a beautiful, calm day of sunshine, I set out over a good surface with a slight down grade.

From the start my feet felt curiously lumpy and sore. They had become so painful after a mile of walking that I decided to examine them on the spot, sitting in the lee of the sledge in brilliant sunshine. I had not had my socks off for some days for, while lying in camp, it had not seemed necessary. On taking off the third and inner pair of socks the sight of my feet gave me quite a shock, for the thickened skin of the soles had separated in each case as a complete layer, and abundant watery fluid had escaped saturating the sock. The new skin beneath was very much abraded and raw. Several of my toes had commenced to blacken and fester near the tips and the nails were puffed and loose.

I began to wonder if there was ever to be a day without some special disappointment. However, there was nothing to be done but make the best of it. I smeared the new skin and the raw surfaces with lanoline, of which there was fortunately a good store, and then with the aid of bandages bound the old skin casts back in place, for these were comfortable and soft in contact with the abraded surface. Over the bandages were slipped six pairs of thick woollen socks, then fur boots and finally crampon overshoes. The latter, having large stiff soles, spread the weight nicely and saved my feet from the jagged ice encountered shortly afterwards.

So glorious was it to feel the sun on one's skin after being without it for so long that I next removed most of my clothing and bathed my body in the rays until my flesh fairly tingled – a wonderful sensation which spread throughout my whole person, and made me feel stronger and happier . . .

[17 January] A start was made at 8 a.m. and the pulling proved more easy than on the previous day. Some two miles had been negotiated in safety when an event occurred which, but for a miracle, would have terminated the story then and there. Never have I come so near to an end; never has anyone more miraculously escaped.

I was hauling the sledge through deep snow up a fairly steep sloop when my feet broke through into a crevasse. Fortunately as I fell I caught my weight with my arms on the edge and did not plunge in further than the thighs. The outline of the crevasse did not show through the blanket of snow on the surface, but an idea of the trend was obtained with a stick. I decided to try a crossing about fifty yards further along, hoping that there it would be better bridged. Alas! it took an unexpected turn catching me unawares. This time I shot through the centre of the bridge in a flash, but the latter part of the fall was decelerated by the friction of the harness ropes which, as the sledge ran up, sawed back into the thick compact snow forming the margin of the lid. Having seen my comrades perish in diverse ways and having lost hope of ever reaching the Hut,

I had already many times speculated on what the end would be like. So it happened that as I fell through into the crevasse the thought "so this is the end" blazed up in my mind, for it was to be expected that the next moment the sledge would follow through, crash on my head and all go to the unseen bottom. But the unexpected happened and the sledge held, the deep snow acting as a brake.

In the moment that elapsed before the rope ceased to descend, delaying the issue, a great regret swept through my mind, namely, that after having stinted myself so assiduously in order to save food, I should pass on now to eternity without the satisfaction of what remained – to such an extent does food take possession of one under such circumstances. Realizing that the sledge was holding I began to look around. The crevasse was somewhat over six feet wide and sheer walled, descending into blue depths below. My clothes, which, with a view to ventilation, had been but loosely secured, were now stuffed with snow broken from the roof, and very chilly it was. Above at the other end of the fourteen-foot rope, was the daylight seen through the hole in the lid.

In my weak condition, the prospect of climbing out seemed very poor indeed, but in a few moments the struggle was begun. A great effort brought a knot in the rope within my grasp, and, after a moment's rest, I was able to draw myself up and reach another, and, at length, hauled my body on to the overhanging snow-lid. Then, when all appeared to be well and before I could get to quite solid ground, a further section of the lid gave way, precipitating me once more to the full length of the rope.

There, exhausted, weak and chilled, hanging freely in space and slowly turning round as the rope twisted one way and the other, I felt that I had done my utmost and failed, that I had no more strength to try again and that all was over except the passing. It was to be a miserable and slow end and I reflected with disappointment that there was in my pocket no antidote to speed matters; but there always remained the alternative of slipping from the harness. There on the brink of the great Beyond I well remember how I looked forward to the peace of the great release – how almost excited I was at the prospect of the unknown to be unveiled. From those flights of mind I came back to earth, and remembering how Providence had miraculously brought me so far, felt that nothing was impossible and determined to act up to Service's lines:

> Just have one more try – it's dead easy to die,
> It's the keeping-on-living that's hard.

My strength was fast ebbing; in a few minutes it would be too late. It was the occasion for a supreme attempt. Fired by the passion that burns the blood in the act of strife, new power seemed to come as I applied myself to one last tremendous effort. The struggle occupied some time, but I slowly worked upward to the surface. This time emerging feet first, still clinging to the rope, I pushed myself out extended at full length on the lid and then shuffled safely on to the solid ground at the side. Then came the reaction from the great nerve strain and lying there alongside the sledge my mind faded into a blank.

When consciousness returned it was a full hour or two later, for I was partly covered with newly fallen snow and numb with the cold. I took at least three hours to erect the tent, get things snugly inside and clear the snow from my clothes. Between each movement, almost, I had to rest. Then reclining in luxury in the sleeping-bag I ate a little food and thought matters over. It was a time when the mood of the Persian philosopher appealed to me:

> Unborn To-morrow and dead Yesterday,
> Why fret about them if To-day be sweet?

I was confronted with this problem: whether it was better to enjoy life for a few days, sleeping and eating my fill until the provisions gave out, or to "plug on" again in hunger with the prospect of plunging at any moment into eternity without the supreme satisfaction and pleasure of the food. While thus cogitating an idea presented itself which greatly improved the prospects and clinched the decision to go ahead. It was to construct a ladder from a length of alpine rope that remained; one end was to be secured to the bow of the sledge and the other carried over my left shoulder and loosely attached to the sledge harness. Thus if I fell into a crevasse again, provided the sledge was not also engulfed, it would be easy for me, even though weakened by starvation, to scramble out by the ladder.

Notwithstanding the possibilities of the rope-ladder, I could not sleep properly, for my nerves had been overtaxed. All night long considerable wind and drift continued.

On the 19th it was overcast and light snow falling; very dispiriting conditions after the experience of the day before, but I resolved to go ahead and leave the rest to Providence . . .

[29 January] I was travelling along on an even down grade and was wondering how long the two pounds of food which remained would last, when something dark loomed through the haze of the drift a short distance away to the right. All sorts of possibilities raced through my mind as I headed the sledge for it. The unexpected had happened – in thick weather I had run fairly into a cairn of snow blocks erected by McLean, Hodgeman and Hurley, who had been out searching for my party. On the top of the mound, outlined in black bunting, was a bag of food, left on the chance that it might be picked up by us. In a tin was a note stating the bearing and distance of the mound from Aladdin's Cave (E. 30° S., distance twenty-three miles), and mentioning that the ship had arrived at the Hut and was waiting, and had brought the news that Amundsen had reached the Pole, and that Scott was remaining another year in Antarctica.

It certainly was remarkably good fortune that I had come upon the depot of food; a few hundred yards to either side and it would have been lost to sight in the drift. On reading the note carefully I found that I had just missed by six hours what would have been crowning good luck, for it appeared that the search party had left the mound at 8 a.m. that very day . . . It was about 2 p.m. when I reached it. Thus, during the night of the 28th our camps had been only some five miles apart.

Hauling down the bag of food I tore it open in the lee of the cairn and in my greed scattered the contents about on the ground. Having partaken heartily of frozen pemmican, I stuffed my pocket, bundled the rest into a bag on the sledge and started off in high glee, stimulated in body and mind. As I left the depot there appeared to be nothing on earth that could prevent me reaching the Hut within a couple of days, but a fresh obstacle with which I had not reckoned was to arise and cause further delay, leading to far-reaching results.

It happened that after several hours' march the surface changed from snow to polished névé and then to slippery ice. I could scarcely keep on my feet at all, falling every few moments and bruising my emaciated self until I expected to see my bones burst through the clothes. How I regretted having abandoned those crampons after crossing the Mertz Glacier; shod with them, all would be easy.

With nothing but finnesko on the feet, to walk over such a sloping surface would have been difficult enough in the wind without any other hindrance; with the sledge sidling down the slope and tugging at one, it was quite impossible. I found that I had made too far to the east and to reach Aladdin's Cave had unfortunately to strike across the wind.

Before giving up, I even tried crawling on my hands and knees.

However, the day's run, fourteen miles, was by no means a poor one.

Having erected the tent I set to work to improvise crampons. With this object in view the theodolite case was cut up, providing two flat pieces of wood into which were stuck as many screws and nails as could be procured by dismantling the sledgemeter and the theodolite itself. In the repair-bag there were still a few ice-nails which at this time were of great use.

Late the next day, the wind which had risen in the night fell off and a start was made westwards over the ice slopes with the pieces of nail-studded wood lashed to my feet. A glorious expanse of sea lay to the north and several recognizable points on the coast were clearly in view to east and west.

The crampons were not a complete success for they gradually broke up, lasting only a distance of six miles . . .

A blizzard was in full career on January 31 and I spent all day and most of the night on the crampons. On February 1 the wind and drift had subsided late in the afternoon, and I got under way expecting great things from the new crampons. The beacon marking Aladdin's Cave was clearly visible as a black dot on the ice slopes to the west.

At 7 p.m. that haven within the ice was attained. It took but a few moments to dig away the snow and throw back the canvas flap sealing the entrance. A moment later I slid down inside, arriving amidst familiar surroundings. Something unusual in one corner caught the eye – three oranges and a pineapple – circumstantial evidence of the arrival of the *Aurora*.

The improvised crampons had given way and were squeezing my feet painfully. I rummaged about amongst a pile of food-bags hoping to find some crampons or leather boots, but was disappointed, so there was nothing left but to repair the damaged ones. That done and a drink of hot milk having been prepared I packed up to make a start for the Hut. On climbing out of the cave imagine my disappointment at finding a strong wind and drift had risen. To have attempted the descent of the five and a half miles of steep ice slope to the Hut with such inadequate and fragile crampons, weak as I still was, would have been only as a last resort. So I camped in the comfortable cave and hoped for better weather next day.

But the blizzard droned on night and day for over a week with never a break. Think of my feelings as I sat within the cave, so near and yet so far from the Hut, impatient and anxious, ready to spring out and take the trail at a moment's notice. Improvements to the crampons kept me busy for a time; then, as there was a couple of old boxes lying about, I set to work and constructed a second emergency pair in case the others should break up during the descent. I tried the makeshift crampons on the ice outside, but was disappointed to find that they had not sufficient grip to face the wind, so had to abandon the idea of attempting the descent during the continuance of the blizzard. Nevertheless, by February 8 my anxiety as to what was happening at the Hut reached such a pitch that I resolved to try the passage in spite of everything, having worked out a plan whereby I was to sit on the sledge and sail down as far as possible.

Whilst these preparations were in progress the wind slackened. At last the longed for event was to be realized. I snatched a hasty meal and set off. Before a couple of miles had been covered the wind had fallen off altogether, and after that it was gloriously calm and clear.

I had reached within one and a half miles of the Hut and there was no sign of the *Aurora* lying in the offing. I was comforted with the thought that she might still be at the anchorage and have swung inshore so as to be hidden under the ice cliffs. But even as I gazed about seeking for a clue, a speck on the northwest horizon caught my eye and my hopes went down. It looked like a distant ship – Was it the *Aurora*? Well, what matter! the long journey was at an end – a terrible chapter of my life was concluded!

SATYAGRAHA

Web Miller

Mahatma Gandhi's campaign of "satyagraha", non-violent civil disobedience, against British rule in India was begun in 1920. Although repressed, assaulted and provoked, Gandhi and his followers steadfastly continued with their peaceful path, in the process becoming an inspiration for the racially downtrodden everywhere. India was granted independence in 1947. Here is an account of a classic "satyagraha" protest, against the Salt Tax, from May 1930. Gandhi himself was in prison but his followers, led by Iman Sahib, marched on the salt pans at Dharsana, and kept marching despite the baton blows and kicks of the British forces. And always the Gandhi people refused to retaliate.

D ungri consisted of a little huddle of native huts on the dusty plain. There were no means of transportation. I could find nobody who spoke English. By repeatedly pronouncing the word "Dharsana" and pointing questioningly around the horizon, I got directions and set off across country on foot through cactus hedges, millet fields, and inch-deep dust, inquiring my way by signs.

After plodding about six miles across country lugging a pack of sandwiches and two quart bottles of water under a sun which was already blazing hot, inquiring from every native I met, I reached the assembling place of the Gandhi followers. Several long, open, thatched sheds were surrounded by high cactus thickets. The sheds were literally swarming and buzzed like a beehive with some 2500 Congress or Gandhi men dressed in the regulation uniform of rough homespun cotton *dhotis* and tri-angular Gandhi caps, somewhat like American overseas sol-diers' hats. They chattered excitedly and when I arrived hundreds surrounded me, with evidences of hostility at first. After they learned my identity, I was warmly welcomed by young college-educated, English-speaking men and escorted to Mme Naidu. The famous Indian poetess, stocky, swarthy, strong-featured, bare-legged, dressed in rough, dark homespun robe and sandals, welcomed me. She explained that she was busy martialling her forces for the demonstration against the salt pans and would talk with me more at length later. She was educated in England and spoke English fluently.

Mme Naidu called for prayer before the march started and the entire assemblage knelt. She exhorted them, "Gandhi's body is in gaol but his soul is with you. India's prestige is in your hands. You must not use any violence under any circum-stances. You will be beaten but you must not resist; you must not even raise a hand to ward off blows." Wild, shrill cheers terminated her speech.

Slowly and in silence the throng commenced the half-mile march to the salt deposits. A few carried ropes for lassoing the barbed-wire stockade around the salt pans. About a score who were assigned to act as stretcher-bearers wore crude, hand-painted red crosses pinned to their breasts; their stretchers consisted of blankets. Manilal Gandhi, second son of Gandhi, walked among the foremost of the marchers. As the throng drew near the salt pans they commenced chanting the revolutionary slogan, *Inquilab zindabad*, intoning the two words over and over.

The salt deposits were surrounded by ditches filled with water and guarded by 400 native Surat police in khaki shorts and brown turbans. Half-a-dozen British officials commanded them. The police carried *lathis* – five-foot clubs tipped with steel. Inside the stockade twenty-five native riflemen were drawn up.

In complete silence the Gandhi men drew up and halted a hundred yards from the stockade. A picked column advanced from the crowd, waded the ditches, and approached the barbed-wire stockade, which the Surat police surrounded, holding their clubs at the ready. Police officials ordered the marchers to disperse under a recently imposed regulation which prohibited gatherings of more than five persons in any one place. The column silently ignored the warning and slowly walked forward. I stayed with the main body about a hundred yards from the stockade.

Suddenly, at a word of command, scores of native police rushed upon the advancing marchers and rained blows on their heads with their steel-shod *lathis*. Not one of the marchers even raised an arm to fend off the blows. They went down like tenpins. From where I stood I heard the sickening whacks of the clubs on unprotected skulls. The waiting crowd of watchers groaned and sucked in their breaths in sympathetic pain at every blow.

Those struck down fell sprawling, unconscious or writhing in pain with fractured skulls or broken shoulders. In two or three minutes the ground was quilted with bodies. Great patches of blood widened on their white clothes. The survivors without breaking ranks silently and doggedly marched on until struck down. When every one of the first column had been knocked down stretcher-bearers rushed up unmolested by the police and carried off the injured to a thatched hut which had been arranged as a temporary hospital.

Then another column formed while the leaders pleaded with them to retain their self-control. They marched slowly toward the police. Although every one knew that within a few minutes he would be beaten down, perhaps killed, I could detect no signs of wavering or fear. They marched steadily with heads up, without the encouragement of music or cheering or any possibility that they might escape serious injury or death. The police rushed out and methodically and mechanically beat down the second column. There was no fight, no struggle; the marchers simply walked forward until struck down. There were no outcries, only groans after they fell. There were not enough stretcher-bearers to carry off the wounded; I saw eighteen injured being carried off simultaneously, while forty-two still lay bleeding on the ground awaiting stretcher-bearers. The blankets used as stretchers were sodden with blood . . .

In the middle of the morning V. J. Patel arrived. He had been leading the Swaraj movement since Gandhi's arrest, and had just resigned as President of the Indian Legislative Assembly in protest against the British. Scores surrounded him, knelt, and kissed his feet. He was a venerable gentleman of about sixty with white flowing beard and moustache, dressed in the usual undyed, coarse homespun smock. Sitting on the ground under a mango tree, Patel said, "All hope of reconciling India with the British Empire is lost for ever. I can understand any government's taking people into custody and punishing them for breaches of the law, but I cannot understand how any government that calls itself civilized could deal as savagely and brutally with non-violent, unresisting men as the British have this morning."

By eleven the heat reached 116 degrees in the shade and the activities of the Gandhi volunteers subsided. I went back to the temporary hospital to examine the wounded. They lay in rows on the bare ground in the shade of an open, palm-thatched shed. I counted 320 injured, many still insensible with fractured skulls, others writhing in agony from kicks in the testicles and stomach. The Gandhi men had been able to gather only a few native doctors, who were doing the best they could with the inadequate facilities. Scores of the injured had received no treatment for hours and two had died. The demonstration was finished for the day on account of the heat.

I was the only foreign correspondent who had witnessed the amazing scene – a classic example of *satyagraha* or non-violent civil disobedience.

THE BIG HITTER

Bob Considine

Lou Gehrig played 2,130 consecutive ballgames for the New York Yankees from 1 June 1925 to May 1939, when his career was cut short by a form of spine paralysis. This became known as "Lou Gehrig's Disease", chiefly in tribute to the valiant way he faced his demise.

The Yanks won easily in 1938, Lou's fifteenth year with the ball team. They went on to demolish the Chicago Cubs in the World Series. But Lou's contribution was modest. During the regular season he hit .295, a highly acceptable figure in today's baseball, but a source of great embarrassment for Gehrig in 1938. It was the first time he had hit under .300 since joining the team. DiMag had beat him in home run production the year before. Lou played through the Series against the Cubs, but the four hits he got in fourteen times at bat were all singles.

The first hint I had that Lou's problem was more sinister than a routine slump that year was provided by a wild-and-woolly Washington pitcher named Joe Krakauskas. After a game at Yankee Stadium he told Shirley Povich of the *Washington Post* and me that a frightening thing had happened to him while pitching against Gehrig. Joe had uncorked his high inside fast ball with the expectation that Lou would move back and take it, as a ball. Instead, Krakauskas said, Lou – a renowned judge of balls and strikes – moved closer to the plate.

"My pitch went between his wrists," Joe said, still shaken. "Scared the hell outta me. Something's wrong with Gehrig . . ."

Lou's salary was cut three thousand dollars a year before he went south with the Yankees in 1939. There was no beef from him. He had had a bum year, for him, so the cut was deserved. He'd come back. After all, the Babe played twenty-two years without ever taking good care of himself . . .

Joe McCarthy started Gehrig at first base on opening day of the 1939 season, contemptuous of a fan who, a few days before in an exhibition game at Ebbets Field, had bawled, in earshot of both of them, "Hey, Lou, why don't you give yourself up? What do you want McCarthy to do, burn that uniform off you?"

Lou hobbled as far into the 1939 season as May 2. Then, on the morning of the first game of a series against Detroit, he called McCarthy on the hotel's house phone and asked to see him.

"I'm benching myself, Joe," he said, once in the manager's suite. McCarthy did not speak.

"For the good of the team," Lou went on. "I can't tell you how grateful I am to you for the kindness you've shown me, and your patience . . . I just can't seem to get going. The time has come for me to quit."

McCarthy snorted and told him to forget the consecutive-games-played record, take a week or two off, and he'd come back strong.

Gehrig shook his head. "I can't go on, Joe," he said. "Johnny Murphy told me so."

McCarthy cursed the relief pitcher.

"I didn't mean it that way, Joe," Gehrig said. "All the boys have been swell to me. Nobody's said a word that would hurt my feelings. But Johnny said something the other day that made me know it was time for me to get out of the lineup . . . and all he meant to do was to be encouraging."

McCarthy, still angry, asked for details.

"You remember the last play in that last game we played at the Stadium?" Lou asked. "A ball was hit between the box and first base. Johnny fielded it, and I got back to first just in time to take the throw from him."

"So?"

"So, well, I had a hard time getting back there, Joe," Lou

said. "I should have been there in plenty of time. I made the put-out, but when Johnny and I were trotting to the bench he said, 'Nice play, Lou.' I knew then it was time to quit. The boys were beginning to feel sorry for me."

At the urging of his devoted wife, Eleanor, Lou checked into the Mayo Clinic in Rochester, Minnesota. In due time he emerged with a bleak "To Whom It May Concern" document signed by the eminent Dr Harold C. Harbeing:

"This is to certify that Mr Lou Gehrig has been under examination at the Mayo Clinic from June 13 to June 19, 1939, inclusive. After a careful and complete examination, it was found that he is suffering from amyotrophic lateral sclerosis. This type of illness involves the motor pathways and cells of the central nervous system and, in lay terms, is known as a form of chronic poliomyelitis – infantile paralysis.

"The nature of this trouble makes it such that Mr Gehrig will be unable to continue his active participation as a baseball player, inasmuch as it is advisable that he conserve his muscular energy. He could, however, continue in some executive capacity."

Lou returned to the team for the remainder of the 1939 season, slowly suiting up each day, taking McCarthy's lineups to home plate to deliver to the umpires before each game. It was his only duty as captain. It was another winning season for the Yankees, but hardly for Lou. The short walk from the dugout to home plate and back exhausted him. But more exhausting was a cruel (but mostly true) story in the *New York Daily News* to the effect that some of his teammates had become afraid of drinking out of the Yankee dugout's drinking fountain after Lou used it.

"Gehrig Appreciation Day" (July 4, 1939) was one of those emotional salutes which only baseball seems able to produce: packed stands, the prospect of a doubleheader win over the Washington Senators, a peppery speech from Mayor Fiorello La Guardia, the presence of Yankee fan and Gehrig buff Postmaster General Jim Farley, and the array of rheumatic and fattening old teammates of yesteryear. And The Family in a sidelines box. Presents and trophies filled a table.

For Lou, now beginning to hollow out from his disease, one basic ingredient was missing. Babe Ruth wasn't there. Babe, the one he wanted to be there more than he wanted any of his old buddies, had not answered the invitations or the management's phone calls.

Then, with little warning, a great commotion and rustle and rattle in the stadium. The Babe was entering. He magnetized every eye, activated every tongue. Lou wheezed a prayer of thanksgiving.

The ceremony between games of the doubleheader was not calculated to be anything requiring a stiff upper lip. Joe McCarthy's voice cracked as he began his prepared tribute. He promptly abandoned his script and blurted, "Don't let's cry about this . . ." which had just the opposite effect among the fans.

When Lou's turn came, he, too, pocketed the small speech he had worked on the night before. He swallowed a few times to make his voice stronger, then haltingly said:

"They say I've had a bad break. But when the office force and the groundkeepers and even the Giants from across the river, whom we'd give our right arm to beat in the World Series – when *they* remember you, that's something . . . and when you have a wonderful father and mother who worked hard to give you an education . . . and a wonderful wife . . ."

His words began to slither when he tried to say something about Jake Ruppert and Miller Huggins, dead, and McCarthy, Barrow and Bill Dickey, alive.

But nobody missed his ending.

"I may have been given a bad break," he concluded, briefly touching his nose as if to discourage a sniff, "but I have an awful lot to live for. With all this, I consider myself the luckiest man on the face of the earth."

Babe, the irrepressible, stepped forward, embraced him and blubbered, an act that turned out to be epidemic.

Gehrig made the trip to Cincinnati that fall to watch his old club clobber the Reds in the World Series. He had a good time, but some of his friends found it a troubling experience being around him. Going out to dinner one night, with Dickey at his side, Lou staggered and was on the brink of plunging down the long flight of marble steps that led from the lobby of the Netherlands Plaza hotel to the street level. Dicky made one of the better catches of his life and saved Lou from a possibly fatal fall.

Then there was a scene on the train that brought the victorious Yanks back to New York. Lou spotted his friend Henry McLemore of the United Press and invited him into his drawing room for a drink. A table had been set up. Lou slowly but surely put ice in the glasses, then reached for the partly filled fifth of Johnnie Walker Black Label. He wrapped a bony hand around the cork and tried to pull it loose. It was not in tightly, but he did not have the strength to loosen it. Henry stopped listening to what Lou was saying about the Series. He was mesmerized by Lou's struggle, and too reverent of the man to offer to help. Finally, Lou raised the bottle to his lips, closed his teeth on the cork, and let his elbows drop to the table. The cork stayed in his teeth. He removed it, poured the drinks, and went on with what he had been saying.

Henry got very drunk that night.

Just before he died on June 2, 1941, Lou called me from his office. Mayor La Guardia had appointed him to the New York City Parole Board to work with and encourage youthful lawbreakers. Gehrig threw himself into the work with everything he had, or had left. He also kept up a lively interest in research into the disease that had driven him out of baseball.

It was a note about the latter that prompted his phone call.

"I've got some good news for you," he said. "Looks like the boys in the labs might have come up with a real breakthrough. They've got some new serum that they've tried on ten of us who have the same problem. And, you know something? It seems to be working on nine out of the ten. How about that?" He was elated.

I tried not to ask the question, but it came out anyway, after a bit.

"How about *you*, Lou?"

Lou said, "Well, it didn't work on me. But how about that for an average? – nine out of ten! Isn't that great?"

I said yes, it was great.

So was he.

THE TRIALS OF GALILEO

John Hall

A profile of the scientist as hero. In 1609 the Pisan inventor Galileo Galilei perfected the refracting telescope. This seemingly innocuous happenstance eventually led to Galileo being tried by the Inquisition.

The most momentous year of the life of Galileo, 1609, was also the source of all his disasters. It began with his telescope, which he produced in that year, having heard of such an instrument in Flanders the year before. He thought its construction out as a scientific problem, from the meagre data which he had been sent from the Low Countries, and soon produced independently an instrument which magnified to three diameters and showed objects twenty-two miles distant on the earth's surface.

The Council of Venice called him to show them his discovery, and when he did so, as a reward for seventeen years' brilliant service to the state, he was granted a life professorship at a new salary of two hundred and twenty pounds a year. The stipend was magnificent and his future secure. All over Europe, copies of his telescope were sent as gifts to ruling princes, potentates and learned men. But Galileo accepted his success coolly, and turned his instrument on the heavens.

There began his greatness, his immortal fame, and his downfall.

Up to this time, there had been one principal system of astronomy, the Ptolemaic, which was based on the earth being the centre of the universe, all the planets, stars and the sun revolving round it, the "immutable sphere." Twenty years before the birth of Galileo, however, another great astronomer, Copernicus, had arisen, and his system, with greater truth, had shown the sun as the centre of the universe, with the earth revolving round it.

The system of Copernicus had been accepted by many learned men, but not by the Church. It had been founded largely on inspired observation, needing proof. Galileo had already espoused the Copernican cause as opposed to the Ptolemaic. Now, with his telescope and his brilliant deductive mind, he turned a new eye to the stars and completed the Copernican revolution.

Alone, night after night, he swept the heavens. The moon he first saw as a world, all hills and valleys; the structure of the Milky Way, the planets – all came under his avid gaze, and their movements and positions were interpreted by his great intelligence. In January, 1610, he first saw Jupiter's satellites, the four moons, which he called the Medicean Stars, in honour of the Grand Duke of Tuscany and his three brothers. Then he discovered the "Ring" of Saturn. Under his hand, the "changeless" heavens were changing. This, as he was to discover to his cost, could not happen without the consent of Holy Church. . . . The Scriptures said: "He hath made the round world so fast that it cannot be moved." By confirming the earth's movement, Galileo was setting his foot on the road to becoming a heretic.

Already a subject for envy among the professors of all Italy, he was now, unwittingly and unwillingly, making enemies among the Jesuits, and attracting the fearful attention of the Holy Inquisition. Finally, he made a fatal mistake which paved the way to the ultimate triumph of his enemies.

At this time, Venice was the only part of Italy which was entirely free from Jesuit influence. Before Galileo entered the service of the Republic, the Senate, finding the Jesuits scheming to gain control of education in its territories, had declared that they were not to teach there. Only in the Republic was freedom of thought complete. With the growth of Galileo, the Tuscan's, fame, it became fitting for him to serve his own Grand Duke, Cosmo II dei Medici. Besides, he needed time for his researches: in Venice and Padua he was too occupied with his pupils, now legion, to follow them properly. When, at length, he was offered the post of first mathematical the University of Pisa, and philosopher and mathematician to the grand duke, at the same salary as in Padua, and in addition with no obligation to lecture or live at Pisa, he accepted it. In 1610, he left the Venetian Republic, and his security.

Henceforward, whatever he did was attacked by the Jesuits, Aristotelians and traditionalists of all kinds; what was worse, he defended himself brilliantly and successfully, with pungent satire.

Deeming it prudent, none the less, to beware of offending the Church openly, he early journeyed to Rome in order to forestall any possible theological accusations. The Pope, Paul V, received him cordially. His "Celestial Novelties," as they were called, were accepted by the Church as real observations, yet without giving them official sanction. The great scientific academy, "Dei Lincei," honoured Galileo by electing him a member. He returned in triumph to Pisa, fearing nothing. In Rome, among those who had supported him and shown himself greatly in sympathy with his cause, was Cardinal M. Barberini, afterwards Pope Urban VIII, later to be one of his chief accusers.

On his return, controversy followed controversy. In April, 1611, Galileo discovered the existence of "sun-spots," announcing that they were actually "blemishes" on the face of the sun, an idea highly repugnant to accepted tradition, which held that the sun was a "perfect body." In the same year a Jesuit, Christopher Scheiner, claimed to have made the same discovery, explaining that the spots were really planets revolving round the sun, a thesis already dropped by Galileo. The Jesuits championed Scheiner's view on theological grounds.

Roused to anger, finally, by these and other doctrinal objections to what he regarded as purely scientific truths, Galileo wrote his famous letter to his pupil Castelli, taking the view that the "language of the Scriptures is suited to the intelligence of those for whom it is written, and that the interpretation must be revised in the light of new facts."

Castelli rashly circulated copies of this letter, and the Inquisition, obtaining one, prepared to attack. Galileo, his fighting spirit roused, went to Rome, determined to defend himself and his doctrines equally. He did not believe his voyage to be dangerous either to himself or his integrity as a teacher. He was wrong.

In February, 1616, the Inquisition reported on Galileo's work on sun-spots, embodying the doctrine that the sun is the fixed centre of the world. To his amazement and uneasiness, they condemned this view as false philosophically and formally heretical, and similarly the doctrine that the earth rotates and also revolves round the sun. At the same time, Copernicus's own book on his system was suspended.

Cardinal Bellarmine sent for Galileo and solemnly warned him of the error of his opinions, and Galileo, as a good son of the Church, bowed his acknowledgement of this error. What he did not know, however, was that when he signed the written copy of the cardinal's admonition, the Commissary of the Inquisition secretly amplified it, adding that from henceforth he "must not hold, teach or defend the opinions in question."

When he returned to Florence, it was with the uneasy knowledge that in future he must be more circumspect in dealing with the Copernican doctrine, but he did not realize that from now on the Inquisition was only waiting for an occasion to suppress him entirely; remove his liberty, and if they could, his life.

The next fifteen years were therefore years of caution and decision. Galileo was growing old. He was one of the most celebrated figures in Christendom, but ill-health and family troubles were for ever with him.

Ever since the far-off days in Padua, he had been a sick man. In his first year under the Venetian Republic, he had gone with some friends to rest in a cave near the city. They slept there, in a cold, possibly a poisonous draught. Two of his friends died of their exposure. Galileo had suffered ever since from a constitutional weakness and tendency to catch chills, colds and ague.

From 1616 until the end of his life, he was constantly weak, constantly in the shadow of death. Only his indomitable spirit and boundless enthusiasm kept him alive, writing of his discoveries and attacking his enemies. When he saw his friends, or his beloved pupil, Castelli, he was the great man, the philosopher, wit and musician, fond of good wine and good company. But he rarely discussed his work with strangers, and alone he was an æsthete and a hermit.

Always tortured by money cares, he supported all his parasitic family with truly philosophic calm and extraordinary generosity. His son by Marina Gamba, Vincenzio, had turned out selfish, idle and good for nothing, like his uncle, Michelangelo. Marina Gamba herself, Galileo married off to a man in her own station in life, providing for her generously and gratefully.

His two daughters he had made nuns. They were his great solace, particularly the elder of the two, Marie Celeste. They had taken the veil because their father, with all his other pressing cares, had not the money to provide for them, and their birth barred them from marriage in their own rank. Marie Celeste was her father's dearest human interest.

When she died in 1634, he wrote to his friend Elia Diodati: ". . . I paid frequent visits to the neighbouring convent where I had two daughters who were nuns and whom I loved dearly; but the eldest in particular, who was a woman of exquisite mind, singular goodness and most tenderly attached to me . . . now she is dead . . ."

Above all family matters, however, in the years following his first condemnation by the Inquisition, Galileo studied, observed, worked and schemed for the publication of his work; schemed, because now publication was for him an act of diplomacy. He had to please his supporters and avoid the ban or too close attention of the hunting, ferreting Inquisition.

In 1623, he obtained the papal sanction to publish his book, *Il Saggiatore*, the Assayer. It was a reply to a Jesuit attack on a work of his concerning comets, which he maintained were atmospheric phenomena. He dedicated it to Cardinal M. Barberini, his former sympathizer, who had lately become Pope Urban VIII. The Pope was well pleased with the work, though the General of the Jesuits forbade even the mention of it to the members of the Order.

Urban VIII was between two fires: his own critical appreciation of Galileo's greatness, and the power of the Jesuits. When Galileo went to Rome in 1624 to pay his respects to the new Pope, the latter received him generously, with gifts and the promise of a pension for his son, while refusing for reasons of policy to remove the embargo of 1616 on the doctrines of Copernicus. He did, however, add a rider that the Church had not condemned these doctrines as heretical, but rash.

Encouraged by the attitude of the Pope, Galileo, between desperate bouts of illness, and overwhelmed by his brother Michelangelo's sending his whole family to live with him in Florence, concentrated his energies on the work which was to be his glory and downfall, the *Dialogues on the Two Principal Systems of the World*.

Month after month he worked at it, until his daughter, Marie Celeste, knowing how his knowledge and concentration was an anodyne to his family cares, beseeched him in letter after letter not to weaken himself and thereby lay himself open to sickness, for on him the whole family depended.

By the time the book was ready, Galileo was an invalid in all save his spirit and mind. His strong face with its white beard and piercing eye remained, but his poor body was a torture. None the less, in 1629, he again journeyed to Rome, where he actually obtained the papal permission to print his masterpiece.

Castelli, his favourite pupil, was now Papal Mathematician. Riccardi, the Chief Censor, encouraged him, by telling him that the Pope was still a Copernican at heart, and sure enough, he returned to Florence in 1630 with the coveted permission to print, provided only that he made it clear that the subject of the dialogues was purely hypothetical, and furthermore, that if anything in the Scriptures appeared to present insuperable difficulties according to the new theory, the Scriptures must not because of this be called impossible.

Nature, however, now took a hand in delaying the publication of the dialogues. The plague was raging in Florence and throughout Italy when he returned. Communications between all the great cities were interrupted, and Galileo decided to have the work published in Florence instead of in Rome. New permission had to be obtained from the censor, and this was not forthcoming until the end of 1631. The Jesuits in Rome, in the absence of Galileo, fought tooth and nail to prevent its publication. It did not appear until February, 1632.

The book was an immense and immediate success. Only by the Jesuits was it received with a howl of execration, headed by Galileo's old enemy, Scheiner. On every possible occasion, the most cunning and persuasive men in the Order were put to work on the mind of the Pope, trying to turn him against Galileo. At last they succeeded.

The scheme of the dialogues is that of an argument between two supporters of the Ptolemaic and Copernican systems, respectively. A third party is introduced as their judge and commentator, supposed to represent the view of the man in the street. To him is given the name of Simplicio.

It was cleverly noted by the Inquisition that the Pope's arguments, the inclusion of which the latter had demanded when granting the permission to print, were put into the mouth of Simplicio, and it was claimed that Galileo wished to insinuate thereby that the Pope was a simpleton. This childish argument struck home. Galileo's publisher received an order from the Inquisition forbidding the sale of the book until further notice. A commission was set up to examine and report on the dialogues. Its composition was grossly unfair. Even the intervention of the Grand Duke of Tuscany himself did not succeed in obtaining the representation of any man of science, such as Castelli. Niccolini, the grand duke's ambassador, in Rome, was told that His Holiness believed himself to have been deliberately deceived into granting his licence to publish, and that furthermore, in the book, Galileo "did not fear to make game of me."

Galileo, sick and in the depths of despair, knowing that he had found truth, yet cursing the light of his mind which had led him to it, awaited his unjust condemnation.

In due course, the whole of the Inquisition proceedings of 1616 were brought up against him, and, principally on account of the false minute forbidding him to "hold, teach or defend" the doctrines of Copernicus, he was condemned and summoned to Rome by the commissary general to recant of his heresy.

The plague was still raging. Niccolini endeavoured without success to arrange for Galileo to be examined in Florence, for he was gravely ill. Ophthalmia and the threat of blindness was on him. The summons was for October. In December, the Pope, impatient at the delay, ordered that he should be brought to Rome immediately, "in irons if necessary." Helpless, the grand duke arranged for his transport in litters to the Eternal City, and for him to be lodged there in the Tuscan Embassy. He left in cold and bitter rain, at the worst season of the year, sick probably to death. He did not expect to see Florence again, but his spirit never failed him. To a friend who came to bid him farewell, he said:

"I go to my death, but what is death to immortal achievement? My dishonour, as a faithful son of the Church, must one day be the Church's shame. Would that it were otherwise. I shall defend myself to the end."

But once in Rome, Niccolini, who knew that there were plans to torture the old man, to discover "his true opinions," managed to dissuade him from this dangerous determination, making him promise to submit to the tribunal.

April 12, 1633: the day fixed for the trial of Galileo. He went to it as to execution, in the full knowledge that he had not long to live, being in his seventieth year and very infirm. His real concern was not for his frail life, but for the coming suppression of his life's work.

He went to the court in mental anguish, aching with revolt, the last words of Niccolini echoing resentfully in his ears:

"Submit: the more completely the better . . ."

He appeared before the commissary general and the procurator fiscal, hard and bitter men, in silent triumph. His spirit and person dominated theirs: white-haired and venerable, thoughtful and strong of face, sublimely simple in his answering of questions.

They asked him: "You know why you are here?"

"On account of my book, the authorship of which I must freely admit, though it be to my own scandal."

"Did you, Galileo Galilei, take cognizance of the admonition of his late Eminence, Cardinal Bellarmine, in the process of 1616, that the doctrine that the sun is the fixed centre of the universe, and that the terrestrial globe rotates and revolves round the sun, is absurd in philosophy and formally heretical?"

"I did, and furthermore submitted to the admonition and signed it as an obedient son of the Church."

"And did you then promise not to hold, teach or defend these doctrines?" The old man hesitated, too wily to walk into a trap.

"Did I promise such a thing," he replied, "my conscience is clear that I have been obedient: but the infirmity of my age makes memory insecure . . . Besides, it has ever been my contention that by publishing my last work, of which you complain, far from glorying in the truth of Copernican doctrines, I have refuted them as weak, and inconclusive, according to the views of our Holy Father Himself . . ." He had promised submission, and therefore, heart wrung with bitterness, he gave it. For reward, and because the eyes of the whole learned world were on Galileo and his tribunal, the procurator fiscal had him confined in his own house, and Niccolini was allowed to send in meals to him.

Three days later, the counsellors of the holy office pronounced his guilt. Next, they demanded, as was the practice in cases of heresy, his full admission of this guilt. The commissary general therefore came to Galileo and persuaded him to promise a full confession "so that the Court could deal leniently with him."

Accordingly, on April 30, with a humility altogether foreign to his nature, he was called to speak a colourless admission of guilt to the assembled court. He still had the strength to deliver his speech in his own manner, not impersonal enough for his soulless accusers:

". . . Sure, sirs, I have fully examined my work and conscience since last I appeared before you . . . I know well of the untruth latent in my defence of the system of Copernicus, witness the fact that in my teachings at various universities throughout my life, I have not neglected assiduously to pay tribute to Ptolemy and Aristotle. Yet I do find that carried away by false pride in my own subtlety, in my present work, I put a lying cause too strongly, so that to the untutored mind, it might appear true. Of this I do repent in all humility, and offer, to satisfy the holy office, to add to my dialogues, with all my poor skill, a full and complete refutation of Copernicus, that men's minds may no longer be in danger . . ."

After this humiliation, Galileo was allowed to return to the Tuscan Embassy. On May 10, however, he was summoned again and forced to sign a written confession of the truth of the minute of 1616, with an appeal for clemency on account of his age and sickness.

Perjury was thus added to the crimes which he was forced to commit against his own conscience and lifelong beliefs.

On June 16, the Pope presided at a meeting of the sacred congregation, at which it was decided that Galileo should be put to the question, under threat of torture, as to his real beliefs;

that he should be made to recant before the plenary assembly of the Inquisition; that he should be imprisoned, and forbidden thereafter to discuss the motion of the earth and sun, under pain of death by burning, as a relapsed heretic . . .

On June 21, Galileo suffered this penultimate indignity at the hands of the court: it saved him from torture. Under close question, a reply was wrung from him which cost him untold agony:

"You order me to abandon these doctrines: gentlemen, I have never held them as true, in my heart. How then can I recant further? I am ready to do so if only you will point the way . . ."

The day of sentence came at last. Bodily utterly broken, yet still unbowed in spirit, he was led before the court to receive his deserts at the hands of the Church.

Ten cardinals' names were prefixed to the account of his trial and works, damning him and them completely. It ended with sentence on the man Galileo, "vehemently suspected of heresy, who will be absolved of his crimes only if he will abjure, curse and detest the said errors and heresies in the form hereunder prescribed . . . and furthermore, as a warning to himself and all others, his works will be prohibited by public edict, he will be formally imprisoned in the Inquisition at the judges' pleasure, and will recite once a week the seven Penitential Psalms; the judges alone reserving the right to mitigate the above penalties . . ."

Grovelling on his knees, therefore, before the Inquisition, in plenary council assembled, Galileo, the greatest man of his age, read aloud the prescribed form of abjuration, then signed it.

By intervention of Niccolini, the Pope permitted Galileo's place of imprisonment to be changed from the Inquisition to one of the grand duke's villas, near Rome. As Niccolini conducted him thither, the grand old man laid a hand on that of the ambassador:

"Do not grieve, Master Niccolini," he said. "My condemnation is nothing . . . The earth moves for all that."

A year after his departure to Rome for trial, he was allowed to return to his villa at Arcetri, near Florence, still under conditions of close confinement. Until the end of his life he was pestered by restrictions. His bitterness over his fate was terrible. In 1632, he wrote to a friend:

". . . When I think that the end of all my labours, after having gained for myself a name not obscure among the learned, has been finally to bring upon me a citation to appear before the Tribunal of the Holy Office . . . I detest the remembrance of the time I have consumed in study. I regret ever having published what I wrote, and I have a mind to burn every composition that I have yet by me . . ."

But despite illness and disappointment, sorrow in the death of his beloved daughter, resentment at his treatment by the Church whose faithful son he had always believed himself to be, he still worked. Worked until blindness took away from him, in December, 1637, the infinite joy of contemplating the unfettered heavens.

His blindness drew forth from him a piteous letter to his friend, Diodati:

". . . Alas, your dear friend and servant Galileo, has been for the last month hopelessly blind; so that this heaven, this universe, which I by marvellous discoveries and clear demonstrations had enlarged a thousand times, beyond the belief of wise men of bygone ages, henceforward for me is shrunk into such a small space as is filled by my own bodily sensations . . ."

Yet when he knew that he would never see again, this man to whom sight was life never complained, only asking his friends to remember him in their prayers.

Broken, weary, blind, he died in 1642 on January 8. His last mechanical suggestion was the application of the pendulum principle to regulate a clock, but his mortal illness interrupted his work on it.

His enemies, unappeased, even struck at him beyond the grave. He was to have been given a public funeral in Florence and a monument in marble, by order of the Grand Duke Ferdinand dei Medici. The Pope forbade it.

But his monument was more lasting than marble, his name imperishably greater than those of his accusers, popes, cardinals and princes. When, a century later, they were all dead and his name still lived, in the church of Santa Croce, in Florence, with money left for the purpose by his last pupil, Viviani, a monument was erected to his memory. His bones were brought thither and laid to rest with Viviani's own, but Galileo no longer stood in need of this recognition. He was immortal.

OBITUARY: BILL REID, V.C.

The Times

A bomber pilot who nursed his badly damaged Lancaster back to base, steering by moon and stars when his navigator was killed by machine-gun fire.

O n the night of November 3, 1943, Flight Lieutenant Bill Reid was the pilot and captain of the Lancaster bomber O for Oboe of No 61 Squadron, flying on a mission to attack German industrial installations in Düsseldorf. Shortly after crossing the Dutch coast the Lancaster was attacked by a Messerschmitt 110 night fighter, which the mid-upper and rear airgunners drove off only with difficulty because their turret heating systems had failed and their hands were consequently numb with cold. In the attack, the Me110's machine-guns shattered Reid's windscreen and wounded him in the head, shoulders and hands.

After establishing that all his crew members were unhurt and without mentioning his own injuries. Reid renewed his course for Dusseldorf. He then discovered that the Messerschmitt's guns had also damaged the rear gun-turret and the elevator trimming tabs, making the aircraft difficult to control.

Reid had barely assessed the total damage when O for Oboe was attacked by a second night fighter. The Lancaster was raked from end to end with machine-gun fire which killed the navigator, fatally injured the radio operator and wounded Reid for a fourth time. The rear-gunner succeeded in driving off the fighter with his one remaining serviceable Browning, but the mid-upper turret was damaged and the aircraft's intercommunication and oxygen systems were put out of action.

Using oxygen from a portable supply operated by the flight engineer, Reid continued towards Düsseldorf, still some 200 miles distant, on a course he had memorised. Meanwhile the bomb-aimer, isolated by the failure of the intercom, remained unaware of his captain's injuries or of the other casualties to the crew.

As they approached the target area he recognised the night's objective and released the bombs over the centre. (The accuracy was verified by photographs taken automatically by the Lancaster's camera 28 seconds later.) His mission accomplished, Reid set course for home, steering by the Moon and Pole Star. Soon the intense cold from the shattered windscreen and shortage of oxygen caused him to slip into semi-consciousness. Helped by the bomb-aimer who had joined him in the cockpit, the flight engineer kept O for Oboe in the air, fortunately avoiding further damage from heavy anti-aircraft fire as they recrossed the Dutch coast.

Reid recovered consciousness over the North Sea and despite his vision being partly obscured by blood from his head wound, resumed control and prepared to land at the nearest airfield. This was accomplished through ground mist and without further injury to the surviving crew, although one leg of the undercarriage collapsed as soon as the aircraft's weight load came to bear on it.

The citation for Reid's Victoria Cross concluded: "Wounded in two attacks, Flight Lieutenant Reid showed superb courage and leadership in penetrating a further 200 miles into enemy territory to attack one of the most strongly defended targets in Germany. His tenacity and devotion to duty are beyond praise." The air vice-marshal commanding the bomber group to which 61 Squadron belonged visited Reid in hospital and asked, "Why didn't you turn back?" He replied that the idea had simply not occurred to him.

The Düsseldorf raid was Bill Reid's tenth bombing mission and he resolved to return to active duty as soon as he had recovered from his injuries. His skill and determination were rewarded by a posting to No 617 (Dambuster) Squadron, then led by Wing Commander Leonard Cheshire, who would later also win the VC to add to his DSO and DFC.

Reid flew bombing missions with 617 Squadron until a daylight raid on a V1 flying bomb storage site in a railway tunnel at Rilly la Montagne, to the east of Paris, brought his wartime career to a dramatic halt on July 31, 1944. (By this time command of 617 had passed to Wing Commander Willie Tait.)

Reid's task was to attack with a 12,000lb "Tallboy" bomb (a revolutionary deep-penetration weapon which was also the brainchild of Barnes Wallis, creator of the Dambusting bomb). His attack was to close one end of the tunnel, the other being sealed by a similar Tallboy attack. A follow-up group of Lancasters was to attack 15 minutes later with delayed-action bombs to crater the approaches to the tunnel.

Unfortunately, as soon as Reid had dropped his bomb (which he did with uncanny accuracy), an aircraft of the follow-up group bombed early from 18,000 ft immediately above him. One of the bombs struck Reid's outer port engine, without exploding, and a second cut through the fuselage, severing control leads to the ailerons and rudder, rendering the control column useless.

As the aircraft began to spin, the nose fell away and Reid found himself falling through the air in an uncanny silence after the roar of the Lancaster's engines. He pulled his parachute cord, landed unhurt in a tree and was taken prisoner within half an hour. Of the seven-man crew, only he and and the radio operator, Flying Officer David Luker, DFC, DFM, survived the most unusual experience of being "bombed down".

First imprisoned near Frankfurt, Reid later found himself in Stalag Luft III in what is now Poland. As the Red Army advanced in early 1945, all the occupants of the camp were marched eastwards for a week before being put on a train to Luckenwalde, southwest of Berlin. They were still there when the Russians captured the place in April and were held for a further month before being released and returned to England. Reid took his service discharge at once to start a degree course in agriculture.

William Reid was born in the Baillieston district of Glasgow on 1921, the third son of William Reid – a second generation blacksmith. After attending the Coatbridge Secondary School in Baillieston, he joined the RAF Volunteer Reserve in 1940. He graduated from Glasgow University in 1949 and joined the MacRobert Trust Farms Ltd in Aberdeenshire on a scholarship which sent him on a tour of agricultural installations in India, Australia, New Zealand, Canada and the United States. After his return, he worked as an agricultural adviser to the MacRobert Trust, 1950–59.

From 1950 he was for twenty years national cattle and sheep adviser for Spillers Farm Feeds and ran the Spillers milk production trial at the national dairy event in London and Kenilworth. He retired in 1980 and moved to Crieff.

He was a founder member and later a life vice-president of the Aircrew Association. He was one of the ten VC holders who accompanied the VC10 aircraft promotional tour of East Africa in 1972 and in recognition of his work for the Aircrew Association he was granted the Freedom of the City of London in 1988.

His death leaves 20 living holders of the Victoria Cross.

Reid married in 1952 Violet Campbell Gallagher, who was completely unaware that he was a holder of the VC until they were married. She was a daughter of William Gallagher, sports editor of the Glasgow *Daily Record*, and survives him with their son and daughter.

Bill Reid, VC, wartime bomber pilot, was born on December 21, 1921. He died on November 28, 2001, aged 79.

THE MIRACLE OF THE JACAL

Bill O'Neal

Elfrego Baca was an Hispanic New Mexican teenager who, in 1884, tired of prejudice, pinned on a mail order deputy's badge and "arrested" a cowboy racist. There ensued the "miracle of the jacal" gunfight, whereby Baca single-handedly fought 80 cowboys for thirty-three hours.

October 1884. Frisco. New Mexico. A cowboy named McCarty was shooting up the town, concentrating his drunken efforts upon making the Mexican populace "dance" by firing at their feet. The nineteen-year-old Baca cockily pinned on his mail-order badge, pulled out his guns, and "arrested" McCarty. He then marched McCarty to the Middle Plaza, intending to leave at daylight for the county seat at Socorro, but several punchers led by McCarty's foreman, a man named Perham, confronted him and demanded that he release their friend. Baca waved his revolvers and retorted that he would give them until the count of three to leave town. He quickly counted. "One, two, three," and began firing. One cowboy took a slug in the knee, and Perham's horse reared and fell, fatally injuring the foreman.

In the morning a group of citizens led by J. H. Cook approached Baca and persuaded him to turn over his "prisoner" to the local justice of the peace. The justice fined McCarty five dollars, and a satisfied Baca turned to leave. But outside he was met by eighty cowboys led by Tom Slaughter, owner of the ranch for which Perham and McCarty worked. A shot was fired, and Baca ducked into an alley. He sprinted into a nearby jacal, a tiny building inhabited by a woman and two children, and pushed them outside just as rancher Jim Herne rushed the dwelling on foot, brandishing a rifle. Baca pumped two bullets into Herne, and the rancher collapsed, mortally wounded.

Herne's body was dragged away, and the cowboys began to pour systematic volleys into the jacal. The flimsy building was constructed only of posts and mud, but the floor was dug out about eighteen inches below ground level, and Baca crouched low as bullets whipped over his head. From time to time he managed to shoot back, and his aim was so deadly that his adversaries tied ropes between nearby buildings and draped blankets over them so that they could walk about in comparative safety. Baca placed a plaster replica of a saint in a window and dropped his hat on top of it to provide an alternate target.

About dusk a volley succeeded in collapsing part of the roof, and Baca was buried under the rubble, managing to dig himself out only after two hours of effort. At midnight a stick of dynamite demolished half the building, but Baca survived in a far corner. At dawn he coolly began to cook breakfast, to the delight of a large group of Mexicans who had arrived to cheer him. One cowboy managed to close in behind a cast-iron shield made from a cookstove, but Baca sent him scampering away by grazing him on the skull.

It was claimed that more than four thousand bullets were fired into the little jacal, that the door had 367 holes in it, and that a broom handle had been hit eight times. But Baca fought grimly on, finally killing four men and wounding several others. At last Cook, followed by a deputy sheriff named Ross and Francisquito Naranjo approached the ruined jacal and persuaded Baca to come out. He emerged at 6:00 P.M. after thirty-three hours under siege, having agreed to let the cowboys take him under custody to Socorro, but insisting that he be allowed to keep his guns. When they set out, the cowboys rode in the lead, followed by a buckboard, driven by Ross, in the rear of which Baca was seated with his guns alertly trained on his captors. Baca was tried twice for murder, but won acquittal on both occasions.

ANNIE SULLIVAN AND HELEN KELLER

Lorena A. Hickok

The name of Helen Keller is familiar, the name of Annie Sullivan is not. It was Sullivan — a near blind, impoverished Irish girl — however, who taught the deaf-and-blind Keller to speak and read.

The day was Washington's Birthday. The year, 1876.

Through the cold February twilight, an ugly black conveyance jolted and rattled on high iron-rimmed wheels over a frozen dirt road through the outskirts of Tewksbury, Massachusetts.

It has only one small window, covered with iron bars, in the padlocked rear door. Along the sides, up near the top, were narrow slits, presumably to let in a little light and air. It was drawn by two dejected-looking horses. It was called "the Black Maria", and it was used to haul criminals off to jail.

The passengers on this trip, however, were not under arrest. There were two of them, a small boy and girl huddled together on one of the long wooden benches that ran along the sides. The Black Maria was borrowed to take people to the place where they were going. It belonged to the town, and it was the only conveyance available.

The bench was worn and slippery, and the children clung desperately to each other to keep from falling off. The boy had a crutch, and he whimpered and sometimes cried out in pain as the cumbersome vehicle swayed and lurched in the frozen ruts.

Outside the town, the Black Maria turned into a driveway, passed through a big gate and stopped in front of a large building that looked run-down and rickety even in the dim wintry dusk. A man who had brought them out from Boston on a train climbed down from the front seat, where he had ridden with the driver, and led the tired, half-frozen passengers up some creaking steps, across a sagging porch, and into a big hall dimly lighted with kerosene lamps. Nine-year-old Annie Sullivan and her little brother Jimmie had arrived at their new home.

It was called the Massachusetts State Infirmary. But there were no nurses about, in starched white uniforms. When doctors came there – and they seldom came unless called in an emergency – they received no pay. Although its name implied that it was a hospital, this was actually the state almshouse, grudgingly supported by the legislature at a cost of one dollar and eighty-eight cents per week for each patient.

The patients were people whom nobody wanted. Some were insane; some were alcoholics. Some were foundlings. Most of the babies did not live long, for there was not enough money to give them proper food and care. Many of the inmates were old people, no longer able to work, without money and with nobody to support them. Here they were sent to die, out of sight and forgotten. In their misery, some of them welcomed death as a release.

Annie and Jimmie were sent there because they had no other place to go. Their mother was dead, and their father had deserted them. Annie's eyes were bad, and Jimmie had a lump on his hip which the doctor said was tuberculous. He was unable to walk without a crutch. Nobody wanted a nine-year-old girl who was going blind, or a little boy who was a cripple.

The trouble with Annie's eyes had started before she was three years old. They became badly inflamed as little lumps began to form on the insides of her eyelids. The disease was trachoma. When a person has trachoma, the lumps inside the eyelids, soft and fuzzy at first, eventually become hard, like callouses. These keep scratching the eyeballs, causing ulcers and scar tissue. Gradually the scar tissue covers the eyes, and blindness results.

Annie was strong, well developed, and healthy except for her eyes. She had thick, soft brown hair, a lovely Irish complexion and beautifully curved lips that gave her face, in repose, a wistful expression. But her blue eyes were scarred and cloudy, the lids red and inflamed. All through her girlhood, people would say of her, "She'd be pretty if it weren't for her eyes."

The children were told to sit down on a bench and wait. Behind a desk, a man wearing a green eyeshade began to make notes, talking with the man who had brought them there. Annie and Jimmie paid little attention until they heard the man with the green eyeshade say, "We'll put the girl in with the women. The boy will have to go in the men's ward."

Jimmie caught it first: they were going to be separated. He began to cry and frantically clutched Annie's arm.

Then in a flash something happened to Annie, something wild, fierce, desperate. She threw her arms around her little brother and held him close, glaring over his head at the men.

"No! No! No! You can't!" she cried, in a voice that was half-scream and half-growl. "He's my brother!"

Alarmed, the man with the green eyeshade jumped up and came over to them. "There, there, don't cry!" he said, clumsily patting Annie's head. "Don't cry! We'll leave you together."

Looking up at the man who had brought them, he said in a whisper, barely moving his lips, "For to-night, at least."

After a skimpy supper, which they were both too tired to eat, Annie and Jimmie were taken to a small room at one end of the women's ward.

There was a narrow iron bed. They crawled in and seconds later were sound asleep, Annie with a protecting arm around her brother. Nobody tucked them in or offered to hear their prayers, but, since nobody ever had, they would have been bewildered by such attention.

In the room was a small altar. Whenever one of the old women died out in the ward, the body would be wheeled in to lie there until the men came with a pine box. Sometimes, if there was a clergyman available, there would be a brief funeral service. The room was called "the dead house".

Had Annie and Jimmie known about it, they would not have been disturbed. Death was no mystery to them. They were used to it. Their mother had taken a long time dying.

After breakfast the following morning Annie and Jimmie waited on a bench in the big dark hall a long time while the superintendent decided what to do with them. Because the foundlings in the maternity ward, in another part of the building, never lived very long, there were no other children in the institution. Finally one of the attendants came to them with a girl's apron – for Jimmie. He started to squirm and howl in protest as they tied it on him, but Annie hurriedly quietened him. If they were to remain together, this was the price he must pay.

Annie and Jimmie settled down happily. They were given adjoining beds, and the dead house was their playroom. Evenings in the women's ward, lighted by only one flickering, smoky kerosene lamp over the door into the dead house, were never dull for Annie and Jimmie. The place was alive with cockroaches and mice, and along the baseboards were some large rat-holes. Cockroaches, mice, and even big, grey rats held no terror for Annie and Jimmie. They had lived with them most of their lives. Jimmie would make a long paper quill and poke it into the ratholes, shouting with glee when an infuriated rat would leap out and race madly around the ward. The bedridden old women would scream, and an attendant would come running to see what was causing the uproar. Annie and Jimmie would be scolded and sent to bed, but it was almost bedtime anyway.

The days grew longer, the ice and snow melted and spring arrived. On April 14, Annie was ten years old, but nobody took note of it: she did not even know it was her birthday.

Annie began to go outdoors to play, riding up and down the driveway in one of the rickety old wheel chairs that were kept on the porch.

Jimmie never went out to play with Annie. He was content to remain in the women's ward, teasing the old women by making faces at them and mimicking them. It was becoming more difficult for him to walk, and the tapping of his small crutch on the wooden floor was heard less and less often. May had come, and the air outdoors was fragrant with lilacs, when one morning, as Annie was helping him to dress, he fell back on his bed, screaming with pain.

The old woman in the next bed said crossly, "Didn't you hear him crying in the night? He kept me awake."

Later that morning the doctor came, and Annie sat fearfully

watching as he ran his hands over her brother's thin little body. The lump on Jimmie's hip had grown much larger. Whenever the doctor touched it, the little boy moaned, "It hurts! It hurts!"

Finally the doctor straightened up and turned to Annie. "Little girl," he said gently, "your brother will soon be going on a journey."

Jimmie did not get up again, and Annie spent the next few days sitting beside his bed, afraid that, if she left him, they would take him away. At night, after Jimmie was asleep, she would drop off herself into the deep sleep of exhaustion. It did not last through the night, however, for once or twice she would wake up with a start and reach out to touch Jimmie's bed. One night she reached out – and Jimmie's bed was gone.

Annie started to get out of bed, but for a second she was trembling so violently that she could not. When a bed was wheeled out of the ward, it was taken to one place only. Her heart pounding wildly, she stumbled to the door under the flickering light and opened it. Groping in the dark, she found the foot of the narrow iron bed and held on to it for support. Her legs were trembling so that she could hardly stand. She shook herself and felt her way along the side of the bed. There was a sheet, covering something. She lifted it and placed her hand on Jimmie's cold little body.

Ten years would have to pass before Annie Sullivan would find another human being to love as she had loved Jimmie.

Some time before Jimmie's death, one of the old women told her that there were places where blind children could be sent to school.

"I'm going to one of those schools," Annie promptly announced.

The old woman grunted disapprovingly and told Annie not to get "uppity". No one else paid any attention. One lonely, cast-off child, a pauper, ward of the state which did not care what became of her so long as she was out of sight! Her chances of getting out of Tewksbury and going to school were too remote to be worth any consideration at all.

But from that day on, Annie lived with her dream. She did not talk about it, because the others only scolded her and told her not to be a little fool. But the dream was always there. Some day, somehow, she would get away from Tewksbury. She would go to school and grow up to be a fine lady.

The weeks, the months, the years slipped by in shadowy procession. Annie did not know when her birthday was, but at intervals she was told that she was now twelve, thirteen, fourteen.

Her eyes had grown worse. She could no longer distinguish one face from another, and could recognize her fellow inmates only by the sizes and shapes of their bodies and by their voices.

She was fourteen years old and had been at Tewksbury for more than four years when the Massachusetts State Board of Charities decided to investigate the place.

Word of the impending visit was quickly picked up on the inmates' grapevine. They did not expect much. From time to time in the past, fashionable ladies had come prying about. Nothing ever came of those visits.

"There's a man named Sanborn who's head of it," the women told her. "Maybe if you can get to him, he'll pat you on the head and call you a poor little girl."

Annie expected more from Mr Sanborn. For days she went about in a dream, going over and over in her mind what she would say to him if she had a chance. But black despair filled her heart at times. How could she, one child, virtually blind, apparently destined to spend the rest of her life at Tewksbury, expect Mr Sanborn to do anything for her?

On a morning in late September, word went around the wards that Mr Sanborn had come. He was with a group of well-dressed men. From ward to ward they proceeded, looking around, asking questions.

All day Annie followed them about, staying as close as she dared. She did not know which of the men was Mr Sanborn. They were all just shadowy figures to her. And voices.

The day wore on. Finally it was late afternoon, and they were down by the gate, about to leave. Annie saw her one chance, her big dream slip away.

Suddenly she sprang into the middle of the startled group of men. "Mr. Sanborn!" she shouted desperately. "Mr Sanborn! I want to go to school!"

"What is the matter with you?" a surprised voice asked.

"I can't see very well," Annie said timidly, frightened now that she was the centre of attention. She expected someone to grab her arm and pull her away.

"How long have you been here?" the voice asked.

Tongue-tied in her embarrassment, Annie could not answer. The men moved a few steps away, stopped, and talked in low voices with the superintendent.

Annie cried herself to sleep that night, convinced that she had failed. Her last hope was gone.

A couple of days later, however, someone came looking for her.

"Annie! Annie!" she cried. "You've got your wish. You're going away to school!"

"What is your name?" the teacher asked.

"Annie Sullivan."

"Spell it."

"I can't spell."

A titter rippled around the class.

"How old are you?"

"Fourteen."

"Fourteen years old and can't spell?"

The whole class laughed.

The Perkins Institute for the Blind, when Annie Sullivan entered it, was the most famous school for the blind in the country. Since all the children and some of the teachers were blind, courses were taught in raised print and in Braille, the "dot language" of the blind. In addition to reading, writing, English literature, arithmetic, geography, and history, all the girls learned to knit, crochet, and do fine needlework. The children were sons and daughters of farmers, well-to-do businessmen, doctors, lawyers, clergymen. Only a few were charity pupils, as Annie was. Their sheltered backgrounds could hardly have been more unlike Annie's if she had landed in their midst from the planet Mars.

She was far behind in her classes. She had to start down at the bottom, weaving mats, which she loathed, a great big fourteen-year-old down among the first graders. Impatient as she was to get ahead, Annie's reach exceeded her grasp. She would make ridiculous mistakes in class, and the other children, and sometimes the teachers, would laugh at her.

The result of all her difficulties was that Annie withdrew into herself, a lonely, unhappy misfit. Her dream world was proving to be a cruel disappointment. Night after night she cried herself to sleep in the first nightgown she had ever owned: a teacher had borrowed one for her from one of the other girls the first night she was there.

The children at Perkins were housed in pleasant cottages, with a fine view of Boston harbour, which of course none of them could see. Living in the cottage to which Annie was assigned was a silent middle-aged woman who rarely left her room. She was Laura Bridgman, blind, deaf, and dumb.

Laura was seven when Dr Howe, the head of the school, discovered her. Scarlet fever when she was three had left her imprisoned within an impenetrable wall of darkness and silence. She could communicate with no one. No one could communicate with her.

Dr Howe took her to the Perkins Institute and set to work trying to find some way of getting through to her. The method he devised was by use of the manual alphabet, the "finger language" by which the deaf and dumb who are not blind talk to each other. Since Laura was blind, he spelled words with his fingers into the palm of her hand and taught her to spell them back to him.

At first, of course, the words had no meaning for her, and it took many months of careful, patient, tedious effort before the moment arrived when it dawned on Laura that the finger letters K-E-Y in her palm meant the object, a key, which she held in her other hand – that everything she touched had a name. Laura learned to read and write as the other blind children did, and to do beautiful, intricate needlework, but she never progressed far beyond that point.

All the children were taught the manual alphabet so that they could communicate with Laura. Most of them were bored, for Laura had no knowledge of conversational, idiomatic English, and the sentences she spelled out with her fingers were stilted, the meaning sometimes obscure. But Annie was fascinated, and Laura Bridgman became the first friend she made after leaving Tewksbury.

Annie Sullivan was entering her fourth year at Perkins when a new matron came to take charge of the cottage where she lived.

She was Mrs Sophia Hopkins, widow of a sea captain. There must have been times when Mrs Hopkins was shocked and dismayed at some of the ideas Annie had picked up at Tewksbury slipped out. And undoubtedly there were times when Annie chafed a little at Mrs Hopkins's gentle, but determined, efforts to make her into a "nice girl". But Sophia Hopkins needed Annie Sullivan, and Annie Sullivan needed Sophia Hopkins. Out of their need developed a friendship that would last as long as they both lived.

Gradually Annie Sullivan was tamed, and as she advanced into her fourth and fifth years at the school, she steadily became a better student. Nobody was surprised when in her sixth and final year she was chosen to be valedictorian of her class. She had earned the right.

Annie Sullivan was now a graduate of the Perkins Institute for the Blind. She must go out and earn her living. But how? She had come a long, long way from Tewksbury. But she had no training that would fit her for a job. And when she left Perkins, as she must, where would she go?

Miss Moore, her English teacher, wanted her to go to a normal school and study to become a teacher. But money would be needed for that. One of the teachers knew someone who might hire her as nursery governess for some young children. But there was nothing definite. Where did people go when they had no home, and could not support themselves?

"I won't go back there!" she told herself fiercely. "I won't! I won't!"

Annie was staying with Mrs Hopkins when a letter came from a gentleman in Alabama. It was a sad letter about his six-year-old daughter, who was deaf, dumb, and blind. Could the Perkins Institute recommend a teacher who could help her?

The little girl's name was Helen Keller.

Ivy Green, the home of Captain Arthur Keller, was set in spacious grounds. The afternoon spring sunshine lay warm upon trees and grass and ploughed fields, and the good smell of earth was in the air, as the carriage turned into the driveway.

In the carriage with Mrs Keller was a young woman wearing a grey woollen costume much too heavy for a mild March day in Alabama. Her eyes were red and swollen, as though she had been weeping. Her expression was anxious, tense. Miss Annie Sullivan had arrived to become Helen Keller's teacher.

Annie had not been weeping. Coal dust and cinders on the long train trip from Boston had left her eyes, still tender from a recent operation, badly inflamed. So impatient was she to meet her little pupil that she could hardly sit still in the carriage.

Captain Keller waited on the lawn with a flowery speech of welcome, but Annie scarcely heard him.

When he paused for breath, she interrupted: "Helen – where is Helen?"

"There on the porch, waiting," Mrs Keller told her.

Annie's weak eyes made out a small figure in the shadow of a creeper, and, almost running, she hurried towards it. As she drew near she slowed down, in order not to startle the child. Now she could see her more clearly.

She was surprised at Helen's forlorn, neglected appearance. Her light-brown hair was unkempt, tangled, her face streaked with dirt and tears, her pinafore soiled. Annie would learn presently that on days when Helen was in a bad mood, as she had been that day, she would not let anyone comb her hair or wash her face.

From the bustle of preparation for Annie's arrival – the guest-room aired and cleaned, extra cooking being done in the kitchen, her mother's departure in the carriage without her – Helen had sensed that something unusual was happening. Since she had no way of finding out what it was, she was resentful and badly behaved.

As Annie approached her with outstretched arms, Helen leaped at her with such force that she would have knocked her off the porch if Captain Keller had not caught her.

Snarling like a little wild animal, Helen wrenched herself loose from Annie's arms. These were not her mother's arms, as she had expected, but the arms of a stranger.

Her groping hands found Annie's handbag and jerked it out of her grasp. When Mrs Keller tried to rescue it, Helen flew into a rage, kicking and scratching.

"She thinks there's candy in it," Mrs Keller panted.

Annie intervened, handing Helen her precious watch, a graduation present from her teachers at the Perkins Institution. Examining this new toy with her fingers, Helen calmed down.

Curious now, she followed Annie into the house and upstairs to her room.

As Annie started to unpack, Helen's grubby fingers were everywhere, into everything.

"Looking for sweets," Annie decided.

She recalled having seen a trunk outside in the hall. She led Helen out to it, placed her small hands on it and tried to indicate by a series of pats that there would be sweets in her trunk, which would be along later.

Helen seemed to understand, and Annie felt a glow of satisfaction at her first apparent success with her pupil. Had she realized at that moment what the next month would be like, she would have been tempted to repack her bags and go back to Boston.

With only six years of schooling, no training, no experience, and a childhood background that would have horrified the Kellers had they known about it, Annie Sullivan was taking on as difficult and complicated a job as was ever undertaken by any teacher. The date was March 5, 1887. Her twenty-first birthday was a month away.

Her own childhood, however, was really in Annie's favour. Annie had never been deaf, but she knew what it was like to be blind, frustrated, and resentful. She was equipped to understand Helen Keller far better than her parents ever could.

Annie's first task was to win the confidence of a miserable little soul who trusted no one because she knew no one. The people around her existed in her imprisoned mind only as hands – hands that were trying to restrain her.

Annie had hoped to win her with gentleness and affection. But almost immediately she realized that this would not work. She had been with the Kellers only a few days when Helen, in a sudden rage, knocked out two of her front teeth. Helen could be as dangerous as a ferocious dog.

At times Helen's tantrums were unpredictable, but in general they followed a pattern. Whenever she could not have her own way, Helen had a tantrum.

This tendency was aggravated by the fact that her parents, rather than fight with her, gave in to her, even to the extent of allowing her to go unwashed and uncombed for days at a time.

She was an undisciplined little tyrant, ruling the household by physical force.

After a few encounters with her, Annie was forced to the realization that the only solution must be discipline. Understanding as she did the reason for Helen's violence, she set to work reluctantly, hoping that she would not break the child's spirit.

Their longest and most violent battle occurred one morning at the breakfast table. No one had ever tried to teach Helen to sit at the table and eat from her own plate with a spoon. Instead, she would run around the table, grabbing food off other people's plates and the dishes that were being passed while the family went on eating and talking as though nothing extraordinary was happening.

That morning Helen started to grab some food off Annie's plate. Annie pushed her greasy hands away. Helen tried it again, and Annie slapped her. Whereupon Helen threw herself on the floor, kicking and screaming. Annie lifted her up, set her down hard on a chair, forced a spoon into her hand, and started to help her scoop up some food on it.

Helen threw the spoon on the floor. Annie dragged her down off the chair, made her pick up the spoon, set her back on the chair and started over again. But Helen hurled the spoon to the floor and threw herself on top of it.

At this point Captain and Mrs Keller, who had been watching in horrified silence, got up and left the room, breakfast unfinished. Annie followed them to the door, locked it behind them, returned to the table and went on eating her breakfast, although it nearly choked her.

Helen jumped up and tried to pull Annie's chair out from under her. When that didn't work, she pinched Annie, and Annie slapped her. This was repeated several times.

Finally, after another fit of kicking and screaming, Helen started feeling her way around the table. When she discovered that her parents' places were empty, she came back to Annie. She seemed puzzled and placed her hand on Annie's wrist. Raising her fork to her mouth, Annie indicated that she was eating. Helen hesitated for a moment, then climbed up on her chair and docilely permitted Annie to help her eat her breakfast with a spoon. Apparently hunger had won.

But the battle was not yet over. As she finished eating, Helen tore off the napkin that had been tied around her neck, threw it on the floor and ran over to the door. Finding it locked, she blazed with fury, pounding and kicking the door and howling.

Annie went over and, after a struggle that required every ounce of strength she could muster, dragged Helen back to the table, forced her to pick up the napkin, and started to show her how to fold it. Helen managed to jerk the napkin away from her, threw it to the floor again and herself on top of it.

This time Annie left her alone. Helen's screams finally subsided into sobs, and she let Annie lift her up and show her how to fold her napkin. It was nearly lunchtime when Annie unlocked the door, and a subdued, quiet Helen wandered out into the garden to play.

From the beginning, there was difficulty with Helen's parents, especially with her father. She very quickly learned to run to her parents for sympathy whenever Annie corrected her.

"I know we shouldn't do it," Mrs Keller said, "but we feel so sorry for her."

"If I could have her alone with me for a while I think I could accomplish more," Annie replied in a discouraged tone. "She's got to learn to obey me before I can help her. I can't do anything with her the way she is."

Mrs Keller found a solution. She had a hard time convincing her husband, but the Kellers were really in desperate straits. Every day Helen was growing larger, stronger, and more dangerous. Unless she could be brought under control, she would have to be sent away. And the only place to send her would be to a home for the feeble-minded – and a strait jacket.

With this in mind, Captain Keller grudgingly gave his consent, and Annie and Helen moved into a cottage a short distance from Ivy Green.

In the meantime, as she fought Helen's tantrums, Annie worked tirelessly, doggedly, unceasingly to communicate with her, using the manual alphabet, as Dr Howe had used it with Laura Bridgman many years earlier. Before coming to Alabama, she had unmercifully abused her eyes, poring over and over the cramped, barely legible notes Dr Howe and her teachers had made as they worked with Laura.

They had had one advantage she did not have. Laura had

been a placid, docile child, who had never given them any trouble.

"But Helen is much more intelligent than Laura was," Annie told herself as she nursed her bruises. "I know she is! I've got to get through to her!"

She started using the manual alphabet with Helen the morning after her arrival. In her trunk was a doll for Helen. The blind children at Perkins had bought it with their pennies, and Laura Bridgman had dressed it.

She took Helen's hand and slowly and carefully with her fingers spelled into her palm: D-O-L-L. She did it several times, then showed Helen how to form the letters with her own small fingèrs.

Presently, like an imitative monkey, Helen spelled the word back to her, D-O-L-L. Tears sprang to Annie's eyes as she patted her small pupil's shoulder.

In the cottage the finger-spelling – which Helen seemed to regard as an interesting new game – continued, along with other things Annie found for Helen to do with beads and a ball of wool and a crochet hook. With these pastimes, Helen seemed more contented. She had fewer tantrums. Although the words as yet had no meaning for her, she learned to spell them with amazing ease and rapidity.

But Annie still had Helen's father to contend with. He was impatient and sceptical. He wanted his child at home. And after two weeks Annie had to give in.

It had been agreed that Captain Keller could look in on Helen every morning on his way to his office, provided she did not know he was there. One morning, a day or two before they moved out of the cottage, he brought Helen's dog Belle, a beautiful setter, with him.

Helen raised her head, sniffed and ran eagerly to the dog. She dropped to her knees, took one of Belle's paws in her hands and began moving her claws about while Captain Keller and Annie stared.

"What's she doing with that dog's paw?" Captain Keller demanded.

There was wonder in Annie's voice as she cried, "She's trying to teach her to spell! Look – she's trying to teach her to spell 'doll'!"

But Captain Keller shook his head. "What's the good of it?" he said bitterly. "She doesn't know what it means any more than the dog does!"

They appeared to be playing in the water on a warm spring day – Annie and Helen in the creeper-covered pump house in the Keller's garden.

Helen held a cup in one hand. As Annie pumped water into the cup, she kept moving her fingers into the unresponsive little palm.

The date was April 5, a month and two days since Annie's arrival to become Helen's teacher. Day after day through that month Annie's fingers had moved in Helen's hand, spelling words – words – words.

Helen knew how to spell them back with her own small fingers, but they still had no meaning for her. And she was becoming bored with what at first had been a fascinating new game.

That April morning had been difficult. Annie was trying to teach Helen to distinguish between two words, "cup" and "water". Since she did not know what they meant, Helen kept mixing them up. She could not understand what she was supposed to do, and she had grown tired and cross. Finally her frustration drove her into a rage, and she smashed her favourite doll, the doll the blind children had sent her from Boston.

To give her a change, Annie led her out to the pump, a place where Helen loved to play. But still the lesson went, Annie's determined fingers pressing insistently in her pupil's palm, spelling one word over and over again: W-A-T-E-R. W-A-T-E-R. W-A-T-E-R. The cool water overflowed the cup and ran down the child's hand and wrist.

Suddenly Helen dropped the cup. Her body stiffened. For an instant she stood transfixed, holding her breath. Like a bright probing sunbeam, a new thought had penetrated the curtain that had held her mind a prisoner within its dark folds.

She stumbled towards Annie, reaching for her hand. With trembling fingers she started to spell. W-A-T-. She had not finished when she felt Annie's approving pat on her shoulder. Groping wildly, Helen ran about touching things and back to

Annie. The ground, the pump, the trellis, the honeysuckle. And as Annie's fingers moved swiftly in her hand, the child quickly spelled them back. She knew these words! They had been spelled in her hand a dozen times! This was it – the Big Secret that had been withheld from her so long! Everything had a name!

She stopped for a moment, looking thoughtful, then placed a questioning hand on Annie's arm. Tears ran down Annie's cheeks as her fingers moved in Helen's eager palm – slowly and carefully, for they had not spelled this word before.

In that shining moment, Annie Sullivan took on a new identity. Henceforth for the rest of her life, to Helen and to everyone they knew, she would be "Teacher".

TIANANMEN SQUARE

Anonymous student

The protest by students in Beijing, China, in June 1989 has become a worldwide symbol of courage in the face of a repressive state.

I am a student at Qinghua University. I am twenty years old. I spent last night sitting on the steps of the Monument to the Heroes of the People. I witnessed from start to finish the shooting and suppression by the army of students and citizens.

Many of my fellow students have already been shot dead. My clothes are still stained with their blood. As a lucky survivor and an eyewitness, I want to tell peace-loving and good people across the world about the massacre.

Frankly speaking, we knew early on in the evening that the troops intended to suppress us. Someone whose status I can't reveal phoned us at four o'clock on Saturday afternoon. (The call was to a neighbourhood phone station in an alley near the Square.) The caller told us that the Square was about to be invaded and cleared. We went on to the alert. After a discussion we took some measures. We did our best to alleviate contradictions and avoid a bloodbath.

We had twenty-three submachine-guns and some incendiary bombs that we'd snatched from soldiers during the previous two days. The Autonomous Students' Union called a meeting and decided to return these weapons forthwith to the martial law troops to show that we intended to promote democracy by non-violent means. On the rostrum at Tiananmen Square beneath the portrait of Chairman Mao we liaised with troops about this, but an officer said that he was under higher orders not to accept the weapons.

So the negotiations failed. At around one in the morning, when things had become really critical, we destroyed the guns and dismantled the bombs. We poured away the petrol so that bad people couldn't use it and the authorities couldn't point to it as "proof" that we were out to kill soldiers. After that, the Union told everyone in the Square that the situation was extremely grave, that bloodshed seemed inevitable, and that they wanted students and citizens to leave the Square. But there were still 40,000–50,000 students and about 100,000 citizens determined not to go. I, too, decided not to go.

The mood was extraordinarily tense. This was the first time we'd ever experienced such danger. I'd be lying if I said we weren't afraid, but everyone was psychologically braced and tempered. (Some students, of course, didn't believe that the troops would shoot to kill.) In a word, we were imbued with a lofty sense of mission. We were prepared to sacrifice ourselves for China's democracy and progress.

After midnight, after two armoured cars had sped down each side of the Square from the Front Gate, the situation became increasingly serious. Official loudspeakers repeatedly blared out "notices". Dense lines of steel-helmeted troops ringed the Square. Despite the darkness, you could clearly see the machine-guns mounted on top of the History Museum. There was not the slightest attempt to hide them.

We students crowded round the Monument to the Heroes of the People. I carefully estimated the crowd. Two-thirds were men, one-third were women; about 30 per cent from universities and colleges in Beijing. Most were students from other cities.

At four o'clock sharp, just before daybreak, the lights in the Square suddenly went out. The loudspeakers broadcast another order to "clear the Square". I suddenly had a tight feeling in my stomach. There was only one thought in my head: the time has come, the time has come.

The hunger-striker Hou Dejian (a Taiwan pop-singer now working on the mainland) and some other people negotiated with the troops and agreed to get the students to leave peace-fully. But just as they were about to go, at 4.40 am, a cluster of red signal flares rose into the sky above the Square and the lights came on again.

I saw that the front of the Square was packed with troops. A detachment of soldiers came running from the east entrance of the Great Hall of the People. They were dressed in camouflage. They were carrying light machine-guns and wearing steel helmets and gas-masks.

As soon as these troops had stormed out, they lined up a dozen or so machine-guns in front of the Monument to the Heroes of the People. The machine-gunners lay down on their stomachs. Their guns pointed toward the Monument. The rostrum was behind them. When all the guns were properly lined up, a great mass of soldiers and armed police, wielding electric prods, rubber truncheons, and some special weapons of a sort I'd never seen before suddenly rushed us. We were sitting quietly. There were two differences between the troops and the armed police: their uniforms were different, and so were their helmets. The police helmets were bigger than the troops' and had steel flaps going down over the ears. The soldiers and the policemen started violently laying about us. They split our ranks down the middle and opened up a path to the Monument. They stormed up to its third tier. I saw forty or fifty students suddenly spurt blood. Armoured troop carriers and an even greater number of troops that had been waiting in the Square joined the siege. The troop carriers formed a solid blockade, except for a gap on the museum side.

The troops and policemen who had stormed the monument smashed our loudspeaker installations, our printing equipment, and our supply of soda water. Then they beat and threw down the steps the students still occupying the third tier. We'd stayed put all along, holding hands and singing the Internationale. We'd been shouting "The people's army won't attack the people". The students packing the third tier had no choice but to retreat under the blows and kicks of such a large body of men. While this was going on, the sound of machine-guns started up. Some troops were kneeling down and firing. Their bullets whizzed above our heads. The troops lying on their stomachs shot up into the students' chests and faces. We had no choice but to retreat back up onto the Monument. When we reached it the machine-guns stopped. But the troops on the

Monument beat us back down again. As soon as we'd been beaten down, the machine-guns started up again.*

The dare-to-die brigade of workers and citizens picked up anything that served as a weapon – bottles, pieces of wood – and rushed towards the troops to resist them. The Students' Union gave the order to retreat to places outside the Square. It was not yet five o'clock.

A great crowd of students rushed toward the gap in the line of troop carriers. The heartless drivers closed the gap. Thirty-odd carriers drove into the crowd. Some people were crushed to death. Even the flagpole in front of the Monument was snapped off. The whole Square was in massive chaos. I'd never thought my fellow-students could be so brave. Some started to push at the troop carriers. They were mown down. Others clambered over their corpses and pushed too. Finally they managed to push one or two carriers aside and open up a gap. I and 3,000 other students rushed through under a hail of fire. We ran across to the entrance to the History Museum.

There were large numbers of citizens in front of the Museum. We joined up with them. Seeing how bad things were, we immediately ran off to the north in the direction of the Gate of Heavenly Peace. But we'd only gone a few steps when rifle fire broke out from a clump of bushes alongside the road. We saw no people – just the bursts of fire from the gun-barrels. So we turned and ran off south towards the Front Gate.

I was running and weeping. I saw a second batch of students running off under machine-gun fire. I saw lots of people lying on their stomachs on the road that we were trying to escape along. We were all crying – running and crying. When we reached the Front Gate, we were suddenly confronted by a batch of troops. They didn't open fire. They were armed with big wooden staves. They beat us furiously.

Then a large crowd of citizens came pouring out of the Front Gate. They clashed violently with these troops. They protected us while we escaped in the direction of Beijing railway station. The troops pursued us. It was five o'clock. Dawn was breaking. The gunfire on the Square seemed to have died down a little.

* This manoeuvre was plainly designed to avoid troops firing directly onto the Monument, and chipping or pocking the stone fresco of heroes (though, as television news has shown, they did hit a few).

PRISONER OF ISLAMIC JIHAD

John McCarthy

On 17 April 1986 television journalist John McCarthy was kidnapped in Beirut by the terrorist group Islamic Jihad. Like Islamic Jihad's other prisoners – among them Terry Waite, Brian Keenan, Tom Sutherland, Frank Reed, David Jacobsen – he was held in isolation, squalor and usually chained. His captivity lasted for five years, during which his then girlfriend Jill Morrell campaigned ceaselessly for his release.

The next morning we were given breakfast by Sayeed and Mustafa and taken to the bathroom. Daylight flooded in, cheering our spirits. Then came the rattle of chains. They brought them into the room with them. They fixed a bolt to the wall, then the chains to the bolt. I couldn't believe it. I knew that the Yanks had been chained up before, but it was such an awful thought that I'd tried to blot out any notion that it could happen to me. Yet here it was. My immediate reaction was to laugh, "You cannot be serious." They were. No humour could break this impermeable human ice. They were set.

Brian was furious. He could easily believe they'd do it.

"I am a human being, not an animal. You are destroying my dignity as a human being."

"We are sorry, this for your security."

"For our security! That's crazy, you're destroying our security completely!"

"No, this is good for your security, if you chained then you won't try escape and we won't have to shoot you, so you safer with chains."

With this surreal logic, they chained us up.

I was a man, and in my mind I knew it, but what was happening to my body told me otherwise. The guards lifted and pulled our legs around as if they weren't attached to a person. They experimented with the length and tightness of the chains as if it were a normal exercise, part of a regular working day, two men working on repairing a bit of office equipment, deciding the best spot for a new piece of furniture. It was bitterly demoralizing that men could do this so naturally, that it was possible for them to ignore our humanity so casually. It also boded ill for any ideas of release.

We'd had our blindfolds on for more than thirty hours. That meant that the guards were permanently around. Any move was tense, but this time we had moved continuously, and the blindfolds had been taped tight over our eyes. Physically this was very uncomfortable, but the torment of going, sightless, to an unknown fate was unbearable. Whenever we were like this I had to loosen the binding so that I could feel, even in the darkness of a metal box or the boot of a car, that I was going out with my eyes wide open.

There was also the difficulty of walking blindfolded. In the prisons we learned the route to the bathroom and anyway would be able to look down our noses and see a small area around our feet. Most of the guards were quite happy with this, even pulling up our blindfolds a little if we stumbled, so that we could move more easily. However, other guards, the nervous or sadistic ones, insisted we had them on tight. The sadists enjoyed pushing us around in our blind confusion.

You never, ever, get used to being blindfolded. It was always a cold shock when talking to a guard, especially if it was a friendly conversation, to realize, "He's talking to me in this pleasant, intimate way, yet he can't see me, and won't let me see him." Any warmth was rendered meaningless. It was so sad to think this was the only level on which these guys could operate. If they felt shame, their fear of us and their bosses overrode it – that's assuming they ever did consider what they were doing. Every time we took them to task for their treatment of us, we got nowhere. The incessant commands for silence, the chains, the blindfolds, all reflected their own insecurity, their lack of real power.

After the first couple of days, life settled back into the usual routine of food deliveries and bathroom runs. The pressure was slightly eased when they put a curtain across our door so that at least we could raise our blindfolds more often. But we still had to keep almost silent, speaking in only the lowest of whispers.

In the mornings, after the guards had finished their dawn prayers, they would usually go back to bed for a while. As the light strengthened outside I often peeked through a crack around the cardboard that had been taped over the window. Just outside I could see greenery, what looked like a privet hedge in the foreground and beyond that a tall tree. The glimpse of trees, the sounds of street life and the thin band of daylight moving across the ceiling and down the walls as another day passed never failed to lift my spirits.

We had no books now, nor even our faithful set of dominoes. We talked as much as ever despite the closeness of the guards – more so perhaps, for we were both highly nervous. The uncertainty of what might come next, Sayeed's insane praying and, above all, the new and terrifying shock of being chained up kept us constantly on edge. Even the homey nature of our cell was a vicious tease emphasizing, through its incongruity, that we might be displaced again at any moment. Our nervousness came not so much from fear, as from the impossibility of calming down, of "settling" in this place. The slightest thing would set us off into uncontrollable fits of giggles.

Our nerves were so stretched that even pet jokes became unnecessary. Merely saying each other's name or just sighing was enough to render us hysterical. This madness became more acute at night, perhaps as subconsciously we prepared ourselves for the eerie ordeal of listening to Sayeed's prayers. Faith, or psychosis, prompted him to pray all night, alternating the praying with readings from the Koran. These would almost immediately reduce him to tears, raving over the words. I know this can happen to fervent devotees, but in Sayeed it didn't seem genuine. He'd switch back to normal in a second if he got up for a drink or to give an order. He made a deafening racket and it was often so alarming that I couldn't sleep through it. Brian was less affected by it and once Sayeed broke off his wailing to pull back the curtain and tell me to make Bri stop snoring. It was crazy.

In the first week of April our guards were joined by a new man who spoke very good English. On his arrival he came and asked us how we were. He seemed more sophisticated than the others and was obviously more powerful. Brian made it clear that we were not happy and that while some of the guards were all right, others were evil men who had beaten us for no reason. He apologized, explaining that some of the "brothers" were poorly educated and couldn't understand that hostages should be treated differently from enemies or criminals. He promised to speak to them and remarked that just as we were being tested by our experience, so, too, was God testing the "brothers" in the way they treated us. Fine sounding phrases, but as meaningless as the claims that the guards were as much prisoners as we were.

The next day Brian was unchained and moved out of the kitchen. I was afraid that we would be separated or that we were in for yet another move. In fact Bri was only moved to the far side of the room next to the kitchen, where the guards initially had based themselves. I heard the English speaker talking to him. He seemed to be asking questions. He then came to me and gave me some sheets of paper with questions written out on them. I had to fill in the answers.

The questions struck me as being rather mundane, but their curious use of English made me smile. "What is a news?" "How you make a news for TV?" I could answer those fairly easily, concerned only that the answers might be too technical or boring. As with Sayeed's interrogation back in November there were questions about my life, family, work and all the places I'd ever visited. After a couple of hours I had worked my way through them. The man returned, thanked me and gave me another great wodge of papers to go through.

I was quite enjoying the limited mental exercise of planning the answers and putting them down coherently on paper, the only such opportunity, apart from the necessarily brief messages we'd exchanged in the Land of Grey and Pink, that I'd had in almost a year. But now the questions were getting more detailed. "Give names for all your organization's offices in the world." I listed as many as I could remember. They wanted to know how the company budgets were organized. This was something I'd never been involved with so said as much, but privately regretted that it took oddly phrased questions from my kidnappers for me to realize how little effort I'd made to understand the workings of my company.

I had a chuckle when they asked, "List all details of corruption in your organization." Apart from the odd lunch on somebody's company credit card, posing as an executive from another TV station, I really didn't know of anything. When the man came back again, I explained that I couldn't answer some of the questions but he seemed unperturbed. He said that he would give me more questions the next day.

I couldn't follow what was going on at all. There had been no threats, no force, indeed the man had been very polite. Nonetheless, I couldn't get one of Tom Sutherland's jokes out of my mind. Hand-talking one day about the difficulties of sleeping, he'd said, "It reminds me of the joke about the guy who says to his wife, 'Be sure and get a good night's rest, honey, there's something very important I want to tell you in the morning.'" Like the woman in the story I didn't sleep a wink.

The following morning, after breakfast and the bathroom run, the man came to me again. My imagination had been working overtime all night, convincing me that things would soon get very unpleasant, that I would be "interrogated" in a more direct and painful way. But no, I was just presented with another batch of written questions.

This time, however, they were more to the point. "List all your contacts with secret services (any country)", "Give the names of all secret people who have spoken to you in Lebanon." This struck me as being quite barmy. If I had been a spy surely I would have known how to dodge the obvious questions? They repeated some of the earlier ones about news so I reckoned that there might be some method in their madness and decided that simple, honest answers would still be best. I wrote that I'd had no contact with any secret service people from anywhere and that if any spies had made contact with me they hadn't told me about their private business. Knowing that I wasn't a spy made it all seem rather pointless, even though it was mildly amusing. What did bother me was that they might find out that WTN was largely owned by ABC, the company who had managed to get an exclusive on the TWA hijack/hostages story in Beirut in 1985. This was widely seen as having been made possible through throwing bundles of money at powerful Shia leaders and having powerful friends in high places in and around Washington, DC. If they knew I was linked to ABC, I feared they would become suspicious, or feel that I was more valuable and hang on to me even longer.

When the fellow came back, I told him I'd answered his questions as well as I could, but that the replies seemed very dull. He didn't seem worried and asked if I would like anything. I said that I wanted to write a letter to my family and my girlfriend. It had been a year since I'd seen or spoken to them. Surprisingly, he agreed and gave me a sheet of paper. How could I convey in such a small space what had happened to me, my fears and my concerns for those I loved? I wrote first to my parents and brother. I wanted them to know that I was all right and that I was in good spirits. I hoped that their fears for me would be eased if my letter sounded optimistic. I said that I was fine and that conditions weren't too bad. I told them how much I loved them and how thinking of things in the past often had me laughing out loud. I said I was sure I would be home soon. I asked them to tell Jill that I loved her very much and that she mustn't worry about the time we'd lost, that we were both young and that we had the whole of our lives to live and enjoy together. The man took the letter away but returned after a while, saying he had read it and thought that my "spirit" was very good. He said his friends felt the same.

I was pleased but felt rather uncertain. It seemed to imply that the guards thought I was co-operative. Brian and I had worked so hard to keep each other's spirits up and work together to maintain our dignity in the face of constant humiliation that it was a mixed blessing to have our success endorsed by the people who were holding us down.

The man also added that he was going to take my answers to some other "brothers". I just hoped they would be as satisfied as he seemed to be. I wanted to believe that all the questions were aimed at proving to the British government that my kidnappers did hold me, although I had to admit to myself that it was a very long-winded way of doing it. With this hope in mind, I asked the man what the "brothers" purpose was in asking all these questions. "We want to be sure you are what you say."

"But I've been here a year, haven't you done that already?"

"No, now we will be sure and hope for negotiations."

"You mean there haven't been any yet?"

"No, but now we hope for a quick solution to your problem."

That quick solution was more than four years away.

It was a great relief when Brian was moved back into the kitchen with me. Our visitor had left, all his questions answered, and we tried to put some positive meaning into the little information we'd gleaned from him. It wasn't easy. In fact, he'd only confirmed our worst fears, that no-one had been negotiating on our behalf and we both had the clear impression that they hadn't made any demands for us. Like me, Brian had been allowed to write a letter. We could only hope that these would be sent so that at least they'd know back home that we were all right.

Mahmoud came in and told us he was very happy that we'd said good things about him. We tried to take advantage of his good mood to get a clearer idea of where things stood.

"Your friend told me that negotiations would now start. What do you want and how long will it take?"

"I am sorry I do not have the order, but I hope you go home very soon." The same old story.

The next day was the first anniversary of Brian's kidnap, 11 April. That night Sayeed came and said we were moving to a better place. He unchained me, told me to pick up my clothes and led me to the front door of the house. Standing on the doorstep he put a gun to my back and said I must walk straight across the road to his friend. The night was very quiet. Underneath my blindfold I could see the rutted track in the moonlight. I sensed the village sleeping around me. Should I make a run for it? Would it be possible in these floppy plastic sandals? How far would I get barefoot with at least two men after me? What would Bri do if I made it without him? Sayeed pushed the pistol in my back. I stumbled across the road.

I knew that there were two guns pointing at me but at least I was walking freely, with no tape or chains binding me. It felt good.

On the other side of the road Mahmoud led me up a flight of

stairs and told me to sit in the corner of a room. Brian joined me a few minutes later. Our mattresses were brought in and we were told to go to sleep – hard to do with the guards staying in the same room. We slept fitfully and at dawn they were up praying.

The next day they fitted bolts to the wall and chained us to them. Then they stretched some wires across our corner and hung curtains from them so that we found ourselves in a sort of tent. This gave us a little privacy and we could raise our blindfolds, but our guards were living in the same room and we never had a moment to forget them. A new man, Abu Salim, joined Mahmoud and Sayeed. The three of them were incredibly noisy. They would have the radio and television going full blast at the same time. At prayer times they would often have a tape machine playing "Nadbars", Moslem chants, so that we found it impossible either to think or to relax. Their mattresses came right up to the curtain so that now I had one or two extra heads snoring within arm's reach.

Abu Salim soon demonstrated that he was one of the would-be holy-macho brethren and would compete with Sayeed as to who could pray the loudest, hissing and clicking his fingers at us if we whispered or even just sighed. He liked clicking his fingers. He'd click at us to indicate that we should leave the bathroom. It irritated me so much that he couldn't even bother to say "*dah*", come, that I would stand in the bathroom doorway clicking my fingers back at him until he either said something or came and grabbed me. One morning I was desperately tired and so furious at the row from the radio that I started clicking my fingers over the top of the curtain. He came over hissing like a goose. I kept on clicking until he put his head through the curtains and then, pointing to my ears, I whispered, "Radio, radio", and made a lowering motion with my hands. He clicked and hissed, but did go and turn the thing down. It was a minor achievement, but it made me feel a hell of a lot better.

AND REMEMBER THE ALAMO

Jon E. Lewis

The stand of Texans at the Alamo is now legend. Like an earlier fight-to-the-death, that of the Spartans at Thermopylae (see pp. 1–8), it inspired a people to resistance and eventual victory. The men at the Alamo died in battle but won a war for liberty. The enemy was an imperial Mexican army under Santa Anna, which sought to keep Texas strictly Mexican property. The time was 1835–6.

Santa Anna determined to put an end to the Texan rebellion. Raising an army of 6,000 men and placing himself at its head, Santa Anna started for San Antonio. The town was nearly abandoned, with the exception of a skeleton force of 187 men holding the ancient mission station of San Antonio de Valero: the Alamo.

As Santa Anna neared, there was initially only confusion at the Alamo. The garrison demanded reinforcements, but Houston wanted them to abandon the station, so the Texan defence could be concentrated elsewhere. Then some of the men, objecting to the youth of the station commander, the studentish William Barrett Travis, staged a virtual mutiny. In democratic American fashion they were allowed to elect a leader. They chose the Tennessee Indian-fighter Jim Bowie, whose elder brother Rezin had invented the famed "Bowie Knife", a one-edged blade with a guarded hilt so perfectly balanced it could be thrown to killing purpose.

Jim Bowie was not a leader of men. He drank and cared

nothing for discipline. When Bowie contracted pneumonia, Travis took over sole and unfettered command. For all their antagonism, Travis and Bowie were agreed that they would make a stand against the Mexicans when they arrived.

As a place to make a stand the Franciscan mission of the Alamo had drawbacks. Situated on three acres a little to the east of San Antonio, it had low scaleable outer walls, with no loopholes. Worst of all, there was a large 50-yard gap in its southeastern face which was secured only by a cedar-post stockade and an earth parapet. But the walled convent yard and the stone chapel, with its walls 22 feet high and 4 feet thick, offered good cover.

The first Mexicans arrived on 22 February 1836 along the Laredo road, the bells of the town clanging the alarm. The Mexican commander, Colonel Almonte, demanded the immediate surrender of the Texan post. As a reply, Travis shot a cannon ball at a group of waiting Mexican soldiers.

The siege operation that followed was conducted personally by Santa Anna, the self-styled "Napoleon of the West". He began by subjecting the post to a 24-hour artillery bombardment, which caused surprisingly few casualties inside the Alamo. During a lull afterwards, Travis drafted an appeal for help, which was sent out with a Mexican *vaquero* (cowboy) loyal to the Texan cause. The message read:

> Commandancy of the Alamo
> Bexar, Feby 24th 1836
>
> Fellow citizens and compatriots,
>
> I am besieged by a thousand or more of the Mexicans under Santa Anna – I have sustained a continual bombardment and cannonade for 24 hours and have not lost a man. The enemy has demanded a surrender at discretion, otherwise the garrison are to be put to the sword, if the fort is taken. I have answered the demand with a cannon shot, and our flag still waves proudly from the walls. I shall never surrender or retreat.
>
> Then, I call on you in the name of liberty, of patriotism and everything dear to the American character to come to our aid, with all dispatch. The enemy is receiving reinforcements daily and will no doubt increase to three or four thousand in four or five days.

.If this call is neglected, I am determined to sustain myself as long as possible and die like a soldier who never forgets what is due to his own honour or that of his country.

Victory or death.

WILLIAM BARRETT TRAVIS

Lt. Col. Comd.

P.S. The Lord is on our side. When the enemy appeared in sight we had not three bushels of corn. We have since found in deserted houses 80 or 90 bushels and got into the wall 20 or 30 head of beeves.

TRAVIS

The next day, the 25th, the Mexicans received reinforcements, and attempted to set up a battery south of the Alamo. This was prevented by accurate fire from the fort's ramparts, to the cheer of the men inside. But the respite was short-lived. On the 26th, two of Santa Anna's batteries were sheltered behind earthworks on the northeast side of the river. From then on they kept up a slow, resolute bombardment. Hardly an hour went past without a cannon ball falling on the fort, and men rushing out with picks and shovels to plug the breach. By now, also, Jim Bowie, fighting despite the grip of pneumonia, had fallen from scaffolding supporting a gun emplacement and broken his hip. He was placed in a cot in a building beside the south gate of the yard.

The lines of earthworks grew around the men of the Alamo. Each dawn the sentries found new entrenchments, until it was ringed by an unbroken Mexican circle.

Despite the encirclement, on the night of 1 March, a small reinforcement of 32 men crept through the Mexican lines to join the defenders. They were from Gonzales, a settlement which numbered only 30 split-plank cabin homes. Their arrival crowned a good day for the defenders. Earlier, a lucky round from the 12-pounder on the roof of the chapel had struck Santa Anna's lodging in the town.

But already the end was in sight for the men of the Alamo. The enemy were simply too many. Understanding this, Travis rallied the men during the sunset of 3 March. According to a drifter named Louis Rose, who escaped the fort that evening, Travis paraded the men in single file and then stood before them, almost overcome with emotion. He declared that he was intent on staying and fighting it out to the end, but that every man must do what he thought best. Then Travis drew a line on the ground with his sword and said: "I now want every man who is determined to stay here and die with me to come across this line." Almost before he had finished, Tapley Howard bounded across saying "I am ready to die for my country." He was followed by every man except the bedridden sick and Rose. "Boys," called Bowie from his cot, "I wish some of you would . . . remove my cot over there." Four men lifted him over. Every other wounded man made the same request, and had his bunk moved over.

This left only Louis Rose. He wrote later in a memoir:

I stood till every man had crossed the line. Then I sank to the ground, covered my face with my hands, and thought what best I might do. Suddenly an idea came. I spoke their [the Mexicans'] language, and could I once get safely out of the fort might easily pass for a Mexican and effect my escape. I stole a glance at Colonel Bowie in his cot. Colonel Davy Crockett was leaning over talking to him. After a few seconds, Bowie looked at me and said, "You don't seem willing to die with us, Rose." "No," I said. "I am not prepared to die, and shall not do so if I can avoid it." Then Crockett looked at me, and said, "You might just as well, for escape is impossible." I made no reply but looked up at the top of the fortress wall. "I have often done worse things than climb that wall," I thought. Then I sprang up, seized my travelling bag and unwashed clothes and ascended it. Standing on top, I glanced down to take a last look at my friends. They were all now in motion, but what they were doing I heeded not. Overpowered by my feelings, I turned away.

In the darkness Louis Rose made it through the Mexican lines and out of San Antonio without incident.

Somebody else escaped the Alamo that night. A woman Mexican non-combatant deserted and told Santa Anna's commanders how small the garrison was. Emboldened, they ordered a mass storm of the fort on the morning of the thirteenth day of the siege, 6 March 1836.

In the pre-dawn darkness of the 6th, the Mexicans approached the barricade surrounding the fort, forming an armed ring through which none could escape.

As daylight broke, Santa Anna sent 1,800 men against the sides of the Alamo while his band blared out the "No Quarter" call of the Spanish battle march, the "El Deguello". Twice the Mexicans charged, and twice they were rebuffed. Then Santa Anna sent in his reserves, and these breached the walls of the fort on the west and northeast. Colonel Travis died in the latter place, slumped next to a cannon, a bullet through his forehead. The outer walls were now abandoned and the survivors, fighting hand to hand, fell back to the convent and the chapel. Davy Crockett apparently fell outside the chapel, using his rifle as a club (although some evidence suggests that he, and six of his Tennesseans, were captured and tortured to death).

What is known of the last minutes of the men of the Alamo comes from the non-combatants in the fort whose lives were spared, particularly the wife of Lieutenant Dickinson, Ham, the Black servant of Jim Bowie, and Joe, the Black servant of Travis. The rooms of the stone buildings were fought for one by one. Armed with his knife and a brace of pistols, Jim Bowie fought from his sickbed in the baptistry. The chapel was the last place to be taken.

At around 7 a.m. with the din of battle dying down, Santa Anna judged it safe to approach the fort. One of the handful of Texans still alive in the chapel fired a last defiant volley, and the dictator retired to his adobe-walled command post. Only when the last Texan was dead did Santa Anna again venture forth to the Alamo, directing that the bodies of the fallen Texans should be burnt in two great funeral pyres.

To capture the Alamo cost General Antonio Lopez de Santa Anna over 1,000 of his men. He had also given the new Republic of Texas a battle cry which would bring it ultimate victory.

SWIMMING NIAGARA

E.J. Trelawny

A friend of the English Romantics Byron and Shelley, Trelawny shared something of their reckless derring-do. At the age of 38 he decided to swim Niagara.

To-day I have been mortified, bitterly. The morning was hot and cloudless, I sauntered along the brink of the Rapids, descended the long tiresome spiral staircase which leads directly to the ferry on the river.

Instead of crossing over in the boat to Canada, I threaded my way along the rugged and rocky shore. I came to a solitary hollow by the river side, about a mile below the Falls. The agitated water mining the banks, had broadened its bed and covered the shelving shore there with massy fragments of dark limestone rocks. The mural cliffs rose on each side two or three hundred feet almost perpendicularly, yet pine trees and cypress and yew managed to scale the steep ascent and to hold their ground, boring into the hard rocks with their harder roots, till, undermined by the continual rising of the water, they had fallen. Even at this distance from the Falls the waters in the mid-channel were still boiling and bubbling and covered with foam, raging along and spreading out in all directions. Pieces of timber I threw in spun round in concentric circles. Then turning and twisting against the rocks like crushed serpents, it flowed on to the Rapids and formed dangerous whirlpools two miles lower down. Above the Falls this river is a mile broad, where I was now it was less than half a mile, above and below me not more than a quarter; so that flowing through a deep ravine of rocks it was very deep even to its brink, and in the centre they say above a hundred feet. The sun was now at its zenith and its rays concentrated into the tunnel made my brains boil, the water was not agitated, was of that tempting emerald green which looks so voluptuously cool like molten jasper flaked with snow.

I never resist the syren pleasure, when she is surrounded by her water nymphs in their sea-green mantles, and my blood is boiling. I hastily cast aside my clothes, with nerves throbbing and panting breast, and clambering up to a ledge of rock jutting over a clear deep pool, I spring in head foremost. In an instant every nerve was restrung and set to the tune of vigorous boyhood. I spring up and gambol between wind and water.

To excel in swimming long and strong limbs and a pliant body are indispensable, the chest too should be broad, the greatest breadth of most fish is close to the head; the back must be bent inwards (incurvated), the head reined back like a swan's and the chest thrown forward; thus the body will float without exertion. The legs and arms after striking out should be drawn up and pressed close together, and five seconds between each stroke, as in running distances so in swimming distances, it is indispensable. Your life depends upon it, avoid being blown, the strongest swimmer, like the strongest horse, is done when his respiration fails. Utterly regardless of these truths, notwithstanding it is the pure gold of personal experience, in the wanton pride of my strength and knowledge of the art, I gambolled and played all sorts of gymnastics; methought the water, all wild as it was, was too sluggish, so I wheeled into mid-channel and dashing down the stream I was determined to try my strength in those places where the waters are wildest. I floated for some time over the eddying whirls without much difficulty and then struck through them right across the river.

This triumph steeled my confidence of "the ice brook's temper," after gaining breath regardless that I had changed the field of action in having been borne a long way down the river, consequently that I was rapidly approaching the Rapids, which no boat nor anything with life can live in.

Well, thinking alone of the grandeur and wildness of the scene I swam on without difficulty yet I felt the chill that follows over-exertion stealing up my extremities, cramping my toes and fingers with sudden twitches. I was again returned to the centre of the vortical part of the river, I was out of sight of the Falls, the water was becoming rougher and rougher, I was tossed about and drifting fast down. I now remembered the terrible whirlpool below me, I could make no progress, the stream was mastering me. I thought I had no time to lose so I incautiously put forth my strength, springing in the water with energy to cross the arrowy stream transversely, conceiving that when I reached the smoother part, out of the vortex of mid-channel, my work was done. I seemed to be held by the legs and sucked downwards, the scumming surf broke over and blinded me, I began to ship water. In the part of the river I had now drifted to the water was frightfully agitated, it was broken and raging all around me; still my exertions augmented with the opposition, I breathed quicker and with increasing difficulty, I kept my eye steadily on the dark-browned precipice before me, it seemed receding, I thought of returning, but the distance and difficulty was equally balanced; the rotary action of the water under its surface, when I relaxed my exertions, sucked my body, heels foremost, downwards. Whilst breathing hard I swallowed the spray, my strength suddenly declined, I was compelled to keep my mouth open, panting and gasping, my lower extremities sank. I looked around to see if there was any timber floating, or any boat or person on the shore. There was nothing, and if there had been no one could have seen me enveloped in spray, and the distant voice of the Falls drowned all other sounds; the thought that my time was come at last flashed across my mind, I thought what a fool I was to blindly abuse my own gained knowledge and thus cast myself away; the lessons of experience like the inscriptions on tombs grown faint and illegible if not continually renewed. Why did I attempt to cross a part of the river that none had ever crossed before? There was not even the excitement of a fool on the shore to see or say he had seen me do it. Why had I not spoken to the man at the ferry, he would have followed me in his boat. I remembered too hearing the thing was not practicable; why, what a wayward fool am I. These things acted as a spur, these truths crossed my mind rapidly, and I thought of all the scenes of drowning I had seen; of my own repeated perils that way. I heard the voices of

the dead calling to me, I actually thought, as my mind grew
darker, that they were tugging at my feet. Aston's horrid death
by drowning nearly paralysed me. I endeavoured in vain to
shake off these thick-coming fancies, they glowed before me.
Thus I lay suspended between life and death. I was borne
fearfully and rapidly along, I had lost all power, I could barely
keep my head above the surface, I waxed fainter and fainter,
there was no possibility of help. I occasionally turned on my
back to rest and endeavour to recover my breath, but the
agitation of the water and surf got into my mouth and nostrils,
the water stuck in my throat, which was instantly followed by
the agonizing sensation of strangulation. This I well knew was
an unerring first symptom of a suffocating death. Instead of air
I sucked in the flying spray, it's impossible either to swallow or
cast out again, and whilst struggling to do either I only drew in
more. The torture of choking was terrible, my limbs were cold
and almost lifeless, my stomach too was cramped. I saw the
waters of the Rapids below me raging and all about hissing. I
thought now how much I would have given for a spiked nail so
fixed that I could have rested the ball of my toe on it for one
instant and have drawn one gulp of air unimpeded, to have
swallowed the water that was sticking in the mid-channel of my
windpipe; any I would have been glad at any risk to have rested
on the point of a lancet. I had settled down till I was suspended
in the water, the throbbing and heaving of my breast and heart
and increased swelling in my throat had now so completely
paralysed my limbs that I thought of giving up a struggle which
seemed hopeless. My uppermost thought was mortification at
this infallible proof of my declining strength, well I knew there
was a time in which I could have forced my way through ten
times these impediments; the only palliation I could think of
was the depth and icy chilliness of the water which came
straight from the regions of the frigid zone. This contracted
all my muscles and sinews, my head grew dizzy from bending
the spine backwards, the blow I had received from the upset I
had not recovered; the ball, too, immediately over my jugular
vein retards the circulation; my right arm has never recovered
its strength and it was now benumbed. All this and much more I
thought of, my body I said "is like a leaky skiff" no longer seaworthy, and "my soul shall swim out of it" and free myself. I

thought the links which held me to life were so worn that the shock which broke them would be slight. It had always been my prayer to die in the pride of my strength, – age, however it approached, with wealth and power, or on crutches and in rags, was to me equally loathsome, – better to perish before he had touched me with his withering finger, in this wild place, on a foreign shore. Niagara "chanting a thunder psalm" as a requiem was a fitting end to my wild meteor-like life. Thoughts like these absorbed me. I no longer in the bitterness of my heart struggled against the waters which whirled me along, and certainly this despair as if in mockery preserved me. For looking again towards the shore I saw that I had been carried nearer to it, and without any exertion on my part I floated lighter, the under-tow no longer drew me down, and presently the water became smooth, I had been cast out of the vortex and was drifting towards the rocks. I heard the boiling commotion of the tremendous Rapids and saw the spume flying in the air a little below me, and then I lay stranded, sick and dizzy, everything still seemed whirling round and round and the waters singing in my ears. The sun had descended behind the cliffs, and my limbs shook so violently that I could not stand; I lay there for some time, and then, as the rocks were too rugged to admit of walking, I swam slowly up along the shore. I was deeply mortified, the maxim which has so long borne me towards my desires triumphantly – "go on till you are stopped" – fails me here. I have been stopped, there is no denying it, death would have pained me less than this conviction. I must change my vaunting crest.

My shadow trembling on the black rock as reflected by the last rays of the setting sun, shows me as in a glass, that my youth and strength have fled. When I had recovered my breath I dressed myself and walked sullenly to the ferry boat. I took the two heavy oars and exerting my utmost strength bent them like rattans as I forced the clumsy boat against the stream. The ferry man where I landed seemed surprised at my impetuosity, he said the sun's been so hot today that he was dead beat, I said, "Why how old are you?" "Oh," he said, "that's nothing" – he was thirty-eight. "Thirty-eight," I echoed, "then you are not worth a damn, you had better look out for the almshouse." I started off running up the steep acclivity and heard him muttering "Why, you aren't so very young yourself; what the devil does he mean?" When I got to the summit I threw myself down on a ledge of rock, instead of over as I should have done, and fell asleep, and thus ended the day; I shall not, however, forget it.

(August 15, 1833.)

BOUDICCA'S BATTLE CRY

Tacitus

A queen of the British Iceni tribe, Boudicca (incorrectly "Boadicea") was flogged and her daughters raped when she dared to oppose Roman confiscations of her property in AD 60. Outraged, Boudicca then led the British in a rebellion that almost ended Roman rule in the isles. Here the Roman historian Tacitus recounts the prototype of women warriors rousing her troops to battle.

Boudicca, with her daughters standing in front of her, was borne about in a war-chariot from tribe to tribe. "We Britons", she declared, "are accustomed to female war-leaders, but I do not now come forward as one of noble descent, fighting for my kingdom and my wealth: rather I present myself as an ordinary woman, striving to revenge my lost liberty, my lash-tortured body, and the violated honour of my daughters. Roman lust and avarice had reached the point where our very bodies – even those of old people and virgins – were no longer left unpolluted. But now the gods are granting us our just revenge: the one legion that dared to stand and fight has been cut to pieces, and the rest either cower in their forts or look about them for a means of escape. The enemy won't even stand up to the shouts and battle-cries of so many thousand men as we have, let alone endure our blows and assaults! Consider our numbers, and the reasons why we are fighting: then you will either conquer or die in this battle. I, a woman, am resolved to do so – you men, if you like, can live to be Roman slaves".

*   *   *

After destroying the Roman centre of Camulodunum (Colchester), sacking Londinium (London) and razing Verulamium (St Albans), Boudicca was defeated in a pitched battle by the Roman governor Suetonius Paulinus. It is reported that she took poison rather than being taken prisoner.

A YANKEE ANTIQUE

Walt Whitman

In which the American poet immortalizes Sergeant Calvin Harlowe, a Union soldier in the Civil War.

March 27, 1865. – Sergeant Calvin F. Harlowe, company C, 29th Massachusetts, 3d brigade, 1st division, Ninth corps – a mark'd sample of heroism and death, (some may say bravado, but I say *heroism*, of grandest, oldest order) – in the late attack by the rebel troops, and temporary capture by them, of fort Steadman, at night. The fort was surprised at dead of night. Suddenly awaken'd from their sleep, and rushing from their tents, Harlowe, with others, found himself in the hands of the secesh – they demanded his surrender – he answer'd, *Never while I live.* (Of course it was useless. The others surrender'd; the odds were too great.) Again he was ask'd to yield, this time by a rebel captain, Though surrounded, and quite calm, he again refused, call'd sternly to his comrades to fight on, and himself attempted to do so. The rebel captain then shot him – but at the same instant he shot the captain. Both fell together mortally wounded. Harlowe died almost instantly. The rebels were driven out in a very short time. The body was buried next day, but soon taken up and sent home, (Plymouth county, Mass.) Harlowe was only 22 years of age – was a tall, slim, dark-hair'd, blue-eyed young man – had come out originally with the 29th; and that is the way he met his death, after four years' campaign. He was in the Seven Days fight before Richmond, in second Bull Run, Antietam, first Fredericksburgh,

Vicksburgh, Jackson, Wilderness, and the campaigns following
– was as good a soldier as ever wore the blue, and every old
officer in the regiment will bear that testimony. Though so
young, and in a common rank, he had a spirit as resolute and
brave as any hero in the books, ancient or modern – It was too
great to say the words "I surrender" – and so he died. (When I
think of such things, knowing them well, all the vast and
complicated events of the war, on which history dwells and
makes its volumes, fall aside, and for the moment at any rate I
see nothing but young Calvin Harlowe's figure in the night,
disdaining to surrender.)

MAN COULD NOT DO MUCH MORE

Geoffrey Winthrop Young

A leading light of Edwardian mountaineering, Winthrop Young recounts below the greatest climbing feat of the age, that of the guide Franz Lochmatter in leading the ascent of the south-west face of the Taschhorn in the Alps. The year was 1906. With Lochmatter were his brother Josef, plus the guides Little J. and Joseph Knubel, along with Winthrop Young himself and with fellow climber V.J.E. Ryan.

Franz Lochmatter's mountaineering feat was the greatest I have witnessed, and after a number of years I can still say the greatest I can imagine. It is right that it should be recorded; for I do not suppose that in its mastery of natural difficulty, in its resistance to the effects of cold and fatigue and to the infections of depression and fear, it has often been equalled on any field of adventure or conflict.

. . . A slight, pricking snow began to drift across us. From the exposed height of our great pyramidal wall, surging above other ranges, we looked out across a frozen and unheeding stillness of white peak and glacier, disappearing under darker clouds to the south. We seemed very much removed from the earth, and very much alone. As I turned back to the rock I could see nothing but antagonism in the ice-wrinkled face of the crags upon which we were venturing; and I had the feeling – it was too formless at the time to take the definite shape I must now give to it – as if somewhere low down beyond the horizon behind me a great grey bird was just lifting on its wings into heavy flight. As the hours wore on, this shadow at our backs seemed to be approaching soundlessly and covering more and more of the sky. Gradually it was enclosing us within its spread of cold wings, and isolating us from all the world of life and movement in our contest with the frigid wall of grey precipice.

. . . I have no clear recollection of the series of traverses up and across the face that followed. After a short easier interval, they became, if anything, more steeply inclined and more outward sloping than before. The snow on them grew slimier and colder, the day darker, the sprinkling pepper of snowfall denser and keener. Hands and feet grew lifeless and lost their touch; and there was never a single sound holding-edge for any one of the party. We began that monotonous beat of any unoccupied toe or hand against the rock which alone kept the blood in circulation during the long cold hours of halt and fight and creep, and creep and fight and halt. On the next day my own toes and finger-tips were bruised blue – though I had felt no pain at the time; and a few fingers still retain the lowered vitality that follows on frost-bite. But during the climb no lesser trouble could get its head above the dark tide of oppression which filled all the spaces of consciousness. The fight went on doggedly, with that determination to take no long views but to make just the next hold good and the one more step secure which enables a human atom to achieve such heights of effort and to disregard such lengths of suffering.

The next clear memory is of finding ourselves inside the second, smaller, chimney, a precipitous narrow cleft up the face, of worn, skull-smooth rock. It was all dirty white and bone-blue in the gloomy afternoon light, with blurred ice-nubbles bulking through the adhesive snow. But at least there was the singular rest for eye and nerves which the feeling of enclosing walls gives us after long hours on an exposed cliff. We even found a nominal stance or two, in ice-pockets on chock-stones, where we could almost hold on without help from the hands. Franz, who was back again above me, resting from the lead, could spare me a few partial hoists with the rope. I began to feel my muscles slackening with the relief, and I became conscious of the cold. I had time to notice that I was climbing less precisely, a symptom of relaxed tension; time, too, to admit ungrudgingly that nothing in the universe but Franz' rope could have got me up to and over some of the expulsive ice bulges in the chimney. Ignorant in my remote position of what the front men saw awaiting us above, I even thawed into a congratulatory remark or so; but I drew no response.

And then, it all ended! The chimney simply petered out; not under the south-east ridge, as we might have hoped, but in the very hard heart of the diamond precipice some six hundred feet below the final and still invisible summit. The vague exit from the chimney faded out against the base of a blank cliff. One of its side walls led on for a little, and up to the left. There it too vanished under the lower rim of a big snowy slab, sloping up, and slightly conical, like a dish-cover. I have reason to remember that slab. It formed the repellent floor of a lofty, triangular recess. On its left side, and in front, there was space and ourselves. On its right, and at the back, a smooth leap of colossal cliff towered up for a hundred feet of crystallised shadow, and then arched out above our heads in a curve like the dark underside of a cathedral dome. A more appalling-looking finish to our grim battle of ascent could hardly have been dreamed in a "falling" nightmare; and we had not even standing room to appreciate it worthily! As I looked up and then down, I had an overpowering sense of the great grey wings behind us, shadowing suddenly close across the whole breadth of precipice, and folding us off finally from the world.

. . . Right up in the angle of the recess there was a rotund blister of rock modelled in low relief on the face of the slab; and round this a man, hunched on small nicks in the steep surface, could just belay the rope. Josef and Franz were crouching at this blister up in the recess. The rest of us were dispersed over freezing cling-holds along the lower rim of the slab. And the debate proceeded, broken by gusts of snow. The man to lead had clearly to run out a hundred to a hundred and fifty feet of rope. He could be given no protection. His most doubtful link would come some eighty feet up, above the roof. If he found a flaw there, and it served him favourably, he would be out on the convex of the dome fully a hundred feet above us, and outside us in a direct line above our heads. If, at this point, he could not proceed – well, it was equally unlikely that he could return!

Franz showed no hesitation. The hampered preparations for the attempt went on hurriedly. We had all to unrope as best we could, so as to arrange for the two hundred feet of possible run-out, and we hooked on to our holds with difficulty, while the snow-frozen rope kinked and banged venomously about us. In the end Little J. and I had to remain off the rope, to leave enough free. Then –

> as a flame
> Stirred by the air, under a cavern gaunt –

Franz started up the corner, climbing with extraordinary nerve but advancing almost imperceptibly. It was much like swarming up the angle of a tower, rough-cast with ice. Ryan and Little J. crept up near the blister; but as there was no more room I remained hanging on to the fractured sill of the slab. In this position I was farther out; and I could just see Franz' two feet scratting desperately for hold to propel him up the tilt of the roof above the corner. The rest of him was now out of sight.
    . . . An indistinct exchange of shouts began, half swallowed by echo, wind, and snow. Franz, it appeared, was still quite uncertain if he could get up any farther. For the time he could hold on well enough to help one man with the rope; but he had not two hands free to pull. I could hear his little spurt of laughter at the question: "Could he return?" He suggested that Josef should join him, and the rest wait until they two might return with a rescue-party. Wait, there! – for at best fifteen hours, hanging on to the icy holds, in a snow-wind! Well, then, what if we four tried to get down, and he would go on alone – if he could? "Get down? Ho, la, la!" – Josef was at his resourceful wits' end. I suggested, pacifyingly, that Ryan might join and reinforce Franz, and that we remaining three could attempt the descent together. This provoked the crisis, which had been long threatening. Josef's competence and control were second to none in the Alps; but the responsibility, the physical strain, and this last disappointment had overstrained the cord. It snapped; and in somewhat disconcerting fashion.
    Harsh experience can teach us that when these accidiae occur, as they may to the most courageous of men if tested unfairly, the only remedy is to soothe or to startle. The first was impracticable in our situation. I spoke sharply in reproach, but without raising my voice. The experiment succeeded surprisingly. Self-

control returned upon the instant, and for the rest of the day Josef climbed and safeguarded us with all his own superb skill and chivalrous consideration.

He was right in so far that, at that hour of the day and upon those treacherous cliffs, now doubly dangerous under accumulating snow, all the odds were against any of us who turned back getting down alive. Franz in any case could not get back to us, and he might not be able to advance. We were committed, therefore, to the attempt to join him, however gloomy its outlook. As many as possible must be got up to him – and the rest must be left to chance.

. . . The end of the long rope hooted down past us. It hung outside the recess, dangling in air; and I could only recover it by climbing down again over the rim of the slab and reaching out for it one-handed with my axe. I passed it up; and then I stayed there, hanging on, because I could no longer trust hands or feet to get me up the slope again. Ryan began the corner; but if I have described the position at all intelligibly, it will be seen that while the corner rose vertically on our right, the long rope hung down on a parallel line from the dome directly above our heads. So it came that the higher we climbed up the corner the more horizontal became the slanting pull of the rope, and the more it tended to drag us sideways off the corner and back under the overhang. Very coolly, Ryan shouted a warning before he started of the insufficient power left in frozen hands. Some twenty feet up, the rope tore him from his inadequate, snowy holds. He swung across above our heads and hung suspended in mid-air. The rope was fixed round his chest. In a minute it began to suffocate him. He shouted once or twice to the men above to hurry. Then a fainter call, "I'm done," and he dangled to all appearance unconscious on the rope. Franz and Josef could only lift him half-inch by half-inch. For all this hour – probably it was longer – they were clamped one above the other on to the steep face of the dome, their feet on shallow but sound nicks, one hand clinging on, and only the other free to pull in. Any inch the one lifted, the other held. The rough curve of the rock, over which the higher portion of the rope descended, diminished by friction the effectiveness of each tug. The more one considers their situation, the more super-human do the co-operation and power the two men displayed during this time, at the end of all those hours of effort, appear. Little J. and I had only the deadly anxiety of watching helplessly, staring upward into the dizzy snow and shadow; and that was enough. J. had followed silently and unselfishly the whole day; and even now he said nothing; crouching in unquestioning endurance beside the freezing blister on the slab.

Ryan was up at last, somehow, to the overhang; and being dragged up the rough curve above. A few small splinters were loosened, and fell, piping, past me and on to me. I remember calculating apathetically whether it was a greater risk to try and climb up again into the recess, unroped and without any feel in fingers and toes, or to stay where I was, hanging on to the sill, and chance being knocked off by a stone. It is significant of the condition of body and mind that I decided to stay where I was, where at least stiffened muscles and joints still availed to hold me mechanically fixed on to my group of rounded nicks.

Ryan was now out of sight and with the others. When the constriction of the rope was removed he must have recovered amazingly toughly, and at once; for down once more, after a short but anxious pause, whistled the snow-stiffened rope, so narrowly missing me that Little J. cried out in alarm. I could not for a time hook it in with the axe; and while I stretched, frigidly and nervously, Josef hailed me from seemingly infinite height, his shouts travelling out on the snow eddies. They could not possibly pull up my greater weight. Unless I felt sure I could stick on to the corner and manage to climb round to them by Franz' route, it was useless my trying! At last I had fished in the rope, with a thrill of relief, and I set mental teeth. With those two tied on to the rope above, and myself tied on – in the way I meant to tie myself on – to the rope below, there were going to be no more single options. We were all in it together; and if I had still some faith in myself I had yet more in that margin of desperation strength which extends the possible indefinitely for such men as I knew to be linked on to me above. And if I were once up, well, there would be no question after that about Little J. coming up too!

I gave hands and feet a last blue-beating against the rock to restore some feeling to them. Then I knotted the rope round my chest, made the loose end into a triple-bowline "chair" round the thighs, and began scratching rather futilely up the icy rectangular corner. For the first twenty-five feet – or was it much less? – I could just force upward. Then the rope began to drag me off inexorably. I clutched furiously up a few feet more; and then I felt I must let go, the drag was too strong for frozen fingers. As I had already resolved, at the last second I kicked off from the rock with all my strength. This sent me flying out on the rope, and across under the overhang, as if attached to a crazy pendulum. I could see J. crouching in the recess far below, instinctively protecting his head. The impetus jumped the upper part of the rope off its cling to the rock face of the dome above, and enabled the men to snatch in a foot or two. The return-swing brought me back, as I had half hoped, against the corner a little higher up. I gripped it with fingers and teeth, and scrambled up another few feet. But the draw was now irresistible. I kicked off again; gained a foot or so, and spun back.

I was now up the corner proper, and I should have been by rights scrambling up the roof on the far side of my gable edge. But the rope, if nothing else, prevented any chance of my forcing myself over it and farther to the right. Another cling and scratch up the gable end, and I was not far below the level of the dome overhanging above and to my left. For the last time I fell off. This time the free length of the rope, below its hold upon the curve of the dome, was too short to allow of any return swing. So I shot out passively, to hang, revolving slowly, under the dome, with the feeling that my part was at an end. When I spun round inward, I looked up at the reddish, scarred wall freckled with snow, and at the tense rope, looking thin as a grey cobweb and disappearing fraily over the fore-spring of rock that arched greedily over my head. When I spun outward, I looked down – no matter how many thousand feet – to the dim, shifting lines of the glacier at the foot of the peak, hazy through the snow-fall; and I could see, well inside my feet, upon the dark face of the precipice the little blanched triangle of the recess and the duller white dot of J.'s face as he crouched by the blister. It flashed across me, absurdly, that he ought to be more anxious about the effect of my gymnastics upon the fragile thread of alpine rope, his one link with hope, than about me!

(Eventually Young and Little J. reached the other three.)

. . . And then, something was happening! There came a mutter of talk from the dusk above. Surely two shadows were actually moving at one time! I was at the foot of a long icy shelf, slanting up to the right. It was overhung by cliff on the left, as usual. It was falling away into space on my right, as usual; and it had the usual absence of any holds to keep me on it. I began the eternal knee-friction crawl. The rope tightened on my waist. "Shall I pull?" – called Josef's voice, sounding strange after the hours of silence, and subdued to an undertone as if he feared that the peak might still hear and wake up to contrive some new devilment. "Why not? – if you really can!" – I echoed, full of surprise and hope; and I skimmered up the trough, to find Josef yoked to a royal rock hitch, the third and the best of the day! And, surely, we were standing on the crest of a great ridge, materialised as if by magic out of the continuous darkness of cliff and sky? And the big, sullen shadow just above must be the summit! It was indeed the mounting edge of the south-east ridge upon which we had arrived; and sixty feet above us it curled over against the top of the final pyramid. Josef unroped from me, while I brought up Little J.; and as we started to finish the ascent together in our old-time partnership, I saw the silhouettes of the other three pass in succession over the pointed skyline of the peak.

We found them, relaxed in spent attitudes on the summit-slabs, swallowing sardines and snow, our first food since half-past seven in the morning. It was now close upon six o'clock. Franz came across to meet me, and we shook hands. "You will never do anything harder than that, Franz!" "No," he said reflectively, "man could not do much more."

HEROISM

Ralph Waldo Emerson

There was something heroic about Ralph Waldo Emerson's own life (1803–82), for he struggled for over fifty years to develop and promote a philosophy that accorded primacy to the individual conscience. Although separated by the Atlantic, he was a close friend of the Scottish historian Thomas Carlyle (see pp. 33–37), another writer who pondered much on the nature of heroism.

S elf-trust is the essence of heroism. It is the state of the soul at war, and its ultimate objects are the last defiance of falsehood and wrong, and the power to bear all that can be inflicted by evil agents. It speaks the truth, and it is just, generous, hospitable, temperate, scornful of petty calculations, and scornful of being scorned. It persists; it is of an undaunted boldness, and of a fortitude not to be wearied out. Its jest is the littleness of common life. That false prudence which dotes on health and wealth is the butt and merriment of heroism. Heroism, like Plotinus, is almost ashamed of its body. What shall it say, then, to the sugar-plums and cat's cradles, to the toilet, compliments, quarrels, cards, and custard, which rack the wit of all society? What joys has kind nature provided for us dear creatures! There seems to be no interval between greatness and meanness. When the spirit is not master of the world, then it is its dupe. Yet the little man takes the great hoax so innocently, works in it so headlong and believing, is born red, and dies grey, arranging his toilet, attending on his own health, laying traps for sweet food and strong wine, setting his heart on a horse or a rifle, made happy with a little gossip or a little praise, that the great soul cannot choose but laugh at such earnest nonsense. "Indeed, these humble considerations make me out of love with greatness. What a disgrace is it to me to take note how many pairs of silk stockings thou hast, namely, these and those that were the peach-coloured ones; or to bear the inventory of thy shirts, as one for superfluity, and one other for use!"

Citizens, thinking after the laws of arithmetic, consider the inconvenience of receiving strangers at their fireside, reckon narrowly the loss of time and the unusual display: the soul of a better quality thrusts back the unseasonable economy into the vaults of life, and says, I will obey the God, and the sacrifice and the fire he will provide. Ibn Hankal, the Arabian geographer, describes a heroic extreme in the hospitality of Sogd, in Bukharia. "When I was in Sogd, I saw a great building, like a palace, the gates of which were open and fixed back to the wall with large nails. I asked the reason, and was told that the house had not been shut, night or day, for a hundred years. Strangers may present themselves at any hour, and in whatever number; the master has amply provided for the reception of the men and their animals, and is never happier than when they tarry for some time. Nothing of the kind have I seen in any other country." The magnanimous know very well that they who give time, or money, or shelter, to the stranger – so it be done for love, and not for ostentation – do, as it were, put God under obligation to them, so perfect are the compensations of the universe. In some way the time they seem to lose is redeemed, and the pains they seem to take remunerate themselves. These men fan the flame of human love, and raise the standard of civil virtue among mankind. But hospitality must be for service, and not for show, or it pulls down the host. The brave soul rates itself too high to value itself by the splendour of its table and draperies. It gives what it hath, and all it hath, but its own majesty can lend a better grace to bannocks and fair water than belongs to city feasts.

The temperance of the hero proceeds from the same wish to do no dishonour to the worthiness he has. But he loves it for its elegancy, not for its austerity. It seems not worth his while to be solemn, and denounce with bitterness flesh-eating or wine-drinking, the use of tobacco, or opium, or tea, or silk, or gold. A great man scarcely knows how he dines, how he dresses; but without railing or precision, his living is natural and poetic. John Eliot, the Indian Apostle, drank water, and said of wine, "It is a noble, generous liquor, and we should be humbly thankful for it; but, as I remember, water was made before it." Better still is the temperance of King David, who poured out on the ground unto the Lord the water which three of his warriors had brought him to drink, at the peril of their lives.

It is told of Brutus, that when he fell on his sword, after the battle of Philippi, he quoted a line of Euripides, "O virtue! I have followed thee through life, and I find thee at last but a shade." I doubt not the hero is slandered by this report. The heroic soul does not sell its justice and its nobleness. It does not ask to dine nicely, and to sleep warm. The essence of greatness is the perception that virtue is enough. Poverty is its ornament. It does not need plenty, and can very well abide its loss.

But that which takes my fancy most, in the heroic class, is the good-humour and hilarity they exhibit. It is a height to which common duty can very well attain, to suffer and to dare with solemnity. But these rare souls set opinion, success, and life, at so cheap a rate, that they will not soothe their enemies by petitions, or the show of sorrow, but wear their own habitual greatness. Scipio, charged with peculation, refuses to do himself so great a disgrace as to wait for justification, though he had the scroll of his accounts in his hands, but tears it to pieces before the tribunes. Socrates' condemnation of himself to be maintained in all honour in the Prytaneum, during his life, and Sir Thomas More's playfulness at the scaffold, are of the same strain. In Beaumont and Fletcher's *Sea Voyage*, Juletta tells the stout captain and his company:

> *Jul.* Why, slaves, 'tis in our power to hang ye.
> *Master.* Very likely;
>   'Tis in our powers, then, to be hanged, and scorn ye.

These replies are sound and whole. Sport is the bloom and glow of a perfect health. The great will not condescend to take anything seriously; all must be as gay as the song of a canary, though it were the building of cities, or the eradication of old and foolish churches and nations, which have cumbered the earth long thousands of years. Simple hearts put all the history and customs of this world behind them, and play their own game in innocent defiance of the Blue-Laws of the world; and such would appear, could we see the human race assembled in vision, like little children frolicking together; though, to the eyes of mankind at large, they wear a stately and solemn garb of works and influences.

The interest these fine stories have for us, the power of a romance over the boy who grasps the forbidden book under his bench at school, our delight in the hero, is the main fact to our purpose. All these great and transcendent properties are ours. If we dilate in beholding the Greek energy, the Roman pride, it is that we are already domesticating the same sentiment. Let us find room for this great guest in our small houses. The first step of worthiness will be to disabuse us of our superstitious associations with places and times, with number and size. Why should these words, Athenian, Roman, Asia, and England, so tingle in the ear? Where the heart is, there the muses, there the gods sojourn, and not in any geography of fame. Massachusetts, Connecticut River, and Boston Bay, you think paltry places, and the ear loves names of foreign and classic topography. But here we are; and, if we will tarry a little, we may come to learn that here is best. See to it, only, that thyself is here; — and art and nature, hope and fate, friends, angels, and the Supreme Being, shall not be absent from the chamber where thou sittest. Epaminondas, brave and affectionate, does not seem to us to need Olympus to die upon, nor the Syrian sunshine. He lies very well where he is. The Jerseys were handsome ground enough for Washington to tread, and London streets for the feet of Milton. A great man makes his climate genial in the imagination of men, and its air the beloved element of all delicate spirits. That country is the fairest, which is inhabited by the noblest minds. The pictures which fill the imagination in reading the actions of Pericles, Xenophon, Columbus, Bayard, Sidney, Hampden, teach us how needlessly mean our life is, that we, by the depth of our living, should deck it with more than regal or national splendour, and act on principles that should interest man and nature in the length of our days.

We have seen or heard of many extraordinary young men,

who never ripened, or whose performance in actual life was not extraordinary. When we see their air and mien, when we hear them speak of society, of books, of religion, we admire their superiority, they seem to throw contempt on our entire polity and social state; theirs is the tone of a youthful giant, who is sent to work revolutions. But they enter an active profession, and the forming Colossus shrinks to the common size of man. The magic they used was the ideal tendencies, which always make the Actual ridiculous; but the tough world had its revenge the moment they put their horses of the sun to plough in its furrow. They found no example and no companion, and their heart fainted. What then? The lesson they gave in their first aspirations is yet true; and a better velour and a purer truth shall one day organize their belief. Or why should a woman liken herself to any historical woman, and think, because Sappho, or Sévigné, or De Staël, or the cloistered souls who have had genius and cultivation, do not satisfy the imagination and the serene Themis, none can – certainly not she. Why not? She has a new and unattempted problem to solve, perchance that of the happiest nature that ever bloomed. Let the maiden, with erect soul, walk serenely on her way, accept the hint of each new experience, search in turn all the objects that solicit her eye, that she may learn the power and the charm of her new-born being, which is the kindling of a new dawn in the recesses of space. The fair girl, who repels interference by a decided and proud choice of influences, so careless of pleasing, so wilful and lofty, inspires every beholder with somewhat of her own nobleness. The silent heart encourages her; O friend, never strike sail to a fear! Come into port greatly, or sail with God the seas. Not in vain you live, for every passing eye is cheered and refined by the vision.

The characteristic of heroism is its persistency. All men have wandering impulses, fits and starts of generosity. But when you have chosen your part, abide by it, and do not weakly try to reconcile yourself with the world. The heroic cannot be the common, nor the common the heroic. Yet we have the weakness to expect the sympathy of people in those actions whose excellence is that they outrun sympathy, and appeal to a tardy justice. If you would serve your brother, because it is fit for you to serve him, do not take back your words when you find that prudent people do not commend you. Adhere to your own act, and congratulate yourself if you have done something strange and extravagant, and broken the monotony of a decorous age. It was a high counsel that I once heard given to a young person, "Always do what you are afraid to do." A simple, manly character need never make an apology, but should regard its past action with the calmness of Phocion, when he admitted that the event of the battle was happy, yet did not regret his dissuasion from the battle.

There is no weakness or exposure for which we cannot find consolation in the thought, – this is a part of my constitution, part of my relation and office to my fellow-creature. Has nature covenanted with me that I should never appear to disadvantage, never make a ridiculous figure? Let us be generous of our dignity, as well as of our money. Greatness once and for ever has done with opinion. We tell our charities, not because we wish to be praised for them, not because we think they have great merit, but for our justification. It is a capital blunder; as you discover, when another man recites his charities.

To speak the truth, even with some austerity, to live with some rigour of temperance, or some extremes of generosity, seems to be an asceticism which common good-nature would appoint to those who are at ease and in plenty, in sign that they feel a brotherhood with the great multitude of suffering men. And not only need we breathe and exercise the soul by assuming the penalties of abstinence, of debt, of solitude, of unpopularity, but it behoves the wise man to look with a bold eye into those rarer dangers which sometimes invade men, and to familiarize himself with disgusting forms of disease, with sounds of execration, and the vision of violent death.

Times of heroism are generally times of terror, but the day never shines in which this element may not work. The circumstances of man, we say, are historically somewhat better in this country, and at this hour, than perhaps ever before. More freedom exists for culture. It will not now run against an axe at the first step out of the beaten track of opinion. But whose is heroic will always find crises to try his edge. Human virtue demands her champions and martyrs, and the trial of persecution always proceeds. It is but the other day that the brave Lovejoy gave his breast to the bullets of a mob, for the rights of free speech and opinion, and died when it was better not to live.

I see not any road of perfect peace which a man can walk, but after the counsel of his own bosom. Let him quit too much association, let him go home much, and stablish himself in those courses he approves. The unremitting retention of simple and high sentiments in obscure duties is hardening the character to that temper which will work with honour, if need be, in the tumult, or on the scaffold. Whatever outrages have happened to men may befall a man again; and very easily in a republic, if there appear any signs of a decay of religion. Coarse slander, fire, tar and feathers, and the gibbet, the youth may freely bring home to his mind, and with what sweetness of temper he can, and inquire how fast he can fix his sense of duty, braving such penalties, whenever it may please the next newspaper and a sufficient number of his neighbours to pronounce his opinions incendiary.

It may calm the apprehension of calamity in the most susceptible heart to see how quick a bound nature has set to the utmost infliction of malice. We rapidly approach a brink over which no enemy can follow us.

Let them rave:
Thou art quiet in thy grave.

In the gloom of our ignorance of what shall be, in the hour when we are deaf to the higher voices, who does not envy those who have seen safely to an end their manful endeavour? Who that sees the meanness of our politics, but inly congratulates Washington that he is long already wrapped in his shroud, and for ever safe; that he was laid sweet in his grave, the hope of humanity not yet subjugated in him? Who does not sometimes envy the good and brave, who are no more to suffer from the tumults of the natural world, and await with curious complacency the speedy term of his own conversation with finite nature? And yet the love that will be annihilated sooner than treacherous, has already made death impossible, and affirms itself no mortal, but a native of the deeps of absolute and inextinguishable being.

THE DEATH OF ADOLFO RODRIGUEZ

Richard Harding Davis

This incident from the Cuban rebellion against Spanish rule occurred on 19 January 1897.

A dolfo Rodriguez was the only son of a Cuban farmer, who lived nine miles outside of Santa Clara, beyond the hills that surround that city to the north.

When the revolution in Cuba broke out young Rodriguez joined the insurgents, leaving his father and mother and two sisters at the farm. He was taken, in December of 1896, by a force of the Guardia Civile, the corp d'elite of the Spanish army, and defended himself when they tried to capture him, wounding three of them with his machete.

He was tried by the military court for bearing arms against the government, and sentenced to be shot by a fusillade some morning before sunrise.

Previous to execution he was confined in the military prison of Santa Clara with thirty other insurgents, all of whom were sentenced to be shot, one after the other, on mornings following the execution of Rodriguez.

His execution took place the morning of the 19th of January, 1897, at a place a half-mile distant from the city, on the great plain that stretches from the fort out to the hills, beyond which Rodriguez had lived for nineteen years. At the time of his death he was twenty years old.

I witnessed his execution, and what follows is an account of the way he went to his death. The young man's friends could not be present, for it was impossible for them to show themselves in that crowd and that place with wisdom or without distress, and I like to think that, although Rodriguez could not know it, there was one person present when he died who felt keenly for him, and who was a sympathetic though unwilling spectator.

There had been a full moon the night preceding the execution, and when the squad of soldiers marched from town it was still shining brightly through the mists. It lighted a plain two miles in extent, broken by ridges, and gullies and covered with thick, high grass, and with bunches of cactus and palmetto. In the hollow of the ridges the mist lay like broad lakes of water, and on one side of the plain stood the walls of the old town. On the other rose hills covered with royal palms that showed white in the moonlight, like hundreds of marble columns. A line of tiny camp-fires that the sentries had built during the night stretched between the forts at regular intervals and burned clearly.

But as the light grew stronger and the moonlight faded these were stamped out, and when the soldiers came in force the moon was a white ball in the sky, without radiance, the fires had sunk to ashes, and the sun had not yet risen.

So even when the men were formed into three sides of a hollow square, they were scarcely able to distinguish one another in the uncertain light of the morning.

There were about three hundred soldiers in the formation. They belonged to the volunteers, with their band playing a jaunty quickstep, while their officers galloped from one side to the other through the grass, seeking a suitable place for the execution. Outside the line the band still played merrily.

A few men and boys, who had been dragged out of their beds by the music, moved about the ridges behind the soldiers, half-clothed, unshaven, sleepy-eyed, yawning, stretching themselves nervously and shivering in the cool, damp air of the morning.

Either owing to discipline or on account of the nature of their errand, or because the men were still but half awake, there was no talking in the ranks, and soldiers stood motionless, leaning on their rifles, with their backs turned to the town, looking out across the plain to the hills.

The men in the crowd behind them were also grimly silent. They knew that whatever they might say would be twisted into a word of sympathy for the condemned man or a protest against the government. So no one spoke; even the officers gave their orders in gruff whispers, and the men in the crowd did not mix together, but looked suspiciously at one another and kept apart.

As the light increased a mass of people came hurrying from town with two black figures leading them, and the soldiers drew up at attention, and part of the double line fell back and left an opening in the square.

With us a condemned man walks only the short distance from his cell to the scaffold or the electric chair, shielded from sight by the prison walls, and it often occurs even then that the short journey is too much for his strength and courage.

But the Spaniards on this morning made the prisoner walk for over a half-mile across the broken surface of the fields. I expected to find the man, no matter what his strength at other times might be, stumbling and faltering on this cruel journey; but as he came nearer I saw that he led all the others, that the priests on either side of him were taking two steps to his one and that they were tripping on their gowns and stumbling over the hollows in their efforts to keep pace with him as he walked, erect and soldierly, at a quick step in advance of them.

He had a handsome, gentle face of the peasant type, a light, pointed beard, great wistful eyes, and a mass of curly black hair. He was shockingly young for such a sacrifice, and looked more like a Neapolitan than a Cuban. You could imagine him sitting on the quay at Naples or Genoa lolling in the sun and showing his white teeth when he laughed. Around his neck, hanging outside the linen blouse, he wore a new scapular.

It seems a petty thing to have been pleased with at such a time, but I confess to have felt a thrill of satisfaction when I saw, as the Cuban passed me, that he held a cigarette between his lips, not arrogantly nor with bravado, but with the nonchalance of a man who meets his punishment fearlessly, and who will let his enemies see that they can kill but not frighten him.

It was very quickly finished, with rough and, but for one frightful blunder, with merciful swiftness. The crowd fell back when it came to the square, and the condemned man, the priests, and the firing squad of six volunteers passed in and the line closed behind them.

The officer who had held the cord that bound the Cuban's arms behind him and passed across his breast, let it fall on the grass and drew his sword, and Rodriguez dropped his cigarette from his lips and bent and kissed the cross which the priests held up before him.

The elder of the priests moved to one side and prayed rapidly in a loud whisper, while the other, a younger man, walked behind the firing squad and covered his face with his hands. They had both spent the last twelve hours with Rodriguez in the chapel of the prison.

The Cuban walked to where the officer directed him to stand, and turning his back on the square, faced the hills and the road across them, which led to his father's farm.

As the officer gave the first command he straightened himself as far as the cords would allow, and held up his head and fixed his eyes immovably on the morning light, which had just begun to show above the hills.

He made a picture of such pathetic helplessness, but of such courage and dignity, that he reminded me on the instant of that statue of Nathan Hale which stands in the City Hall Park, above the roar of Broadway. The Cuban's arms were bound, as are those of the statue, and he stood firmly, with his weight resting on his heels like a soldier on parade, and with his face held up fearlessly, as is that of the statue. But there was this difference, that Rodriguez, while probably as willing to give six lives for his country as was the American rebel, being only a peasant, did not think to say so, and he will not, in consequence, live in bronze during the lives of many men, but will be remembered only as one of thirty Cubans, one of whom was shot at Santa Clara on each succeeding sunrise.

The officer had given the order, the men had raised their pieces, and the condemned man had heard the clicks of the triggers as they were pulled back, and he had not moved. And then happened one of the most cruelly refined, though unintentional acts of torture that one can very well imagine. As the officer slowly raised his sword, preparatory to giving the signal, one of the mounted officers rode up to him and pointed out silently that, as I had already observed with some satisfaction, the firing squad was so placed that when they fired they would shoot several of the soldiers stationed on the extreme end of the square.

Their captain motioned his men to lower their pieces, and then walked across the grass and laid his hand on the shoulder of the waiting prisoner.

It is not pleasant to think what that shock must have been. The man had steeled himself to receive a volley of bullets. He believed that in the next instant he would be in another world; he had heard the command given, had heard the click of the Mausers as the locks caught – and then, at the supreme moment, a human hand had been laid upon his shoulder and a voice spoke in his ear.

You would expect that any man, snatched back to life in such a fashion, would start and tremble at the reprieve, or would break down altogether, but this boy turned his head steadily, and followed with his eyes the direction of the officer's sword, then nodded gravely, and with his shoulders squared, took up the new position, straightened his back, and once more held himself erect.

As an exhibition of self-control this should surely rank above feats of heroism performed in battle, where there are thousands of comrades to give inspiration. This man was alone, in sight of the hills he knew, with only enemies about him, with no source to draw on for strength but that which lay in himself.

The officer of the firing squad, mortified by his blunder, hastily whipped up his sword, the men once more leveled their rifles, the sword rose, dropped, and the men fired. At the report the Cuban's head snapped back almost between his shoulders, but his body fell slowly, as though someone had pushed him gently forward from behind and he had stumbled.

He sank on his side in the wet grass without a struggle or a sound, and did not move again.

It was difficult to believe that he meant to lie there, that it could be ended without a word, that the man in the linen suit would not rise to his feet and continue to walk on over the hills, as he apparently had started to do, to his home; that there was not a mistake somewhere, or that at least someone would be sorry or say something or run and pick him up.

But, fortunately, he did not need help, and the priests

returned – the younger one with tears running down his face – and donned their vestments and read a brief requiem for his soul, while the squad stood uncovered, and the men in the hollow square shook their accoutrements into place, and shifted their pieces and got ready for the order to march, and the band began again with the same quickstep which the fusillade had interrupted.

The figure still lay on the grass untouched, and no one seemed to remember that it had walked there of itself, or noticed that the cigarette still burned, a tiny ring of living fire, at the place where the figure had first stood.

The figure was a thing of the past, and the squad shook itself like a great snake, and then broke into little pieces and started off jauntily, stumbling in the high grass and striving to keep step to the music.

The officers led it past the figure in the linen suit, and so close to it that the file closers had to part with the column to avoid treading on it. Each soldier as he passed turned and looked down on it, some craning their necks curiously, others giving a careless glance, and some without any interest at all, as they would have looked at a house by the roadside, or a hole in the road.

One young soldier caught his foot in a trailing vine just opposite to it, and fell. He grew very red when his comrades giggled at him for his awkwardness. The crowd of sleepy spectators fell in on either side of the band. They, too, had forgotten it, and the priests put their vestments back in the bag and wrapped their heavy cloaks about them, and hurried off after the others.

Every man seemed to have forgotten it except two men, who came slowly towards it from the town, driving a bullockcart that bore an unplaned coffin, each with a cigarette between his lips, and with his throat wrapped in a shawl to keep out the morning mists.

At that moment the sun which shown some promise of its coming glow above the hills, shot up suddenly from behind them in all the splendor of the tropics, a fierce, red disk of heat, and filled the air with warmth and light.

The bayonets of the retreating column flashed in it, and at the sight a rooster in a farm-yard near by crowed vigorously, and a dozen bugles answered the challenge with the brisk, cheery notes of the reveille, and from all parts of the city the church bells jangled out the call for early mass, and the little world of Santa Clara seemed to stretch itself and to wake to welcome the day just begun.

But as I fell in at the rear of the procession and looked back, the figure of the young Cuban, who was no longer a part of the world of Santa Clara, was asleep in the wet grass, with his motionless arms still tightly bound behind him, with the scapular twisted awry across his face, and the blood from his breast sinking into the soil he had tried to free.

SIR THOMAS MORE
UPON THE SCAFFOLD

Anonymous

A man of supreme conscience, Sir Thomas More, the Lord Chancellor of England, refused to support Henry VIII's shady schemes to jettison one wife in favour of another, Anne Boleyn for Catherine of Aragon. And so More found a sure route to the executioner. Many have trodden there, before and since, but rarely has anyone left the world with such elan.

The bitter question of Henry's divorce from Catherine of Aragon soon came to disturb More's peace of mind. At first he was silent on the point, but when Henry taxed him he could not agree to the king's views. In March, 1531, the decisions of the universities were read out to the House of Lords by More, who, when asked his own opinion, cautiously said that he had already told it to the king. But the chancellor saw the trend of events, and in 1532 he resigned. He went home and informed his wife with light-hearted indifference, and at once made plans for a new life in straitened circumstances.

A year later he was named as one of the disciples of the Holy Maid of Kent, and was charged as guilty of treason. He was called before four privy councillors, and in spite of his danger, treated them with cool disdain. Only his great popularity saved him then, and Henry grudgingly struck his name out of the Bill of Attainder.

But in April, 1534, Sir Thomas More refused to take the oath of adherence to the new Act of Succession, by which Anne Boleyn's issue became heirs to the throne. He was willing to take an oath of loyalty to the king, but he could not swear one which abrogated the authority of the Pope. So he was committed to the Tower.

He was a sick man. Congested lungs, gravel, stone and cramp made his body a torment, but his spirits were as cheerful as ever. His wife asked him to take the oath and regain his liberty, but More answered: "Is not this house as nigh heaven as mine own?"

In 1535, Henry was declared supreme head of the Church of England, and in April, Thomas Cromwell went to the Tower to ask More whether this were lawful in his eyes. More replied that he was a faithful subject of the king. In May and June, Cromwell repeated the visits, and then sent the solicitor-general to interview More.

Meanwhile, More was still cheerful, believing that: "A man may live for the next world and yet be merry." He wrote to his wife and daughters, but when it was discovered that he had exchanged notes with his friend and fellow-prisoner, John Fisher, Bishop of Rochester, his writing materials were taken from him. From that time More closed the shutters of his cell.

On June 25, Fisher was executed. More knew what to expect. He was charged with high treason at Westminster Hall on July I. The evidence was based on the solicitor-general's reports of his conversations and on the notes to Fisher. More, seated as a sick man, denied the charges with great dignity. He was found guilty and sentenced to be hanged at Tyburn, but five days later Henry commuted the method to decapitation.

His behaviour at the final scene on Tower Hill on the morning of July 7, 1535, was as magnificent as it was moving. As he reached the steps of the scaffold, he said to the lieutenant there: "I pray thee see me safely up, and for my coming down let me shift for myself." With a joke he told the executioner to do his job fearlessly, and then he moved the beard, which he had grown during his imprisonment, away from the block, saying: "It has never committed treason."

THE GREAT ESCAPER

Tom Moulson

Squadron Leader Roger Bushell was the Houdini of British POWs in World War II. Despite ever growing threats and sanctions by his German captors, he escaped time and again. For Bushell, escape was a matter of personal honour and patriotic duty. And required rare nerve. He was the principal organizer of the breakout from Stalag Luft III in 1944, the event on which the film The Great Escape *is based. This account of Bushell's escaping career begins with his shooting down over Dunkirk in 1940.*

The first place to which they took him was Dulag Luft, a transit camp for aircrew prisoners near Frankfurt. After a period of solitary confinement, Bushell made a survey of the camp. In the playing field, and just outside the compound wiring, there was a goat in a kennel. If a hole were dug in the floor of the kennel and a trapdoor fitted to support the goat, a man could remain concealed from the sentries and stay outside the compound as the prisoners returned from the playing field after exercise. The hole was dug by relays of prisoners hiding in the kennel one by one, the sand being taken away in vessels used for feeding the goat. If the guards had counted the number of times the goat was fed their suspicions would have been aroused, but they did not. Bushell planned to hide in the kennel on the evening before a separate tunnel escape involving a number of prisoners; to climb the single wire surrounding the sports field as soon as it was dark, and thus to confuse his pursuers with the twenty-four hours' start over the tunnelers.

On the prospect of staying in the kennel until dark, someone asked him, "What about the smell?" and Bushell replied, "Oh, the goat won't mind that."

It was an easy matter to falsify the roll call, and he got away smoothly. With his fluency in German and experience of the winter sports areas he set course for Switzerland, travelling by day in a civilian suit bought from one of the guards at Dulag Luft. He was able to engage safely in brief conversations, and navigating with the aid of guide books purchased from shops along the way he went to Tuttlingen by express train, and from there to Bonndorf by suburban line. His plan to throw the Germans at Dulag Luft off the scent was entirely successful, for none of the eighteen men who escaped by tunnel got farther than Hanover before being arrested, by which time he had out-distanced the radius of search.

From Bonndorf Bushell reached on foot the point he was making for, a few kilometres from the Swiss border. Things had gone almost too well and, being aware of his habitual over-confidence, he sat down for two hours and made himself generate caution for the last decisive stage. He had the alternatives of waiting for nightfall, with all its problems, or of bluffing it out by daylight. He chose the latter.

In the border village of Stühlingen he was halted by a guard. Pretending to be a drunken but amiable ski-ing instructor, Bushell was being conducted towards a check-point for an examination of his papers when he broke loose and bolted, dodging bullets, into a side street. The side street proved to be a cul-de-sac and he was run to earth within a minute. The officer to whom he was taken turned out to be a German he had known in his ski-ing days, and Bushell ventured to suggest that for old time's sake he be set free with a ten minutes' start. For once his persuasive charm had no effect, meeting only with a stony, Teutonic refusal.

Bushell served a punitive sentence in a Frankfurt goal, intended to soften his morale; but he was made of firmer stuff and on being moved to Barth, near the Baltic coast, he escaped again with a Polish officer.

The two men separated, and Bushell was stumbling along a road near the concentration camp at Auschwitz on a dark night when he blundered into a sentry he had not seen, knocking him to the ground. With an instinctive courtesy he helped the soldier to his feet, handed him his rifle and said, "Sorry!" The game was up once again.

It was decided to move this troublesome officer to a new camp, and he was herded into a cattle truck with several other prisoners and taken from Lübeck to Warburg. What pleasures awaited him there Bushell did not stay to see, and with five others prised open the truck's floorboards and dropped on to the track as the train was moving. One of the prisoners dropped on to the rail and lost both legs as a truck rolled over him.

With a Czech named Zafouk, Bushell reached Czechoslovakia where the Resistance boarded them with a courageous family in Prague. Bushell appreciated this limited freedom and would dress in civilian clothes and take daily walks around the city while waiting for the Resistance to complete arrangements for his transfer to Yugoslavia. But the assassination of the tyrant Heydrich activated a house-to-house search for students suspected of the crime. At the time, Bushell happened to be in a cinema with the daughter of the household where he was staying, and the audience was ordered to file out for a check on identity cards. As Bushell could not speak the language, his girl companion did the talking, but he was suspected and sent to a Gestapo prison in Berlin.

Bushell's cell was one of a number on either side of a corridor, and when they had locked his door and withdrawn he put his face to the grill and asked softly: "Is anyone here British?" A voice four cells away in the direction of the latrines replied, "Yes, Flight-Lieutenant Marshall, RAF."

Marshall, who had known Bushell before the war, was also an escaper and had been captured in the same cinema and at the same time. Conversation between the two was restricted to furtive whisperings of a few seconds' duration whenever Bushell passed Marshall's cell. It took several days for Bushell to explain that he was refusing to admit his identity for fear of repercussions on the Prague family, which would be telling the same story as his. He was tormented by the thought of what would happen to them. One evening he whispered that he had left a note in the lavatory. When Marshall found it tucked behind the cistern it contained Bushell's service number, rank and full name. "They are going to shoot me," it stated; "Please pass full particulars to the Red Cross."

But Bushell learned that the Prague family had been executed and he admitted his identity. Until he did so he had consciously forfeited his right to protection by the Geneva Convention. Again a bona fide prisoner-of-war, he was sent to Stalag Luft III at the end of 1942, and it was here that he received his ultimatum: if he ever escaped again he would be shot.

Stalag Luft III, the large prison camp at Sagan, eighty miles east of Berlin, was a good camp and had only been opened the previous spring. The north compound to which Bushell was committed could almost have been a luxury camp; it held a thousand prisoners, was spacious and boasted private kitchens and washrooms with every barrack. There were excellent facilities for entertainment, and the commandant, Baron Von Lindeiner, hoped the British prisoners would enjoy their stay and even wish to remain in Germany after the war. His prisoners regretted that they had no desire to stay in Germany, war or no war, and bent their entire energies – diverted every useful item of food or material, subverted every sport or educational group, directed every imaginative talent – towards the predominant objective of escape.

The commandant and the senior British officer at Sagan both advised Bushell to take no further chances. "I can't possibly stay here for long," he replied; "the winters are terrible." But first he had a spell in "The Cooler", the camp gaol, to undergo.

"The Cooler" was so overcrowded with delinquent prisoners that those assigned to it had to wait their turn until a cell was available. When Bushell was called he again found himself a few cells away from Marshall, and while the guards were not paying much attention they resumed their discussion. Bushell was obsessed by the prospect of being mysteriously liquidated, or of the circumstances surrounding his death being mis-represented. He was less afraid of dying, though he cherished life, than of being shot in cold blood on a false pretext such as resisting arrest, a thing he was far too sensible to do. "If anything goes wrong," he told Marshall, "you'll know what to think." He gave Marshall names and addresses of people to be informed in such an event.

Upon his release from "The Cooler" Bushell flung himself

with such intensity into the theory and practice of escape that, after playing minor roles in several escape bids, he rose rapidly through posts of ascending seniority in the Escape Organisation to Intelligence Officer, and finally to its top position – Chief Executive or "Big X" of the North Compound. He studied case histories and learned from past mistakes; organised departments to take care of clothing, forged documents, rations, logistics, engineering and security, presiding over his cabinet like a prime minister. His nimble brain cut through to essentials quickly. Three tunnels were to be constructed, and they were to be of such refinement that discovery of any one would lead to the belief that it must be the only one. To avoid danger of a security leak the word "tunnel" was banned from all discussion. They were to be called "Tom", "Dick" and "Harry".

As "Big X" Bushell introduced a new and important concept – that of collectivism, the abandonment of unco-ordinated private enterprise and concentration on a highly efficient and centralised organisation. As a corollary, there were to be no more inflexible timetables, and if for any reason the guards' (or "ferrets") suspicions were aroused, all work was to cease immediately and not to be resumed until the security department gave the all-clear.

New arrivals at the compound were always impressed by their first encounter with Bushell, when he grilled them on what they had seen of the local area. His rather sinister appearance, with the gash over one eye, his forceful personality and well-developed powers of interrogation lent an awe-inspiring quality to the grim and clandestine surroundings of an improvised headquarters.

His intensity of purpose partially concealed a gentleness that was very real. "Goon baiting" – playing practical jokes on the guards and undermining their morale – was an understood responsibility of the prisoner, not just a game. Despite his mastery of the art, Bushell sometimes expressed a compulsive remorse. "It's not really fair," he would say, "some of these poor bastards are so simple they haven't a chance."

"Tom" was discovered by sentries, and "Dick" was then used solely as a repository for sand as work proceeded with "Harry", now the only chance. Food and escape equipment was provided by the organisation for over two hundred escapers, considered the most optimistic estimate of the number which would get through the tunnel before it was discovered. If everything worked perfectly it would be possible for one man to go through every two minutes, making a total of two hundred and fifty during the eight hours of darkness. Long experience had taught, however, that there would always be hitches beyond the planners' control.

"Harry" was a miracle of planning and improvisation. With a length of 336 feet, 28 feet deep at the entrance in the north compound and 20 feet high at the exit among trees outside the double electrified wiring, it was furnished with electric lighting, manually operated air conditioning and relays of trolleys connecting three "half-way houses" to carry prone escapers singly to the far end. "Harry" had taken two hundred and fifty men working full time a year to dispose of the sand it displaced. A highly co-ordinated teamwork was devised to despatch the maximum number of men in the minimum time. Except for about forty priorities who were thought to have the best chance of reaching England, each man on the escape list got there by drawing from a hat. He had his belongings checked by the inspection committee to obviate jamming in the tunnel through the carrying of excessively bulky packages, was given an allotted time to arrive at Hut 104, which housed the entrance, and was thoroughly indoctrinated in his drill.

The organisation fixed the night of 24th March 1944 as the one for the break-out, twelve months after the commencement of work on "Tom", "Dick" and "Harry". Every known factor had been weighed: the weather would be suitable for travellers on foot ("walkers"); there would be no moon; a strong wind would disturb the adjacent pine forest and drown any sounds made by leaving the tunnel.

From mid-day the engineers finished off final details, connecting wiring and installing extra lights, while the forgery department filled in dates on the forged papers. A little after nine o'clock two engineers went to open the exit. Every man was in his place, and zero hour was nine-thirty. Then there occurred a train of mishaps: there was a delay in opening the shaft, and not until ten o'clock did those waiting down the shaft feel the gust of cool air which told them the surface had been broken. Word was then passed back that the exit, contrary to plan, was several yards short of the trees. As the papers were all date-stamped Bushell decided that the escape must continue, and hurriedly conferred with his colleagues on the escape committee to work out a revised method of control at the exit, necessary to avoid detection by the guards in their look-out posts. As the escapers moved forward on their trollies, further delays were caused by those who had broken the baggage regulations and got stuck in the tunnel with the bulkiness of their suitcases. The rate of departure dropped from two to twelve minutes per man. To add to these complications, an unexpected air raid on Berlin caused the camp electricity to be switched off, and with it the tunnel lighting. Over half an hour was lost as margarine lamps were substituted.

Bushell was noticed to be calm but more thoughtful than usual. Dressed as a businessman he had teamed up with Lieutenant Scheidhauer of the Free French Air Force, with whom he planned to travel by train to Alsace. Both were on the priority list and were among the first to leave. As the delays multiplied Bushell, in smart civilian suit and converted service overcoat, with astrakhan collar and felt hat, an efficient-looking briefcase in his hand, glanced at his watch and called down the shaft: "Tell those devils to get a move on; I've got a train to catch."

Bushell and Scheidhauer caught their train at Sagan station. Two days later, during the most extensive search the Reich had ever been forced to mount for escaped prisoners of war, they were recaptured at Saarbruecken railway station by security policeman and taken to Lerchesflur gaol. There they were interrogated by the Kriminal-polizei and admitted being escapers from Stalag Luft III.

When he learned of the escape, Hitler was incensed; he was angered at the tying-up of German resources in a time of great national stress and particularly afraid of an uprising among the foreign workers. At a stormy meeting with Goering, Himmler and Keitel, he gave instructions for the prisoners to be shot.

On orders received by teleprinter from Gestapo headquarters in Berlin, Bushell and Scheidhauer were handcuffed behind their backs and driven in a car along the autobahn leading to

Kaiserslauten. The car was stopped after a few miles, the handcuffs removed, and the prisoners allowed to get out and relieve themselves. They must have known what was coming. Both were shot in the back, Scheidhauer dying instantly, Bushell after a few minutes. It was 28th March 1944.

Seventy-six prisoners escaped through the tunnel. Three made "home runs", the rest were recaptured. Of these, the Gestapo shot fifty.

OMDURMAN

Winston S. Churchill

At Omdurman, fought on 2 September 1898, the British crushed the Sudanese separatists of the "Mahdi". Some 20,000 Mahdi died; British losses were 500. The battle was not quite the "piece of cake" the figures suggest, as Churchill's account of the charge by the 21st Lancers (in which he served as subaltern) makes plain.

I took six men and a corporal. We trotted fast over the plain and soon began to breast the unknown slopes of the ridge. There is nothing like the dawn. The quarter of an hour before the curtain is lifted upon an unknowable situation is an intense experience of war. Was the ridge held by the enemy or not? Were we riding through the gloom into thousands of ferocious savages? Every step might be deadly; yet there was no time for over-much precaution. The regiment was coming on behind us, and dawn was breaking. It was already half light as we climbed the slope. What should we find at the summit? For cool, tense excitement I commend such moments.

Now we are near the top of the ridge. I make one man follow a hundred yards behind, so that whatever happens, he may tell the tale. There is no sound but our own clatter. We have reached the crest line. We rein in our horses. Every minute the horizon extends; we can already see 200 yards. Now we can see perhaps a quarter of a mile. All is quiet; no life but our own breathes among the rocks and sand hummocks of the ridge. No ambuscade, no occupation in force! The farther plain is bare below us: we can now see more than half a mile.

So they have all decamped! Just what we said! All bolted off to Kordofan; no battle! But wait! The dawn is growing fast. Veil after veil is lifted from the landscape. What is this shimmering in the distant plain? Nay – it is lighter now – what are these dark markings beneath the shimmer? *They are there!* These enormous black smears are thousands of men; the shimmering is the glinting of their weapons. It is now daylight. I slip off my horse; I write in my field service notebook, "The Dervish army is still in position a mile and a half south-west of Jebel Surgham." I send this message by the corporal direct as ordered to the Commander-in-Chief. I mark it XXX. In the words of the drill book "with all despatch", or as one would say, "Hell for leather."

A glorious sunrise is taking place behind us; but we are admiring something else. It is already light enough to use field-glasses. The dark masses are changing their values. They are already becoming lighter than the plain; they are fawn-coloured. Now they are a kind of white, while the plain is dun. In front of us is a vast array four or five miles long. It fills the horizon till it is blocked out on our right by the serrated silhouette of Surgham Peak. This is an hour to live. We mount again, and suddenly new impressions strike the eye and mind. These masses are not stationary. They are advancing, and they are advancing fast. A tide is coming in. But what is this sound which we hear: a deadened roar coming up to us in waves? They are cheering for God, his Prophet and his holy Khalifa. They think they are going to win. We shall see about that presently. Still I must admit that we check our horses and hang upon the crest of the ridge for a few moments before advancing down its slopes.

But now it is broad morning and the slanting sun adds brilliant colour to the scene. The masses have defined themselves into swarms of men, in ordered ranks bright with glittering weapons, and above them dance a multitude of gorgeous flags. We see for ourselves what the Crusaders saw . . . From where we sat on our horses we could see both sides. There was our army ranked and massed by the river. There were the gunboats lying expectant in the stream. There were all the batteries ready to open. And meanwhile on the other side, this large oblong gay-coloured crowd in fairly good order climbed swiftly up to the crest of exposure. We were about 2,500 yards from our own batteries, but little more than 200 from their approaching target. I called these Dervishes "The White Flags". They reminded me of the armies in the Bayeux tapestries, because of their rows of white and yellow standards held upright. Meanwhile the Dervish centre far out in the plain had come within range, and one after another the British and Egyptian batteries opened upon it. My eyes were riveted by a nearer scene. At the top of the hill "The White Flags" paused to rearrange their ranks and drew out a broad and solid parade along the crest. Then the cannonade turned upon them. Two or three batteries and all the gunboats, at least thirty guns, opened an intense fire. Their shells shrieked towards us and burst in scores over the heads and among the masses of the White Flagmen. We were so close, as we sat spellbound on our horses, that we almost shared their perils. I saw the full blast of Death strike this human wall. Down went their standards by dozens and their men by hundreds. Wide gaps and shapeless heaps appeared in their array. One saw them jumping and tumbling under the shrapnel bursts; but none turned back. Line after line they all streamed over the shoulder and advanced towards our zeriba, opening a heavy rifle fire which wreathed them in smoke.

Hitherto no one had taken any notice of us; but I now saw Baggara horsemen in twos and threes riding across the plain on our left towards the ridge. One of these patrols of three men came within pistol range. They were dark, cowled figures, like monks on horseback – ugly, sinister brutes with long spears. I fired a few shots at them from the saddle, and they sheered off. I did not see why we should not stop out on this ridge during the assault. I thought we could edge back towards the Nile and so watch both sides while keeping out of harm's way. But now arrived a positive order from Major Finn saying "Come back at once into the zeriba as the infantry are about to open fire." We should in fact have been safer on the ridge, for we only just got into the infantry lines before the rifle-storm began . . .

As soon as the fire began to slacken and it was said on all sides that the attack had been repulsed, a General arrived with his staff at a gallop with instant orders to mount and advance. In two minutes the four squadrons were mounted and trotting out of the zeriba in a southerly direction. We ascended again the slopes of Jebel Surgham which had played its part in the first stages of the action, and from its ridges soon saw before us the whole plain of Omdurman with the vast mud city, its minarets and domes, spread before us six or seven miles away. After various halts and reconnoitrings we found ourselves walking forward in what is called "column of troops". There are four troops in a squadron and four squadrons in a regiment. Each of these troops now followed the other. I commanded the second troop from the rear, comprising between twenty and twenty-five Lancers.

Everyone expected that we were going to make a charge. That was the one idea that had been in all minds since we had started from Cairo. Of course there would be a charge. In those days, before the Boer War, British cavalry had been taught little else. Here was clearly the occasion for a charge. But against what body of enemy, over what ground, in which direction or with what purpose, were matters hidden from the rank and file. We continued to pace forward over the hard sand, peering into the mirage-twisted plain in a high state of suppressed excitement. Presently I noticed, 300 yards away on our flank and parallel to the line on which we were advancing, a long row of blue-black objects, two or three yards apart. I thought there were about a hundred and fifty. Then I became sure that these were men – enemy men – squatting on the ground. Almost at the same moment the trumpet sounded "Trot", and the whole long column of cavalry began to jingle and clatter across the front of these crouching figures. We were in the lull of the battle and there was perfect silence. Forthwith from every blue-black blob came a white puff of smoke, and a loud volley of musketry broke the odd stillness. Such a target at such a distance could scarcely be missed, and all along the column here and there horses bounded and a few men fell.

The intentions of our Colonel had no doubt been to move round the flank of the body of Dervishes he had now located, and who, concealed in a fold of the ground behind their rifle-men, were invisible to us, and then to attack them from a more advantageous quarter; but once the fire was opened and losses began to grow, he must have judged it inexpedient to prolong his procession across the open plain. The trumpet sounded

"Right wheel into line", and all the sixteen troops swung round towards the blue-black riflemen. Almost immediately the regiment broke into a gallop, and the 21st Lancers were committed to their first charge in war!

I propose to describe exactly what happened to me: what I saw and what I felt. The troop I commanded was, when we wheeled into line, the second from the right of the regiment. I was riding a handy, sure-footed, grey Arab polo pony. Before we wheeled and began to gallop, the officers had been marching with drawn swords. On account of my shoulder I had always decided that if I were involved in hand-to-hand fighting, I must use a pistol and not a sword. I had purchased in London a Mauser automatic pistol, then the newest and latest design. I had practised carefully with this during our march and journey up the river. This then was the weapon with which I determined to fight. I had first of all to return my sword into its scabbard, which is not the easiest thing to do at a gallop. I had then to draw my pistol from its wooden holster and bring it to full cock. This dual operation took an appreciable time, and until it was finished, apart from a few glances to my left to see what effect the fire was producing, I did not look up at the general scene.

Then I saw immediately before me, and now only half the length of a polo ground away, the row of crouching blue figures firing frantically, wreathed in white smoke. On my right and left my neighbouring troop leaders made a good line. Immediately behind was a long dancing row of lances couched for the charge. We were going at a fast but steady gallop. There was too much trampling and rifle fire to hear any bullets. After this glance to the right and left and at my troop, I looked again towards the enemy. The scene appeared to be suddenly transformed. The blue-black men were still firing, but behind them there now came into view a depression like a shallow sunken road. This was crowded and crammed with men rising up from the ground where they had hidden. Bright flags appeared as if by magic, and I saw arriving from nowhere Emirs on horseback among and around the mass of the enemy. The Dervishes appeared to be ten or twelve deep at the thickest, a great grey mass gleaming with steel, filling the dry watercourse. In the same twinkling of an eye I saw also that our right overlapped their left, that my troop would just strike the edge of their array, and that the troop on my right would charge into air. My subaltern comrade on the right, Wormald of the 7th Hussars, could see the situation too; and we both increased our speed to the very fastest gallop and curved inwards like the horns of the moon. One really had not time to be frightened or to think of anything else but these particular necessary actions which I have described. They completely occupied mind and senses.

The collision was now very near. I saw immediately before me, not ten yards away, the two blue men who lay in my path. They were perhaps a couple of yards apart. I rode at the interval between them. They both fired. I passed through the smoke conscious that I was unhurt. The trooper immediately behind me was killed at this place and at this moment, whether by these shots or not I do not know. I checked my pony as the ground began to fall away beneath his feet. The clever animal dropped like a cat four or five feet down on the sandy bed of the watercourse, and in this sandy bed I found myself surrounded by what seemed to be dozens of men. They were not thickly packed enough at this point for me to experience any actual collision with them. Whereas Grenfell's troop next but one on my left was brought to a complete standstill and suffered very heavy losses, we seemed to push our way through as one has sometimes seen mounted policemen break up a crowd. In less time than it takes to relate, my pony had scrambled up the other side of the ditch. I looked round.

Once again I was on the hard, crisp desert, my horse at a trot. I had the impression of scattered Dervishes running to and fro in all directions. Straight before me a man threw himself on the ground. The reader must remember that I had been trained as a cavalry soldier to believe that if ever cavalry broke into a mass of infantry, the latter would be at their mercy. My first idea therefore was that the man was terrified. But simultaneously I saw the gleam of his curved sword as he drew it back for a ham-stringing cut. I had room and time enough to turn my pony out of his reach, and leaning over on the off side I fired two shots into him at about three yards. As I straightened myself in the saddle, I saw before me another figure with uplifted sword. I raised my pistol and fired. So close were we that the pistol itself actually struck him. Man and sword disappeared below and behind me. On my left, ten yards away, was an Arab horseman in a bright-coloured tunic and steel helmet, with chain-mail hangings. I fired at him. He turned aside. I pulled my horse into a walk and looked around again . . . There was a mass of Dervishes about forty or fifty yards away on my left. They were huddling and clumping themselves together, rallying for mutual protection. They seemed wild with excitement, dancing about on their feet, shaking their spears up and down. The whole scene seemed to flicker. I have an impression, but it is too fleeting to define, of brown-clad Lancers mixed up here and there with this surging mob. The scattered individuals in my immediate neighbourhood made no attempt to molest me. Where was my troop? Where were the other troops of the squadron? Within a hundred yards of me I could not see a single officer or man. I looked back at the Dervish mass. I saw two or three riflemen crouching and aiming their rifles at me from the fringe of it. Then for the first time that morning I experienced a sudden sensation of fear. I felt myself absolutely alone. I thought these riflemen would hit me and the rest devour me like wolves. What a fool I was to loiter like this in the midst of the enemy! I crouched over the saddle, spurred my horse into a gallop and drew clear of the *mêlée*. Two or three hundred yards away I found my troop all ready faced about and partly formed up.

SPARTACUS

James Chambers

Spartacus is surely the most famous freedom fighter of the Ancient World. He led the slaves of Rome in revolt, he bested armies of legionaries, and even when he had the chance to escape entrapment he remained with his men.

O ne of the abhorrent domestic benefits of Roman imperialism was an inexhaustible supply of slaves. In the cities family servants, particularly educated Greeks, were often valued members of their households, but the easily replaceable prisoners who laboured in gangs on the country estates were on the whole treated no better than the animals and, in spite of their enormous numbers, the Romans did not even regard them as a threat to internal security: when Asian slaves rebelled in Sicily, they were so disorganized that they were soon suppressed.

In 73 BC, however, seventy-four gladiators, who had been trained to a peak of excellence in the art of killing each other for their masters' entertainment, broke into the armoury of their training camp in Capua, stole all the weapons and fled to take refuge on the summit of Mount Vesuvius. When thousands of slaves from the neighbouring estates escaped to join the revolt, the praetor Caius Claudius Glaber marched south with a legion and confidently began to surround Vesuvius. But these rebels were not the wretched and servile products of eastern slave markets, they were Thracian, Gallic and Teutonic prisoners of war, organized and instructed by formidable gladiators and led by an instinctive military commander – a Thracian gladiator called Spartacus, who had once served as an unwilling conscript in the Roman army and had been enslaved for desertion. One by one the Roman units were cut to pieces and by the end of the year the whole of southern Italy was under the control of an army of slaves.

In the following spring the consuls Lucius Gellius Publicola and Gnaius Lentulus Clodianus took the field with two legions each. The rebel army, which had been swollen to nearly 100,000 strong by the slave population of southern Italy, was divided into two corps, one commanded by Spartacus and the other by a Gallic gladiator called Crixus. Crixus was carried away by the temptations of easy plunder; exposing themselves to the inevitable attack of a Roman army, his men roamed aimlessly from town to town until they were isolated and annihilated by Gellius at Monte Gargano. But Spartacus was not interested in plunder or vengeance; his only objective was the freedom of his followers and, knowing that they could not survive in Italy for ever, he decided to lead them north to the Alps, where they could split up and escape over the mountains to their homes. As they marched north with more slaves joining them every day, Gellius followed and Lentulus raced past to intercept them. The destruction of Crixus had been no more than the Romans had expected and what followed was as terrifying as it was incredible. In Picenum Spartacus halted his slaves, fell on the following legions of Gellius and then turned to attack the army of Lentulus a few days later. Both the consuls were crushingly defeated and half their soldiers were killed.

The last army that stood between the slaves and freedom was the army of Caius Cassius, proconsul of Cisalpine Gaul, and when that too was defeated the roads through the mountains lay open. But by then their own success had convinced the slaves that, once they scattered, the humiliated Romans would track them down relentlessly. Believing that so long as they remained united they could always defeat a Roman army, they decided instead to return to the south and take over Sicily for themselves with the support of the Sicilian slaves and eastern pirates. It was a suicidal ambition: the slaves could never hope to hold the island against a republic that was capable of conquering Spain and most of the Middle East. Nevertheless, although his own chance of freedom was as good as it would ever be, Spartacus would not desert them and he led them south again.

The Romans were the masters of the Mediterranean, but their homeland seemed to be as vulnerable as it had been in the days of Hannibal and, already demoralized by political unrest and the first violent tremors of civil war, they began to blame their self-seeking leaders and demanded that soldiers be recalled from the outposts of the empire. When the rebels reached Rhegium, in the toe of Italy, Roman ships prevented them from crossing into Sicily and the praetor Marcus Licinius Crassus came up behind them with no less than eight legions. Hoping to contain the rebels until they starved, Crassus built a wall from coast to coast across the peninsula, but in spite of the size of his army it was ridiculous to imagine that he could hold all thirty-seven miles of the wall at once. Spartacus broke through and headed east to escape out of Italy from the port of Brundisium, in the heel. Before he reached it, however, it was occupied by Marcus Lucullus, who had sailed across with an army from the Black Sea. There was now no alternative but to return to the Alps. Yet the slaves were still so confident that two dissident groups, led by the Gallic gladiators Castus and Cannicus, began to make bandit raids as Crixus had done, and Spartacus lost valuable men extricating them from Roman ambushes until they were finally cut to pieces by Crassus.

Spartacus's army no longer had numerical superiority and at last the full military might of the Roman republic was closing in on him. Lucullus was behind him, Crassus was somewhere on his left flank and ahead of him Gnaeus Pompeius (Pompey), who had just returned in glory from Spain, was marching south from Rome. There was little left to do but hide in the mountains, but the slaves were eager to attack Crassus before Pompey arrived and once again Spartacus gave in to them. He knew that their chance of victory was slight, yet so now was any hope of freedom, and a glorious death was better than slavery or torture. Before the battle he rode out in front of his army and killed his horse so that he would have no means of escape. "If I am victorious," he said, "I shall easily get another, and if vanquished I shall not need one." By the time Pompey reached him, Crassus had already defeated the rebels and the body of

Spartacus had been found in the middle of the field, covered in wounds on a pile of slaughtered Romans.

Along the roadside from Rome to Capua, 6,000 prisoners were crucified in hideous vengeance. A catastrophe had been averted and when the two victorious commanders returned the jubilant citizens elected them consuls. To the Romans, Spartacus was the dangerous bandit who had threatened their republic with revolution when it was already weakened by political rivalries, and it was not until their empire had fallen that he was remembered as a hero. All he had ever wanted was freedom and to that end he had defied the most powerful nation in the world, dominated southern Italy as Hannibal had done and defeated three Roman armies in open battle. It had taken more than a dozen legions to destroy him and his downfall had been due at least in part to the aimless indecision of the desperate fugitives whom he refused to desert.

ORDINARY HEROES

Richard Jerome, Susan Schindette, Nick Charles and Thomas Fields-Meyer

A roll call of "everyday" heroes compiled by People *magazine, America, in 1999.*

There are many kinds of heroes in the world. There are the epic figures whose bold deeds alter the course of humanity. There are those who thrill us with their unique talents or who inspire us with lives of exceptional purpose and character. And there is a special category, one that never ceases to intrigue us, made up of people whose heroism crystallizes in a single moment of selflessness – who tempt fate for the sake of others. These are just the people you'd want around when the going gets tough. What sets them apart? Hard to say, observes Temple University psychology Prof. Frank Farley, who has made a study of heroism: "Often they have shown some propensity to take risks in the past. The big moment comes along, and they are ready for it. But I wish I understood them better, because we need much more of this kind of heroism." One thing we do understand, however, is that their selflessness seems to them to be entirely uncomplicated. Asked where he found the courage to race into a burning house in Wichita, Kans., to save six children (see below), Willie Gantt says simply, "I didn't think about it being dangerous until after. If somebody needs help, I help. It's the way I was raised."

* * *

In the following pages we tell the stories of Gantt and others who became heroes when the moment presented itself – ordinary people, to all outward appearances, who risked their lives or their safety to help neighbors, friends and strangers in peril. Some of those they rescued weren't even human, suggesting that, sometimes at least, man is dog's best friend. And some we honor are those of whom heroism is more routinely expected – firemen, for example, and police officers – yet who went beyond duty's call in moments of terrible stress.

Out of the Ordinary? They're just regular folks – except that in the face of danger or dire need they put themselves in harm's way to help others

CROSSING GUARD JILL COOK, 66
Taking a hit to save a child

As usual, Jill Cook's post at North Crystal Lake Drive and Lowry Avenue in Lakeland, Fla., was busy on the morning of Aug. 16. With Cook's guidance, 7-year-old Amber Stringer had just stepped onto the curb, with her big brother Tony, 10, lagging close behind. But before he could reach the safety of the sidewalk, a pickup truck, out of nowhere, came speeding toward him. Instinctively, Cook pushed Tony out of the way. But she had no time to save herself, and the truck struck her with terrible force. "She flew up, landed on the hood, hit the windshield, and when the truck stopped it threw her off," says Christine Stringer, Amber and Tony's mother, who saw what happened from her nearby backyard and rushed to Cook's side. "I thought she was dead." Cook remained conscious but recalls little of the impact. "The only thought I had was, 'Are the kids okay?'" she says. The pain was excruciating, and small wonder. She'd broken her pelvis, right knee, hip, tibia and fibula and five ribs. (Police say driver Chester Lepriol, 28, was doing about 46 mph in a 15-mph zone; charged with criminal reckless driving, he pleaded not guilty.) A retired nurse and widowed mother of six, Cook is staying with her daughter Jennifer, also a nurse, and faces months of rehab. "She may have a limp, but all her fractures should heal," says her surgeon Dr George Letson.

The grateful Stringers visit Cook often. "There's a special bond," says Christine, 34. Adds Amber. "I love her very much." Cook downplays her heroism and hopes her story serves as a lesson. "That's my whole goal – for people to be more cautious," she says. "Obey those flashing lights. Don't put on makeup while driving. Don't read the newspaper. Please be careful."

STEELWORKERS IN ILLINOIS
Braving a fiery wreck, they pull victims out alive

Just before 10 p.m. on March 15, the Birmingham Steel plant in Bourbonnais, Ill., shook with a deep rumble. No one on the night shift seemed concerned; steel mills often reverberate with "wet charges" – explosions set off as chunks of scrap metal, moist from sitting outdoors, strike the furnace where they're melted down. But this time was different. Crane operator Mark Lapinsky peered outside the plant grounds and to his horror saw a jumble of railroad cars engulfed in fire and smoke. He sprinted to the shipping office.

"Amtrak wreck! Call 911!" he screamed, then ran through the plant summoning coworkers. Heading south from Chicago with 216 people aboard, the train, the City of New Orleans, had collided at a crossing with a truck carrying 18 tons of steel. Driver John Stokes, 58, escaped with cuts and bruises, but 11 people on the train died and 116 were injured. (The cause of the crash remains under investigation.) Terrible as the toll was, it would have been worse but for Lapinsky and 34 fellow steelworkers. "They were the major heroes," says Bourbonnais Fire Chief Mike Harshbarger. "They were there first, willing to wade into the mess."

When Lapinsky reached the crash site, 100 yards from the mill, he found people crawling out of a ditch, drenched in water and blood. "Out comes a crew member holding a little girl," he recalls. "He hands her to me and tells me to get help. I look down, and her left foot is missing." Lapinsky wrapped her wound in his jacket until he spied a nurse. (Though the girl, Ashley Bonnin, 8, of Nesbit, Miss., survived, her mother, June, 46, was killed, along with a cousin and two friends, all between the ages of 8 and 11.) Crane operator Dale Winkel, 41, and shipping clerk Joe Brown, 29, joined Lapinsky in pulling out survivors as fire spread through the wreckage. At one point, passenger Greg Herman, 40, of Memphis crawled out, handed off Kristen, his 8-year-old daughter, then raced back to the sleeping car where his wife, Lisa, 39, and their other children, Kaitlin, 5, and David, 3, remained. Lapinsky, Brown and Winkel intercepted him. "One of them said, 'You can't go in there,'" Herman recalls. "I grabbed him and said, 'My wife and kids are in there.' He said, 'Let's go.'" The steelworkers crawled in and got out Herman's family, all of whom suffered only minor injuries. "They wouldn't be alive today if it weren't for them," Herman says of the steel men.

Moments later, the plant's night supervisor Bob Curwick, 39, and millwright Jack Casey, 41, entered the dining car to find Susan Falls, her right leg crushed by debris. Falls told them her husband, John, and their 19-year-old daughter Jennifer were somewhere inside. At the time of the crash, the family had been eating cheesecake. Afterward, Falls, 46, called out their names but heard nothing. "I'm not going to make it," she told Curwick and Casey. "If you're going to die, I'm going to die with you," Curwick replied. "And I'm too ornery to die." John, 56, had escaped on his own, and after searching the car, Curwick was startled when a hand reached out from a pile of tables and chairs and grabbed his ankle. It was Jennifer, who has Down's syndrome, immobilized by fractures of the ribs and spine. Curwick and Casey stayed with mother and daughter as the flames drew closer and firefighters cleared debris. Finally a hose appeared, and water came pouring in ("The sweetest sound I ever heard," says Casey).

On the scene until 3:30 a.m., the steelworkers took the next day off. When they returned, they met with counselors and talked of their trauma – especially the lives they couldn't save. "There were a bunch of tough guys in there," says Casey. "But there were plenty of tears."

SECURITY TECHNICIAN GUY BURNETT, 27
He rescues two trapped babies from a roadside canal

Last June 13 was a brilliant Sunday in South Florida, and Claudia Cox, in the backseat of a friend's Mitsubishi, was going from Miami to Naples to visit her boyfriend Otasha Barrett with their year-old twin daughters, Kendia and Kenisha, strapped into car seats beside her. Heading west through the Everglades on I-75, Cox, 23, a hospital lab assistant, was singing gospel tunes with her cousin Simone Hyatt, who was sitting in front with driver Tashana Brown. But just after 3 p.m. a front tire blew, and the car crashed through a fence, flipping over and landing upside down in an alligator-infested canal. "All I could think was 'I'm going to die,'" says Cox. "Then I thought, 'Please, God, don't let anything happen to my babies.'"

The answer to her prayers was Guy Burnett, who had been just minutes behind Cox, driving with his wife and two children. Burnett pulled over and saw that all three women were out of the car, but that Cox was standing in the water screaming, "My babies!" Then a serviceman for a security firm, Burnett dove into the murky canal and tried vainly to open the car doors. "It was like pea soup," he recalls. "I wouldn't have seen my hand if I'd held it in front of my face." Finally, finding an open window, he unlocked a door and freed Kenisha from her car seat and brought her to safety. That's when he heard Cox screaming, "There's two of them!" Diving back in, he found Kendia and brought her to the surface. But it seemed too late. "She was like a rag doll," Burnett says. Cox's friend Brown, a flight attendant with first aid training, began administering CPR. Then Burnett, who learned the technique as a lifeguard in high school, took over. "C'mon, baby, breathe!" he exhorted. After a couple of minutes, Kendia whimpered. "That progressed to a good cry," he says. "It was like music to my ears."

GIRL SCOUT KORTNEY CAMPBELL, 13
A tough cookie pulls a pit bull off her little brother

Max the pit bull had never caused any trouble. Or so his owners assured their wary friends, the Campbells, and three other Phoenix-area families when they brought their pet along for a summer camping trip last year. But as soon as they chained him to a pine tree at a campsite 40 miles south of the Grand Canyon, the dog grew agitated, then vicious. He leaped at one child, knocking off his glasses, then he went after 6-year-old Rusty Campbell, knocking him to the ground and biting his face. Blood gushed from the wound as the boy lay screaming, and Max seemed ready to move in for a second attack.

Sizing up the danger in an instant, Kortney sprang into action. She grabbed the dog's chain and, with a mighty yank, pulled the animal away. ("I don't usually freeze up when something bad happens," she says.) Grabbing Rusty, their mother, Jennifer, 30, was shocked to see that his nose was gone. Her husband, Luther, 41, shot Max dead, then drove their son to a nearby motel and called 911. As paramedics rushed Rusty to a hospital, Luther sped back to search for the nose. "It's a miracle I found it," he says. "It was rolled up in some pine needles." Doctors reattached it, and after reconstructive surgery it appears almost normal. "She really protected me." Rusty says of his sister. Awarded the Girl Scouts bronze cross for valor last June, Kortney – an A student who plays basketball and runs track at her elementary school – was asked if the incident made her feel any closer to her little brother. "Yeah," she said with a grudging smile, every bit the big sister. "Sometimes."

COLLEGE STUDENT BARRETT BABER, 19
At a crash site inferno, his cool action saves lives

On the night of June 1, Barrett Baber, a sophomore at Ouachita Baptist University in Arkansas, had settled back in his seat on American Airlines Flight 1420, eagerly awaiting his arrival home in Little Rock after a two-week tour of Germany performing with 24 other members of his college choir. But as the plane approached the runway, it was jolted by winds from a violent thunderstorm. "I was sitting there, buckled up, and we were shaking," says Baber. "I thought, 'Here we go. We're coming down.'"

The pane, carrying 139 passengers and six crew members, touched down hard, then went into a gut-wrenching skid. "They turned those back-thrusters on full blast, but we kept going forward," he says. "Then the lights flashed off and on, and the stewardess screamed, 'Brace yourself!'" The plane careered toward the end of the runway and, just short of the

Arkansas River, crashed into a metal support for approach beacons and split apart. "I looked out, and I could see flames outside the airplane," says Baber.

Escape wouldn't be easy. As fire began engulfing the plane, panicked passengers tugged at a jammed exit door. "I grabbed the door and pulled on it as hard as I could," says Baber. "It wasn't budging." But through the thickening smoke, he spied an 18-inch break in the fuselage. "I picked a stewardess up and pushed her through the hole," says Baber, who quickly did the same for three others. "Then it got really smoky," he says. "I couldn't breathe or see, and I got really scared." In spite of that and despite cuts on his legs and torso, Barrett squeezed his 6'4", 225-lb. frame headfirst through the crack and found himself outside the plane knee-deep in water near the river's edge. "I thought for a while I was the only survivor because I couldn't see anybody. All I could see, taste or breathe was black smoke," he says. "It was freezing cold and hailing something terrible."

After helping two more survivors out of the same hole in the fuselage, Baber joined three fellow passengers, including the flight attendant, in the cold water. "I got to the stewardess and started sobbing, just crying uncontrollably," he says. "She said, 'Come on, Barrett. Stay with me.' " He shook off his terror and helped guide others away from the fiery wreck.

In the end the crash of American Airlines Flight 1420 killed 11, injured 80 and changed Barrett Baber's life forever. "You hear it all the time, people saying that every day is a gift. But it really is, you know," he says. "I drive the speed limit. I spend more time with people. And relationships mean a lot more to me now." As they no doubt do to those whose lives he helped save. Says Luke Hollingsworth, Baber's friend and fellow passenger. The Bible says to sacrifice your life for a friend is the greatest gift. But to do it for a stranger takes it a step farther. And that's what Barrett did."

TECHNICIAN WILLIE GANTT, 42
Carrying precious cargo from a raging house fire

Working on his tax returns in the wee hours of Feb. 28, Willie Gantt was startled by an urgent banging at the door of his

Wichita, Kans., home. It was a breathless Sharanda Beard, 12, clutching a baby and shaking with fear as she blurted out that the house next door, where she was babysitting seven younger cousins and siblings, was on fire. Gantt, 42, barefoot and in boxer shorts, dashed out the door and "leaped over the fence," says his wife, Vera, 32. "He looked like a lion." Opening the door to the neighbor's house, "the fire knocked me to my knees," says Gantt, the father of three. Racing to the side of the house and crawling through the basement window that Sharanda had broken to escape, Gantt found the children and carried them to safety one by one. The fire, started by clothes near a space heater, gutted the house. "A few more minutes," says fire investigator Don Birmingham, "we'd be talking about eight fatalities."

ELEMENTARY SCHOOL STUDENT
AUSTIN PAYNE, 8 With his principal
in trouble, he applies a big squeeze

Bantering in the cafeteria last month with students at Northridge Elementary School in Oklahoma City, principal Ron Christy noticed a child wasn't eating his Tater Tots. So he asked for one. Then another. Christy's chatting and chewing prompted a pupil to wonder aloud if his mother hadn't told him not to talk with his mouth full. Too late. By now, Christy, 50, was in distress, a Tater Tot stuck in his throat. "I looked around for another adult," says Christy, whose face was turning blue, "and saw only a roomful of children."

With the other students oblivious, Austin Payne sprang into action. Rushing behind Christy, he wrapped his arms around the principal and gave a sudden squeeze, performing the Heimlich maneuver his father, Charley, 30, had taught him last year. Out popped the Tater Tot. A whirlwind of attention has since come the third-grader's way, including a visit to Late Show with David Letterman. But the straight-A student and budding right fielder is most impressed by the Thank You pin Christy gave him. "He told me he thought he was going to die," says Austin, "and that he was real proud of me."

COURIER WILSON DAVIS, 27
Refusing to walk away

Walking along a side street near St. Nicholas Avenue in Harlem on March 30 to visit his mother, Wilson Davis saw the shadowy figure of a man towering over a little girl. Ignoring her screams, the man had pulled her pants down and was straddling her. Another passerby just kept on walking. Not Davis. "I couldn't just walk by," he says. "That girl could have been killed."

Containing his anger ("I really wanted to hit the guy"), the amateur heavyweight boxer pinned the man, then yelled to a woman looking down from an apartment, "Call the cops!" The relieved 12-year-old hugged Davis repeating "Thank you! Thank you! Thank you!" Even the arresting officers embraced him.

A Virginia native whose family moved to The Bronx when he was 7, the imposing 6'4", 230-lb. courier spends most of his evenings at the gym, training for hours in hopes of winning a professional championship belt. As for his personal triumph last spring, Davis modestly shrugs and shakes his head. "I have a sister, I have a mom who lives in that area," he says. "It could have been one of them. Even so, I would have done it for anybody."

CABBIE WILLIAM SPIVEY, 50
Defending the road

Leaving Helen, Ga., on the night of Feb. 27, cabbie William "Bubba" Spivey drove over a hill and found himself face to face with an oncoming car on the wrong side of Interstate 20. Knowing a drunk driver had recently killed a father and his two children on that same stretch of road, Spivey decided on the spot to stop the oncoming car with his own. "If I stop dead still, I could block it," he said to himself, "and I believe I could survive the impact."

As others sped by, Spivey forced the other car off the road, then shouted to the driver, "Lady, you're on the wrong side of the interstate!" "No, I'm not," insisted Martha Bracken, 55, who tried to drive around him. But steering his car into hers,

Spivey pushed her off the highway and jumped out to grab her keys.

Weeks later, Bracken pleaded guilty to driving under the influence and driving on the wrong side of the road. "I'm glad he stopped me," says the Crawfordville, Ga., resident. Spivey, a divorced father of two from Langley, S.C., felt he had no choice. "If I didn't try to stop her," he says, "and she killed somebody, I might as well have been driving that car."

PARAMEDIC TERRY HOBEN, 37
In a hurricane's wake, he ferries neighbors to safety

After wrapping up a brutal 17-hour shift Sept. 17 at a hospital in Newark, N.J., paramedic Terry Hoben thought he'd take a look at what Hurricane Floyd had left behind before he headed home. Entering downtown Bound Brook, where he lives with his wife, Sally, 45, and their two children, Hoben found chaos. Floodwaters from the Raritan River had risen more than 10 feet on Main Street, inundating homes, shorting out power lines and setting off fires. "It was hysteria at that point," recalls Hoben. "There were fire trucks running all over the place state police were arriving with boats, 10 to 12 feet of water." And the water was still rising.

Spotting a friend, police Lt. Steven Cozza, Hoben asked how he could help. Cozza urged him to get home as fast as he could, put his fishing boat into the water and start emptying houses. Soon after, in the 16-foot skiff he had left parked on a trailer in his driveway, Hoben teamed up with officer Diana Paczkowski and pushed off into the eerie landscape of half-submerged buildings in search of stranded residents. "You put 16 feet of water on an area you usually walk around, and you can't recognize a thing," says Hoben. "We were scared to death." Adds Paczkowski, 29: "I'm not an avid water lover, first of all."

Navigating fast-running murky waters where familiar streets once lay, the two were soon hard at work. Taking aboard babies and children first, they plucked whole families from upper floors, attics and even rooftops where they had sought safety. Hoben sometimes entered a house where residents had been reluctant to leave or were waiting for the waters to subside. But water wasn't the only worry. The floods had risen to the point that Hoben and his passengers had to duck beneath high-voltage power lines, some of them still surging with current. And in one area a gas main had broken. Hoben carefully eased his boat along, hoping nothing would set off the potentially lethal fumes. "A mistake could not just have cost my life or Diana's, but the 8 or 10 people in the boat," he explains.

He and Paczkowski made nearly 50 trips over 13 hours, taking people to safety. Mary Anne Baloy, 42, remembers him well. She, her husband, Roger, 39, and their three children thought they could wait out the flood. Then it rose to their first-floor ceiling and kept on climbing. In the distance, she says, "you heard people screaming." When Hoben and another team of rescuers arrived, he lifted Baloy's kids into his boat. "It was incredible what they did," she says. "I have no idea how to repay them." But Hoben says he was just one of many residents and police officers who helped that night. "My town was in trouble," he says. "And this disaster pulled this community together."

COLLEGE STUDENT MARIAN NEAL, 40
Broke and out of a job, she gives a child the gift of life

Troubled by back problems in 1996, Marian Neal gave up her job handling freight in Washington, D.C., for a shipping company. Broke and homeless, she moved in with a friend two years later in nearby Alexandria, Va. There she befriended Terrance Varner, a 7-year-old who lived with his grandmother Elaine Harris and whose kidneys were failing. To keep her little friend company, Neal, now 40, often accompanied him on his three weekly trips to dialysis at Washington's Children's National Medical Center. "I saw all the suffering the children went through there," she recalls, "and wondered what I could do to help." Then she had an idea.

Last December, Neal donated one of her kidneys to Terrance – an unusual offering in that only 4 percent of transplants come from people unrelated by blood or marriage. Thankfully medical tests showed that Neal and Terrance were a match. "I didn't think it was a big step," says Neal. "I just wanted

Terrance to be able to eat, drink and play like a normal boy."
Grandmother Harris saw the December operation as a much
bigger deal. "It's the best Christmas present I could ever have,"
she told *The Washington Post*.

Good deed aside, Neal again found herself homeless last
August when her friend's brother moved back in. But her
plight did not go unnoticed. Hearing about Neal, U.S. Secretary of Housing and Urban Development Andrew Cuomo
secured a one-bedroom apartment for her in Southwest D.C.
Says Cuomo: "In an age when many people think only about
themselves, she was totally selfless."

In addition to the apartment, Neal also received a free car
from a local auto dealer so she could drive to classes at Northern
Virginia Community College, where she is studying to become
a social worker. "I made a way for Terrance," says Neal
gratefully, "and God made a way for me."

Saving Grace Humans aren't the only ones in need of a hero;
it's a dangerous world out there for animals too. When three
creatures found themselves in big trouble, three determined
men pitched in to help:

WILDLIFE SUPERVISOR ART YERIAN, 42
Olga the Otter's brave savior

Just past noon on New Year's Eve day, staffer Art Yerian was
making his rounds at the Homosassa Springs State Wildlife
Park on Florida's Gulf Coast when he noticed something amiss
in the alligator pond. There, where 17 of the carnivorous
amphibians are kept, "I could see bubbles," says Yerian, "like
a little submarine." Scanning an adjacent pen, Yerian quickly
realized what had happened. Olga, an 8-year-old sea otter, had
pried loose a grate in her enclosure and paddled through a 6-ft.
barrier into the gator pond. As a crowd of visitors gathered,
Yerian grabbed a net and ladder, hopped a 4-ft. fence (catching
a shoelace and crashing onto his back) and waded into the knee-
deep pond. "There was no way I was going to let Olga get
munched in front of 3,000 people – not to mention kids," says
Yerian, the father of two. Struggling for footing on the slippery
bottom, he used the ladder to sweep the water for Olga and to

keep the alligators at bay. But in chuming the water, Yerian got the attention of a 15-ft. gator, which rushed him, mouth wide open for the kill. Scrambling to safety, Yerian asked for a long pole to ward off further attack. "Since he came after me," he explains, "I was going to go after him so he wouldn't charge again." Finally steering Olga back onshore, Yerian scooped her into his net, to the cheers of the crowd, and hauled her to safety. How to explain the risk he'd been willing to take for an otter? That's easy, says colleague Susan Lowe: "He treats every one of the animals like it's his own."

SCHOOLTEACHER GEOFF HALEY, 50
His dog trapped in a drain, a loyal owner digs him out

Their daily walks near home in Medomsley, England, were a relaxing ritual for schoolteacher Geoff Haley and his mixed-breed Lakeland-Border terriers Billy and Ben. But on the afternoon of May 3, Ben suddenly darted into the woods. "I thought he might be chasing a rabbit," says Haley. But when Ben didn't return after several hours, adds Haley, "I knew he had met with some kind of trouble."

Haley's best guess was that Ben had disappeared into a long-disused 18-in. drainpipe that had so fascinated the dog that Haley had blocked it repeatedly with wire fencing. But sure enough, the fencing was gone. Investigating, Haley discovered the pipe had recently been connected to the drainage lines of a new subdivision. When he and a friend, John Bell, began lifting manhole covers from a newly built road directly over the pipe, their worst fears were confirmed. "I listened at the drain," recalls Bell, 61, "and I could hear Ben yapping."

Firemen tried to dislodge the dog with a high-powered stream of water, but that didn't work. Finally, Haley, along with wife Bobbie, 50, daughter Helen, 24, and a group of volunteers, took matters into their own hands. "I couldn't wait," says Haley. "I didn't know how much air Ben had, and any rain would have drowned him." Throughout the night they dug up more than a foot of tarmac and concrete, then broke through the pipe itself. Friends lowered Haley headfirst into the pipe but he still couldn't free the dog – and the hole was caving in. It wasn't until 8 a.m. when a construction crew arrived for work that the hole was widened and Ben was freed. "He was stuck in goo like the cork in a wine bottle," recalls Haley. "It took a massive heave to get him out."

With no more damage than a dirty coat, Ben, after a brief turn in the family shower, was soon wagging his tail but offering no word on what had prompted his excursion. "He's a bit of a daft dog," says Haley affectionately. "What possessed him that day is a mystery."

FISHERMAN SHAUN CURNOW, 32
A helping hand for a deer in deep water

As he headed out at dawn last June off the coast of Cornwall, England, fisherman Shaun Curnow of the village of St. Keverne was hoping for a standard day's haul of 500 pounds of mackerel. Instead, as he scanned the sea a quarter-mile offshore, he spotted a disturbance in the water. "The gulls were really going in on something," says Curnow. "I could see this little brown blob. I thought it was a bit of driftwood at first."

But it wasn't. As Curnow pulled his 19-ft. fishing boat, the Bold Venture, toward the scene, he made out an object moving against the tide. "As soon as I saw the antlers, I knew what it was," he says. "'That's a blinkin' deer!'" After several attempts to pull alongside the flailing animal, Curnow finally managed to grab hold of the exhausted creature and haul him over the side. "He was huffing and puffing and panting," says Curnow, who offered the deer a bit of a Kit Kat bar. "He kept looking at me, and he was a sad little thing." Onshore in 20 minutes, Curnow, who had radioed ahead, was met by local veterinarian David Cromey, who examined the winded but healthy 3-year-old male – which weighed in at 65 lbs. – and later released him into the nearby woods.

To date no one in St. Keverne, where few deer are ever seen, has been able to explain how the hapless animal wound up in the sea. But his rescue briefly made Curnow, a divorced father of two, a national celebrity. "They were all ready for big brown eyes and a story with a happy ending," says Cromey. "And that's what they got."

All in a Day's Work Honors don't come with the badge. These professional lifesavers earned them:

POLICEMAN ERICH KESSINGER, 29
The right call saves a life

It was supposed to be a birthday celebration – a night of barhopping just after the stroke of midnight Aug. 24, when Kristine Lurowist would officially turn 21. In honor of the occasion, the Penn State University senior consumed 21 shots of booze – one for each year. Fortunately, by the time Lurowist staggered out of her last State College saloon that night, officer Erich Kessinger was on routine duty nearby. "I watched her go from stumbling and staggering to being held up by a guy on each arm to the point where her legs started to drag," says Kessinger. When he approached to help, Lurowist's companions put up a stink. "They said, 'She's 21. We're legal. Get out of here, cop,'" he recalls. Over her friends' initial protests, he called an ambulance. By the time it arrived she was unconscious. When he learned later that night that her blood-alcohol level was an astonishing .682 – more than six times the legal limit for driving – "I never envisioned that she was going to pull through," he says. In fact, she survived only because she was placed on emergency dialysis. In a letter to the local *Centre Daily Times*, Lurowist thanked Kessinger and wrote, "I am doing fine and am eager to make up the class work missed and pursue my studies." More gratifying were her personal thanks; when Kessinger visited Lurowist the next day in the hospital, she greeted him as the man who saved her life. "It's not like I took a bullet," says Kessinger. "But for someone to say that, well, that makes a career."

DETECTIVE INSPECTOR HOWARD GROVES, 42
Visiting the U.S., an English tourist catches a thief

It was supposed to be a welcome break from work for British police officer Howard Groves, who arrived last March for a week of sightseeing in New York City with girlfriend Rachel

Double. But stepping out of their Manhattan hotel on just their second morning in town, the pair heard shouts from a nearby store. "I went into police mode right away," says Groves, a detective inspector in the London suburb of Uxbridge. "I started to walk across the street, but I remember thinking, 'Whoa, this is New York, be careful.'"

Very careful. Next thing he knew a man burst out of the shop. "He was running toward me covered in blood, shouting, 'Help, help, they're trying to rob me,'" says Groves. When two suspects emerged from the shop and began walking calmly down the street, Groves barked at them. One took off, but the other glared at Groves, than pulled a gun from a paper bag. "Without saying anything – bang!" recalls Groves. "The shot echoed around the buildings."

Unhurt, he and Double, 28, ducked back into their hotel lobby. But Groves, who like most British policemen has never carried a firearm on duty – and had never before been shot at – refused to give up. He followed the two men and quickly came upon a parked patrol car. Hailing an officer and identifying himself as a cop, he headed toward a subway stop where the suspects had fled. "I ran into the subway thinking, 'This is not happening to me,'" he says. One suspect jumped onto the tracks and escaped, but Groves – now with three NYPD cops – spotted the other and helped wrestle him to the ground, seize his gun and handcuff him. Only later, during a press conference, did fear get the better of Groves. "There was a sea of photographers clicking away," he says. "My knees were shaking."

FIREFIGHTER TIM DENEEN, 41
Digging deep for Jessy

Just that morning, last May 13, Tim Deneen's squad in the Wichita (Kans.) Fire Dept. had taken a special class on making rescues in confined spaces. Then at 7 p.m. the call came in: 17-month-old Jessy Kraus had tumbled into a well being dug in the backyard of his family's new home in nearby Mulvane. By the time Deneen and his technical rescue team arrived at 7:30, nearly two dozen rescue workers and neighbours were on the scene, and a local chemical company had set up a video camera to lower into the well – but that was not enough. "I saw that picture of his hand and this little head," Deneen, the father of two young girls and a firefighter since 1991, says of the video image. "I knew we had to get him."

Rescuers used a backhoe to dig a 20-ft.-deep pit next to the nearly 17-ft. well, then dug 7 ft. across to Jessy, who, by then exhausted, had fallen asleep. Deneen wedged himself into the 2-ft.-wide opening and grabbed the boy by the foot. "I asked him if he liked Barney," says Deneen. "And he said, 'No! No!'" Fifteen minutes later – five hours after the ordeal began – Deneen wrested the toddler from the pit, much to the relief of the boy's parents, Jerry Kraus, 30, and Karen, 28, who have another son, Cody, 8. (Karen was in the kitchen making dinner, and Jerry was with Jessy watering trees in the backyard when the toddler, walking toward him, tumbled into the well.) After a night in the hospital for observation, the little boy was released in the morning with just a minor bruise on his forehead and scratches on his elbow. "Thankfully it was one of those nights when everything worked like clockwork," says Deneen. "I could feel God all around."

ACKNOWLEDGMENTS AND SOURCES

The editor has made every effort to locate all persons having any rights in the selections appearing in this anthology and to secure permission from the holders of such rights. The editor apologises in advance for any errors or omissions inadvertently made. Queries regarding the use of material should be addressed to the editor c/o the publishers.

"Bomb Disposal" by Anonymous is an extract from *Blitz* by Constantine Fitzgibbon, W.W. Norton and Company, Inc., 1952.

"Tiananmen Square" by an Anonymous Student is from *New Statesman & Society*, 16 June 1989.

"The Habit and Virtue of Courage" is an extract from *Nicomachean Ethics* by Aristotle, trans. W.D. Ross, The Internet Classics Archive.

"George Washington and the Cherry Tree" by J. Berg Esenwein et al is quoted in *The Book of Virtue*, ed. William J. Bennett, Simon & Schuster, 1993.

"The Hero as Priest" and "Hero Worship" are extracts from *Sartor Resartus/On Heroes, Past and Present* by Thomas Carlyle, Chapman and Hall Ltd., n.d.

"The Heroes of Eyam" by Paul Chadburn is from *Fifty World Famous Heroic Deeds*, Odhams Press Ltd, n.d.

"Spartacus" by James Chambers is an extract from *Heroes & Heroines*, ed. Antonia Fraser, Weidenfeld & Nicolson, 1980. Copyright (C) 1980 Weidenfeld & Nicolson.

"The Evacuation of Kham-Duc" is an extract from *Life on the Line* by Philip D. Chinnery, Blandford Press 1988. Copyright (C) 1988 Philip Chinnery.

"Omdurman" is an extract from *My Early Life* by Winston S. Churchill, Heinemann, 1930. Copyright (C) 1930 the estate of Winston S. Churchill.

"Cobbett in the Dock" by William Cobbett is quoted in *Courage: An Anthology* edited by Hugh Kingsmill, Geoffrey Bles, 1939.

"The Front of the Bus" is an extract from *Rosa Parks: The Movement Organizes* by Kai Friese, Silver Burdett Press, 1990.

"The Darlings of the Life-boats" is from *Dictionary of Phrase and Fable*, E. Cobham Brewer, 1898.

"The Big Hitter" is an extract from *They Rose Above It* by Bob Considine, Doubleday, 1977. Copyright (C) 1977 Millie Considine as Executive of the Estate of Bob Considine.

"Obituary: Digby Tatham-Warter" is from *Daily Telegraph*, 30 March 1993. Reprinted by permission.

"Heroism" by Ralph Waldo Emerson is quoted in *English Prose* Volume IV, chosen and arranged by William Peacock, Oxford University Press, 1921.

"Lieutenant Philip Curtis wins the Victoria Cross" is from *The Edge of the Sword* by Anthony Farrar-Hockley, 1956. Copyright (C) 1956 Anthony Farrar-Hockley.

"The Face of Courage" is an extract from *Six Faces of Courage* by M.R.D. Foot, Methuen, 1978. Copyright (C) 1978 M.R.D. Foot.

"The Candle That Shall Never be Put Out" is an extract from *Foxe's Book of Martyrs*, ed Rev. T. Pratt, 1858.

"The Storming of Ciudad Rodrigo" is an extract from *Adventures with the Connaught Rangers 1809–1814* by William Grattan, ed Charles Oman, Edward Arnold, 1902.

"Let's Roll" (originally published as "The quiet executive who defied hijackers") by Toby Harnden is from *Daily Telegraph*, 18 September 2001.

"The Death of Adolfo Rodriguez" is an extract from *A Year From a Reporter's Notebook* by Richard Harding Davis, Harper, 1897.

"Britain is a Land of Unsung Heroes" (originally published as "Britain is a land of unsung heroes, says the Humane Society") by Robert Hardman is from the *electronic Telegraph*, 5 May 1999.

"Moral Fibre in Bomber Command" is an extract from *Bomber Command* by Max Hastings, Michael Joseph, 1979. Copyright (C) 1979 Romadata.

"On Trial" is an extract from *Scoundrel Time* by Lillian Hellman, Macmillan, 1976. Copyright (C) 1976 the estate of Lillian Hellman.